Richard Smitten lives ⬝⬝⬝⬝⬝⬝⬝⬝⬝⬝⬝⬝⬝⬝⬝⬝⬝
currently involved in ⬝⬝⬝⬝⬝⬝⬝⬝⬝⬝⬝⬝ to his
books. He is the author of *The Godmother*, the story
of Griselda Blanco and her crime empire, and co-
author with Robin Moore of *The Man Who Made it
Snow*, about the Colombian drug trade. *Legal Tender*
is his second novel.

Legal Tender

Richard Smitten

First published in Great Britain in 1992
by HEADLINE BOOK PUBLISHING PLC

First published in paperback in 1992
by HEADLINE BOOK PUBLISHING PLC

A HEADLINE FEATURE paperback

10 9 8 7 6 5 4 3 2

ISBN 0 7472 3703 4

Typeset by Medcalf Type Ltd, Bicester, Oxon

Printed and bound in Great Britain by
HarperCollins Manufacturing, Glasgow

HEADLINE BOOK PUBLISHING PLC
Headline House
79 Great Titchfield Street
London W1P 7FN

This book is for Gordon Badger —
a man never had a better friend.

The love of money is the root of all evil. Some men in their passion for it have strayed from the faith, and have pierced themselves through with many sorrows.

(1 Timothy 6   7–11)

DEFINITION OF A DOLLAR

In 1784 there was a furious debate in the United States Congress over money.

Thomas Jefferson cleared the air: 'If we determine that a dollar shall be our unit of exchange then we must say with precision exactly what a dollar is.'

The Founding Fathers heeded Jefferson's advice and in 1792 they defined the dollar as a precise weight of either silver or gold.

In 1971 the US Government abandoned the gold standard.

WEEK ONE

Monday night 7:00
LONDON, ENGLAND

Zed's Chief of Security was returning to his office one more
time tonight before he went home. He nodded at Heather
Harrison and the man she was with as they walked past him
down the long cool halls lined with Plexiglass. Zed was one
of the world's largest manufacturers of copying machines.

It was Zed corporate policy that there were no closed offices
in the research section, only open spaces; no secrets when
everything is a secret. Private offices and dark corners made
it easy to copy secrets about copiers.

The Chief stopped to check the sign-in book.

J.M. Keynes had been scribbled in after Heather's name.
Nice enough looking fellow, the Chief thought, looking up,
watching them disappear. The slicked-back dark brown hair
made him look almost like a thirties character, obviously an
American, judging from the loafers and open shirt he wore.
Heather's long legs were almost fully visible under her short
skirt; they were slim and sleek, not muscular, like a high-
fashion model's. 'Nice ass for an egghead,' the Chief thought.
He wondered why she wore such a short skirt and running
shoes tonight. It wasn't her style.

After 'Occupation', J.M. Keynes had written 'Consultant'.
The Chief grimaced and decided to call the 'Black Room',
the maximum security room. He told Stanley, the guard on
duty, to let him know if anyone tried to enter the room.

It was Monday night. Heather nodded at the few people

who were working late as she and Keynes walked toward her office. She was Head of Research and this was her section.

She slowed to glance into her own expansive work area as she passed, and couldn't help smiling, pleased with herself; she had come a long way in a short time. Her area showcased a rectangular glass and chrome desk, shiny and clean, clear of all papers, with only a framed eight-by-ten photo of Heather as a young girl standing confidently on a pair of racing skis, holding a blue ribbon, smiling, hugging her father. Thoughts of her father crept into her mind. Her mouth went dry. Her throat constricted and tears began to well up in her eyes. She shook her head quickly from side to side as if she could shake the thoughts of him out of her head.

'Tonight is for you, my precious father,' she said silently to herself, and took a deep cleansing breath to steady her trembling body. 'Tonight we get even.'

The Black Room loomed up suddenly ahead of her. It was enclosed by cloudy black Plexiglass. You could see out, but no one could see in. A sign in red letters said: NO ENTRY.

She gently slapped her palm print flat onto the glass lock-box at the entrance and looked back over her shoulder at Keynes. He stared at her; there was a twinkle in his deep blue eyes. His physical presence, his nearness, sent a flash of electric adrenaline through her body to her groin. Her palm was sweaty, cool on the glass. She hoped the moisture wouldn't distort the palm print.

They waited.

The door slid suddenly and silently into the wall; a security guard filled the space, blocking any entry.

'Problem, Stanley?' She was pleasantly shocked at how normal her voice sounded.

'No, Ma'am. Just orders from the Chief: no unauthorized personnel allowed entry without his personal okay. Sorry, Miss Harrison, but those are my orders.'

'They're really my orders, Heather.' The Chief was

4

standing directly behind them now. Heather could smell the pungent, stale tobacco smell of the unlit cigar in his mouth. He seemed bigger and broader than she remembered.

'You should know the rules: no one in the Black Room without security clearance. No exceptions!'

'Of course I know the rules, Chief. I wrote them!' She fumbled in her purse and dug out a red card that had Priority Clearance written across the top in yellow, with John M. Keynes typed in across the middle of the card. It was signed by Heather and the Chairman of the Board of the Zed Corporation.

The Chief examined it carefully, flipping it over twice in his hand. He shrugged his shoulders and handed it back, muttering, 'We usually get these at least a day ahead of time.'

'Mr Keynes is one of our investment bankers on the project. He arrived today unexpectedly,' Heather countered.

The Chief waved the guard off, turned on his heel and strode quickly down the hall, chewing angrily on what was left of his unlit cigar stump. She should have turned the damn priority card in at the sign-in desk. He decided to call the Chairman at home when he got back to his office.

The Black Room was empty except for a small computer and a powerful color copier, the most advanced digital model manufactured by the Zed Corporation. The computer was coupled to the copier by a shiny black box of metal about the size of a small portable TV set. The machines were lit softly from the ceiling by three spotlights that cast an eerie glow.

Heather hit a tiny toggle switch. The three machines hummed into life, waiting patiently for an order.

Keynes looked over at the guard, who was now engrossed in reading the London *Sun*, before he handed a fifty-dollar bill to Heather. He held open a handful of fingers then closed it into a fist and opened it again. She nodded and fed the currency note into the copier, then hit the 'Wait for Instructions' button.

She sat down at the computer and entered her password, Jason, her father's name. She waited for the OK, and typed: US DOLLARS . . . PRINT TEN COPIES . . . FIFTIES . . . FULL COLOR . . . PRINT BOTH SIDES . . . SEQUENTIAL NUMBERS . . . GUILLOTINE. THAT'S ALL FOR NOW. BYE.

The computer screen flashed back: THANK YOU HEATHER. HAVE A NICE NIGHT. BYE. The screen became solid black as the yellow letters washed away.

Heather looked over at the guard; he was still reading. She heard the familiar thump-clump as the pre-cut rectangular bills hit the FINISHED box of the copier.

Keynes reached in and picked out ten fifty-dollar bills. He held them up toward the overhead spotlights, examining both sides, out of the guard's sight. Each bill had a separate serial number. They were perfect copies.

He nodded his head up and down slowly, smiling, pleased, exhaling evenly in almost a whistle as he slipped the notes into his jacket pocket. Heather flashed a quick grin and winked.

It was all the proof he needed. They would do it tonight, as planned.

The Chairman's wife told the Chief of Security that her husband wasn't at home, to try the phone in the Rolls, and No she couldn't remember the damn number; it surely must be on file somewhere. The Chief quietly hung up, sorry now that he had called. He walked over to his computer terminal to dial up the Chairman's car-phone number.

Keynes dipped into his pocket and extracted a thin plastic pistol, about the size of a child's water pistol; a mean-looking dart syringe extended half an inch from the end of the muzzle.

He slipped off the membrane-like sheet of Saran that protected the chemical tip as he silently walked up behind the guard, who was still engrossed in the *Sun*. He spotted

6

some white flesh just between the stiff uniform collar and the hairline, took aim and fired. The dart struck deep, drawing a few drops of blood. The guard swatted at the back of his neck as if he had been stung by a bee, and fell forward into the bikini-clad young girl in the center section of his newspaper. He slumped to the floor in a fetal position, the newspaper framing his head and shoulders. Keynes brushed the papers aside and got busy stripping him.

Heather dropped to her knees in front of the Black Box, took out a small set of precision Allen key wrenches and went to work.

The metal box disassembled into four equal sections of ten inches by ten inches. A second set of outer walls had been previously hidden by Heather, under the metal skin. She slipped these panels out and set them aside.

Next, she carefully re-assembled the box using the hidden walls. She lined them up carefully and screwed them together, simulating a perfect Black Box, a Black Box with no insides.

She then connected the main power cables directly to each other with a cable from her purse that had been disguised to look like a false hair braid. The computer was now joined to the copier but the union was basically ineffective for printing money once the Black Box had been removed.

She then went to the IBM computer and ejected the floppy disks from the power drives, dropping them into the paper protective sleeves that read, 'US Dollars'.

Heather moved to the main file cabinet that stood next to the computer. She unlocked it and took out the floppy disks under the headings: Pound Sterling, Italian Lire, French Francs, Swiss Francs, German Marks, Japanese Yen, South African Rand, Canadian Dollars and Russian Rubles. She took the back-up disk copies as well. They all fitted easily into her purse.

'We don't have investment bankers. You should know that. We have one bank in England. Have had for over twenty

7

years. The same bank. Barclay's. Chief, don't you ever look at your paycheck?' the Chairman asked.

'Yes, sir, sorry to bother you. Have to go.'

'There's no trouble, is there, Chief?'

'I hope not,' the Chief mumbled, cutting the transmission.

He automatically hit the Black Room intercom buzzer and picked up the receiver.

Keynes heard the phone buzz as he was putting the four quadrants of the Black Box into the guard's attaché case, the large square type of bag used by airline pilots. He looked at the flashing red light and then over to Heather. She shrugged and picked up the receiver.

'Hello.' Her voice quivered.

'Where's Stanley?' the Chief yelled so loudly into the phone that Keynes could hear him from six feet away.

'The loo,' Heather almost whispered.

'Not bloody likely.' The Chief slammed the phone down and ran out of his office, hitting the general alarm button on the console as he passed through the door.

Keynes finished inserting the sections of the Black Box into the attaché case, looked at his Rolex. He was fully dressed now, in the guard's uniform.

'Twenty seconds, Heather.' They heard the clanging of the bells and the wail of the sirens as the general alarm system kicked in.

Heather went to the wall and pressed the 'Door Open' panel. The door slid aside as she and Keynes stepped out into the corridor. Keynes easily handled the attaché case. It weighed about thirty pounds.

They heard the Chief's voice down the hall behind them.

'Hold it right there, goddammit!' Keynes gently took Heather's hand as they turned to face the Chief, who was running down the hallway with two security men behind him.

'Just where the hell do you think you're going with that bloody bag?' the Chief bellowed.

Keynes glanced nervously at his watch again, as if he could urge the second hand to move faster. Only three seconds to go.

They all heard the dull thud of an explosion outside the building and felt the floor shudder as the entire building went dark and quiet.

The transformer that fed the entire complex had been blown.

Keynes and Heather took off running. After a short distance, Heather took the lead. These corridors had been her home for years.

The people working late were shuffling aimlessly around the long dark corridors, confused and upset. Keynes and Heather settled into a fast walk, melding in with the cleaning staff, office workers and security people, trying not to bump into anyone in the blackness.

In the dark, in his guard's uniform and with an arm round Heather's waist, John Keynes looked perfectly normal and protective of the Head of the Research Department. Twice he stopped to tell the guards they met: 'Head for the Black Room, protect the Black Box at all costs.'

'Less than two minutes till the back-up generators kick in,' Heather whispered as they headed down a long hall.

The outline of the exit door was barely visible at the end of the corridor. They ran for it. Keynes hit the emergency crossbar on the door with the flat of his hand. It popped open onto a small park where the employees ate their lunch. The door slammed shut behind them as they ran full speed for the perimeter fence. It was thick chain-link with three electrified barbed wire strands running along the top.

The back-up generators kicked in; spotlights illuminated the outside grounds.

Heather searched in her bag for her set of keys as they reached the fence. She found the right key quickly and opened the gate. They left it flapping in the wind behind them as they ran for the dark forest only twenty feet away, threading their way through thick stands of oak and sycamore, following a path well worn by lovers.

Minutes later they found the clearing and the helicopter.

The pilot didn't have to be told what to do. He took one look at them and the blades started to spin, giving off a low-pitched whumping noise, the wind force beating down in their faces, almost driving them back.

Over the helicopter noises, they could hear voices behind them through the forest. Keynes was glad police didn't carry guns in England.

Heather looked out of the dark bubble of the helicopter as they rose, to see the Chief standing there, his hands on his hips, as the rest of the security people followed him into the clearing. They looked up helplessly as the helicopter disappeared into the black night, the Chief only moving to yank his cigar out of his mouth and slam it onto the ground.

In fifteen minutes the helicopter touched down at a private airstrip near Gatwick. Keynes paid the helicopter pilot in cash. He and Heather ran for the waiting Gates-Learjet that seemed to be airborne before the door closed.

Destination Nassau.

The Chief strode into the Black Room. Stanley, the guard, was groggy but sitting upright now in the computer swivel chair, being ministered to by two para-medics.

The Chief breathed a long sigh of relief when he looked over to see the Black Box still glistening in the grey light. He was even more relieved when he hit the power button and both the computer and the copier lit up and hummed.

His concentration was broken by the Chairman who burst into the room with Barsley, the Assistant Head of Research in tow.

'They didn't get it. Good show, Chief.' The Chairman ran his hand over the smooth black surface of the Box, smiling, as he off-handedly waved Barsley forward to check it out.

* * *

At twenty thousand feet, Keynes popped the Cristal, watching the cork ricochet around the inside of the cabin. Heather giggled nervously as she accepted her glass, holding it in front of her, pinching the base, watching the champagne bubbles sparkle as they danced up the hollow stem.

They clinked glasses, smiled at the same time and burst out laughing.

'I can't get the bloody machine to do as it's told, sir. And it doesn't sound right. The wrong hum . . . hollow,' Barsley explained almost in apology. He and Heather Harrison had worked on this project together for almost three years. He somehow felt like an accomplice.

'The floppy disks?' the Chairman asked.

'Gone, I'm afraid, sir.'

'The back-ups?'

'Gone too. Sorry,' Barsley said sheepishly, looking over at the Chief, who turned away disgustedly.

'You mean the back-up disks were here for all ten currencies? Here in this room?' the Chairman stammered.

'Yes, sir. We brought them in here this morning, on Heather Harrison's orders, to do a consolidation, a few minor corrections in the software programming.'

'Brilliant. Absolutely bloody brilliant. Barsley, why the hell do we bother with any security? You people in research just do what you damn well want anyway.'

'The Box,' the Chief of Security blurted out.

'Barsley, open it up!' the Chairman moved back away from the Black Box, afraid of what they would find.

Barsley opened the small leather case that housed his tools: sets of delicate screwdrivers, stainless steel Allen keys, and fine tungsten splicing pliers. Slowly, like a surgeon, he undid the screws with the Allen key wrenches, laying them carefully on the console of the computer, one by one. Finally, he removed the first section, then the second panel slipped off.

There was nothing inside but a strange connecting cable

11

that looked like a braid of Heather Harrison's long ash-blonde hair.

Heather sat cross-legged in the large passenger seat facing Keynes. He moved across and sat beside her, filling her glass with the last of the champagne. The Black Box sat alone, glistening, on the small galley table in front of them, lit only by the dim interior reading lights of the cabin. The gray moonlit night flashed by, visible through the portholes.

'About four hours till we reach Nassau,' he whispered, undoing the buttons on her blouse.

'Do you really think they'll stay up forward?' Heather said hoarsely, eyeing the cockpit door. She freed her hair from the tight bun on top of her head; it cascaded down, framing her exquisite face, accentuating her high cheekbones and perfect teeth. She knelt in front of him and undid his belt, pulling it through the loops. She liked the slapping, snapping sound the leather made. A year ago she never would have thought herself capable of doing anything like this.

'At the rates they charge, they'll do anything we want,' Keynes said. His hand moved down her silk blouse as he undid the buttons; he pressed her flat bare stomach with his hand.

'Let's hope so,' she said, removing the bottle from his free hand.

The Zed Chairman was dreading this call. He waited for the satellite to connect him through to New York and Phillip Sturges, head of the Federal Reserve.

The Chairman cleared his throat. 'Mr Sturges, I'm afraid I have bad news. I'm afraid the Black Box project has gone awry.'

'Awry?' Phillip Sturges asked.

'The Black Box is gone. Stolen, actually. Just a few hours ago. Inside job. The Head of Research was involved.'

'Disks gone too?'

12

'Yes. They blew the main power line with C-4 plastique. The entire facility was blacked out for almost five minutes; very professional job. The gentleman she was with was an expert; the whole thing was very well planned.'

'They got all the US dollar software, all denominations, twenties, fifties and hundreds?'

'I'm afraid so.' There was a brief silence until Sturges spoke again.

'What else?'

'We tracked them to a small airfield near Gatwick. Their plane filed a flight plan for the Channel Islands but cancelled it when they got airborne. We don't know where they're headed. I'll put our Chief of Security on the line.' The Chairman handed the phone over to the Chief like it was hot.

'We want no publicity on this, it's too sensitive. No leaks. Is that clear?' Sturges said to the Chief.

'Yes, sir.'

'Did the man have a name?'

'Yes, J.M. Keynes was the name he gave.'

'J.M. Keynes?'

'Yes. John M. Keynes,' the Chief said importantly, remembering the priority card.

'John Maynard Keynes?' Some smart joker rubbing it in, Sturges thought.

'Could be the very same, sir. I'll have Interpol check it out,' the Chief blurted, nervously.

'You do that, Chief! Keep me posted.' The line went dead.

'Good luck,' Phillip said to himself as he hung up the line. 'The esteemed John M. Keynes has been dead for fifty years.'

The Black Box had great power. It was like having a key to the Treasury of the United States.

Phillip reached for the red phone on his desk to inform the President.

Monday afternoon 3:00
FEDERAL RESERVE, NEW YORK CITY

The Federal Reserve is located at 33 Liberty Street in New York City. The 'Gold Vault', buried below, ninety feet deep in the bedrock of Manhattan Island, holds the gold reserves of eighty nations in spartan iron cages with bars like prison cells. Countries often settle international debts by requesting that the Fed physically move the gold from one cage to another. The Fed holds more gold than Fort Knox; four thousand and six tons were currently in inventory. This represented sixty-four billion dollars at the current market price of five hundred dollars an ounce.

Phillip Sturges lived on the top floor of the Federal Reserve building in an apartment. The apartment was connected to his office by a short narrow hall.

Phillip sat behind his office desk reading the gold inventory report. He felt safe and comfortable with all that gold buried in the vault below him and surrounded by the heavy dark panelling of his office; a warm glow from the green-shaded gooseneck lamp illuminated his massive oak desk. The desk had been Teddy Roosevelt's when he was Police Commissioner of New York City.

Like Roosevelt, Phillip also believed in fundamentals.

The red phone on his desk buzzed into life.

'Hello.'

'Phillip, is that you?' It was the voice of Ralph Cobb, the head of the Secret Service.

'Yes.'

'I just found out about the theft in England, the magic copier that would do it all, revolutionize the printing of money. And now the fucking thing has been stolen.' His high voice irritated Phillip. And when Cobb got excited, Phillip found the voice even more irritating.

14

'We know it's been stolen, Ralph.'

'I've been working with the FBI, and we have a name on this asshole, J.M. Keynes, the perpetrator.' He let the news hang there until Phillip broke the silence.

'What's the name, Ralph?'

'John St John.'

'Recognize the name? He goes by the nickname Books.'

'Yes. We were roommates in college,' Phillip answered coolly.

'And prep school, from what we've learned. His grandfather donated a wing of the Princeton library, didn't he?'

'Yes, that's why he's called Books. I haven't seen him in years,' Phillip added quickly, regaining his composure. Cobb was certainly fast and thorough in his investigations.

'Well, the next time you see him, Phillip, it will be in Federal prison. We have a positive ID on him from the Zed security videotapes. Books St John and this Heather Harrison have been lovers for some time.' His shrill voice emphasized the word 'Books'.

'Do you have enough to arrest him?'

'No, not really. It's under British jurisdiction, and who knows where he is? But I'll try to get Justice to issue a warrant anyway. Can you give us any more information on the case, help us complete the file?'

'I haven't seen your file,' Phillip said.

'No, of course not. It's classified, for the President's eyes only. Why don't I send our chief investigator over to interview you, to make sure we have all the details. Maybe you could clue him in on everything you know about Books St John: family background, personal habits, men . . . women, who knows who's fucking who anymore. Hard to believe he's an heir to the Oberson banking fortune, and he pulls a goddamn stunt like this. How's tonight for you?'

'No good. Make it tomorrow morning at seven. I'll have some uninterrupted time then. My office.'

'He'll be there. Any photos, yearbooks, letters would be helpful.'

'I'll do my best.'

'I know you will.'

'Goodbye, Ralph.' Phillip slowly slipped the receiver into the cradle. He knew Ralph Cobb was persistent, tenacious, and would dig deep.

Cobb had personally kept two presidents alive through three turbulent terms of office. And counterfeiting fell under the jurisdiction of the Secret Service. There hadn't been a serious case in twelve years, and Phillip knew that Cobb wanted to keep it that way.

Phillip moved into his bedroom and sorted through his personal files for the next hour, carefully taking out all photos, letters and yearbooks that had pictures of Books. The pictures went back to when he had first met Books at the age of ten in Connecticut, their years together at Groton, the exclusive New England prep school that prepped the men of the Ivy League for their pre-destined lives. He stopped at a picture of them in their bathing suits on winter vacation frolicking in the surf at the Oberson Palm Beach estate. He flipped through the pages of the Princeton yearbook and the team pictures when Nick had joined them as the third Musketeer.

Phillip made a neat pile in the center of his bed, cataloguing the photos, letters, and yearbooks for the Secret Service investigator. He inhaled slowly and deeply as he studied a picture of the three of them, Books, Nick, and himself in yellow racing slickers, standing on the dock in Fort Lauderdale on the beginning day of the Nassau race. He picked up a second picture of Big Books embracing the three boys behind the helm of *Wanderlust*, a look of pride on his face, embracing them like they were all his sons.

Phillip's hand began to tremble slightly. He stuffed the two photos in with the others, in the center, to hide them from his view as quickly as he could; he picked up the phone to order the Federal Reserve Learjet to be ready for him at nine in the morning. He would leave as soon as he had finished talking to the Secret Service investigator.

Then he slipped into his specially tailored robe and prepared himself for Veronica's visit. Maybe she could empty his mind of the bloody images of that fateful day, and the stormy weather that he knew lay ahead.

Tuesday morning 9:00
MARTINIQUE, CARIBBEAN

Nick Sullivan was anchored-off on the reef line in a small cove of a deserted island just south of Martinique.

He carefully finished bolting down the hookah rig directly ahead of the console on the sixteen-foot Whaler that he used as a tender. He had waited almost two months for a hookah rig to be built to his exact specifications and delivered from the Florida Keys.

The hookah rig was a small on-board air compressor that could take three divers down to a hundred feet, using only second-stage mouthpieces attached to long half-inch hoses. When Nick ran out of hose or got bored he could return to the boat, pick up the Whaler's anchor, and walk along the bottom until he found another spot.

There was a slight west wind, less than ten knots; it would be just enough to make sure the air-hose would drift clear of the Whaler without tangling as he uncoiled it. The long bright yellow hose, an endless drifting worm, floated on the surface, waiting.

He pulled the starter cord and the compressor spat several times, then coughed into life, violating the silence. He twisted the long exhaust pipe so the fumes would blow away from the fresh-air intake, then he gently somersaulted backwards off the gunnel, sinking through the aquamarine sea, pulling himself down the Whaler's anchor line hand over hand to the clear white sand below. He planted the anchor securely and headed for an enormous coral head.

The coral rose from the ocean bed like a stalagmite. It was an underwater city of life and prosperity, with room for all his finned friends. Angel fish peeked out of their apartments, glowing blue, yellow and black. Two Beau Gregorys, fierce little one-inch fighters, swam up to Nick and belligerently took a peck at his face mask, decided humans were of no interest to them, and swam away. Pairs of yellow and black four-eyed butterflies swam around in tandem, too much in love with each other to notice him. Black and white spotted morays watched beady-eyed from their caves, toothy mouths opening and closing as they pumped water gently through their gills.

Nick inhaled deeply and exhaled slowly as a fat olive-green moray stuck its head out of its cave to give him the once-over; the spiny lobster that lived underneath the moray waved its two antennae wildly in the air, conducting two orchestras at once.

Nick swam slowly up to the top of the coral head until he was less than four feet from the surface. He rolled on his back and looked skyward. The hot midday sun glowed red-orange, sending down a wild prism of molten iridescence, a shattered rainbow that permeated the blue-green ocean.

He explored for another two hours, going back twice to pick up the anchor and replant it as he moved along the reef line.

At three he surfaced for lunch. He carefully set the seat in the Whaler and served himself smoked marlin, conch salad, and ham sandwiches on fresh French bread from the bakery in Martinique. He washed it down with a half bottle of chilled Meursault from the Igloo cooler.

Nick had been living alone like this for almost two years

18

now, a recluse in a self-imposed exile. He saw himself as a lone pelagic dolphin roaming the West Indies, skimming along aimlessly on the surface of the ocean past Dominica, Antigua, Barbados, unable to stop, unable to find peace.

He opened the Ziploc bag that was in the Igloo cooler and looked, once again, at the strange telegram that had been delivered to him by the dockmaster in Martinique that morning.

'Nick need to see you ASAP on most urgent matter STOP Will be in La Fitte Cove near Eleuthera STOP Don't let me down this is a matter of the highest importance STOP Your friend Books.' He folded the telegram into a neat square, tucked it back into the Ziploc bag, sealed it, and tossed it into the Igloo cooler.

'What the hell does that mean?' Nick said out loud.

He swished his hand through the clear Caribbean Sea over the side of the Whaler and looked down between the Vs of his fingers at the white sand below.

The beach in Nigeria was white, glistening almost silver in the sun; it ran for miles, as far as the eye could see, empty, primeval. There was no sign of life except the birds: gulls walked the beach, only springing to life to hammer the small bait in the surf. Frigate birds made lazy circles high in the sky, brushing against the clouds. Pelicans rode sleepily on the edge of the breaking surf, indifferent to all around them.

The man appeared on the beach like a black apparition; he was just suddenly there. His tribal colors were visible on his ceremonial shield. He was dressed in full regalia, looking stately and proud. The only thing out of place was his formal black silk top hat. It was well-worn, had been battered, and carefully reshaped. He spun three times and started to dance, raising both his bare black feet at the same time, then pounding them down hard into the fine hot sand as he chanted.

It was the signal they were looking for.

The rubber Zodiac landing craft with the Evinrude engine was lowered into the calm blue ocean. There was hardly any surf breaking. The recon team of six armed men crabbed down a rope cargo net that hung on the side of the freighter and jumped into the rubber boat. The leader, Alfred the Cockney, called up to the Greek captain, 'Lower those lifeboats and the small barge and get ready to fill them.'

The tired old freighter was carrying ten thousand Kalashnikov AK-47 automatic rifles that had been picked up in Yugoslavia, and ten million rounds of ammunition. The arms were for the Nigerian rebels.

Alf rode a curling wave onto the beach with his crew of five men, and they pulled the Zodiac up on the dry sand. The men checked their weapons and cautiously approached the dancing black man on the beach, who seemed oblivious of them, possessed.

There was something quietly electric in the air; the birds were gone, there was only a humid stillness. Alf had noticed it before in the Congo and Angola: the static silence before death.

The black man had stopped dancing and was shuffling slowly backward toward the tall waving palm trees and the bush line that formed the edge of the jungle. The man stared at them, smiling at Alf as he retreated.

'Hold it, you bleedin' Wog!' Alf yelled. The recon team had formed an extended V behind their leader; they were all alert, carrying their weapons at port arms. 'I don't like this, boys.'

The black man spun suddenly, tossed his shield and broke for the jungle at a full run. Alf started to run after him. The other men in the landing party stood still, feet planted in the sand, mesmerized, as Alf took careful aim and squeezed the trigger of his Kalashnikov AK-47, letting off a long burst. The first three rounds splattered in the sand behind the running man, small puffs blown upward. Alf used these rounds to track his victim, raising the fire-spitting muzzle of his gun. The following shots ran up the black man's back like a dark red zipper. They tore through his body, hurling the man forward into the thick bush. His black top hat flew into the air as the bullets climbed his neck and his head exploded like a ripe melon. Alf was running full speed by now and had almost caught up to the body.

The surrounding jungle suddenly burst into life; bullets flew from every direction. The Nigerian Army had been waiting in ambush. The still, tropical air was filled with the cacophony of machine gun rounds being fired. Alf dropped and crawled into the bush. The firing went on for a full two minutes although the five men on the beach had died in the first ten seconds. The soldiers continued to pump hundreds of rounds into the mercenaries' bodies.

Three Nigerian gunboats appeared out of tiny coves; they had been camouflaged the night before. The Nigerian regulars converged on the helpless freighter like flies on a dead body, and scuttled up the cargo nets that hung over the side.

The entire cargo was lost, along with the ship.

Four weeks later Alf sat in Nick's office in London. 'It was that fuckin' Sean O'Reilly, Nick. I seen him with my own eyes.'

It was one of the few major African ordnance deliveries that Nick hadn't handled personally.

Alfred saw him looking at the stump that used to be his arm. 'Don't worry, Nick, I got my right arm still, and that's the one I need. I'm better off than those poor bloody blokes on the beach.' Two of the men were Alf's best chums, boyhood mates, good men.

'You sure it was O'Reilly?'

'Hey, do Irishmen fuck donkeys? Sure I'm sure. I used to work for the prick. I knew when I seen him.' Alf smiled. 'I'm sorry, Nick. I know you're half Irish.' He patted Nick's forearm with his remaining hand.

It had cost Nick twenty-five thousand dollars to ransom

21

each dead body out of Nigeria so he could send the remains home to friends and family. That plus the loss of the freighter and the cargo just about broke him. He had barely enough left to lay low in the islands for a couple of years . . . after he took care of Sean O'Reilly.

Nick's reverie was broken by the whoosh of a giant manta ray sailing straight up out of the water, arching through the air, landing with a resounding belly flop to shake off parasites.

Nick retrieved the long yellow hose, coiling it neatly in the bow of the Whaler, then he covered the compressor. In ten minutes he was back to where his Rybovich sportfisherman was anchored. In a matter of minutes Nick was on his way towards Fort-de-France harbor, Martinique, towing the Whaler. It skidded around in the wake, bobbing from side to side like a playful dolphin.

His berth at the marina required that he moor stern to. He slowed down to let the Whaler catch up to him as he approached the marina, gathered the tow line and cleated it to the bow.

A man sat in a wheelchair at the far end of the dock. He started to roll slowly down the pier into view as Nick made his U-turn in front of the mooring, gently slipping one engine into forward, the other into reverse, then backing into the slip. The Rybovich responded easily in his hands.

The wheelchair was stationed squarely at the stern as Nick pulled in. The man waved, motioning for Nick to throw him the lines. He caught the lines and wheeled himself to both stern cleats to make them fast.

Nick jumped the two feet from the stern to the dock, extending his hands and a big smile.

'I can't believe it. You! Here! No notice, no warning. God, I'm glad to see you.' Nick hugged the man's shoulders, squatting to get his arms round him in the wheelchair.

'Decided to come this morning; commandeered the company plane and here I am.' Phillip Sturges couldn't stop smiling. Neither could Nick. They hadn't seen each other in three years.

'I thought you never left your ivory tower, or mountain of money, I should say. But I'm sure glad to see you. You look good.'

'I'm only staying the night, Nick. We need to talk. Any bars or restaurants in this part of the world?'

'A few; not the kind you're used to, but I know a couple that are fair to middlin'.'

Nick absently circled the wheelchair to grab the two handles and push. Phillip slammed the brake on full. It caused Nick to lift the rear wheels off the ground, almost dumping Phillip. He lowered the wheels just in time.

Phillip leaned back, tilting his head up at Nick as he slipped the brake off. 'I'm self-propelled at all times. Shrink's orders.'

'Okay. Sorry. Let's go . . .'

Nick led the way, a deep frown creasing his forehead. He was wrestling with the accident again, an accident that had happened twenty years ago, an accident that had put Phillip in a wheelchair. It was like it had happened yesterday. It took a few seconds to get his mind together; but he was used to fighting this old ghost. Phillip caught up with him where the pier joined the main street of Fort-de-France.

They came to Pierre's, an outdoor cafe Nick knew well. He chose an isolated table and ordered two rum punches as Phillip settled in to the table. Nick didn't know whether or not to move a chair to make room for Phillip; at the last moment he moved it to the next table.

'Thanks,' Phillip said, wheeling in. He felt more comfortable now that they were at the same eye level. Nick knew Phillip hated having to look up at people he used to look down at. It was one of the reasons he hardly ever left his office. 'Rum? You've gone native, Nick.'

'Specialty of the house. If you don't like it, I'll drink both of them.' Nick smiled, still ill at ease.

23

'I've never sent a drink back in my life,' Phillip laughed, 'and you know it.' He was facing the sun, basking in the last warm light before sunset.

The sun lay on the western horizon over the spit of land that formed the harbor. It was framed by two royal palms, two splayed hands and bent arms placed in exactly the right spot to embrace and swallow the molten orange solar-ball for the night. Both men watched the red glow in silence as it sank into the flat sea.

'You arrange that?' Phillip asked, adjusting his wheel chair.

'Yeah. At great expense.' Nick looked away from Phillip and the wheelchair.

'Nice.' Phillip signalled for two more rum punches.

'So . . . how big is it?'

'What?'

'Your problem,' Nick said, finally facing Phillip. 'You didn't leave your money mountain for a rum punch and a tropical sunset.'

Nick could feel Phillip forming the words in his mind before he spoke. He was always precise and exact. Phillip's looks belied his background; his thick features were the antithesis of an Ivy League gentleman. They were sexual, animal, the rough looks of a peasant on the Steppes of Russia. But his mind was highly developed, refined, and exact, a precision instrument. Phillip's exactness was a trait Nick had always admired. Phillip didn't make mistakes. Nick hated his own impulsiveness, sometimes willfulness.

'It's Books.'

'In trouble again?'

'Big-time.' Phillip paused, then continued. 'He's stolen something very important. It was being developed for the Federal Reserve by the Zed Corporation. A device that has the ability to get a computer to talk to a copier. It's called the Black Box.'

'And the language is money,' Nick added.

'Right.'

24

'With you two it's always money.'

'This Black Box uses a digital copier and advanced laser technology to print currency, a copier-computer-printer that eliminates color separations, expensive artwork, and engravings. The production runs can be set up and changed instantaneously by the operator, an operator with minimal skill; it takes about the same skill level as operating a word processor. And it can all be installed in an area about the size of the saloon on your boat.'

'Who is Books in this with?'

'He had a woman with him, the Head of Research for Zed in England. We don't know much about her or her motive.'

Nick looked out over the harbor. He could see the royal palms, now gray spidery silhouettes in the moonlight, softly waving like fans in the trade wind. 'Do they know at the Fed that you and Books go back for years?'

'The President was informed. He wasn't pleased.'

'Do they have enough to arrest Books?'

'It was a secret project, and very sensitive. Books would have to be extradited from wherever he is and put on trial; all the details of the project would come out. It could be extremely embarrassing to all concerned.'

'Knowing Books, this Black Box is well hidden.'

'Yes. He could hold it ransom, blackmail the hell out of us.'

'So, how am I about to be manipulated?'

'Same subtle self, huh?' Phillip grinned.

'Did Books' family ever get over that Arab stuff?' Nick asked, changing the subject, wanting a few minutes to think about what Phillip had said, what the strange telegram from Books was about, and what web he was being drawn into.

'No, not really, but it hurt the family in the one place it trains its generations to protect.'

'Preserve capital. Protect the cash stash.'

'Right. Even Books' family noticed losing fifty million,' Phillip said.

'Where is he now?' Nick asked.

'No one knows. But he has a house in Nassau and a small bank there. I think he's there, or on one of the islands. You two had a favorite spot somewhere south of Eleuthera, near Harbor Island, didn't you?'

'Yes,' Nick said. He didn't volunteer any information about the telegram. He let the silence hang over them. He wanted to know what Phillip was really after.

'Can you find him? I'm prepared to pay and pay well.'

'Maybe.' Nick studied Phillip's broad, flat, peasant face. It showed no emotion.

'I'd like you to see what he's up to. See if we can settle it quietly,' Phillip said.

Nick looked at the sailboats anchored off, the tall masts swaying in rhythm with the lazy swell. 'Do you want to help him or hurt him?'

Phillip glared at Nick. 'Stupid question.' He let a few minutes pass.

'Not so stupid. Answer it!'

'I don't want to hurt him. And I don't want to be hurt.'

'How can you be hurt?'

'The Black Box was my idea. I promoted the use of new technology to print money and my ex-best friend steals it. I don't look so good.'

'Did you ever discuss it with him?'

'Once. Briefly.'

'Apparently once was enough!'

'He's very clever and he knows about money.'

'Like you,' Nick muttered.

'Better, maybe. In school, he was the first to understand monetary theory, to understand John Maynard Keynes and Adam Smith.'

'No one understands Keynes and Adam Smith,' Nick said.

Phillip looked away and fingered the lip of his glass. 'That's true.'

They both thought of Books and the great influence he had always had on their lives. 'Will you go, Nick? Will you try?'

26

Nick hesitated, not wanting to respond; these were complex men who dealt with complex issues, and often what appeared on the surface was no more than the eyes of the alligator.

There was something about Phillip's request that made him shiver inside with a combination of fear and anticipation. But he was bored and almost broke. He wondered if Phillip knew how broke he really was. Probably he did know. He always seemed to be able to figure out how much money people had, real money, cash money.

Both men let the ocean breeze roll in off the bay in silence.

Nick wondered why he hadn't told Phillip about the telegram.

Wednesday morning 7:00
SECRET SERVICE, WASHINGTON, D.C.

Ralph Cobb sat alone in his spartan office at seven in the morning. He was usually finished with his administrative work when everyone was just beginning. Then he would concentrate on what he thought was the most important part of the job – personal strategy. He had climbed to become head of the Secret Service by knowing who was really orchestrating the action.

The Black Box presented an enormous potential problem; it had the ability to ruin his impeccable record. Counterfeiting was under the domain of the Secret Service, and therefore he was the one to lead the investigation. Cobb knew the power of the media; if they ever got hold of this story . . .

He concentrated on trying to develop a lead, to transport himself into the mind of Books St John. He studied his handwritten check list:

1. Distribution . . . who, where, how?
2. Ink . . . special qualities, where
   can it be purchased?
3. Location . . . where will they set
   up manufacturing?
4. Personnel . . . prepare a list of
   potential personnel requirements.
5. Paper.

Cobb circled this final item on his list in red. It was critical; paper was the area where counterfeiters always got careless and confused, an area where they inevitably failed.

Fledgling agents in the Secret Service academy were taught that currency was made from special paper: fifty per cent linen and fifty per cent cotton stock, interlaced with tiny red and blue threads. The paper had to be able to withstand a pressure of sixty-five pounds per square inch and tolerate two thousand double folds without breaking. It also had to have an opacity of sixty-five per cent. When examined under a microscope, an agent would see tiny pinpoints of light showing through the paper if it was the real thing.

There was only one plant in the United States that was authorized to manufacture currency paper, Crane and Company of Massachusetts, and their security was too tight for anyone to steal from them.

Cobb went to the map of the United States that hung on his wall, carrying a fistful of green tacks. He stepped up onto his footstool and stabbed the tacks into seven specific locations around the country, grinding the green heads in tight, flush to the wall, as he read from the computer printout that he had requested from the US Mint – a secret list of the seven paper manufacturers with the machinery and capability that were necessary to produce currency paper.

Books St John would need to have a steady source of paper if he was really going into the business of counterfeiting in a big way. The paper would have to come from one of these mills.

'Maybe he's not in the business of counterfeiting,' Cobb thought. 'Maybe he's in the business of blackmail. Maybe he will try to get the United States Government to buy the Black Box in order to take it out of circulation. If he does ransom it, if he does try blackmail, then it's someone else's problem. If I'm wrong about the paper, I'll only have wasted some time. But if I'm right . . . Goddammit . . . if I'm right!'

The pain flashed through Cobb's brain. He opened his fist and looked at the remaining green tacks; they were red with blood.

'Shit!' He mumbled out loud as he extracted the bloody tacks from his palm, one at a time, and threw them into the wastebasket. He looked back up at the map. He re-mounted his footstool and slapped the wall map dead center with his bloody palm, leaving a red paw print in the Midwest.

He made a blood oath. 'Whatever it takes!'

At ten that morning he met with seven teams of Secret Service investigators; four men were assigned to each team. Cobb gave them their instructions personally. They would stake out each mill location, one team per factory, and infiltrate.

He was a good hunter, with good instincts. His prey would have to come to him sooner or later. The paper was the key to success for a counterfeiter, and no one had ever found a way to get round it. No one.

Wednesday morning 8:00
MARTINIQUE, CARIBBEAN

Nick heard the jet thrust, and looked up to watch the silver flash of wings as Phillip Sturges' jet climbed, rising almost straight up into the blue Caribbean morning sky.

Nick's Rybovich sportfisherman sat at the fuel dock swallowing thick black liquid from a long hose. The diesel fuel pump bell broke the early solitude, ringing each time a gallon of fuel was fed into the tanks. It would take another half hour to get the full thousand gallons loaded for the trip to the Bahamas.

Nick took a slow walk to the end of the pier. The three of them had never resolved the accident, never discussed it. Maybe they never would.

Phillip had spent the evening in deep concentration, filling Nick in on the last three years: how he had worked to become head of the Fed; how he had been seduced away from a major Wall Street merchant bank by the President himself, to become the youngest Chief of the Federal Reserve Bank in US history. Phillip told Nick how he loved the job and everything about it; he could immerse himself totally in his work, forget everything else.

Nick and Phillip skirted the issues, the real issues of the accident and their friendship.

It had taken Phillip almost six months in the hospital with operations and therapy until he could climb into his wheelchair. He had refused visitors during that time.

And their conversation last night gave Nick an empty, hollow feeling in the pit of his stomach, as if he was dropping into a dark abyss in a dream. But he had decided to do it, to find Books, so he might as well do it properly.

These were his best friends, his only friends. But they were tricky, devious, cunning products of wealth and privilege . . . highly intelligent monsters. Why did he doubt everything these days? Why couldn't he simply take things at face value and just go and find his friend Books; after all, that was all Phillip had asked of him.

Phillip was strong and persuasive; even crippled he exuded raw power. His handicap seemed only to emphasize his indomitable will. His arms and upper body were thick and strong from maneuvering the wheelchair. He had the torso of a body builder. He had always been the biggest and the strongest of the three of them; that hadn't changed. 'And there are probably depths and intrigues going on here with these men that I will never comprehend,' Nick said to the open ocean at the end of the dock.

Nick found a piling and sat. He silently observed two seagulls perched on the next piling; they were watching a fisherman cleaning fish in a boat below.

He opened the chart he was carrying and started to plot his course to the Bahamas, but he couldn't concentrate on the chart. All he could think about was the accident.

Wanderlust was quick and unpredictable, a slick spoiled bitch of a boat. She had left Fort Lauderdale at dawn in force 8 winds. The maxis were always first out of the harbor. Eighty feet along the waterline, they were the fastest sailing machines afloat.

Wanderlust had been first in her class all season.

She was beating hard against the chop, heaving, slamming down on the curling breakers, torquing, twisting, trying to bend to the will of the gale-force northwest wind. The main was reefed to catch less wind, but still the mast was straining, the sails whining against the torture of the wind.

Phillip and Nick were in the bow fighting with the spinnaker, trying to furl the sail and secure the pole. Phillip was tall, with the body of a linebacker. He battered and buffeted his body against the sail, the pole, and the wind.

Nick was slim and agile, surer of foot, quicker, deft. He followed Phillip, wrapping the lines faster than Phillip could gather the spinnaker and bear-hug the sheet to the pole.

Finished, they held onto the windward stanchions, looked at each other and grinned. Nick was bareheaded, his blonde hair streaming out with the wind; his sharp features – high cheekbones and aquiline nose – seemed to cut the salt spray as it hit his face. Phillip's face was stolid, broad, and Slavic: a wall against the wind.

The wind seemed to be watching. It hit the mainsail with a gust that threw them off balance for a second, until Books and his father could fight the helm back to center, back on course.

Books turned the helm over to his father and fought his way forward to his two friends in the bow. The wind and spray pressed the slicker into his body and squeezed the skin on his face tight against the bone, making slits out of his deep blue eyes. He looked like a yellow devil, possessed and powerful.

The three boys, Nick, Phillip and Books were inseparable. They had trained steadily in small boats for two summers but until now had never been invited to crew on a maxi racer. They saw this heavy wind as a chance to test themselves and prove their abilities to Big Books.

Books' father, Big Books, owned the maxi boat and manned the helm during all races. For two years he had refused their constant request to crew, telling them to forget racing, leave it to the pros, it was too dangerous. But his son had persisted with his nagging until finally in his junior year at Princeton, Big Books relented and agreed that the three boys could fill in for the regular crew on this Fort Lauderdale–Nassau race.

Only ten nautical miles lay ahead before the Northeast Providence Channel and Nassau. They had a substantial lead.

The three friends stood on the bow pulpit, plunging in and out of the breaking waves as the boat lunged ahead. They held tight to the railing, laughing into the wind, young healthy animals challenging life and nature, bonded in danger, closer than brothers. They let go of the stanchions with one hand for a fleeting second, just enough time to raise a united victory fist, joining hands high to salute each other against the wind.

Phillip suddenly grimaced and dropped his hand, pointing to the stern.

Sundancer, a fast maxi from Hawaii, was beating down in

their wake. She had raised all her sails full, including the spinnaker. She was going for it. She was catching them.

Big Books waved his son back to the wheel and gave Phillip and Nick the signal to raise the spinnaker.

The boys could see the red slickers of *Sundancer*'s crew now as they danced in and out of their positions. She was racing against them only, balls to the wall; the storm spinnaker was in full balloon, and the main was reefed to the first notch.

Nick and Phillip waved the other two bow hands forward to assist, and the four of them unlashed the spinnaker pole and reconnected it to the main mast.

Getting the spinnaker raised in forty knots would be the final test for them. If they could get it hauled properly, they would be permanent crew for the rest of the season.

They were using the chicken chute, the same storm spinnaker that they had just furled round the pole. The other hands worked the foreguy and the afterguy, carefully feeding the cable through the pulleys.

As the spinnaker shot up the mast, Books misjudged the gusting wind. The boat lurched and the sail filled with heavy air, jerking the chute open. It billowed like a parachute, snapping the bow hard over, breaking the directional stability of the boat.

Nick couldn't unravel the spinnaker fast enough as the wind took over, ripping it out of his hands. They all knew what would happen if they lost control of the spinnaker and Books lost control of the rudder at the same time: a Chinese leap-jibe, when God's finger reaches out and flicks so hard the main mast kisses the sea; it was the worst thing that could happen when a boat was running downwind in dirty weather.

Nick looked to the stern and saw Books fighting the wheel, his father anxiously standing by the helm, but not interfering.

Nick cringed when he heard the foreguy cable crack under the strain and snap loudly, like a gunshot. He was afraid to look over his shoulder; he knew the cable was alive now, a deadly, angry, steel snake, whipping and biting crazily all over the bow.

When Big Books heard the cable snap, he knew the boys in the bow were in serious trouble. He broke from the helm, leaving the wheel to his son, and pulled himself along the safety ropes hand over hand towards the bow.

Nick smelled the smoke as the cable burned through the pulley. He stood ready in anticipation, imagining the sharp bite of the unforgiving steel wire tearing his flesh.

Without the foreguy cable to hold it, the spinnaker collapsed, swallowing Nick as the boat started to twist off the wind and broach broadside to the curling breakers. He fought, punching at the spinnaker with both his hands as he tried to pull the sail off his body, but it enveloped him, a cold white shroud pressed hard against him by the fierce northwest wind.

He finally beat the spinnaker off his face and came eye to eye with Phillip.

Phillip was hanging upside down, swinging, suspended at the base of the mast by the foreguy cable that was coiled tight around his ankle almost to his knee. He was dangling by a thin stainless steel thread, a silver thread spotted red with blood.

Phillip's eyes were wide, pleading for help, his mouth open, jaw moving, but no sound coming out. Nick lunged for Phillip's groping hand. The fingers of their hands locked and their eyes met in horror. The cable wrapped round Phillip's ankle started to strain and groan with the motion of the boat; it was pulling Phillip up the mast. Nick wrapped one arm around the mast and used his other arm to pull Phillip towards him with all his might, but he was losing. Their lives flashed before them both like the hollow snapping of a deck of Tarot cards.

The bow finally broke full over, hard to the windward side, into a full Chinese leap-jibe. Books had lost control of the helm, oversteered.

Phillip's mighty arms were no match for the wind. The force of the jibe broke their grip. Nick screamed Phillip's name as their palms separated, pulled apart by the strain; Phillip shot up the mast, feet first, and disappeared into the grayness above.

The waves cascaded over the bow and the boat heeled hard-over to the port side, tipping the gunnel deep into the water. The boat was close to capsizing, the tip of the main mast touching the crest of the breaking waves. Nick clung to the base of the mast and hugged it as the water cascaded over him.

The wave passed, and *Wanderlust* popped upright, the weight of the huge keel automatically righting her. Nick looked up the mast and saw Phillip hanging forty feet in the air above him, swinging in a slow pendulum motion. He had hit the first stay of the mast and was stuck there, his brown eyes turned black with fear, arms outstretched pleading for help, swinging by the ankle like a grotesque hanged stick-man.

Suddenly the bow plowed over in the opposite direction, full starboard; there was no control at the helm. As the bow lurched, Phillip was snapped by the cable off into the sea, like the crack of a whip. Nick watched the cable cut into Phillip's leg as it uncoiled, spiraling him off into the wild ocean, a yellow bullet shot into the storm, a human projectile.

Nick clung to the mast, screaming toward the stern, 'Man overboard!' But the wind drowned out his cries.

Books stood alone in the stern, fighting the helm, no match for the wild ocean, lost, pathetic in his struggle.

Big Books, a huge yellow form, was clawing his way towards Nick, towards the bow, slipping on the teak deck, coming hand over hand up the storm line, trying to help. He had seen Phillip fly up the mast. The screaming wind drowned out all sounds, but Nick could see his own name form slowly on Big Books' lips. And above the wind he heard Big Books yell out, 'Nick, hold on, don't let go!' just as a green wave caught him square in his massive chest. When the wave cleared, the deck was washed clean. There was no sign of Big Books.

Nick held tighter to the mast, squeezing it with all his might. He hammered his head hard against the thick aluminum mast over and over again, until he felt warm blood run into his eyes. He had to get the evil furies out of his brain, the terrible images of death. His chest heaved and his shoulders rolled, his hands clawed the smooth aluminum mast.

And he cried, the desperate, deep way a man cries when he loses his family.

The seas were ten foot and breaking. There would be no chance for either of them out there in that unforgiving, savage sea.

Wanderlust was wallowing, out of control. Nick fought his way back to the stern and Books, who was wrestling with the runaway helm.

Nick pushed in next to him and together they wrestled the wheel until the bow turned directly into the wind, to luff the mainsail; the sail went limp and then snapped in loud cracks like a mighty bull whip as it was caught by sporadic gusts. The main boom swung across the gunnels in a deadly sweep as the crew tried to drop the luffing mainsail and harness the runaway boom.

Books abandoned the helm and stood in the stern, screaming into the wild, howling wind for his lost father. His screams disappeared into the blistering wind.

Suddenly, off the stern, the race-photography boat emerged, smashing through the breaking waves; it was a sixty-foot Hatteras sport fisherman that carried the press and the magazine people. The Hatteras had been trailing *Wanderlust*, taking photographs of the race leaders. The press-boat passed twenty feet off the port side, plowing full speed through the boiling ocean, giant plumes of spray cascading off the bow and over the bridge.

Phillip Sturges lay limp and bleeding in the cockpit. His legs were splayed in an extended V, jutting out from his torso.

When *Wanderlust* had broken into the Chinese leap jibe, Phillip had been catapulted from the mast out into the ocean, landing only feet from the bow of the photography boat. They had pulled him aboard. The bottom half of his left leg, from his knee down, was gone. The fore-guy cable had eaten through the calf when it snapped him off into the sea. The first mate was twisting his belt into a tight tourniquet round Phillip's knee, to squeeze the pumping artery shut.

The Hatteras moved closer and passed only ten feet away from *Wanderlust*, plowing through the Northeast Providence Channel toward Nassau.

Phillip looked up at Nick from the cockpit, his eyes wide with fear and shock. Phillip made a hardly discernible movement with his fingers, a feeble wave. Nick tried to will him to hold on. 'Don't die, Phillip!' The cockpit was swishing red with seawater and blood. 'Please, God, don't let him die!'

The captain of the Hatteras, using the bullhorn, shouted down from the bridge as he passed. 'We're taking him into the Nassau Hospital.'

The Hatteras veered off and disappeared into the cresting waves and the whistling wind.

Nick turned to see Books standing in the stern, oblivious of everything, screaming into the ship-to-shore transmitter ordering the US Coast Guard to get a plane up, or a helicopter . . . to find his father.

They all knew it would be useless.

With no sail power, *Wanderlust* was foundering in the breaking seas. Nick put his arms round Books and held him in a bear hug. He nodded for *Wanderlust*'s first mate to start the engine.

Books twisted towards the railing, crying out, when he heard the diesel come to life, coughing black smoke off the stern.

Nick held him tighter, whispering, as if to a child: 'It's going to be all right, Books. They'll find him. It's going to be all right.'

But they both knew it wasn't all right. And it never would be again for any of them.

The two seagulls stood silently on the piling watching the charter captain clean fish as though they weren't interested, as though food was the last thing on their minds.

The captain flicked his wrist, sending the filleted fish carcass high into the air, end over end. Both birds rose screaming and squawking. They fought, ripping the fish apart in mid-air.

It made Nick shudder to see, again, the suddenness of violence. He listened to the ring of the fuel pump bell. He needed to go for a walk. He felt a sense of doom and foreboding, getting back into Books' life again.

And he wasn't sure he trusted Phillip, but he had to go. They were family. He hated to take the money, but he was almost stone broke.

Wednesday midday 12:00
NASSAU, BAHAMAS

Books St John took the steps to the Governor's mansion two at a time, impatient, not wanting to be late for a meeting that had already been cancelled twice.

The success of this meeting was integral to his plan.

Built by the English in colonial times, the mansion gleamed white in the noon sun. Two guards stood fixed at attention in crisp starched white uniforms, a black ribbon of skin separating their knee socks from their shorts. They gave no acknowledgement of him as he walked past them into the marble foyer.

Books asked for the Prime Minister. In seconds a small Bahamian man appeared, dressed in an impeccable pin-striped suit, and silently led him down the hall to two hand-carved floor-to-ceiling doors. He pushed the doors open without knocking, let Books pass, closed the doors softly behind him and disappeared.

It was an impressive, overpowering room with much history. The wooden blades of two white Hunter ceiling fans orbited lazily, pushing the warm tropical air out of the open windows and french doors. A dark mahogany table glistened the length of the room. All the chairs were empty except for the one at the head of the table. The Prime Minister was seated with two thick, legal-sized folders in front of him, both closed. He stood as Books walked in.

'Nice to see you, Books.' The Prime Minister still spoke with the lilting rhythm of the islands, although it was England and Oxford he wanted you to hear.

'Nice to see you, Mr Prime Minister.' Books made a point of lingering on 'Prime Minister'. Eliot Chandler had a big ego.

Chandler was a full six-foot-two, trim and elegant in vest, blue mohair three-piece suit and polka-dot tie. Books extended his hand and received a firm grasp in response. He sat in the first chair on Chandler's right without waiting to be asked. The legal files in front of the Prime Minister were thick. They had been negotiating now for three months and had made little progress as far as Books was concerned. He was used to the small talk and slow rhetorical ways of the Bahamas, but his patience was almost used up on this issue.

'Tea?' Chandler offered.

'Thanks.'

Chandler moved to the silver service behind him, stopping for a diversionary second to admire the garden. He spoke as he poured. 'I love the Bahamas, they are God's playground, don't you think?' Not waiting for an answer, he continued, 'The royal poinciana are exquisite right now.' He made a

39

sweeping gesture toward the garden outside the open window where a dozen flame trees blazed crimson, in full bloom. He handed Books his tea and sat down.

'So the Morgan Bank of the Bahamas continues to want Anguila Cay in the Cay Sal chain for a secret commercial mariculture project, do they?' Chandler smiled. Books remained expressionless. He wanted it resolved. It had to be resolved. It was the key to his plan. Books was the sole secret shareholder of the Morgan Bank of the Bahamas, a small private bank he had capitalized in Nassau five years ago, with the last of the trust fund his father had left him. He smiled to himself every time he heard the name Morgan. He had named his bank after the famous pirate Henry, not J.P. the banker, as everyone thought.

'Yes. We're still interested,' Books said slowly, taking a deep breath to keep his temper down. He rose and walked to the silver service and plopped two sugar cubes into his tea with the tiny silver pincers; he sat down and waited to get down to business.

Chandler owed Books a big favor, and so did half his Cabinet. It was time they paid. They had been working together on the sovereign rights' acquisition for a long time now.

'Our Bahamian bankers are screaming bloody murder. They do not want another tax haven on their doorstep. They are already losing millions to the Caymans, Panama, and the Dutch Antilles. I get impassioned phone calls from them every day about you.'

'Eliot, you know we have already agreed – no banking.'

Chandler rose and walked to the window again to look at the hibiscus and watch the gardeners at work. After a silence he returned to his seat and said, 'Books, getting this through Parliament is a major challenge; putting the votes together has been far tougher than we anticipated. Certain guarantees have been requested.'

'Such as?'

'A strongly-worded clause that states there will be no drug

smuggling from the island. If there is, the charter will be revoked, cancelled immediately. That will also apply to the manufacture of any controlled substance against the laws of the Bahamas or the United States.'

This had already been covered in previous meetings. Books wondered when Chandler would get to the real point.

'I've already agreed to that, Mr Prime Minister. I told you and the Cabinet that we are going to engage in high-tech mariculture projects that require the utmost secrecy and no interference.' Books worked to keep the anger out of his voice.

'I am aware of what you told me.' Chandler set his tea cup down smartly; the cup and saucer rattled in the quiet afternoon air.

They both knew the full implications of ceding the sovereign rights to the island. It meant no country would have any legal jurisdiction over the island or its population.

Chandler continued. 'This is an unprecedented move, one I'm not sure we can get approved. With sovereign rights, you become your own country, subject only to your own laws.'

Chandler was fishing for something. But what?

'Do you have enough funds left in your account to lobby this through?' Books asked.

'The money you have provided so far is almost depleted.'

They watched the two black gardeners slowly pruning the hibiscus and bougainvillea, laughing and chatting to each other in that easy-going Bahamian style Books liked, except when he was doing business.

He looked at Chandler. 'How much will you need to do the job?'

'Half a million more. And I don't want to mislead you. I cannot absolutely guarantee success.' Books stared at him. All it meant was the price would keep rising. This made a total of two million US dollars paid out so far for a desolate piece of coral that he still didn't own, an island that stood in the center of the blue Gulf Stream, bleaching in the hot tropical sun.

The tiny island was in the Cay Sal Bank located due west of the Florida Keys, standing alone, on the edge of the Great Bahama Bank.

'I'll wire the funds to your account in Zurich today.' Books almost sighed, hating to have to give in again to Chandler's extortion.

Books took a deep breath as he went down the steps of the mansion, shaking his head. He wondered how much longer Chandler would walk the fence? And what would happen if Chandler was deceiving him? Suppose in the end the Bahamian Prime Minister said no, that he was sorry, but Parliament had voted against relinquishing the sovereign rights.

Books' plan would fall apart and his money would be gone. 'Maybe I should have waited,' he thought. 'Maybe I should have waited to take the Black Box until after I had the damn island.'

Wednesday evening 9:00
ELEUTHERA, BAHAMAS

Heather Harrison was sitting in front of the mirror in her stateroom aboard *Desperado*, Books' yacht, waiting for his return from Nassau. She wondered what life would be like if you could live on the inside of yourself and look out without being touched. If only she could live behind the mirror she was staring into, see herself go through life as if life were only reflections, not reality. She would never have to react, never be hurt. Pure reason without emotion; why couldn't life be like that?

She focused on her image, raising her head, showing her

long soft neck. She caressed her skin with the tips of her fingers, looking down her perfectly shaped nose. She was more curious than vain as she twisted her head from side to side. She knew she was pretty but she didn't think she was sexy.

Heather began her ritual: one hundred strokes of her long blonde hair every night. She used an ivory-handled brush that her father had given to her. She stopped to finger the soft bristles. She rubbed them lightly against her cheek, making her skin tingle. The bristles had been replaced many times over the years. Jason Harrison had told her the brush handle had come from the tusk of a rogue bull elephant that had been shot by a friend of his in Kenya, after the elephant had rampaged a native village.

She'd never believed the story; days before, she had seen the hairbrush for sale in the window of the antique store in the storybook town where they lived, in upper New York state. But she loved the story, and made her father repeat it to her almost every night for years. She liked the part of the story where, when the shooting was over, the female elephant came out of the jungle looking for her mate and found him dead and wouldn't let anyone near the dead body for a full day, bellowing and charging those who tried to approach.

Heather stopped brushing her hair to examine the picture of her father on the table beside her bed. He was smiling proudly, standing next to a very complicated machine with several layers of metal pans, pulleys and a water pump. It was his invention to extract the floating gold particles that are suspended in ocean waters. The machine, like all his other inventions, had failed.

All except his process for color copying.

Heather finally understood what was really going on within her family one wet grisly afternoon when she was in her last year of high school . . .

*   *   *

'Jason, you have no choice but to accept the offer!' Rachel Harrison, Heather's mother insisted.

They were seated at the shiny black walnut dining room table, occupying three of the eight thick, high-backed chairs. The chair padding was stiff and uncomfortable and made Heather squirm.

'My copier represents four years of hard work, Rachel, and no one has a color copier on the market. They should pay more,' Jason said in a low voice.

'So what? They'll have one soon. And it's been four years of no income. I'm tired of working five days a week, typing letters and hauling coffee just so we can stay alive.' Rachel Harrison worked as an executive secretary to a vice-president of the Zed Corporation headquarters. Zed employed almost half the people in the town they lived in, and treated the county as its fiefdom.

There was a long silence, the pregnant kind of silence that Heather recognized. It happened between them often now, after years of arguing and bickering, chipping away at each other's souls. The gritty silence gave Heather the feeling that she had lost control of her stomach, a stomach full of glass that was grinding itself to pieces in its own black bile.

Rachel broke the silence. 'Heather has to go to college next year. Who's going to pay for that? And you're working on another harebrained invention; who's going to buy all that crap you always need? You, with your endless trips to the hardware store. I'm sick and tired of waiting. We need money, Jason, and we need it now.' She rose from the table and stormed into the kitchen. Somehow Heather felt that the whole scene was a planned act, contrived by her mother; there was something that rang hollow in her voice, as if she were acting. Heather immediately covered her father's hand with her own. 'Don't worry, Dad. I can get a scholarship. I can work. Please do what you want.'

'Don't mollycoddle him,' Heather's mother warned, coming back to stand in the door frame. 'I've been doing it for twenty years and it's time for him to face facts and stop his goddamned dreaming.'

'Mother!'

'She's right, Heather; this is the first decent offer of money I've had in almost ten years. It isn't fair to either of you.'

'No, Dad! Please . . .'

'Jason. Take the offer!' Rachel broke into tears. 'You must stop your dreaming or it will ruin us all.'

He looked so weary that afternoon, so beaten down, that Heather actually thought she saw the wrinkles begin to form on his face, life's essence drain out of his eyes.

He was always so happy, so cheerful, working in 'Invention Central' as he called his basement workshop. Together, Heather and her father had spent hundreds of hours tinkering. They had entered new worlds under the house, letting their imaginations soar unfettered.

All that ended at the dining room table that afternoon seventeen years ago.

The Zed Corporation had stolen Jason Harrison's color copying process. And he still had to deal with them.

A month prior to the scene in the kitchen, Jason had trudged over to the research center in the Zed complex to show his color copying process to the Head of Research. Zed kept it there for two days and gave it back to him, saying they had already developed everything he had, and his machine had no commercial viability. Too bad.

But Jason had filed a patent in the US patent office. When the Zed lawyers found the patent, they came to him with an offer of ten thousand dollars. In return, he was to give them a full release.

Jason gave in to the Zed Corporation and his wife's demands. He had no resources for a long legal battle, and he hated conflict.

Three days after he received the settlement, Rachel moved out. She sat them down again at the same dining room table. 'I have news,' she said firmly, as if she were addressing strangers. 'I am leaving you, Jason. I'm leaving this dreary household. I can't stand it anymore. I will send for Heather and my things when I'm settled.' That was it; she left, carrying twenty years of bitterness, disillusionment and anger as baggage. Twenty years summed up and spat out in a speech of less than a minute.

But Rachel hadn't told the whole truth. She had been having an affair with her boss for over a year. And although it was never proven, there was no doubt in Heather's mind that her mother had been working for Zed's interest against her father. The Zed vice-president was quickly promoted, and Heather's mother moved into a grand house on the other side of town; a week later she was driving around in a beautiful white Buick convertible.

She quit her job at Zed and never worked again.

The fight for custody of Heather was ferocious, and Jason used most of his ten thousand dollars in legal fees. He loved his daughter and fought for her as hard as he could. Finally, with no other regular income, his money ran out and the bank threatened foreclosure on the house. He had no hope.

One afternoon Heather came to visit and found him sitting at that same dining room table, immobile, a silly carefree look on his face that was mirrored in the shiny walnut surface. There was nothing in his eyes.

'Dad, how about we go downstairs and do some work?' Heather asked.

But there was no reply. Jason Harrison was dead.

Crushed by the death of her father, Heather buried herself in work. Heather went to MIT on a Zed scholarship. She lived with her mother and the Zed vice-president in the large house on the other side of town. They never once mentioned her father. After graduation she went to work for Zed.

Jason hadn't shown Zed everything when he had trotted his invention over to them, but he had shown Heather. She had inherited his creative, inventive mind, and she absorbed mechanical concepts quickly. It was his gift to her. But she was different from her father and in many ways she was like her mother: flinty and cold. So much so that sometimes it scared her. She felt like a turtle, thick shelled with only her head extended, the rest of her feelings hidden and protected. She had often wondered if she could really feel, feel deeply in her core, or if she was a heartless bitch like her mother.

She vowed that when the time was right she would slowly unveil more secrets to Zed, secrets about his invention that her father had taught only her, secrets that would open new worlds for photocopying. She would use Zed's money to develop these new techniques, then she would use the same secret against Zed. She didn't know exactly how she would do it, or when, not until she happened to meet Books St John that night in London.

Heather put her ivory hairbrush down and smoothed her hair back. She smiled to herself as she remembered her father's 'crystal ear', a tiny insert of pure quartz crystal that would receive transmitted messages from anywhere in the world. A miniature telephone message center, an audible beeper-receiver that you could wear like an earring.

Another great idea that didn't work. But Heather never cared that his inventions didn't work. The thrill was being with him when the concept was born, witnessing life being infused into a new idea, and the way his eyes shone as he explained his next wild invention to her.

But there were no more ideas from Jason Harrison and there never would be.

Heather turned off the lights and resumed brushing her hair in the golden moonlight that streamed through the open porthole. 'What is justice, anyway,' she asked out loud to the calm ocean that glistened outside her porthole. 'If there's no justice, there's always revenge.'

Heather dropped her brush and cradled her head in her

arms on top of the vanity, the moonlight glowing soft yellow on her fine hair.

Softly, she began to sob and sob; the muted sounds rolled across the still ocean.

Wednesday night 10:00
FEDERAL RESERVE, NEW YORK CITY

Phillip sat alone with only the green glass-shaded bankers' desk lamp illuminating the dark office.

He was waiting for Veronica. She visited him two or three times a week. He had called her as soon as he returned from Martinique that morning.

He pushed his red phone aside, dreading the last call of the day, the one to Ralph Cobb. Instead of placing the call he switched his attention to a report that lay on his desk. He had asked for it from the economic experts within the Fed; he wanted to know how much cash was in circulation. The report stated that in total there were 240 billion dollars in US cash floating throughout the world. This amounted to cash per capita of 1,000 dollars for each American. It was a startling statistic, because the report also stated that American citizens and businesses held the equivalent of only $250 per person. So 180 billion of the 240 billion in circulation was missing. Where the hell was it?

Phillip had come to accept this amazing fact; other studies had been conducted over the years to try to determine where the missing money was. The conclusions drawn were no more than educated guesses: the money was used by other countries such as Argentina and Israel as a semi-official second currency, hidden under mattresses by hoarders, squirreled

48

away in safe deposit boxes by dope dealers and criminals, used as the common acceptable currency in every black market in the world, or simply lost or destroyed over the years.

It was a huge amount of cash to be unaccounted for, and most of it was in big bills. Fifties and hundreds made up 150 billion of the missing money.

Phillip set the report aside and just sat waiting for Veronica. Her visits had become a major part of his life. He questioned himself about it; seeing her was becoming a necessity, almost an obsession. He sat waiting for the sound of the elevator doors popping open.

She would be escorted up the private elevator by the night duty officer, who would let her in then return when summoned, to escort her down to the waiting limousine that Phillip always ordered for her. She never stayed overnight.

He never let her.

He headed for the bedroom; using his strong arms and the cross-bar, in one motion he pulled himself into bed to wait for her. He picked up the phone and dialed Ralph Cobb's home number. It would be his last chance to call in private while Veronica was visiting.

'Yes?' The unpleasant voice resonated over the line.

'Phillip Sturges.'

'Phillip? Didn't recognize you. Your voice sounds strange. Do you have a cold?'

'No, Ralph. Listen. The President has called a special meeting at the Oval Office for Saturday evening at eight thirty; he wants to give us some time to gather more leads and information. Six people have been invited, including you.'

For some perverse reason Phillip wanted to make Cobb ask for information. But Cobb had played this game before. He let the silence hang on the line until Phillip broke it. 'It seems that the Zed management didn't tell us everything about what they were doing with the Black Box.'

'Yes?' Cobb said impatiently. 'Go on.'

49

'They liked the concept of printing money on a copier so much they decided to expand our contract on their own, without informing us about it.'

'Oh shit,' Cobb whispered.

'The Zed Chairman told me that they took the Black Box idea, and on Heather Harrison's advice they expanded it to include the currencies of nine other countries as well as ours. They were going to sell the basic technology to other nations after they developed it for us.'

'Developed it for us, at our expense. Nice. The software programs were complete?'

'Yes. Nine plus ours; they were stolen, too.' Phillip prepared himself for an outrage from Cobb, but there was only a long silence.

'So, they can print everybody's money, everybody that counts. Do the other nations know?' Cobb asked calmly.

'Not yet. Zed feels it would be better if we told them.'

'I'll bet they do; and just how do we inform them?'

'Don't know.'

'Well, Phillip, this was a pet project of yours, a project I was dead against. I hope you can come up with a way out for us.'

'Maybe you'll catch them, Ralph, and we won't have to tell anyone,' Phillip countered.

'I doubt it. Your buddy Books St John is laying low, although we do have one lead that I'm working on; should have some news soon. I'll see you Friday morning, at our regular briefing,' Cobb said, and hung up.

Phillip placed the phone back in the cradle as Veronica came through the front door, dropped her fur coat and strode over to him naked, climbed up on his chest and straddled him with her legs.

'Miss me?' she whispered.

'Always,' he smiled at her as she gently kissed him.

As he disappeared in Veronica's magic, he wondered what Cobb's lead was.

Books looked over at the attaché case strapped into the seat next to him and mused about the secrets contained inside. It had been a long two years of planning and plotting.

The chartered single-engine Cessna was given clearance by the Nassau tower for takeoff. There were five seats altogether, but Books was the only passenger. He sat behind the wing where he could just see the pontoons under the wing struts, the small wheels spinning inside the pontoons as they lumbered clumsily down the tarmac runway. They would need the pontoons to land at Harbor Island, North Eleuthera.

Eliot Chandler always set him off. Books didn't trust him, and hated depending upon Chandler to champion his cause with the Bahamian politicians.

Chandler reminded Books of someone else: Mohammed Akbar, the smarmy Arab, smooth as silk, cunning as a fox, with a conscience as black as the oil under his land.

Once they were airborne, Books struggled forward to the Igloo ice chest and extracted a dripping bottle of Smirnoff vodka; he tossed some loose ice into a styrofoam cup and poured the vodka until it was almost full. He threaded his way back to his seat, trying not to spill any of the clear liquid.

He forced thoughts of Akbar from his mind and looked down and watched Nassau and New Providence Island disappear below him as the Northeast Providence Channel appeared off the starboard wing. He thought of that stormy afternoon and wondered again what had happened to his father's body: if it had been eaten by the sharks and crabs as it drifted and decayed in the warm Gulf Stream current.

He gulped his vodka and went for a refill. There would be just enough time to finish the second drink before they would be in North Eleuthera. But memories of Akbar crept back into his mind.

Books had told the disastrous story in the Manhattan penthouse on Park Avenue five years ago. He phoned his mother, the Duchess, and asked to see her alone. It was her family's money. The money he had lost was hers. She was the main heir to the Oberson banking fortune. And she was the one he had to tell.

It was two in the morning when he finally arrived at the apartment. Shaky and jet-lagged, he had flown in from Abu Dhabi through London, in a straight shot – twenty-six real-time hours in airports and airplanes.

When he walked in, his new stepfather Horace was there as well, drunk, trying to act sober. They were both sitting at the dining-room table, waiting for him. New York was spread out below, sparkling in the giant window like a live electric canvas. His mother had already called London and talked to the Managing Director. She knew the news wouldn't be good.

Books sat at the table and tried to will his stepfather away, but Horace wasn't going anywhere. Books could never understand why the Duchess kept Horace around, with his pasty face, his slim toneless body, his inane remarks at all the wrong times. Books cringed every time his stepfather appeared, ashamed for himself and for his dead father.

'Go ahead, dear, tell us what it is that's on your mind.'

'I just lost fifty fucking million dollars. That's what's on my mind,' he felt like saying. But didn't.

He told them as coolly as he could that he had rushed through a large high-interest loan to an Arab state in the Gulf. After the loan had been made, there had been a revolution sponsored by Mohamed Akbar. A new religious leader had taken over who had no intention of honoring some 'usurious' loan to a greedy American bank.

And there was more. Books had put the loan through

without the board's approval. He had used his mother's family name to ram it through on his own, and now the money was gone.

He looked at his mother. Her beautiful, brittle face broke into a forced smile; she patted his hand and said, 'We all make mistakes, dear. I'll take care of it. Now you go get some rest.' She rose and left the room, leaving Horace sitting there staring at Books, a vacant look on his chinless face.

'There's always some light at the end of the tunnel . . .' Horace offered meekly. Books ignored him, staring out of the window overlooking Manhattan. Horace smelled Books' weakness and plunged on: 'But I'm afraid in this case it may be a train coming from the opposite direction.'

Books ignored Horace's weak, patronizing smile.

She might as well have plunged a blunt-ended spear into his chest. Books knew his mother. She would remove all his power now, quietly stripping him of his manhood. And he would become like Horace, walking three steps behind the Duchess, with no credit cards of his own. She gave no second chances.

She had been looking for an excuse, any excuse, to punish Books, and now she had one. She had never forgiven him for his father's death, or for being born.

He was an only child, a mistake. She wanted only Big Books and the fairytale life they had together. When her son was born, her husband became a devoted father, spending as much time with young Books as he could, time that he should have been spending with her in Paris, New York, Newport, and attending all the gala events to which she was always invited. She resented her son, and she hated herself for what he made her face. Books made her face the fact that she wasn't a mother. She was a woman with no maternal instincts, and she hated herself for it.

It was Books who had insisted that his parents let the three boys race. And reluctantly, against her will, the Duchess had agreed to let the boys crew on the Nassau race. She believed it was their inexperience and panic that had cost her Big Books, the true love of her life, the only person she had ever loved.

After his bungled loan adventure, Books tried calling her for several days but received no response to his calls. On the fourth day he got a letter from the board of directors with a check for a year's wages. The letter asked him to move from the bank's offices within twenty-four hours. The Duchess had scrawled a large red 'SORRY, BOARD'S DECISION' across the bottom of the letter.

Books 'resigned' from the bank the next day and had not spoken to his mother since that night five years ago. He knew he had been cut off for ever.

The Duchess *was* the board of directors.

The plane lurched forward as it touched down, sending a spray of salt water up and over the fuselage. Books was so deep in thought he automatically ducked as the water splashed against the porthole next to him.

The aircraft skipped along the surface of the water, sinking to the tops of the pontoons. The pilot feathered the engine and opened the forward door. He waved for Heather to approach the plane in the dinghy as he motioned Books forward.

Books stepped out onto the pontoon, tossed his briefcase toward the Whaler's bow and hopped down into the center seat.

'Problems?' Heather asked, pushing the Whaler clear of the pontoon.

'Same old shit. Mañana, always mañana,' he said, wrestling with his tie.

Heather leaned forward, opened the top two buttons of his waistcoat and undid his tie. When she was done, she pushed the throttle of the Whaler to full and headed offshore to where *Desperado* was anchored.

Desperado was a converted maxi racer. World-famous at

one time, the flagship of the fleet, state of the art, she was now retired from ocean racing. Maxi racers were the largest racing sailboats on any ocean, less than twenty of them ever actively racing on the world circuit at any time. She had a gleaming white aluminum hull with a single tall mast that stood like a proud needle, one hundred and twenty feet in the air.

Owning *Desperado* was a challenge to Books; it was getting back up on the horse that had thrown him. It was on a boat like this that Phillip Sturges had been hurt and his father had been lost. He had been taught that fear and pain were to be challenged and beaten. This axiom had been drilled into Books by both his mother and his father. He admired the purity of *Desperado*'s lines as they sped toward her. Heather brought them smoothly to the stern.

After they climbed aboard, Books disappeared below to slip into his bathing suit. He noticed that the broken radar he had removed from the mast was completely dismantled in the navigation room, laid out on the chart table in assorted pieces. Heather had been busy while he was in Nassau. He shrugged his shoulders. Maybe she could fix it.

He went forward to change. When he reappeared in the cockpit she had two frosty vodka and tonics waiting.

Heather was dwarfed by the giant stainless steel helm. Only half the wheel showed above decks, a five foot-high semicircle, finger-touch sensitive to the rudder.

'So, wanna talk?' she asked.

Books stared down at his drink, then out at the horizon. Finally he spoke. 'Eliot Chandler wanted more money. I'm almost tapped; maybe we should just print him up what he needs.'

'Don't be ridiculous. We have to follow the plan. Your plan.'

Books shook his head in frustration. 'Parliament has only three days left in session before it closes for winter break. Chandler promised me he would deal with it before they

closed. I think he will, but if it doesn't come out our way . . .'
He let the sentence drift off.

'We wait. That's all we can do.' She stood behind him
massaging his neck muscles, then gently rubbing his temples.
He seemed distant, his thoughts far away.

'We'll go to La Fitte Cove and wait, as we planned,' he
said, pulling her round in front of him, kissing her, placing
his hands on her hips. Her lips tasted salty. 'You've been
swimming,' he said, running his finger roughly along the top
of her bikini bottom, licking the salt off his finger. His hands
dropped and he squeezed the top of her slender thighs. She
was lithe as a doe, fragile and agile at the same time, strong
in the lean sinewy way he liked. She shuddered under his
rough touch; her face flushed as his hand darted into her
bikini bottom.

His rough virility aroused and fascinated her. He never
asked first. He just did what he wanted with her and she let
him, not quite sure why. She melted in his hands in a way
she had never experienced before. She had been with few men
and sex was not something she had thought much about, until
she met Books.

She undid the black bandanna from her forehead, letting
her ash-blonde hair fall forward over her shoulders. The
tropical sun had bleached it, leaving streaks of gold shining
in the afternoon light.

She tossed her head back as she undid her top. Her full
firm breasts were as brown as the rest of her body. Books
stared at them, moving his free hand up to gently squeeze
and twist her erect nipples.

'Swim?' she teased, slithering out of her bikini bottoms,
sliding free of his grip. She didn't wait for an answer. She
dove off the stern, knifing the water cleanly.

Books followed, his bathing suit crumpled in a heap on top
of hers.

Phillip was restless. His fingers drummed a silent rhythm on the arm of his wheelchair as he rode down to the main floor. Each elevator in the Fed serviced only two floors. Security alternated these floors every day, randomly, so it would be impossible for a thief to know what floors any elevator serviced. All floors could be cut off and isolated with the flip of a switch.

Phillip's mind wandered as he connected to a second elevator that would take him below street level, to level nine, the gold vault.

He wondered where Nick was right now, and if he'd located Books in the Bahamas.

The Bahamas. Summers spent sailing the small Oberson family sloop across the Florida Straits from the Palm Beach inlet to the Bahamas, just the three of them, practicing to get good enough to be invited to crew *Wanderlust*. Letting their imaginations soar.

Books always pretending he was Captain Morgan entering the Isthmus of Panama with his motley crew of two thousand pirates, men and women, preparing to cross the tiny strip of impassable snake-infested jungle to pillage and plunder, to sack the city of Panama.

Nick would move quickly in the bow, navigating like Magellan on his magical voyages around the world, discovering new races of people and unspoiled lands forgotten by time.

And Phillip acting his version of Admiral Horatio Nelson, the youngest Lord Admiral of the Fleet, meeting the mighty Spanish Armada in the English Channel, outnumbered ten to one, defeating the Spaniards with a brilliant battle strategy that had never been tested before.

Each boy moved in silence on the twenty-three-foot sloop as they crossed the Straits of Florida, each lost in his own world. And when they came back to reality, their unspoken camaraderie would bond them together yet more tightly.

The elevator stopped suddenly on the first underground floor and Phillip wheeled off; it was the wrong goddamn floor. They must have changed the designations and not given him a new schedule.

This was the floor where they compacted and bagged the shredded paper money. He watched as the men stacked the heavy-duty green plastic bags. They were waiting for the trucks from New Jersey. Garbage trucks were contracted to cart the shredded cash off for land fill in the Jersey Meadowlands. For health reasons, currency paper couldn't be burned. It gave off toxic fumes. Additional bags were set aside in the corner for pick-up by souvenir companies that manufactured novelty items with the shredded money.

The security men were shocked to see him. Phillip Sturges never visited this floor. They interrupted their work to stare at him.

'Carry on, fellas. I'm just a little lost.'

'Yes, sir,' the leader nodded. 'Trucks are coming this morning, sir.'

'Heavy?' Phillip asked, curious, pointing at one of the green garbage bags.

'Heavy enough,' the man said as he struggled to swing the bag up to the top of the pile.

They both looked up as the heavy steel door to the outside street slammed upwards with a resounding clang as four guards armed with M-16s walked past Phillip, nodding at him and closing the floor-to-ceiling doors behind his wheelchair, banging them shut, then locking them. This cut off the elevators, preventing any possible entry into the building while they loaded the trucks.

'Sorry to lock you in here, sir, but the garbage trucks are waiting to back into the loading platform.'

The uniformed men started throwing the bags of shredded paper into the hoppers of the two trucks, pausing every once in a while as a hopper flipped up to compact the green bags into the front of the truck.

The sergeant-at-arms stood next to Phillip as if he was guarding him. There were over two thousand security people inside the building during the day. Philip was touched by the man's protectiveness. He looked up at him and spoke. 'How much do you figure is in each bag, Sergeant?'

'About a million would be my guess, based on how heavy these bags are,' he said, grunting as he lifted a bag off the floor. 'A million dollars in small bills weighs sixty pounds.'

'Seems ironic that a king's fortune is headed for the garbage dump,' Phillip offered idly, fingering a green bag.

'It's just shredded paper, sir,' the guard answered, dropping the bag.

'Yes, of course.' Phillip wheeled closer to the loading dock; each garbage truck was carrying about one billion dollars in shredded paper. He marvelled at how much human effort that would buy in its original state. And how much faith and hope people put in the mystical power of paper currency.

The last bag was thrown into the hopper and the garbage trucks eased out of the garage. The guards stopped traffic as the two trucks slipped into the narrow sunless laneway of Nassau Street, emerging out of the concrete canyon into the downtown New York morning sun.

They opened the doors behind Phillip, pressed the elevator button for him, and waited until he was safely aboard the correct elevator before they went back to their stations.

As the elevator descended, a flash of the indigo-blue water of the Gulf Stream shot through his mind: the pink sand of Eleuthera and the wonderful beach at Harbor Island where the three of them used to spend a few weeks every year. The visit always ended with the final foot race, a ritual that had to be completed before they left, from one end of the beach to the other, three miles, winner take all, a conch shell. And how hard they trained!

Phillip always won.

Nick and Books were faster in the beginning, but it was Phillip who always cleared the finish line first. He needed the distance, the three miles, to beat them. He had the stamina, the strong legs; he could run for ever on that pink sand.

Phillip's hand shot out; his extended finger held the red elevator STOP button compressed into the panel. Thoughts of that day wouldn't leave him.

Phillip was lifted as gently as possible from the cockpit of the photography boat in Nassau and rushed by helicopter to a waiting ambulance in Miami. He remembered looking up, lying flat on the gurney as they ran him through the halls of Jackson Memorial Hospital, the wheels squeaking, the long tubes of fluorescent lights flashing by overhead like a glowing snake. The pain in his legs was almost overwhelming him, even with the shot of morphine, but he fought to stay conscious. He was sure he would die if he drifted off to sleep.

Just before he was wheeled into the operating room they stopped. She was there in the doorway. He never knew how she got there so fast; maybe she was vacationing in Miami.

They stopped the gurney for a second so she could speak to him. He hadn't seen her in seven years. She had run off with a South American playboy. She was beautiful, not just pretty, but a wild, sexy beauty. Thick pouting lips and almond shaped eyes. Her dark hair was pulled back severely, her sunglasses planted on top of her head. She was the female version of Phillip and he saw his reflection in her face.

'Oh my God, my poor Phillip,' was all she could say. Phillip saw her young lover standing behind her in the well lit corridor, leaning sulkily against the wall. He was built like Phillip, big and rugged. He was looking away, away from the pain and carnage.

Phillip beckoned his mother forward to him with his hand.

She leaned down, almost touching her ear to his lips. She smelled of Shalimar perfume and her hair had the pure aroma of baby shampoo. His voice came out like a gurgle, like a death rattle. 'It's too late, Mother. You're too goddamn late.'

He could hold the elevator for only another minute more before security would red-alert and come after him. And a minute more wasn't long enough for him to compose himself.

Friday morning 9:00
LA FITTE COVE, BAHAMAS

Heather sat bathing in the morning sunlight, breathing the saline air, the bosun's chair swinging lightly, brushing easily against the mast as the soft trade winds gusted. She felt like a bird high in its eyrie, surveying its domain, safe from harm.

The coral reefs showed below as mottled brown areas buried under the blue-green water. The cove was a natural harbor with a dangerous reef line. To enter was as tricky as threading a needle with a shaky hand.

On their way in, Heather had held her breath, her heart pumping with excitement as she stood in the bow pulpit of *Desperado* watching for hidden reefs as Books carefully followed the depth gauge and the chart, the deep keel barely skimming over the jagged coral heads.

She used her foot to kick off from the aluminum mast, swinging in a wide arc in the wafting breeze, watching Books swim and snorkel in the cove below.

Heather couldn't understand why he had put up such a fuss when she had asked to go up in the bosun's chair and hang from the mast.

He had finally, reluctantly, agreed to let her go up, but after he had helped her into the bosun's seat he angrily grabbed his mask, fins and snorkel and dove overboard without another word.

She thought it was the pressure of waiting for the Bahamian Parliament's decision that was getting to him. There were times when she felt totally isolated from Books, times when he was cold and secretive, in another world, oblivious of her and her needs. And she resented the fact that he had hidden the Black Box – for security reasons, he said – and hadn't told her where it was.

But he excited the wild side of her, a side that had been buried deep within her all her life. A side she never knew she had.

The entire atoll couldn't have been more than half a mile square, secluded, a long way from the shipping lanes, and it lay in the center of miles of flats that had to be navigated. You could see your enemies coming from a long distance. It was safe haven.

The far horizon was clear except for the small silhouette of a boat. She watched as it slipped easily onto the flats from the edge of the Tongue of the Ocean.

She let her mind drift, remembering the first time she met Books.

London in the fall, two years ago. It was the opening night party for the Picasso exhibition in the Tate Gallery. She had gone only because the Zed Corporation was a major sponsor and had asked her to make an appearance. Restless after half an hour, she was trying to escape quietly when Books had appeared next to her with an extra glass of champagne in his hand.

'Bored with the pictures?' he had asked, handing her the glass.

'Not really.' She paused, drawn by his smile. 'Well, actually, I'm not a fan of Picasso, so, yes, I guess you could say I'm bored with the pictures.'

'Hungry?' he asked.

'No.'

'Good. I know a swell place just round the corner.'

'A "swell" place?' She had to laugh. 'They don't say swell over here.'

'I do.' He took her untouched glass of champagne, set it down and gently squeezed her elbow. 'Let's go.'

That was how it had started, almost as if she had no control over the situation. But somehow she liked it. He was very tall and fit, casual and elegant, with chiseled features, slicked-down dark brown hair, a thin straight nose, and piercing blue eyes. He had a special way of smiling, very confident, and macho in an easy, old-fashioned way. Even his clothes somehow reminded her of the thirties, the Great Gatsby, grand parties on Long Island estates.

Unconsciously, from the beginning, she wanted to be spirited away by this man, so she let herself go, drifting along. It was fun, exciting, and she felt good with him as though she could just lean back and it would all happen.

And she did.

And it did.

She spun in little circles in the chair, letting the line that held the bosun's chair form a tight twist, then swivel her back in the opposite direction.

It wasn't until the second week that they had made love. They had seen each other almost every night. They went to the theater; trendy discos; the fun restaurants; Hyde Park on Sunday morning, watching the orators on their soapboxes.

It happened in Brighton, in a stately seaside hotel. It was the off-season and they were the only guests in the massive old place, with its tall spires that looked like derelict battlements defying the wild north wind and the dark, never-ending breaking waves.

The rooms were old and they had a pleasant smell. Books

had made the reservation, and he sent the bellman up with the luggage when they arrived, not showing the suite to her.

There was that deep sweet tension as they ate dinner and made small talk, both of them really wanting to get to the room. Finally they were there. And Books took over, like he always did. She was suddenly in his arms, kissing him as he roughly tore off her clothing and then they were rolling naked in the king-sized bed and he entered her easily.

They couldn't get enough of each other. Happy and exhausted, they drank champagne and started again, insatiable, feeding off their desire until the gray dawn rose over the English Channel.

They walked the beach in the dawn light, cold, bundled in Irish turtleneck sweaters and woolen greatcoats, then returned to the room to make love one more time on the rumpled sheets before breakfast. Words were unnecessary; their desire was enough.

She tightened the muscles in her thighs as she swung in the chair, feeling the wetness come back between her legs. She wondered why they didn't talk anymore, and she hated it when he slipped away from her, disappearing into his own thoughts.

Books yelled up from below, waving a big lobster at her and pointing. 'Dinner.' She waved back, happy he was over his little tantrum about her hanging from the mast.

She had moved into his flat after Brighton, on weekends only, still keeping her own flat in Hampstead Heath near the Zed Research Center.

His flat in Mayfair was beautiful, small, almost tiny. He kept it neat and comfortable, with luxurious down-filled sofas and chairs facing a small working fireplace where they lay naked, reading the *Sunday Times* on the floor, sipping champagne and orange juice for breakfast, eating big delicious omelettes and fat English sausages.

He often drifted off in his mind, his eyes becoming almost lifeless as his thoughts consumed him. There was an ever-present air of mystery for her, a dark zone buried deep in the recesses of his mind, a sadness that he kept to himself. She sensed that he had suffered a great loss, and knew it was an area she had never entered . . . maybe no one had ever entered.

She had never talked about her work to anyone, but she opened up to Books one Sunday when they were at loose ends after champagne and a long brunch in the King's Road. He had asked her about her work, and she wanted to show him what she did. She wanted him to be proud of her; for some reason she suggested they go look at the project she was working on.

It was just beyond the early development stage; the contract had only recently been let on the project by the Fed. She was able to sneak them in for a look, only a look. They never turned the machine on because once they were inside she had felt guilty, and insisted that they hurry out of the building. But it gave her a rush, a thrill, to be doing something naughty, breaking the rules. It was the same feeling she always got from being with Books when they made love. They made love in elevators, in ladies' rooms, in airplanes. And they had made love in the car in the restricted Zed parking lot that afternoon after they had seen the Black Box.

Something brought her back. She kicked off the mast again and spun one hundred and eighty degrees. The speck on the horizon was a speck no longer. It was a boat, and it was headed their way, directly below her. It was threading the slim needle of the channel, roaring in at full speed.

She yelled to Books, who was face-down, snorkeling on the point, unable to hear her. She was trapped in the chair. And they were trapped in the cove.

Each second the boat bounded closer. She felt the mast shudder from the strong vibrations of powerful diesel engines;

her chair shook. The blue bottom paint stood out as the water split off the yacht's bow in a high arc. The boat was following the small snaking channel, doing at least fifteen knots.

Books must have felt the vibrations. She saw him jettison his speargun and his goody bag with the lobster as he started to swim for *Desperado*. She held still, hoping for invisibility, willing Books to hurry, hurry.

The high-powered boat heeled hard over, skimming past the last barrier reef. There was only one man visible, and he stood at the helm on the flying bridge.

Heather saw Books reach the dive platform, catapult over the transom and disappear below, pausing only a second to look up at her trapped in the bosun's chair.

The yacht burst into the cove and throttled down, sending out waves in rippling circles. The heavy wake shook *Desperado* from side to side, causing Heather to have to fend off the mast.

'Stupid shit,' Books said out loud at the intruder. He tucked a .357 Magnum inside the towel he was now carrying.

Nick Sullivan stood on the bridge; he removed his peaked New York Yankees baseball cap. Books still didn't recognize him. Nick flipped the Bimini top back and took off his sunglasses. He stood clearly in the center of the flying bridge and waved, smiling.

'Nick! You shit,' Books called. 'I should have known. Of course it would be you; thanks for coming. Throw me a line.' The sportfisherman was within twenty feet of *Desperado*, inching closer.

Nick threw Books the line. 'You always hang naked women from the mast?' Nick shouted, and immediately regretted his choice of words. He had blurted it out, without thinking. He watched the expression on Books' face change into a scowl as he bent to cleat the line.

Books moved quickly to lower the line that held the bosun's chair until Heather was on deck. He threw her a towel which she immediately wrapped round herself and then she disappeared below.

Nick jumped aboard *Desperado* and gave Books a big hug. The tense moment had passed. They couldn't stop patting each other on the back and smiling.

Heather resurfaced wearing an oversized sweatshirt.

'Heather, this is Nick Sullivan, a great friend of mine from college, and everywhere. Christ, Nick, it's great to see you. Thanks for coming. You scared the shit out of me, barrel-assing in like that.'

'I knew it was you, Books. You don't see a lot of converted maxis around these waters, especially in La Fitte Cove, our personal gunk-hole,' Nick said, sitting on a winch, noticing the .357 Magnum barrel sticking out of the towel. Books pushed the stainless steel barrel out of sight with his forefinger.

'Can't be too careful,' he said, handing Nick and Heather a beer from the Igloo cooler.

After they finished the drinks, Books dove back to retrieve the goody bag and speargun while Nick secured his boat, rafting it tight against *Desperado*'s hull.

Before sunset Nick and Books went out to a small reef and speared a grouper for dinner.

Heather slipped overboard after dinner for a quiet moonlight swim in the cove. She swam in to the beach and sat alone on the sand. She had eaten little at dinner and made Books do most of the cooking and serving. She resented a stranger invading her secret hideaway. Books had said, 'Thanks for coming,' to Nick. He had obviously invited Nick to join them. Why hadn't he told her?

She knew they were three now, not two.

She smacked the sand with her fist. For the first time since she had been with Books she felt real anger. This was their space, their cove, and it had been violated by this stranger; how could he know about this place and why now, why now? He might be Books' friend but he wasn't her friend. Maybe it was all planned, maybe they had secretly planned to meet here and they were using her somehow. She hated herself for distrusting Books. She shook her head to try to shake these thoughts out of her brain. But now she felt alone on this barren little coral atoll.

No. She was just being a possessive bitch. She rose and walked along the tiny beach line, letting her feet get covered to the ankles in the warm tropical sea.

But she couldn't help wondering: wondering where the Black Box was hidden, what Nick was really doing here with them. Why had he been invited to join them in their secret hiding place, buried on the Great Bahama Bank deep inside the Tongue of the Ocean?

She swam back to the boat and went to bed unnoticed, without saying goodnight. She could hear the pleasant murmur of their animated conversation out on the deck. It was warm and friendly but it unsettled her even more. Things would be different from now on and she knew it. She positioned herself so that her back would be towards Books when he came to bed.

After her early morning swim, Heather sat on the bow of *Desperado*, drinking her coffee alone. She noticed Nick was already up and ashore on the small beach, just sitting there, meditating.

Nick was mysterious, as if he too held dark secrets: distant, calm, almost mystical in some way, as though he had managed to get deep within himself and wasn't sure about what to do with what he had found.

But the stunt with the boat was impulsive and wild.

He was a strange man.

She slipped below to the galley table where she had repaired the radar. She now had an RDF radio dissected and spread out on the table; she was adjusting the frequencies to pick up more stations, to take her mind off things.

Nick made breakfast on his boat, *Ubiquitous*, and after they finished they loaded Nick's Whaler for an all-day excursion on the flats and reefs around them. Books wanted to use Nick's hookah rig on some coral heads he had seen.

The marine phone rang at almost exactly the same time as Nick fired up the Evinrude.

'I better answer it,' Books said, disappearing below.

Minutes later he reappeared. The smile was gone. 'Sorry, guys, I got a problem.'

'Nassau?' Heather asked.

'Yes. Now they say no deal, and there are only two days of Parliament left in session after today. I called Chalk's for a plane. They'll be here in an hour to take me to Nassau.'

'Should I come?' Heather asked hopefully.

'I'd better handle this alone. You and Nick stay here and relax, get acquainted; no sense in wasting this beautiful day.'

An hour later Books was waiting on the foredeck of *Desperado* in his business suit with binoculars in his hands, scanning the sky for the seaplane.

Minutes later the plane arrived and he was gone.

And she was left alone with the stranger.

Friday morning 10:00
SECRET SERVICE, WASHINGTON, D.C.

'Shit, shit, shit,' Ralph Cobb muttered, studying the field agent reports. He walked to the wall map dotted with seven green pins that designated the paper mills under surveillance. He was alone in his office.

'Not one sniff of a lead. I'm not wrong. They have to have a source of paper. If it's blackmail, we would have heard from them by now with a demand. Where are they going to get

69

the currency paper they need?' Cobb had been monitoring the reports of his surveillance teams personally, with no results. But he knew he was right, paper was the key.

Cobb compressed the heads of two of the green pins flush against the wall with his thumb. 'Maybe I'm just jumping the gun. I'll give them another week. Maybe something will break by then.'

Cobb walked slowly back to his desk. He didn't feel optimistic. Either they were skirting his surveillance, or he was looking in the wrong places. But how, how the hell were they going to get the currency paper they needed? And where were they? Where were they operating from? They had to surface soon. And who was in this with them? They had to have connections. They couldn't be doing all this on their own. Two people against the world.

Maybe it was time. Time to call on a confidential informant. A man he had buried deep in the bowels of the underworld years ago. He had left the informant undisturbed for almost five years now. Maybe it was time to call him out, collect his marker.

Cobb looked through his coded phone book. He dialed the number and waited for an old familiar voice.

When he was done he grabbed his files and headed over to the Oval Office.

It had been five working days since the Black Box had been stolen. The President began the morning meeting by addressing his remarks to Phillip Sturges. Ralph Cobb sat directly in front of the President's desk taking notes. They were the only people in the room.

'I'm reluctant to bring in any other countries right now because of the media.' The President paused to sip from his ever-present white coffee cup with the word 'DUKE' slashed across it in bright red letters. 'Duke' was a nickname reserved for a very small circle of friends. He continued, 'Leaks to the media have plagued me from the first day I sat in this chair; even the law enforcement agencies have let me down.

70

I've decided to keep information on this investigation in this room, for now.

'The last thing we want is an international monetary scare. If the media ever gets hold of this story we're all in dire trouble. Even the hint that there is someone out there with the potential capacity to print large quantities of currency will send shudders through the balls of every banker in the world.'

'Maybe it's a blackmail scheme,' Cobb returned, though he didn't believe it was.

'I doubt it,' Phillip replied. 'Too much potential in using the technology; they're better off printing the money, especially if this Heather Harrison is involved. She's the expert.'

'And your pal, Books St John. Don't forget him. He knows his way around where banks and money are concerned,' Cobb remarked.

The President raised a hand, palm out, in a calming gesture. 'The first priority is to locate them,' he said, raising his eyebrows. 'I want some action. And I want it soon. I'll see you tomorrow.' He rose. The meeting was over.

Friday afternoon 4:00
NASSAU, BAHAMAS

It was four in the afternoon, and Books had been sitting in the anteroom for two hours. He was finally escorted down the hall to the conference room in the Governor's mansion.

The large carved doors swung open and Books entered, to be greeted by twelve black faces, all smiling, as he made his way to the head of the table. Eliot Chandler stood; the seat to his right was empty and he pointed at it with the back of his hand, inviting Books to sit down.

There was no apology offered for keeping him waiting.

They were all taking a tea break. The silver service was centered on the long mahogany table. Books nodded when he was asked if he would like a cup. They sat around making small talk for another fifteen minutes until the meeting was called to order. Chandler spoke first.

'I'm very sorry, but we felt we should tell you in person. There is great resistance in Parliament to the deal you have proposed. For us to hand over the sovereign rights to Anguila Cay means that it is lost to us for ever. The members of Parliament have voted against it.' Chandler paused, caught up in the mellifluence of his own voice. He was an eloquent orator, and he knew it.

'We do, however, have an alternative.' Chandler paused to sip the last of his tea. Books noticed that Chandler's pinky finger was extended like an English gentleman's. 'We are willing to give you a ninety-nine-year lease.'

'That doesn't work,' Books said bluntly.

They had already discussed a ninety-nine-year lease, and Books had rejected it; he needed the sovereign rights to the island and they knew it. 'Is it the amount of money?'

'Not entirely. Our brothers in the banking business have complained bitterly about your proposal.'

'I have explained to you all in prior meetings that I have no plans to do any banking from the island,' Books countered.

'But you *are* a banker, Mr St John,' Godfrey Turner, the Minister of Finance, chimed in. 'And you are related to the Oberson family, one of the most prominent banking families in this hemisphere.'

'Can we discuss the sovereign rights?'

'We can discuss them, but there isn't much point in the discussion.' Godfrey Turner was assuming the role of spokesman for the group. Books wondered if it had been set up beforehand, to get Chandler off the hook. Turner continued, 'You are asking us to sign over our national heritage, all rights and controls over the island. It is simply not possible.'

'It sets a precedent we can't live with,' Chandler added gently.

Books needed time to think. He would have to talk to Eliot Chandler in private.

'Could you give me overnight to come up with a solution to your problems? I'll make a proposal in the morning,' he said.

'They're your problems, Mr St John, not ours,' Eliot Chandler said with quiet authority. 'Parliament will be meeting this Saturday to expedite closing of sessions for the winter break; we open the meeting at ten.' He turned to the group. 'Why don't we take a light breakfast here at eight thirty and see what Mr St John has to say?'

'I'm not in favor of waiting any longer,' Godfrey Turner objected. 'I don't see the point. It's just too hard to sell to the Bahamian people.'

'Well, maybe I can make it easier to sell.'

'Perhaps; we owe it to you.' Chandler acknowledged the favor that many of the men in the room owed to Books. 'We will allow you a last appeal in the morning.' They all stood as the Prime Minister stood, signalling that the meeting was over.

'Mr Prime Minister . . .' Books started to say.

'I'll be available to you at eight tomorrow morning,' Chandler said in a quiet voice, anticipating Books' request for a private audience. 'I'll have a private half-hour for you then.'

Books drove his rented Ford Escort slowly through the streets of Nassau, past the crowded Straw Market and the bustling docks. He stopped at the toll booth of the Paradise Island bridge and paid the dollar. His brain was racing as he drove over the bridge. Without sovereign rights to the island the basic legality of his plan to print money was impossible, and all hope of succeeding on a worldwide basis was doomed. Money alone wouldn't buy the rights. He had underestimated the bankers' opposition and Bahamian national pride.

It was his last chance. He had to calm down and think. He had no plan to offer Chandler.

Books gave the hotel switchboard instructions to dial the marine operator. He gave the operator *Desperado*'s code letters and waited.

It was five thirty and the sun was just starting to drop into the ocean when Heather heard the buzz of the marine phone. She had modified the phone speakers in order to hear the phone ring anywhere on the boat. She picked up the receiver in the galley, where she was tinkering with the RDF.

'Hi. The problem continues here.' Books sounded discouraged.

'Bad?' Heather asked.

'Bad enough; I have until eight tomorrow morning to come up with a solution, and I don't have a clue what it will be.'

'Are you coming back to the boat?'

'No. I'd have to leave too early tomorrow to get back to Nassau. I need all the time between now and then to figure this damn thing out.'

'OK.' Heather tried to hide the disappointment in her voice. She understood the importance of obtaining the sovereign rights.

'Are you OK there with Nick?' Books asked.

'I suppose. Yes, of course. I'll be fine,' she added quickly.

'I'll be back tomorrow by noon.'

'Want to talk about it?'

Books paused. 'This line is loose so you'll have to fill in the blanks, OK?'

'Sure, I know.'

'First, the price. As usual, they want more money. Second, the Bay Street boys are screaming that we will set up a tax haven in competition with them but I think I can handle that one. It's the last one, the sovereign rights themselves, that is apparently insurmountable. They simply can't justify it to the people. It's a real tough pill for them to swallow.'

'At least money's no object.' She laughed. 'Remember, we can always pay in installments once we're in production.'

'Any ideas?'

'Only one.'

'Which is?'

'If you can't win, give up. Give them what they want, just alter it slightly.'

'Thanks for the great advice.'

'You're welcome, no charge.' Then, 'I miss you,' she whispered.

'Me too; gotta go now.'

The line went dead in her hand. She shrugged and hung up the phone. She stared out of the porthole window and saw the sturdy white hull of the sportfisherman lashed up against *Desperado*. She aimlessly fingered the phone receiver and wondered why Books had never told her that he loved her, not even once.

Books opened the curtains and watched the last beach stragglers make their way back to the hotel. He stayed there at the window after the sun had set and stared out onto the dark beach and the breaking waves as they hit the shore.

It was almost dawn when an idea struck him. It was something that Heather had said.

Waiting for Books to return from Nassau, Nick and Heather carefully stayed away from real conversation, dancing around any subject that might lead anywhere. They busied themselves with maintenance chores on the boats, and stayed out of each other's way.

It was six when Heather told Nick that Books wouldn't be returning that night. It caused an uneasiness between them that embarrassed them both – strangers thrust together by circumstance.

Nick cleared his throat and spoke. 'So it's dinner for two?' He smiled, turning to look over towards his own boat. She liked his nose. It was almost perfect, except that it had been broken at least once. He was lean, tanned and sinewy; his light brown hair was streaked with gold. His broken nose gave him a strange, rugged look. He turned, catching her staring at him.

'Who cooks?' she asked, blushing slightly.

'I'll cook. It's men's work anyway.'

'Men's work?'

'Ever see a female head chef?'

'Only one.' She smiled.

'Who?'

'My mom! What time?'

Heather spent the next hour getting ready for dinner. It was almost like a date. She took her time preparing her make-up and dress, fussing with her toilette. She and Books were too busy now. They didn't seem to have time for the ritual of romance anymore; romance had been replaced by adventure.

Why couldn't she have both?

She smudged her mascara and blotted it off, staring deeply

into her eyes, wondering what she was doing sitting in the salon of an ocean-racing sailboat about to have dinner with her lover's best friend. A man whose presence she had resented yesterday. Her clear blue eyes stared back at her as if they belonged to someone else, offering no answers, only more questions. She concentrated on getting ready.

Heather showed up aboard *Ubiquitous* at seven exactly. The table in the salon was set: white tablecloth, simple white plates, strong durable stemware. 'He likes things natural, unadorned; No-frills Nick, maybe that's what I should call him,' Heather thought to herself. Her eyes wandered to the bookracks and the collections of Aristotle, Plato and Sartre; first editions of Hemingway, Kipling, and Jack London. She noticed how neat and organized everything seemed to be, not like Books at all. Books always needed someone to pick up after him.

Nick was in the galley preparing dinner, wearing an apron that said: 'I'd rather be selling Avon.' He turned from the galley stove and noticed her fingering the books.

'I just started to read those classics again. Keeps the brain from atrophying when you're alone as much as I am.' He smiled.

Heather smiled too, turning to face him, her dress billowing out slightly from her movement. 'Nice apron.'

'Books gave it to me. Private joke about my old business. Why don't you play bartender?' He pointed over at the fully stocked bar.

Dinner consisted of stone crabs for an appetizer, a conch salad and broiled grouper.

They ate in awkward silence. Heather pushed her plate aside and finally spoke. 'You and Books go back a long time.'

'Over twenty years; he staked me to my first business venture.'

'What was that?' Heather asked.

'I was in the import-export business for twelve years; I'm retired now. I've been in the West Indies for the last couple of years, diving, fishing, just bumming around watching the coral grow.'

'What did you import-export?'

'Death and destruction,' he said matter-of-factly, sipping his wine. 'I was an arms dealer.'

Heather stared at him, her mouth open.

'Don't look so surprised,' he said smiling. 'It's big business and mostly legit. Books arranged for my first major loan with the Oberson Bank. God, how his mother screamed when he told her. Have you met the Duchess – the deadly Duchess?'

'Books has never discussed his family with me,' Heather said sharply.

'He guaranteed my loan with the trust fund his father had left him.' Nick closed his eyes for a second and saw Big Books struggling against the wind, trying to get to him. 'Big Books, Books' father, now there was a great guy.'

Dinner was over. Nick stood and gestured towards the flying bridge. 'I made coffee; let's have it with some Calvados on the bridge.' He stacked their dishes in the sink while Heather looked for the cognac and snifters. She poured for them.

They climbed the stainless steel stairs to the bridge and were greeted by a silver moon that hung in the sky, its light reflected on the surface of the ocean like a shimmering highway.

'Looks like the silver brick road to infinity, doesn't it? I've followed it many long nights in this boat.'

'Does it lead to infinity?'

'No.'

Heather slipped off her shoes and parked her bare feet up on the console, wiggling her toes in the tropical breeze. She looked at Nick, then over at *Desperado*, the greyhound, poised at anchor, ready to run silent and fast. She liked hearing Nick talk. She felt she was hearing precious secrets.

'Tell me more,' she asked.

'Books was my silent partner for the first three years. I

78

finally bought him out and went on my own. Large mistake! I did better when he was my partner. He has a nose for the future, for where the action will be, where it will heat up. He's truly intuitive, know what I mean?' Nick decided not to mention the tragic 'oil loan' that Books had made to Mohammed Akbar, the loan that made him an outcast from the Oberson fortune and an outcast from his mother.

'I think so,' Heather said, but that was all she said. 'Go on, keep talking. Tell me more. I've never met an arms dealer.'

'Not much to tell, really. I had small offices in all the major cities: London, New York, Paris, Berlin, Beirut, Brussels, Zurich. The arms business is a small, tight community, trading in a commodity. The key is not to stockpile the ordnance. But sometimes you have to, in order to get the best price; then you're forced to warehouse the merchandise until you get a call for it. You hope it doesn't become obsolete in the interim. I had warehouses full of American ordnance after Vietnam. It took me five years to blow it all off. I finally sold the last five hundred M-16s to the Christian Militia in Beirut.'

'Vietnam? I don't understand,' Heather said.

'The USA left warehouses, hangars, fields full of brand-new ordnance behind, billions of dollars in hardware, everything from M-16s to bulldozers. Right up to the end, the US military command wouldn't believe that the Viet Cong were at the front door knocking the gates down. They abandoned billions of dollars in equipment, almost like a gift to the Viet Cong.

'The Viet Cong needed cash real bad after the war. They still need cash. Anyway, they put their spoils of war on the world market for sale, for cash, good old US greenbacks. It was probably the largest auction ever held. It was held in secret, with only arms dealers and selected ministers of defense invited.'

'You were there?'

'Yes, with suitcases full of cash. The sale took place on the island of Phu Quoc near the Cambodian border. We all brought our own bodyguards and were assigned two good Vietnamese security men to ensure our safety. Most countries were represented there, except the United States, but the rumor was we had envoys present, probably the Israelis, buying back our own brand-new or used ordnance for twenty cents on the dollar.'

'Ironic. Did it bother you, dealing with them?'

'Bullets have no conscience.'

'And the people who deal in them? They have no conscience?' Heather asked.

'A few do.'

'What made you quit?'

'I ran into some trouble on a beach in Nigeria one spring morning about three years ago. It's a long story, not for tonight. And getting back to your original question, what about you?' Nick asked. Nigeria was not a subject he wanted to talk about.

'Like you, I'm retired. I worked in England for a long time.'

'You're young to be retired,' he said, wanting her to open up to him.

'So are you,' she said.

She didn't want to give out any information until she asked Books. Instead, she talked about how she and Books had met in London and how Books had changed her life; how he had introduced her to new worlds. Now they were retired, just travelling, sailing the Bahamas, and enjoying life. Nick listened attentively; a feeling crept into him, slowly at first, until he recognized it. It was jealousy; only a twinge, a flutter, but it was there.

She was so beautiful and animated in the moonlight that he had to look away. There was something calm and serene about her, yet she was energized, confident in her abilities.

'Would you ever go back into your old business?' Heather

asked abruptly. Nick wondered if she was fishing for something.

'I doubt it, not unless I had to; it's not a very noble profession,' he said.

'What is?' She smiled, the moonglow radiating from her face.

'Beats me,' he said, laughing.

'Tell me more about you.'

'Why?'

'I'm interested.' She smiled and toasted him. 'I'm fascinated by adventurers.'

'It's not very interesting; in fact I often wonder how I finally wound up where I did.'

'Fate? Karma?' she asked.

'Maybe.' Nick stood, slipped down the ladder and returned with the bottle of Calvados. He refilled her glass and his own. 'Little more grease for the jaw bone. I haven't talked about myself for years.'

Heather got up from her chair and sat on the instrument panel, letting the wind catch her hair. It flowed out around her, a golden mane in the breeze. She put her feet on his chair, looked directly at him and smiled. 'Tell me from the beginning.'

'Well, my mother worked as a waitress at the Horn and Hardart on Forty-second Street. I can remember her getting up and leaving very early in the morning, wearing her brown apron and white doily hat. I can remember the smell of the automat; Dad took me there once in a while for breakfast and my mother would wait on us: clean up the table, make change for the machines. They loved each other deeply, but he rarely mentioned her after she died. She collapsed and died on the marble floor from a brain hemorrhage. That doesn't happen often with women, you know.'

Nick took a sip and looked out to sea. When his father got the news, he was working, tending bar; a neighbor told him. His father made the sign of the cross, put his head in his arms on the bartop, and cried like a baby. Two neighbors brought him home. It was the only time Nick had ever seen him cry.

Nick continued, 'My father never remarried. He devoted his life to me. I look a lot like my mother, the fair Mary, he called her. "When you're with me it's almost like she's still here," he used to say. He took me everywhere on his days off, bragged about me constantly; called me the Great White Hope: it used to embarrass me a little. We went on excursions to Central Park, the Bronx Zoo, the Museum of Natural History, and on cold, freezing, winter days we went to Rockefeller Center and watched the skaters gliding in tight circles, the girls spinning, with their stiff, waist-high skirts, and the boys wearing trousers with stirrups. I liked the way they moved in a perpetual circle on those steel blades, a slow perfect orbit. Only the hockey players broke the rhythm, getting chased off the ice by the attendants.'

Nick let a small silence fill the air before he continued. 'It was there in Rockefeller Center under the giant bronze Atlas, struggling with the world on his shoulders, that my dad explained to me that there really was a man named John D. Rockefeller and his family owned all this and the Chase Manhattan Bank too.'

It had been a hard concept for Nick to absorb. How could one man own so much? He and his father lived in two small windowless rooms in the East Village. He didn't tell Heather that part.

'I lived with my old man for two years and never attended school during those years. I stayed at home and read, waiting for my dad. I did the shopping, talked to the neighborhood people, kept the rooms as best I could.' Nick paused. 'I never told anyone this before – I guess I felt guilty – but I never missed my mother, never thought about her after she died. I had my father and I had him all to myself. I think he knew it and that's why he never got married again. We had something special. God, we had fun. Lots of laughs, laughing all the time.

'Then it happened; my tiny world ended.' Nick rose, and looked out to sea. He talked with his back to her.

'It ended suddenly and finally when I was eight. My father was shot to death as he was wiping his bartop. He was shot by an unhappy Puerto Rican regular whom he had thrown out earlier that afternoon. The Puerto Rican came back, weaving and stumbling through the glass doors with a sawn-off twelve gauge double-barrel shotgun in his hands. My dad was shot in mid-air leaping over the bar after the man. The Puerto Rican fired both barrels at once.

'The next ten years are kind of a distant dream for me. My aunt came and collected me and took me to Georgia. I attended military school and hated the South. When a chance came to go to Princeton on a scholarship, I grabbed it; that's where I met Books.

'Books and his family showed me new worlds: penthouse apartments in New York, estates in Connecticut, massive homes on Long Island's North Shore, and mansions in Newport. And they liked me.' Nick let his voice drift off.

'You sound surprised that they liked you.'

'I was. Maybe they liked me because I was raw, different from them, street smart. I was not affected by the trappings of wealth and the privileges they assumed were naturally theirs. I never had those privileges; I never expected them, so I never missed them. I think I was the reality of life and they were the fantasy, and my presence made their fantasy better, sweeter.'

'Tell me about Books' mother. The Duchess.'

'The Duchess is a tough cookie. She always seemed to resent Books, but she sure loved his father, Big Books; he was the only one who could soften her up, take the edge off. Mothers are supposed to have an automatic, biological love for their children, but I'm not sure it's always true.

'She liked me all right, and even invited me down to their Palm Beach estate every year. I can remember the place very well. Royal Palms lined the driveway and cool white marble floors reflected the pink wicker chairs, particularly at sunset. The chairs always seemed to be empty. I would go down and sit in them for long stretches, and look out at the white beach. On windy days you could see the deep blue water of the Gulf Stream brush the beach in long, easy strokes. I always wanted to jump in and go with the flow, all the way to Africa. Just kid stuff, you know.' Nick smiled and fell into silence.

It had been during winter break in Palm Beach that Nick had seen his first maxi racer. The Duchess drove the three boys to Derektor's ship yard in Fort Lauderdale where *Wanderlust* was up on the ways, being repaired and fine-tuned for the summer racing season.

Her crew was disgruntled, working hard in the blistering tropical sun. She had been demasted on the way back from the Jamaica race. The winds had gusted to sixty knots on the final leg and Big Books had pushed her to the limit until her mast twisted under the strain and fell. The first mate told Books and Nick, muttering under his breath, that she was an evil bitch: slim, beautiful, and fast, but unlucky, unpredictable, and willful; a whore who did what she wanted no matter what the cost.

But the three of them all fell in love with *Wanderlust* and the adventure of high-speed racing under full canvas. They worked hard for two long summers on Long Island Sound, training on smaller boats, to impress Big Books, to convince him to let them crew in the Nassau race.

Finally, in late August, Big Books gave them a sea trial before *Wanderlust* left for Florida and the winter racing season. He was a tough captain, working them hard, testing them far into the night, stretching them further than the rest of the crew.

They sailed to Block Island and back with Big Books at the helm, shouting orders at them all the way. At one in the morning they pulled the maxi into the Stamford Yacht Club and made the boat secure. They waited patiently on the dock for the verdict.

Big Books walked over to them and simply said, 'Have your gear on the Oberson jet Friday. We'll pick up the boat in Fort Lauderdale. I'll send three of the regular crew on to Nassau by plane to make room for you boys. Books will man the tiller with me; Phillip, you'll be on the bow and the coffee grinder, and Nick, you're lighter and faster, so you take the bow; work the spinnaker and the jib. We're expecting heavy wind this time of year, so be ready for a rough ride, boys.'

Big Books disappeared off the dock without waiting for an answer, leaving the boys to whoop it up.

It was heavy wind all right, Nick thought.

'Almost midnight, maybe we better turn in,' Heather said, breaking his reverie.

'Books looked upset today before he left for Nassau. Is it a big problem?' Nick asked, trying one last probe.

'Big enough,' Heather said.

'Well, thanks for listening. I don't think I've talked about myself that much in ten years.'

'I enjoyed it.' She took a deep breath and stood, ironing the wrinkles of her thin cotton dress against her body with the palms of her hands. His honesty had caught her off guard, had moved her. She stared at him for a fleeting second, smiled, then stepped down the ladder to the cockpit of the Rybovich and over the gunnel onto *Desperado*. Her movement was fluid as she jumped from one boat to the other, the wind pressing her white dress against her body like a fine rice-paper veil.

Nick felt a little cheated. She had got him to talk, but she had said nothing of herself or her plans to him.

He remained on the bridge, watching the moon roll unfettered through the night sky. At midnight he saw the light flash off in *Desperado*'s stern, where the master stateroom was located. The only light that remained lit on *Desperado* was the white mast light, a small lonely beacon high up on top of the mast.

Remembering Heather swinging halfway up the mast in

85

a bosun's chair, naked, brought a frown to his face. She was Books' girl, but God she was beautiful.

The moon had moved and now hung directly above the mast, clouds streaming by, streaking the silver with fingers of darkness. Nick went below, poured himself another Calvados, and flopped onto the couch. He couldn't sleep, wondering what Books was doing in Nassau, where the Black Box was hidden, and how to squeeze the vision of Heather out of the recesses of his mind. He saw her jumping from one boat to the other, her flowing white dress waving airily like her hair in the moonlight.

Nick was pulled by the magnetic force, a force that he thought he had beaten. But these men, Books and Phillip Sturges, were his family. They had a power over him that he couldn't understand, and sometimes hated. They were blood brothers, welded together by life and by the accident.

Nick fell into a restless sleep. He dreamed of melting into the Gulf Stream and flowing with the current, floating with the Stream on its journey up the East Coast, past Cape Hatteras and New York, flowing steadily to Cape Cod, and finally north to Nova Scotia and the Grand Banks of Newfoundland, then east across the Atlantic to the British Isles where it turned south and disappeared off the coast of West Africa. No one knew where it came from and why it flowed as it did, a constant river in the vast ominous ocean. Nick felt close to the Stream, on an odyssey unknown.

Friday night 9:00
SECRET SERVICE, WASHINGTON, D.C.

'Where the hell are they?' Cobb threw the mill reports into the TO BE SHREDDED basket on top of his desk. 'My best guys on the job and not one sign of them. But they must have a paper supply if they are going into the currency business.'

He had almost told Phillip Sturges and the President about the Secret Service surveillance teams he had assigned to the paper mills, but thought: 'Fuck it. I'll wait until I have something before I say anything about it, no point now.'

Then he had an idea. Cobb grabbed the phone and dialed. 'Phillip?'

'Yes.'

'Cobb here. I got a great idea.'

'Yes?'

'You have banking connections in the Bahamas, right? And St John's last known destination was the Bahamas?'

'The Federal Reserve has no jurisdiction in the Bahamas, but the Canadians have connections down there through their banking system, and the Royal Canadian Mounted Police operate undercover. They might co-operate; they owe me some favors. What's the idea?'

'Money transfers in or out – Switzerland, Panama, Grand Cayman, Antilles, any unusual activity to any tax haven. They have to go through a wire transfer system, so maybe they are going to use the wire somehow to get rid of cash, or pay people off; shit, I don't know exactly, but if they are in the Bahamas, a guy like this Books St John will have to be interwoven into the banking system; maybe he owns one of those small banks, since he's always been a banker.'

'It's good, Ralph. I'll get on it immediately. What made you think of it?'

'Intuition and common sense,' Cobb quipped.

'Right, Ralph. 'Bye.' The line went dead.

Cobb flipped on the switch for the shredder, and fed the mill surveillance reports into the teeth of the machine. He liked the dry slurping noise the machine made as it ate the paper.

He did his own shredding; he trusted no one else.

Saturday morning 7:45
NASSAU, BAHAMAS

Books was at the Governor's mansion at a quarter to eight. He had spent the last two hours drafting up a revised proposal on Anguila Cay. He'd left the document at his lawyer's office at seven, and instructed his sleepy-eyed lawyer and yawning secretary on the format of the document for presentation to Parliament.

At eight sharp he was led down to the Prime Minister's private office where coffee and rolls were waiting on the table. Eliot Chandler sat in a leather wing-backed chair, looking crisp and shiny.

They greeted each other with a handshake, and Books sat on the couch facing Chandler.

'I'll get right to it, Eliot.' He purposely didn't use Chandler's last name or title. 'We have three problems and I would like to offer three solutions.'

Chandler sat back and listened attentively.

'Let's try the easy one first. Money. I've offered two million for the Cay. I'll raise the ante to four, two million at closing and two million in ninety days, US funds.

'Second, the Bay Street boys. I will agree that no commercial banking will be carried on from the island. It can be written in a strong proviso that would allow you to cancel the charter if violated. No loans, tax advantages, secret accounts, no commercial banking whatsoever.'

'That should make the bankers happy, but we still have the big problem of the sovereign rights.'

'Yes. The solution I'll offer is a limited term for the agreement, like a lease, but with full rights. You deliver full sovereign rights to me, but they revert back to the people of the Bahamas in five years.'

'And we keep the four million.'

'Of course, and all the improvements made on the island will be left for the Bahamian people.'

Chandler leaned forward. 'You must want these rights very badly, Books.'

'I do.'

'Perhaps it can be done.' He took a sip of his coffee. 'Perhaps.'

'There's one more thing. There are two million more in it for you personally, Eliot, on the same terms. One million on the passing of the resolution, and another million ninety days after approval.'

'Thirty days on the second million,' said Chandler promptly, placing his cup down, his hand shaking slightly, but showing no emotion. He was an expert at extortion.

'Okay,' Books said.

'You have given us a lot to work with here. I'll pass this on to my colleagues.' He checked his watch. It was almost eight fifteen. The rest of the Cabinet would be assembling in the conference room. 'There's no need for you to stay.'

'The amended resolution is at my lawyer's office. He will have a completed version to you by ten, for the opening of Parliament.'

'Yes. Well, I'll do the best I can for you.'

Books rose and closed his attaché case, reaching inside his coat for his card.

'I can let myself out. Will you call me on *Desperado* this afternoon after the vote?' He handed the Prime Minister a card with the marine phone numbers pencilled in.

'Of course.' Chandler looked at the slip. 'Where are you anchored?'

'A small island off Eleuthera,' Books said. 'Enjoying a little holiday.'

'That's nice. I'll be in touch.'

Books pushed the door open. His back was to the room when Chandler said, 'You wouldn't care to tell me what you're actually going to do on that island, would you? I might be of some service to you.'

'I've already told you, mariculture — a seafood farm.'

'Expensive fish fillets,' Chandler said, his face expressionless.

'I'll send you the first sample batch, Eliot.' Books looked back at Chandler, their wary eyes locking, challenging each other for a fleeting second.

Books gently closed the door behind him.

He returned his car to Hertz and walked to the nearest phone booth. He dialed a collect call through to an apartment behind a small paper mill on the Gatineau River about thirty miles north of Hull, Quebec. The mill sat on the bank of the river, nestled deep in the clustered trees that grew so well on Canada's pre-Cambrian shield.

A sleepy voice answered, 'Jean Valjean Mill.'

The operator spoke. 'Yes, I'll accept,' replied the weary voice on the other end of the line.

'Percival! How are things?' Books asked.

'Fine, Books. You?'

'Nervous. I'm still waiting on the Bahamian Parliament!'

'We're about there with the production.'

'Good. Be ready. I'll know in the next twenty-four hours.'

'Well, I ain't going anywhere!'

'See ya, Perce.'

'Sure,' Percival said, hanging up the phone and walking over to his desk. He took a long swig out of his breakfast bottle of Molson's. Several drops ran down the green neck of the bottle and plopped onto the pure white sheet of currency paper that lay in front of him on his desk. The drops of water turned the paper gray. Percival placed the base of the bottle on the paper over the drops, and pressed hard, slowly turning it by the neck, blotting the base of the bottle. He raised the bottle to look at the perfect little gray circle he had made, smiling to himself.

Saturday morning 11:00
LA FITTE COVE, BAHAMAS

Nick hadn't slept well and couldn't seem to shake the night off. When he climbed up to meet the day, he was surprised to see that Heather had already been for her swim. She was tinkering with the single-side band radio. It was dismantled, lying in pieces on *Desperado*'s teak deck in front of her. Nick stood on the flying bridge of his boat looking down at her, fascinated by her total concentration and the sureness of hand that came only from natural mechanical aptitude. She looked like an innocent young girl, her ash-blonde hair cascading over her shoulders, sitting fixed in a lotus position, her bikini bottom forming a solid black V between her thighs, her breasts swelling slightly out of the bikini top. He took a breath before he spoke. When he finally did, it startled her.

'Can you fix a Loran?' he asked.

'Maybe,' she answered, a little flustered, realizing he had been watching her.

'Mine went out in the Windward Passage, near Haiti. I checked the fuses and wiring, but it seems to be a deeper problem.'

'Take it out and leave it on your galley table. I'll have a look later.' She smiled. 'We fix anything at Harrison's appliance repair.'

At noon the seaplane carrying Books back from Nassau touched down in the cove, skimming over towards the boats. Heather jumped into the Whaler, picked Books up off the pontoon, and brought him over to *Desperado*. Nick helped him climb aboard.

'Great to be back. God, I hate the big city!'

'Success?' Nick inquired.

'We'll know by four today.'

Nick returned to his own boat to pull out his Loran and give them some time together.

'What's your bet?' Heather asked, laying her hand on his arm.

'Even money, no better,' Books murmured quietly. He tried to smile but his heart wasn't in it. There was no sure bet with Eliot Chandler and his gang of thieves. Books stood with his hands in his pockets, looking out over the stern, wishing the breeze could sweep his anxiety away.

'How about that hookah rig dive that I promised you?' Nick yelled over at Books and Heather from his boat. 'Books, you look like you could use a diversion.'

'Sure. Let's go now; I need to be back by four.'

An hour later they were over the coral head; it loomed up thirty feet from the bottom like a stone phallus, a hazard to navigation, the top of the coral head hidden only four feet below the surface. It was buried just deep enough to rip the bottom of a fast-moving yacht.

Nick had connected the second and third hoses and mouthpieces so they could all use the compressor. Books was the first overboard wearing a weight belt and his mask, bubbles floating out of his mouth as he purged the mouthpiece. Heather pointed at the noisy compressor, stuck two fingers in her ears, and somersaulted backward off the gunnel of the Whaler. Nick joined them both at twenty feet.

Books and Heather were studying a pair of banded coral shrimp, red and white candy-striped, beautiful, sitting on the wing of a purple sea fan. The male was making threatening gestures with his tiny claws, protecting his bride.

Nick wondered if Books and Heather knew that banded coral shrimp mate for life. If either lost their lover they would be doomed to wander alone for ever. Nick motioned for them to follow him and leave the little guys alone.

He took them down to the bottom of the coral head and examined a few loose rocks, turning one over. Books and Heather were startled by the life underneath the rock. Brittle starfish skittered and spidered their way off to safety while a giant hermit crab lugged its oversized stolen shell to the nearest cave. A small school of blue-headed wrasse burrowed deeper into the fine coral sand and disappeared.

Then Nick took them up the coral head to the caverns where the morays lived. There were over twenty of them sticking their heads out of caves. Heather's hand instinctively went to her mouth.

Books took her hand and motioned for Nick to take the other. They hung there suspended, the three of them holding hands, watching the morays while the morays watched them.

Heather held tight to Nick's hand, squeezing it. He glanced over at her, but she was studying the morays. He wondered if she was squeezing Books' hand.

At three they surfaced for lunch, cold chicken and white wine. Nick retrieved the hookah lines and at four sharp they were securing the Whaler to *Desperado*'s stern.

It was four fifteen when the marine phone finally buzzed. Books disappeared down into the 'war room' to answer it.

Nick heard the phone slam into its cradle, then silence. Finally, a 'Yaahoo' came screaming up from below decks. It made Nick jump, reminding him of that night on the dock in Long Island Sound when Big Books had said they could race. It was their rebel yell of victory. Nick couldn't help smiling as Books reappeared.

Books' grin was ear to ear. 'We nailed the old pirate. They passed it by one vote. But it's done, and can't be undone. Chandler thinks he screwed me royally. He put one extra clause in the proposal, a ringer, that he thought would queer the deal. But I accepted. He nearly fell off his throne.'

Heather cringed; she did not want Books to speak so freely in front of Nick. She tried to get Books' attention to silence him. But he continued.

'They reduced our sovereign rights down to only three years and kept the price the same. Shit, one year would have been plenty for what we have in mind. We just leased ourselves an island, a kingdom! What do you say we have a party tonight, a big party?' He smiled broadly at Nick.

'Sounds good,' Nick said, wanting to hear more, but Books disappeared down the galley steps.

Heather followed. She caught him up in the galley. 'Books, are you out of your mind? Why did you say so much to Nick, a stranger? I thought it was just going to be you and me. And why did you ask him here?'

'He's no stranger,' Books said, going over to the bar.

'He's a stranger to me!' she countered. 'And how dare you invite someone to come with us and not consult with me beforehand? I hate this kind of bullshit. Why did you tell him so much?'

Books poured them each a tall drink, taking his time to cut the limes and squeeze them into the vodka and tonics. He turned and handed Heather her drink. He had that smug victorious look on his face that Heather hated, that strong, spoiled, willful look he got after he won his way.

'I invited him here because we need him now, Heather, that's why!' Books said, not smiling, his eyes like slits, evil slits. He clinked the glasses together so hard that they almost shattered.

Saturday afternoon 4:00
FEDERAL RESERVE, NEW YORK CITY

Phillip read the report. The information originated from the Royal Canadian Mounted Police headquarters in Ottawa. Their mole, buried like an information tapeworm deep in the stomach of the Bahamian banking system, had reported a series of wire transfers from the Morgan Bank of the Bahamas to a numbered account in Switzerland. A CIA mole planted in the Swiss banking system confirmed that the money was being deposited into Eliot Chandler's personal account.

And the news got worse.

The Canadian police also informed Phillip that the Bahamian Parliament had, that very day, granted Mr St John the sovereign rights to an obscure Bahamian island, effective immediately.

Ralph Cobb had been informed and was checking into exactly what the granting of sovereign rights meant in this case.

Things were moving fast. It was time to inform the President and consider immediate disclosure to the other countries involved.

Phillip picked up the phone and dialed the President's private line.

Saturday evening 7:30
LA FITTE COVE, BAHAMAS

Books had requested a formal evening aboard *Desperado*, a celebration of the culmination of two years' work. Both men loved to dress formally and, along with his one suit, Nick always had a tuxedo stowed in the closet. The only change in the dress code Books made for the evening was that shoes were banned.

The evening began at eight sharp, with dinner to be served at nine thirty after cocktails. A table had been set on the bow of *Desperado* so they could take advantage of the cool trade wind.

Dinner was cooked entirely by Books, who considered

himself a great amateur chef. He had prepared lobster bisque to start, followed by veal Cordon Bleu, fettuccini Alfredo and Caesar salad; dessert was a baked Alaska, served flaming out of the galley by Heather.

They spent the evening laughing and making small talk, and toasted to their sovereign rights. Heather and Books didn't offer any details, and Nick didn't ask.

They all moved across to the flying bridge on the Rybovich for after-dinner drinks. Nick turned up the music from a 'Best of the Seventies' tape he had in the stereo.

Nick glanced over at Heather, who was standing looking out to sea. She was dressed in the same long, thin, white cotton dress that she had worn the night before, when it was just the two of them at dinner. The slight gusts from the trade wind pressed the dress against her slender body. She turned slowly and looked at Nick, no expression on her face.

Books finally got down to business. 'Nick, we have a proposition for you to consider. It's why I sent you the telegram. I bought a small island today, located in the Cay Sal Bank. I acquired the sovereign rights to the island; these rights put us out of everyone's legal jurisdiction.'

'Sounds illegal.'

'Not for us,' Heather said quickly.

'Tonight is not the night for details; but you know me, Nick, I'm not a dreamer.' Nick heard the pitch of excitement rising in Books' voice as he continued, 'Your skills are important to us. You have expertise in areas where we have no experience or knowledge.'

'My nefarious contacts?' Nick asked quietly.

'Let's just say you have access to another world, an underground world that is unavailable to us.'

'Want to be a little more specific?' Nick looked at the small line of breakers on the reef just outside their tiny lagoon. He thought about the coral head and the three of them that same afternoon, floating in a dream world, holding hands. Nick watched the waves break.

'No questions tonight, Nick. We're leaving for our island tomorrow. Will you come? Just trust me like I trusted you when you said you wanted to get into the arms business; you can pull out at any time.'

Nick watched Heather move over to *Desperado* and disappear into the galley, to emerge with a bottle of champagne. She turned and looked at Nick after she handed the bottle to Books, a curious look in her eyes, a challenge and a plea at the same time.

Books popped the cork and filled the glasses. He broke the silence. 'I'm asking you to come along on blind faith in our friendship. When we get to the island I will fill you in on all the details. For now, trust me. Please come with us.'

'Isn't that what the sailor said to the girl, trust me?' Nick smiled. 'Sure. I'll go along for a while. Why not?' He held up his glass to salute them.

Nick sat in the salon of the Rybovich with only the desk lamp lit; he watched the lights go dark on *Desperado* and poured himself a Calvados. It tasted sour in his mouth, but he swallowed it anyway.

What a disgusting role I've accepted, he thought. I'll call Phillip in New York right now, and tell him the whole damn thing is off.

Then he'll tell me that if the Secret Service, or any of their sister agencies, get their hands on Books, we can kiss him goodbye for ever – if he lives. Besides, I can't call Phillip from my marine phone, rafted right up against *Desperado*; clever Heather probably has a way of bugging the line.

I lose all the way around . . .

Books was always there for me. When I ran out of money in my last year at Princeton, it was Books who handed me an envelope filled with cash and said: 'From the Oberson Foundation scholarship fund. Problem with those assholes on the board of directors is that they wouldn't know a real scholar if they fell over one; so every once in a while Dad and I have to intervene and tell them what to do.'

I tried to hand the money back, but Books said: 'It's for you, Nick. Keep it. And let's never discuss it again. Maybe someday you can do a favor for me.'

'It's all too much for me tonight,' Nick said out loud, flicking off the salon lights. He sat in the darkness and twirled his brandy snifter and stared out of the porthole. He knew he wasn't going to call Phillip, not yet, not tonight. There was still something that was gnawing away at his insides, something visceral, something about the whole set-up that wasn't quite right, like a jigsaw piece that should fit together with the rest of the puzzle but didn't no matter how hard he tried to squeeze it in. There was something about this situation that had the same feeling as Nigeria. Something sour.

He quaffed the brandy in one gulp. He wondered how they were going to proposition him when the time came.

Saturday evening 8:00
WHITE HOUSE, WASHINGTON, D.C.

Phillip wheeled his chair into a place at the table and nodded at the President who was finishing some last-minute paperwork.

The President closed a folder and looked round at the group: the Secretary of the Treasury, the head of the FBI, the head of National Security, the Attorney General, Phillip, the White House Chief of Staff, the Chief of the CIA; and Ralph Cobb of the Secret Service.

The President looked tanned and healthy, patrician; he was

wearing a white monogrammed shirt, the sleeves rolled up. 'Phillip, I have informed everybody about the theft of the Black Box. Why don't you spell out all the ramifications.'

Phillip nodded. 'The Federal Government has been printing paper money for only one hundred and twenty-five years, since the Civil War in 1860. All currency up to the present has been printed using engraved metal plates. The metal plates carry a finely-etched, recessed design.' Phillip handed out three engraved plates of twenty-, fifty-, and hundred-dollar denominations. He continued, 'Ink is mechanically rubbed on the plates, then all the excess is removed. This leaves the ink buried only in the fine, recessed lines. The plate is then pressed firmly against paper; this causes the design to transfer not onto the paper, *into* the paper.'

Phillip paused to sip his coffee. He knew most of these men had already learned about currency engraving once, but the importance of the method as it applied to the problem about to be put before them necessitated reminding everyone of the details of the process. As the plates circulated, some of the men ran their fingers over the engraved plates, tracing the lines. He continued. 'The only change that has developed during the five hundred years that paper drafts and currencies have been traded in the world is that now the work is performed on machines run by electricity, and the plates themselves are no longer engraved totally by hand. Otherwise, the technology is the same.

'This system has worked well in the past because no matter how talented the engraver of a counterfeit plate was, he could never perfectly duplicate every single line and detail of the original plate.

'Even the Germans in World War Two, when they were counterfeiting the English pound, couldn't do a perfect job, and they had unlimited resources. The concentration camps provided the finest engravers in Europe to work on the plates. The banknotes were magnified one hundredfold on a screen

99

and the forgeries they produced were good, but never perfect. Fine details were either lacking or distorted.

'There is never a distortion on a Federal bill, because the plates are original and perfect. And there is never a distortion on a bill produced by the technology inside this Black Box.' He tossed a picture of the Black Box on the table.

'In front of each of you is a folder containing currency from ten countries; there's one real bill and one counterfeit for each. They were sent to us by the Zed Corporation. If you'll open the folders you'll see what I'm talking about.'

Each of the six men reached forward and opened the folders to examine the bills. The President and Phillip watched in silence as they held the currency up to the light and flipped the bills over, whistling a chorus of admiration and amazement.

The President spoke: 'It's no trick, gentlemen. One of the bills for each currency has been made with the Black Box, the other has come from the country's own mint. Other than minute discrepancies in the paper, the experts in our lab were unable to see any differences.'

'That's because there are no differences,' Phillip added. 'A counterfeit bill, up to now, when photocopied, always had distortions. The fine border detailing has what is called "blackground" because the pattern is printed white out of solid black. Much of this extra-fine engraving is blurred by a conventional photocopier, but that's not so if the Black Box is used.'

'The woman we're looking for, Heather Harrison, developed this new technology for the Zed Corporation,' Cobb interrupted.

Phillip took back the floor. 'What she invented was a revolutionary process. Starting with a small powerful selenium cell, containing strongly photosensitive metalloids, she added advanced laser beam technology and digital-microwave techniques and put them all inside that Black Box. The system basically burns the ink into the bill so that it comes out exactly like an engraving. She uses her own software inside a regular IBM PCT/XT computer to tell the Black Box what to do. And it prints faster and better than a conventional press, because she uses the Zed 3600 advanced color copier.'

It was Ralph Cobb's turn. He stood before he spoke. 'The RCMP has a mole planted inside the Bahamian banking system. This mole has discovered that large sums of money have been transferred from the Morgan Bank of the Bahamas to a numbered account in Switzerland. We know that this money was transferred to Eliot Chandler's private account there.' Cobb paused to look around. 'The owner of the Morgan bank is John St John, the perpetrator of the Black Box theft.'

The head of the FBI yawned. He had been up most of the previous night working on another case. Everyone in the room knew that Eliot Chandler was on the take from anyone who would give.

'I know that's not particularly surprising,' Cobb said, almost in answer to the yawn. 'What is startling is the fact that the Bahamas voted today, this very afternoon, to allow a shell company owned by John St John to acquire the sovereign rights to a little-known Cay in an obscure chain of uninhabited Bahamian islands.'

Cobb had their attention now. He continued, 'I had an agent in Nassau fax me a copy of the legislation that was passed. Sovereign rights, in this case, means that they can do whatever they like and we don't have a legal foot to stand on if we try to move against them. Just like they were Monaco or Liechtenstein or any of those tiny countries that do whatever the hell they feel like.'

Cobb unfolded a Coast and Geodetic Survey Chart of Anguila Cay, in the Cay Sal Bank. He spread the chart out, pointing to a thick red circle drawn round the location of the islands.

'Can't we arrest him now,' the Secretary of the Treasury asked, 'for the English theft?'

101

'No,' the CIA chief answered. 'We have no jurisdiction, and there is no British extradition treaty covering the theft. And if he's on his own island outside normal law, we can't lay a glove on him.'

'There can be no leaks on this one, gentlemen. I don't have to explain what would happen if the press got hold of his information.' The President sat circling the little chain of islands with his forefinger.

'And the other nations involved?' the Chief of Staff broke the silence. 'What about them?'

'Nothing has happened yet; as far as we know, St John hasn't produced a single dollar, so we don't need to inform them until they need to know.'

'Maybe they will never know,' Cobb muttered.

'What's that, Ralph?' the President asked, standing.

Cobb looked up at the President and said, 'If we move quickly and correctly, we may stop this catastrophe before it starts, sir.'

Cobb was thinking of paper, and paper mills, specialty mills that he had under surveillance; without the proper paper they were finished before they started, and no counterfeiter had ever solved the problem of duplicating currency paper. Paper was a subject that had not been discussed at the meeting, and Cobb had no intention of bringing it up now. If he was right and he nipped them at one of the mills, he would be a hero; if he was wrong, no one would ever know what he had done. He couldn't lose either way. He was covered. It was just the way he liked it.

He smiled, staring into his black coffee, trying to hide his secret. He was going to destroy these fucking counterfeiters.

The face of his confidential informant appeared in the black shiny coffee and he wondered why he hadn't had any information from him. Maybe no news was good news.

Nick could barely see *Desperado*, but she was well within radar range, about six knots north of his position. They had decided to make the voyage to the Cay Sal Bank together.

Nick spotted the giant mainsail on the horizon. Books had *Desperado* hugging the Great Bahama Bank as tight as he dared. The breeze was stiff, thirty knots from the northeast; it gave *Desperado* a chance to strut her stuff, to dangle. Nick watched them through his binoculars. *Desperado*'s portside deck rail was submerged as she heeled over, tacking, cutting the water clean and steady, leaving a waveless wake.

He could see Books hard at work, trimming the sails constantly, using the hydraulic control board at his finger tips while Heather walked the starboard high-side railing, clipping her lifeline to the stainless steel stanchions as she moved forward to the bow pulpit. Nick could see her hair, wet and dark from the spray.

He secured the binoculars and started the second engine, deciding to go on through directly to the Cay Sal Bank; by his calculations he would get there two hours before *Desperado*. There would still be some light left so he could secure a good anchorage and do a little exploring.

To Heather, Nick's Rybovich looked like a lonely silhouette on the horizon, a tiny life form among the forces of nature. The sportfisherman was picking up speed, churning its wake into larger waves.

Heather eased herself off the bow pulpit, moving carefully along the teak deck, holding onto the high side stormrail. She thought of Nick alone on the ocean, always alone. How could he be so self-contained, so strong within himself. Or was it just an act, a facade?

Heather was snapped back into reality with a crackling gust of wind. Books was keeping the pressure on, tightening the halyards, bringing *Desperado* in tighter to the wind until the entire boat was straining and groaning. It was as if he were driven to test himself against the ocean.

With full canvas flying and thirty knots of dirty northeast wind pushing them on toward the Cay Sal bank, Heather was alert, on the edge of fear. She went to the stern to join Books.

He pointed at the stainless steel helm as she sat down next to him. She shook her head 'No', but he roughly took one of her hands and placed it on the wheel, then he moved over, almost forcing her to slide into his spot. Books put his hands over hers to steady her and give her confidence. He spoke in her ear. 'Nice and easy, do everything slowly; give her a chance to follow your orders. There's always a few seconds' delay before she responds. Keep this course.' Books pointed at the red flashing digital readout that showed their exact course. 'I'm going to talk to Nick on the satcom phone,' he said, going below.

Heather could feel the raw power of the wind and the sails. The boat was trimmed perfectly. It responded to her as she massaged the wheel, a living extension of her arms, the sails whining and moaning in the wind. It was complete and total power, not theory, not daydreams, not discussion. It was pure action.

She settled in, edging the wheel to each side just to see what would happen. The boat responded as if they were one, like a lover.

It pleased her, but she also resented the way Books seemed to force her into doing things she never thought she was capable of doing. Then she did them and surprised herself.

No, she had a will of her own. No one really ever got forced into things; she was where she wanted to be. Maybe it was just that his will was stronger, more powerful, and it overwhelmed her; or maybe he didn't force her at all, maybe these powers were just latent within her, and he triggered them out of her psyche, just as he had brought her to life sexually. It was all connected, and all complicated.

Nick was the opposite of Books: he was quiet, assured power, straight, clear in his thoughts. But why had he agreed so easily last night to go with them to the Cay Sal Bank? Did he really love Books that much, or did Books have the same kind of magical power over Nick as he did over her. Or was there something else going on that she wasn't aware of?

Books had power that came with great wealth and a superlative natural intelligence; true dominance that allowed him to get up over anybody, anything.

He emerged from below, and yelled above the wind that was howling at his back, 'Nick is going on his way. He'll meet us at Cay Sal, says he will keep us in the radar scope in case of any trouble.' He smiled. 'Hungry?'

Heather nodded her head emphatically. Books disappeared below to shove a frozen pizza into the microwave that hung swinging from gimbals. He grabbed a couple of apples and hunted for cheese.

She thought about the Black Box again and wondered where it was. Books had taken it for safekeeping when they had arrived in Nassau. It was her baby, her invention, her and her father's invention; she should know where the hell it was.

And she pondered the reasons why she had said yes when he had suggested that they actually steal it.

Books and Heather reached the top of the Cay Sal Bank at four in the afternoon. They passed Dog Rocks and Damas Cays and a dangerous shoal area.

Anguila Cay was dead ahead, the largest cay in the tiny group of coral islands. Books crossed Anguila Cay off the chart, smiled, and idly wrote in 'Treasure Island' in bold black letters.

The island was a sandy mangrove-covered key, no more than half a mile in length and quarter of a mile wide. A few lonely palm trees stood tall above the white coral sand.

The only hint of life on this bleak island was an old tar-paper driftwood shack that faced the harbor. It stood on the beach, listing like a drunk. It looked as if a strong wind could finish the job, but the shack had withstood the fierce gales and wild hurricanes that blew in off the Atlantic.

It was where Caleb, the Bahamian Customs Inspector, used to live before Books bought the island. A bottle of Scotch, some conversation or an old issue of *Playboy* was the toll he collected from fancy yachtsmen or rugged tropical fish divers who came to dive the Cay Sal wall.

The drug smugglers and boat pirates gave Cay Sal Bank a wide berth. It was too open and easily surrounded, sitting alone in the center of the Gulf Stream; there was no place to hide.

Nick was at anchor, waiting in the natural harbor of Anguila Cay. He helped them cover the sails and rig the big tarp to give them shade.

They finished a seafood dinner and two bottles of wine by sunset, slowly unwinding from the journey. They were too keyed up to sleep. Books made coffee and began.

'It's time to tell you, Nick, but I want you to swear to me that you will never tell another living soul what I am about to tell you today. And if your answer is no, you will stop me as early as you can, so I don't say too much. If the answer is no we will pretend this conversation never occurred. Agreed?'

'Agreed.'

'We plan to make money.'

'Most people do,' Nick answered.

'Yeah! Only we plan to manufacture it. Print it.'

Nick let out a long low whistle of feigned surprise. He wondered what kind of an actor he was. He didn't feel like a very good one.

'The reason the acquisition of this island is so important is that it gives us total privacy.'

'And puts us out of everyone's legal jurisdiction,' Heather added.

Books carried on, 'We are going to manufacture paper money here. There is nothing inherently illegal in the manufacture of currency on this island, because it is a sovereign country, independent in every way. It is only the *selling* of bogus currency that is illegal.' Books took a sip of his coffee as Heather got up to make a fresh pot. He paused and studied Nick.

'It sounds impossible, Books. How can you handle the technology, the paper, the ink, and the distribution channels? And what will you take for payment, more paper? No one can buck an entire government. I don't think so, no chance.'

'It's not just one government, we have the capacity to do the currency of nine other countries besides the US dollar.'

Great! Just great! Nine other countries, Nick thought to himself. Phillip Sturges hadn't mentioned nine other countries. Nick thought Phillip had a very convenient memory.

'We handle the major technology with this.' Books slid a photo of the Black Box over to Nick.

It was the same one Philip had shown him in Martinique.

Books continued, 'Doesn't look like much, does it? It needs a computer on one end and a deluxe color copier on the other end. But it can perform magic, alchemy, it turns paper into gold. The computer directs the Black Box and the Black Box directs the color copier. Makes perfect currency, good as the US Mint.'

'You have samples?'

Books nodded at Heather. She went forward to the safe in the bow and returned with ten fifty-dollar bills. She handed them to Nick.

Nick walked over to the light above the chart table and studied the bills. He shook his head in genuine admiration as he handed them back to Heather. 'How do you get currency paper?'

'That's the most difficult thing of all, but the paper is covered. I own a paper mill. One of my worst investments up to now, but this year it will make a great contribution to profits,' Books said.

'And ink?'

Books nodded at Heather to explain.

'The computer measures the ink density and controls the flow through the Black Box. Ink used for currency is special magnetic ink. The copier, with the aid of the Black Box, is able to funnel this ink through very thin plastic coils, exactly the way teller machines on every corner of America measure ink density, so they don't give out bills of the wrong denomination or two bills instead of one. We use the same process to get exactly the right color and density on the bill.'

'Distribution?'

'This is where you come in. Are you interested?'

'I agreed I would tell you to stop when I had heard enough; carry on, Books.'

'I have two very large organizations in mind to distribute. And I would like you to deal with them: the Mafia and the Corsican Brotherhood.' Books waited for Nick.

'Go ahead.'

'I also want you to help me fortify the island. I need it armed to the tits. We'll need radar, ground security, mines, ground-to-air missiles, the works.'

'Fort St John,' Heather said weakly. 'Isn't that overdoing it a little?' The concept that there might be real physical danger was just beginning to become real to her.

'No,' Books said, sensing her fear. 'If trouble comes, we want to be ready, and Nick knows that business better than anyone,' he said.

Books turned to the chart table in front of him. On it was an enlargement of an aerial shot of Anguila Cay, covered with clear acetate. Several buildings had been sketched in on the plastic, and the proposed locations for the armaments. A large ship was marked anchored offshore. Nick laid his finger on it and looked up at Books, a question in his eyes.

'It's a liberty ship. That's where we'll live. I want you to buy one out of Government surplus.'

'How will you power this operation?' Nick asked, rising to place his cup in the sink.

Heather answered. 'Electricity will be supplied by three GM 451 diesel generators, one on the liberty ship, two on the island. We'll keep a small fuel barge offshore with five thousand gallons of diesel fuel. The barge is ready now to be towed down from Miami. Belcher Oil will bring it in next week.'

'We have thirty days to set up,' Books said. 'We live on our own boats and eventually the liberty ship. We'll erect two pre-fab Butler buildings on concrete pads. A Miami firm is on the way here. They will erect them in twenty days. One building will house the Black Box, the other will act as a warehouse.'

'We have an IBM PC/XT and a Zed 3600 copier on the way from Nassau,' Heather added.

Books continued, 'We trade paper for gold, twenty-five cents on the dollar.'

'That's why you need me?' Nick asked, 'You want to use the Mafia in the US and the Corsican Brotherhood in Europe?'

'Yes.'

'Twenty-five cents is high,' Nick said, opening a bottle of red wine and dropping the cork into the wastebasket. 'They're used to paying between ten and fifteen cents on the dollar. And gold, how do they get the gold?'

'The streets. The open market. It's their problem. Show them the samples; how can they argue with perfection?' Books smiled. He slowly and carefully placed the ten sample fifty-dollar bills, printed on US Mint paper, that they had stolen from Zed on top of the coffee table, face up. Ten pictures of Ulysses S. Grant looked up at them, his chest puffed, a dour, defiant, almost drunken look on his face.

'There's nothing like cash,' Nick said, meaning it,

fingering one of the fifties. 'Nothing like it in the world.' His fingers tingled, electrified by the feel of the paper and what it represented.

'Financing the project, getting the paper and the ink will be my responsibility,' Books said, starting to slide three bills around in front of him in a circular motion as if he was playing three-card monte.

'Delivery? How do we make the swap? The paper for the gold?' Nick asked.

'We use fifty-foot Magnum offshore racers for the US deliveries, powered by two turbo diesels; twelve-cylinder engines turning twin screws that can power them up to sixty knots in ten-foot seas. The hulls have been stripped so they are hollow bullets. We'll stuff the paper in the forward hold, just the way they run dope, and exchange the paper for gold on the high seas.' Books searched in his file and produced a picture of a fifty-footer at full speed jumping the crest of a wave. 'I have five of these sitting in a boatyard in Fort Lauderdale, on Fifteenth Street, in the marina right next to the US Customs station.'

'And the Brotherhood? How do we exchange with them?' Nick asked.

'Subs.' Books dug deep into the fat file at his feet and picked out a picture of the Brooklyn Navy Yard. A line of twenty-five Second World War vintage submarines sat in a row, with fiberglass caps over the conning towers.

'Diesel-powered subs in mothballs that haven't seen action in years? Books, you really think the General Services Administration is going to sell us a submarine?' Nick asked, incredulous.

'Not one submarine, Nick, four. And not to us, to you. You used to find a way to buy everything else from them. I'm sure you can find a way to buy a sub.'

The photo of the submarines lay on top of the bills. Heather studied the picture. They looked like vicious gray sharks to her. She flipped the photo over. The back

110

said 'Property of US Navy – Confidential'. It made her shudder.

'And sub-mariners, men able to handle a non-nuclear-powered sub, where do I find them?' Nick asked.

'They're around, probably bored and broke. You found those British ex-Special Air Service men to train the rebels in Nigeria, didn't you?'

Heather saw a look of anger flash across Nick's face that startled her, scared her. It was a look that seemed out of character for Nick, but he quickly got hold of himself. She wondered what Books was referring to.

'If we exchange paper for gold at twenty-five cents on the dollar, where do we store the gold?' Nick asked.

'I don't know. I'm still working on that one, but I've got time to sort it out. If you have any suggestions let me know.' Books paused and looked at Heather, then over to Nick.

'Are you in? Are you with us?'

'You're taking on the most powerful governments in the world, they're going to be pissed off and come down on you like the hammer of Thor, and your chances are probably one in a thousand, but yeah, I'm in. You can count me in. I'll give it a shot.'

'So we're three?' Heather asked.

'We're three,' Nick answered, hating his own deceit, raising his glass in a toast.

Nick looked over at Heather. Her eyes had wandered back to the coffee table; she was fingering the photo of the subs. She didn't look up. Nick wondered how much of the whole plan she really knew. She had seemed surprised to hear about the subs.

Monday and Tuesday passed quickly. They walked the island in every direction. They dove the tiny oval natural harbor and the channel leading into it through the flats, double-checking the depth to make sure the liberty ship could be towed into the harbor by tug.

Nick sketched out the defenses and discussed them with

Books. They made a shopping list of armaments and ordnance they would need and Nick made a few calls.

The personnel requirements took the longest time; they decided on a minimum crew. The final list came to twenty-eight people.

On Tuesday, the eve of his departure from the island, Nick lay for hours in his bed and stared at the ceiling. Deceit. There was no other name for it. He was deceiving Books and himself. 'Books is the same as he has always been. He had just assumed I would say yes and join him. He trusts me. I have to find a way out of this.'

It was five in the morning when he decided that he would go to see Phillip in New York and stop this stupid charade. He fell asleep with a picture of Heather in his mind, staring wide-eyed at the photo of the submarines.

The next day Nick and Books took off in a Chalk's Airlines charter flight to Miami, and from there to their separate destinations, New York and Canada.

Heather waved goodbye to them both from the Whaler in the harbor, and watched them disappear into the fluffy white clouds.

A CIA reconnaissance plane was also watching, snapping photos of the seaplane as it headed west to Miami.

WEEK TWO

Wednesday morning 8:00
SECRET SERVICE, WASHINGTON, D.C.

'Sons of bitches!' Ralph Cobb mumbled to himself as he held a photo under the light. He had been busy the last two days, weaving his information network, setting up satellite surveillance. Now he had his results. The photo in his hand showed three people sitting in the stern of *Desperado* having a drink. All the pictures were so clear that Cobb could almost read the printing on Books' cigarette pack. Cobb recognized Heather from the photos of her that he had seen in the *Zed Gazette*. But it was the third person that held his attention. 'I've seen that face before, somewhere, but where?' he mused.

After Cobb knew that the location of the island was the Cay Sal Bank, he had instructed the CIA to send a recon aircraft to take satellite photos. He ordered the surveillance reports delivered directly to him, and only to him.

Cobb's concentration was interrupted by a call from Langley, Virginia. The CIA had picked up a verbal transmission from the island, ordering Chalk's Airlines to pick up two passengers for delivery to Miami. The two passengers were in the air right now.

Cobb spent the next sixty seconds in deep thought about what he would do if Books St John actually landed in the United States. His brain whirled through his options. There were no charges he could level against St John in the United States, and the English charge for theft of the Black Box was non-extraditable. Besides, it was the Black Box they wanted, and for sure Books St John wouldn't have that with him.

'Goddamn them,' Cobb whispered to the empty room skimming the recon photos across the room one at a time like frisbees.

He phoned the Secret Service Chief of Operations, and twenty minutes later two surveillance teams were waiting at the Chalk's Airlines terminal at Government Cut in Miami. Cobb instructed the teams to contact him every two hours on the movements of the two suspects.

He called his wife and told her he wouldn't be home for the next few days. Then he called housekeeping and asked for a cot and a small refrigerator for his office.

'If these guys fart, I'm going to hear it,' he swore as he hung up the phone.

Cobb went to the corner, knelt, and gathered up the photos he had thrown. He walked back to his desk and sat down. He studied the photo of the three of them again, concentrated on it for a full five minutes. Who was the third person?

He slapped the photo with the palm of his hand. 'Gotcha! I gotcha, you son of a bitch. I knew I had seen your face before.' He had seen it in the pile of photos and yearbooks that he had received from Phillip Sturges.

Cobb bolted from his desk and headed for the security vaults in the basement of the building where they kept the physical evidence on open cases.

'What next?' he wondered. 'What fucking next?'

Wednesday morning 9:00
FEDERAL RESERVE, NEW YORK CITY

The M1 and M2 reports were lying open on Phillip's desk. The reports provided an accounting of the amount of cash floating in the nation's monetary system. Phillip always thought of it as checking the country's bank balance. M1 and M2 supplied key information on whether the interest rate charged by the Fed should be increased or decreased.

Phillip was looking for large amounts of cash entering the monetary system. There was nothing interesting in this month's figures. It was too early.

He closed the file as the private phone line buzzed. There were only four people who had the number: Cobb, the President, Nick, and Veronica. He hit the button shutting off the red light and raised the receiver.

'Phillip?'

'Yes, Nick,' Phillip said, recognizing the deep quiet voice. 'Where are you?'

'The Seaport,' Nick said, slamming the telephone booth door closed against the biting wind.

'You're in New York?'

'Yes.'

'You want to meet?'

'Yes. Let's go for a boat ride. The Staten Island ferry.'

There was a hesitation on the line. Nick could feel Phillip thinking. Phillip would have to appear in public, go through the turnstiles with the masses, be seen in his wheelchair, struggle.

'When?' Phillip finally answered.

'Now.' Deep in his subconscious, Nick wanted to punish Phillip for making him betray their friend. Even though it was in Books' best interest to try to resolve the situation before it got out of hand, there was something else, something strange in the air, something Nick couldn't put his finger on. He felt he was being used, manipulated; he didn't like it but he had to see it through.

'I'll meet you at the main terminal entrance in thirty minutes,' Phillip said, responding to the unspoken challenge.

He buzzed down to the Head of Security and told him to get the truck ready.

Phillip arrived on the loading platform minutes later. A converted armored car was waiting. The door swung open as four plainclothes bodyguards moved in behind Phillip. Two of the guards stepped onto the truck, a third started to push Phillip's wheelchair into it. The Head of Security silently stopped him, intercepting the guard's hand in mid-air behind Phillip's back. He shook his head.

'Four men today?' he asked Phillip politely.

'Two men will be fine, Harold. I'm just going out for a little fresh air and to meet an old friend.'

'Yes, sir.' Harold motioned two attending guards away with a wave of his hand, and closed the metal doors behind Phillip.

The armored car fought its way through the congealed traffic of Wall Street and Broad, until it reached South Street and the Staten Island ferry terminal where it stopped.

Phillip could see Nick through the dark, one-way glass, waiting at the entrance, his collar pulled up against the bitter fall winds. Nick had a deep salt-water tan; the strong wind pushed his skin tight against his face, highlighting his sharp features. His face was angular and defined, set, almost as if it had been chiseled out of bronze. Philip knew the color of the eyes: light gray, soft but resolute, with great depth. He remembered looking into those eyes that stormy day before he flew up the mast; fierce and determined eyes as Nick fought to hang on to his hand.

Phillip took a deep breath then snapped, 'Open the doors!' He looked at the startled guards, adding, 'Please.'

He wheeled out onto the hydraulic platform that lowered him onto the streets of Manhattan Island.

Nick walked over as Phillip wheeled towards him. He couldn't help smiling at his friend. He was sorry now that he had put him through this petty ordeal. They shook hands, the wind from the Hudson River whistling, blustering between them. It was gusting so hard that Phillip had to apply the brakes to keep his chair steady.

Phillip motioned for the two plainclothes guards to go

ahead. They would already have alerted the Port Authority Police from the armored car that a VIP passenger was boarding the ferry. Nick dropped his quarter into the turnstile while Phillip wrestled himself through the handicapped entrance. They met again at the ramp that spilled down onto the decks of the ferry. Phillip let himself go, speeding down the steel ramp onto the upper deck. He hit one brake slightly, spinning in a tight little circle, a grin on his face, that same grin he used to flash when they were boys.

The ramp was raised as the clumsy ferry lurched out into the dirty waters of the Narrows, where the Hudson and the East River married. They steamed towards the Statue of Liberty and Staten Island.

They waited in silence for the World Trade Center to drop into the foreground. Nick spoke first with no preamble.

'Phillip, I can't handle this duplicity. Books is my friend; you two are the only family I have. I can't betray him.'

'Nick, I know all that. This is bigger. If you don't help him, he's doomed. He'll be apprehended and prosecuted to the limit, or killed.'

'You know where he is. Why don't you send a team in and grab him?' Nick asked.

'You know why! There are no formal charges against him, and now he has the sovereign rights to the island. Besides, we don't know where the Black Box is.'

Nick looked out of the open window as the ferry passed a garbage scow that was chugging its way out to sea to dump its load. The seagulls were buzzing the garbage, looking for dinner. The smell wafted up over the ferry, dank and stale, like the breath of Death. Nick slammed the window closed to shut out the smell, but it was too late. 'I still think it stinks. There are things I don't understand. I feel like I'm being manipulated by you both, for different reasons. Are you telling me everything?'

'Why do you think I'm holding something back?' Phillip asked, and waited. He let the silence hang, then spoke:

'We've both been through worse, Nick.' He stared up at Nick from the wheelchair.

'Yeah, I suppose.' Nick plopped down on one of the hard wooden benches. 'Fuck it, the whole thing; it stinks worse than that garbage.'

'See it through, Nick. It's the right thing. Things are heating up in Washington, but no direct action has been ordered yet. Books is going to need paper, and distribution, that's where he's going to come apart; maybe we can grab him in the process. If we do, we can charge him with conspiracy to counterfeit, a charge he may beat or plead out. It's best this way. Stick with it. Keep playing the game until we can make a move.'

'We?' Nick asked, staring at Phillip. 'Who's this we? Who's going to make a move?'

'We is me. Until I can make a move.'

The ferry blew a long, shrill, sorrowful note, splitting the morning sky as it approached the Staten Island docks. The ferry jarred them both as it bounced and skidded its way along the wooden pilings and boards. They both waited silently as the ferry unloaded and reloaded with late commuters rushing into the city. It wasn't until they were halfway back to Manhattan that Nick broke the silence.

'There are a couple of other things,' Nick said.

Phillip wheeled to face him, almost as if he had anticipated the question.

'The accident.' They had never discussed the accident before.

'Go on, Nick.'

'We both know that Books blew it; he lost the helm. If he had –'

'Kept his head? Kept her steady on course like Big Books would have?' Phillip interrupted. 'If he hadn't panicked, then you would have had time to get me down from the mast in one piece. And we wouldn't have lost Big Books.'

'Yes.'

'And do I really want to hurt him, not help him, because he hurt me, crippled me? Is that it, Nick?' Phillip asked in almost a whisper.

'Yes.'

'If I wanted to hurt him, Nick, I would just let him carry on with this stupid scheme, sit back and watch the Secret Service demolish him one way or the other. There are special teams that are trained to do that kind of work.' Phillip looked hard at Nick. 'I want your help, Nick. We're all he has. Even the Duchess has walked away from him, for ever. She tells people she has no son. She's the one who's bitter, Nick, not me. Believe me when I tell you we're all he's got. If we don't help him, he's gone.'

Nick got up and re-opened the window, letting the cold wind rush down the corridor. Several people looked over at him disapprovingly, pulling up their collars and buttoning their coats. But no one asked him to shut the window.

The World Trade Center loomed larger as they approached the Manhattan mooring where they had started.

'So she blames him for losing Big Books?' Nick asked, turning to face Phillip who had adjusted his chair so the cool breeze was blowing over him. His hair was damp, slicked down by the wind. He reminded Nick of a character out of a Hemingway novel, a ruffian, a heavyweight boxer in a custom-made blue suit.

'Always has, Nick.' Phillip locked the brake on his chair as they bounced into the mooring. 'I think she was glad when Books screwed up that Akbar deal; it gave her a chance really to put the boot in, kick him right out of her life.'

The ferry careened into the slip and locked into its mooring with a thud. After the crowd thinned out, Phillip and Nick proceeded slowly towards the exit ramp.

'The Duchess is some lady!' Nick said.

'She was, once, long ago; she was always good to me and you, Nick. Shit happens. What's the next thing on your mind?'

'I think I was followed, after I landed in Miami. They were good, real good, pros; but I lost them in Atlanta.'

'You sure?' Phillip looked up at Nick and then automatically scanned the crowd.

'Yeah. I'm sure.'

When they got to the ramp Phillip stopped. It looked like an inverted bowling alley, the uphill pitch was formidable. Nick looked down at him.

'I can make it, Nick,' he said without looking up.

Phillip pushed off, his muscular arms pistoning the wheels. He was doing fine until the horde of boarding passengers came streaming down on him. The ferry was reloading for the trip back; passengers cascaded down on Phillip. Some of them in their haste to get on board jostled him and bumped into the front of his chair. He slowed down, but continued to creep steadily up the incline. He was doing well until two kids wearing 'Manhattan Bloods' gang jackets appeared like black apparitions in front of him.

'What's the hurry, man, take it slow,' the taller one said as he handed his ghetto blaster over to the short fat one. His hand darted out in a smooth fluid movement to slip into Phillip's jacket pocket and lift his wallet.

The grasping hand was seized in mid-air and twisted behind his back. He was thrown face first against the wall.

The short fat one made a lunge to help his friend, but his feet were swept out from under him. He landed on the ramp, twisting, looking up at one of the security men who had been following ten steps behind Phillip. The ghetto blaster was strapped on his chest, the speakers blaring out a rap tune, vibrating his black shiny polyester jacket.

'Hey, man, cool it, you're hurting the tune box,' he said, gently lifting the blaster off his fat stomach, unclipping the strap.

The security man grabbed the blaster out of his hands, raised it into the air, and shattered it, just missing the second kid pinned to the wall. The music died in a high squeal.

Phillip's bodyguard reached down, lifted the fat kid off the concrete by his throat and pushed him up against the wall next to his friend. The fat kid lunged at Phillip's chair, kicking it with all his might.

'Nick!' Phillip called as his chair started to gain speed and slide backwards down the ramp. Nick ran, moving in behind the chair to stop it.

The two kids were handcuffed behind their backs and the security men ran them up the ramp by their wrists, their Converse sneakers hardly touching the concrete.

'Let them go,' Phillip said. He didn't want any publicity.

The two men turned at the top of the ramp and looked down at Phillip, then at each other. They nodded at Phillip and kicked the men's room door open, throwing the two Manhattan Bloods in ahead of them.

As Nick and Phillip went past the door they could hear grunting and a slight scuffling. The 'Bloods' would think twice before they ever did anything like that again.

Nick was startled to realize how much power Phillip had, how important he was.

They waited fifty feet from the men's room until the bodyguards were finished with the boys. Phillip was breathing hard, his face rigid, hands locked onto the arms of his chair.

In seconds the security men were back, one in front of the wheelchair, the other a few steps behind as Phillip wheeled himself through the terminal. The Federal Reserve truck was waiting in the entrance to the terminal, the engine idling, the driver smoking a cigarette. The wind hit them as they opened the door. Phillip stopped and spun the chair round, against the wind, facing Nick.

'So how come you never mentioned the girl, Nick? It isn't like you,' Phillip said, looking up quizzically. He was back to normal. It was business again.

'Nothing to mention. She's a nice kid. I think Books talked her into it,' Nick said, avoiding Phillip's eyes.

'Sure. A nice sweet kid who could bankrupt the country,

123

ruin the monetary system. She's a real all-American sweetheart all right. Nick, you don't have a thing for her yourself, do you?'

'No,' Nick answered, angry now. 'Fuck you, Phillip.'

'Don't get hot. I look for omissions, it's essential. With bankers, it's not what people say, it's what they don't say that counts. I was just asking, Nick, that's all. Sorry if I hit a nerve.' Phillip was smiling now.

'No. I'm just a little sensitive about the whole damn thing. I liked it better the way it was between us.'

'Me too,' Phillip said, looking out over the bay, the wind rocking his chair. 'I liked it better the way it was.'

'I'll keep in touch,' Nick said, standing back as Phillip wheeled himself onto the hydraulic ramp. It hummed into life, raising him until he was level with the bed of the truck, eye level with Nick.

'I'll look forward to hearing from you, Nick.'

The driver closed the first door, but as he reached for the second door the wind caught it, and slammed it shut with a resounding clang, metal on metal. The driver opened the door an inch to mumble, 'Sorry, sir, it was the damn wind,' then locked it shut.

Nick stood on the edge of the curb as the truck pulled away, the wind shoving against the back of his neck. He stood there until the truck disappeared down Wall Street. He turned to watch a fuel barge slowly being nosed out to sea by an ocean-going tug. The barge and the tug were black. They formed a dark silhouette on the horizon as they inched their way seaward with the creeping tide.

He was being pushed, too. But why? And to where? How could he have been followed and by whom? Was Phillip playing some enormously complicated game with him, manipulating him somehow, or was he just getting paranoid? Nick spun round and looked for a cab to take him uptown to the Plaza Hotel. He had to change and get down to the

Village by seven to meet Don Saverese, an old friend. If you could ever call Don Saverese a friend.

As the taxi sped by Battery Park, Nick thought about Heather. Phillip *had* hit a nerve.

Nick missed her.

Wednesday midday 12:00
SECRET SERVICE, WASHINGTON, D.C.

'I'm afraid we lost Nick Sullivan, sir.' The voice was subdued, waiting for the berating that was sure to come.

'Where?' Cobb grunted.

'The plane was destined for Los Angeles with a stop in Atlanta. Sullivan got off the plane in Atlanta and never returned.'

'Jesus H. Christ. Didn't you follow him off the plane?'

'It looked like he was going to the forward bathroom then he darted out through the front exit door at the last minute, and left his luggage. When he didn't return, and they did the headcount, they found him missing. The airline thought it was a bomb; they made each passenger get off the plane and identify their luggage. No exceptions.'

'Didn't you tell airport security that you were Federal agents?' Cobb's voice was rising.

'Yes, but they didn't believe us, all they said was no exceptions, and they took our IDs and phoned to confirm our status.'

'So, he obviously boarded another plane. Did you check the names on all outgoing flights?'

'Of course. But he must have used an alias. He's a real pro, from what we could see.'

'More than I can say for you!' Cobb snapped. 'What about the other team, the guys following St John?'

'They are still with him; he took a plane to Canada.'

'Where in Canada?'

'Ottawa, the capital.'

'I know it's the goddamn capital. Get back here!' Cobb hung up.

'Canada. Why Canada?' Cobb spoke to himself. 'What the hell is in Canada? Snow, Mounties, Canadian whiskey and Christmas trees . . . trees.

'That's it. Trees! They have millions of trees and trees make paper. And paper makes money. He's got a fucking mill in fucking Canada. That's why my agents never picked anything up at the American mills. His mill is in Canada. Don't lose him, boys. Don't lose him now.'

Cobb took the helicopter from Washington to the heliport at the World Trade Center in New York; a waiting limo took him to the Federal Reserve building.

He strode into Phillip Sturges' office unannounced and tossed two photos on the desk. The first photo was of three people sitting in the stern of *Desperado* having a drink, two men and a woman. The second was a photo Phillip had given to him of three young men dressed in yellow slickers, standing in front of a maxi racer on the Pier 66 dock in Fort Lauderdale.

'Recognize these people?'

'Yes, they're friends of mine,' Phillip said, picking up the photo of the three of them standing on the dock.

'I hope they're ex-friends. Your pals keep growing, like topsy. Any more of your friends going to join this gang?' There was no questioning the inference.

'Be careful, Ralph, you're way out of line. If you have something to say, spit it out. We were classmates, that's all.'

'Then you know that Nick Sullivan was a major international arms dealer up until a few years ago. What the hell is he doing with them?'

126

'Beats me. Maybe Books wants to buy a few guns. Ralph, it's logical that you go to your friends, people you can trust, in a deal like this.'

'Yeah. This still stinks.' Cobb spun on his heel to leave. 'I'll be in touch.'

'Hey, Ralph,' Phillip called out. 'Where'd you get the pictures of them on the boat?'

'Recon plane, CIA,' Ralph answered. 'I'll see you get copies.' He slammed the door behind him.

That was the second time in one day Phillip had heard the word 'stinks'. He wondered how far Cobb's surveillance penetrated. And whether Cobb knew of his meeting with Nick that afternoon.

Wednesday afternoon 2:00
OTTAWA, CANADA

Books landed in Ottawa at two, having flown from Miami directly to Montreal and connected through. He hailed a taxi and told the cab to take him over the bridge to the Quebec side, then on to Lac Saint Marie in the Gatineau Hills above Wakefield.

Hull and Ottawa are sister cities split by the Ottawa River. Ottawa is English, the capital of Canada, the seat of government, but that fact is scrupulously ignored by the French Canadian people living in Hull. As far as they are concerned, the Ottawa River separates two countries, Quebec and the rest of Canada.

The main industry of Hull is pulp and paper mills.

Books sped across the bridge that spanned the Ottawa river. He marvelled at the triangular mountains of logs on the shore, piled fifty stories high, giant pyramids of brown splinters. The logs were spat high into the air at the apex of the pyramids by tall snaking conveyor belts. He watched the logs spiral skywards then tumble down the pyramids until they found their level.

The driver entered the city of Hull. Suddenly all the signs were in French, and the colors were brighter: yellows, purples, greens, and reds, in contrast to the conservative gray tones of English Ottawa. The driver took the mountain highway and headed up the Gatineau River road. Business was slow; he was happy to have this fare. Books had explained that he would only be about an hour and the cab was to wait for him.

Books looked out of the cab window at the chain log booms in the Gatineau River and the tiny tugs wheezing and puffing as they strained to keep control of the sea of logs. Thirty minutes later the cab pulled up to the Valjean mill. The day after he bought it, one year ago, Books named the mill after Jean Valjean, the lead character in *Les Misérables*; Books had anticipated a great struggle.

It was a small mill with seven employees. Most mills turned logs into mushy pulp, then processed the pulp into 'slurry' by adding sulfites and other chemicals. The 'rolling pin' machine did the rest, flattening and drying the slurry into sheets of paper.

But the Valjean mill got its slurry from a very different source.

The mill was run by Percival Smathers, a friend of Books' from school. He was referred to by Books as the 'defrocked mad chemist of Princeton'. He had been fired by every important chemical company in the United States. Percival loved his drink.

He had found a long-awaited home in the Gatineau Hills. He was overpaid by Books, and didn't ask any undue questions. The technical part of the job was easy for him, and he had plenty of free time to enjoy himself. The French

Canadians understood and liked him. He never pushed them too hard. After a few months, he spoke French fluently.

He stood waiting for Books on the steps of the office. It was a long thin wooden building with raw insulation stuck in all the holes and stapled to the ceiling, giving an orange hue to the unpainted wood. His living quarters were directly behind the office.

They shook hands and walked into the office. Percival blinked bloodshot eyes at Books and waved a quart bottle of Molson's beer in the air. Books nodded, and Percival poured them each a drink.

'Perce, you look great. On the Weider fitness program?'

'Fuck you, Books, and the horse you rode in on. No jokes, okay? It's too early. I'm sorry I'm not prettier!' Percival washed his forehead and eyes with the palm of one hand.

The smell of pulp had been in the air from the time Books had crossed the Ottawa River, a combination of burning old sweaty socks and ammonia, but somehow Books always liked the aroma. He used to come to Quebec La Verendrye Provincial Park to fish for pike and pickerel with Big Books once a year. The smell had good memories for him. Percival noticed Books' nostrils flare.

'I can't smell that shit anymore; my nose is burned out from the fucking stench.' He absently squeezed his nostrils together.

'I don't mind it,' Books said, looking out of the window. 'Have all the deliveries been made?'

'The last truck is still unloading. Want to see?'

'Yes. And the currency sheets?'

'All done and in the warehouse. They can be airlifted to you whenever you're ready, four bloody tons of the best paper you ever saw.'

'Let's go,' Books said, standing, leaving his beer, and walking out of the door towards the mill. Percival refilled his glass, took another swig and followed Books, glass in hand.

They rounded the corner of the mill; the earth crunched firm under their feet. Winter was only weeks away and the ground was already frozen, the air so cold and crisp it hurt to take a deep breath. The river would freeze soon and the mills would have to live off their stockpiles of logs. Books watched the Valjean stockpile being fed by a conveyor belt from a logjam in the river. The pyramid of logs was for show only.

They moved on to the mill itself, a dilapidated, sprawling wooden building that had been constructed in the thirties.

A garbage truck had its back flush to the loading dock; it carried New York, New Jersey and Quebec license plates. The truck was modern, with a hydraulic compacter; shiny and new, it looked out of place high in the Gatineau Hills. It was pushing its insides of shredded paper out onto the dock, like a fat maroon beetle laying eggs.

The men were pitchforking shredded Federal Reserve currency notes into square bins, then rolling the bins into the mill and over to giant steel vats that were bubbling and boiling. The men tossed the shreds from the square bins directly into the swirling vats of swill with their pitch forks, like feeding hay to cattle. They carefully avoided any contact with the boiling acid bath that bleached out the ink.

Books watched for a while as the men went about their chores. The garbage truck driver leaned against the front fender smoking a Gauloise. It had been a long drive for him from the landfill site in the New Jersey Meadowlands, where he picked up the shredded currency, to the Valjean mill. It was the mill's truck, carrying New Jersey tags. It was used only for this task.

Books stopped to watch two large vats as the slurry gurgled and spluttered like a congealed mass of white oatmeal.

'Here, hold this a second.' Percival handed Books his beer and walked over to a shelf where he removed two large canisters; one canister held tiny blue threads, the other held red threads. Percival walked over to two cooling vats further inside the room and shook the canisters; the thin threads sprinkled out into the gelatinous mass like salt and pepper. 'That's how I solved the thread problem, Books. Simple but deadly!' He laughed, walking over to replace the canisters on the shelf.

He retrieved his beer from Books and took a fast sip, then grabbed Books' arm and guided him to the locked door that led to the finished paper warehouse. It was old and wooden, but well-built, and newly temperature-controlled.

As they walked in, Percival hit the light switch and illuminated over a hundred skids; each skid was full and covered with a tarpaulin. He went to the nearest pallet and pulled the tarp off with a flourish, like a magician uncovering a beautiful girl. The paper sheets were twenty inches wide and twenty-four inches long, designed to print thirty-two bills per sheet, exactly as the US Mint did, and the sheets were a perfect fit for the slightly modified Zed color copier. The paper was stacked in five-foot-high bundles tied by half-inch black plastic strapping. The exposed paper glistened pristine white in the overhead fluorescent lighting.

Books went to a second pallet hidden in the corner and whipped the tarp off. He motioned for Percival to get the knife and cut the binding straps. After the black plastic straps were removed, Books took a sheet off the top and went to the light, holding it up, studying the texture through the opaque glare.

'This stuff any good, Perce?'

'Better than Crane and Company.'

'I'll be the judge of that.' Books smiled. He considered his idea brilliant: to re-cycle the Treasury's own paper into 'slurry' and use Percival's skill with chemicals to bleach out the ink. It was because of the linen content that genuine notes did not fade or tear. Books arranged for the purchase of the shredded paper in New Jersey from Waste Control Corporation for two hundred dollars a ton. There were no restrictions on the sale of the shredded paper.

Books tore the recycled sheet of paper and examined the edges for linen shreds. Then he took a magnifying glass out of his pocket and looked for the tiny strands of red and blue cotton; they were what the Secret Service looked for first in verifying counterfeit money. The problem with Books' idea had been that the original threads bleached out along with the ink as the shredded recycled paper became slurry, until Percival sprinkled them back in, using his canisters, like shaking spice into soup.

They were clearly there, strands of red and blue thread filaments.

'Well done, Perce.'

'It's exactly the way Crane and Company does it for the Fed; I researched it!'

'I still think it's brilliant,' Books grinned, and finished his examination. 'I remember how we labored over the problem.'

He replaced the sheet on top of the pile, pulling the tarp over it. He went to a third pallet and cut the black plastic binding strap with the knife himself. He took ten sheets off the top.

Books hesitated at the warehouse door. He couldn't help but look back at the stacked pallets of paper. They were blank and meaningless now, but once they were printed they would take on life of their own. What rectangular pieces of paper could represent, what they could do, what men would do for them! He flipped the light switch, casting the warehouse into total darkness. It wouldn't be long now.

Percival broke the silence as they walked back to the cab. 'So?' he asked.

'So, the US Mint had better watch their ass.' Books hoped that Percival wouldn't slack off, go on a bender. He needed Percival straight, especially now.

As they reached the cab, Books motioned for the driver to open the trunk. He slipped the ten currency sheets into an artist's portfolio that he had brought, and zippered them

132

up. He reached into his overcoat and pulled out an envelope and handed it to Percival.

'Shipping instructions. They must be followed exactly.'

'Okay, I'll give them to Claudine, my secretary.'

'No, Perce. You'll do them yourself. I want all the bills of lading collected and destroyed; there can be no paper trail on the shipment. No one can know the destination, or the amounts.'

'Sure, Books. I'll do it myself. What else?'

'Lay off the damn bottle until this is over. When I get the shipment and all the backup paperwork, you can collect your bonus and go on a world-class bender for a week if you want. I'll put the funds on deposit in your account in Nassau. You can come down to pick up the cash. Then you return here, and stand by at the mill for six more months.'

'We carry on with the paper processing?'

'No. We should have enough inventory. Just buy raw slurry from the other mills and carry on with the regular mill production until you hear from me.'

Books slammed the lid of the trunk shut and extended his hand. 'The paper is bleached but not burned. And you solved the problem of the strands; there they are, big as life. You've done an amazing job, Perce.'

Percival gripped Books' hand and stood there expressionless; slowly a smile crossed his face. 'Faith! That's all I needed Books, someone to have faith in me.'

'Don't celebrate yet. It's not over till it's over.'

'How well I know. I won't let you down, Books.'

'Better not, Perce! Take care.'

Books slid into the back seat. He watched the gray Gatineau Hills flash by as he drove back to Ottawa.

'No fuck-ups now, please, Perce,' Books muttered to himself. 'We're almost there.'

So was Ralph Cobb.

Books was high in the air over Ottawa, flying down the
Gatineau River on his way back to Miami when Ralph Cobb's
phone rang in Washington. Cobb tapped his pencil against
the rim of his cold coffee cup as he listened to the leader of
the surveillance team that had followed Books. The rhythm
increased to a crescendo as the report was completed.

'You're absolutely sure that the paper is in the warehouse?
You saw it with your own eye, stacked, ready for shipment?'

'Affirmative, sir. They may already have shipped some.'

'How's their security?'

'Minimal.'

'What's the warehouse building made of?'

'Wood.'

'Wood?'

'Yes, sir.'

'Where's your partner?'

'He's following St John, sir. I thought it best to stay here
and confirm the find, keep an eye on the mill,' the agent said,
hesitating, waiting for Cobb's approval. He continued, 'St
John is on Air Canada flight 711 direct to Miami.'

'He's probably going home to his island. Let him go. I got
what I want.'

Cobb paused to think. He had been a field agent for seven
years and had won every major commendation offered by the
Secret Service. The reason for his success was action. He took
action, sometimes without official sanction. But it had turned
out well, and he always left the door open for his superiors
to take the credit, along with himself. It was time for action
now.

He made his decision.

'You go back to the mill site and wait. I'll come to you;

I'm bringing a specialist with me. We'll settle these bastards. In the next twenty-four hours they'll be out of business.'

He hung up the phone and called Langley. He was put through to the Director of the CIA. Five minutes later he was told that the specialist he requested would be waiting at the Secret Service jet hangar in two hours.

'Clever. Real clever, having the mill in Canada, but the party's over!' Cobb said out loud to the map with the little green pins. 'No paper, no counterfeits.' His voice reverberated against the gray paint and pictureless walls of his office.

Wednesday evening 7:00
NEW YORK CITY

The private and exclusive Club Siracusa was located on the corner of Thompson and Bleeker in the heart of The Village. The doorman filled the doorway. His collar was too small and strangled his twenty-inch neck, setting the bow tie askew. His name was Alfonso; no one got inside without his approval. The cab carrying Nick pulled in behind the empty six-door Mercedes that was moving forward to park and wait.

Alfonso closed the entrance door to the club behind him and held a straight arm out to Nick, the palm upturned as if he were stopping traffic. He stared, not moving, not speaking.

'I'm here to see Mr Saverese,' Nick offered.

Alfonso flipped through the pages of his clipboard and spoke. 'Name?'

'Nick Sullivan.'

Nick started to walk in. The doorman whipped out a

hand-held metal detector and waved it over Nick's body like a magic wand, while he frisked him lightly with the other hand. He did it so quickly that Nick didn't know what Alfonso was doing until he had finished.

Two men in tuxedos stood in the small vestibule just inside the entry. The taller of the two looked over Nick's shoulder and received an approving hand signal from Alfonso. He spoke to Nick.

'Mr Saverese is downstairs. He said for you to join him there. Guillermo, take this guy down to Don Saverese.'

The shorter man adjusted his cummerbund and bow tie and led the way down a flight of stairs to the basement. At the basement level he opened a large metal door. Nick had been in the Club Siracusa before. He knew the first door was made of lead. There was a second door, a few steps beyond, made out of a soft, sound-proof material. The gunfire couldn't be heard until the second door was opened.

Don Saverese stood in position 'One', his back to Nick. His white-on-white silk shirt fitted in perfectly round his waist. There was no fat. The Don was small and slim, barely five foot five; the ear mufflers protruded from the side of his head like grasshopper eyes. It gave the illusion that he could see behind his back. The room was filled with a light gray mist and smelled of cordite: strong, pungent.

He was firing a long-barreled .357 Magnum; his little hands were dwarfed by the gun. Nick saw the barrel rise slightly, just a fraction, six times, six blasts, as the Don squeezed off each cylinder. His arms were strong. They hardly flinched with each shot. Nick saw the black center of the target at the end of the shooting alley disappear as the rounds tore into the paper. There was only a white hollow center left when he was through. Don Saverese turned to a stocky, swarthy man who stood next to him and nodded.

The man squeezed off six fast rounds from his model 1934 Beretta, a classic pistol used by the Italian Army. Nick had found and purchased a warehouse full of them in Addis

136

Ababa, Ethiopia, years ago, and had given six to the Don as a present.

Don Saverese turned to look behind him and smiled at Nick, slipped off his ear protectors and extended his hand. 'Just shooting for Sambuca. Nice to see you, Nick.'

The Don turned to the man he had been shooting with and nodded, noticing that the center of the target had disintegrated. He made a point of not introducing the man. Don Saverese's manners were impeccable; therefore, he had a reason for withholding the introduction. The man turned and walked over to the reloading section at the far end of the gallery, passing the six cubicles used for shooting. The shooting gallery covered the entire basement of the restaurant, a restaurant that was officially licensed as a private gun club by the City of New York.

The walls were covered with glass cases filled with handguns. Under each gun was a set of initials. Don Saverese walked over to the case and opened the glass, slipping the pistol back onto the clips over the initials D.S. He stuck a little red tag on the Hackmayer grips to signify that the gun should be cleaned in the morning. Nick noticed a dozen pistols with the initials D.S. under them. The Don didn't invite him to fire any rounds or to handle any of the pistols.

'Have to keep my hand in. You lose your eye if you lay off for too long. Shall we go upstairs?'

As he spoke, the door opened and three men walked in to shoot. When Don Saverese was on the range the red light over the door was always lit. It ensured exclusive use of the gallery for the Don, with no unfriendly hands on the pistols. A Mafia chieftain had been shot to death on this range in the thirties and his body dumped in the Jersey Meadowlands.

The three men waited patiently for Don Saverese to leave. They each mumbled a respectful greeting as he walked by. The Don spoke to each of them individually, using their first names as he passed. He spoke in a low, restful voice.

Each of the three men took a long look at Nick. They didn't like strangers in their club.

Nick and Don Saverese made their way upstairs to a quiet corner booth that was permanently reserved for the Don. It was swept for listening devices every day. Nick looked around. There were few women in the club; the ones that were visible were flashy; some were obviously hookers and showgirls, others were actresses or mistresses – no wives. This was a men's club. Nick sat quietly as the Don ordered for both of them in Italian.

'It has been a long time between meals for us, Nick. You look a little thin, but healthy. I heard you were retired,' the Don said, tucking his napkin into his collar under his chin. The Don didn't have to worry anymore about spilling marinara sauce on his Countess Mara tie, but old habits died hard.

Nick spread his napkin out on his lap. 'I have a business situation that I think will interest you.' He reached into his jacket pocket and pulled out an envelope. Nick slipped it across the table under his palm.

The Don studied Nick for a second before he opened the envelope and carefully extracted five fifty-dollar bills, one at a time. He rubbed each of them between his thumb and forefinger, testing the paper. The light at the table was dim, making it difficult to study the bills carefully. The Don excused himself and went to the men's room where it was fully lit. He was gone for several minutes.

He returned as the appetizers of daintily fried squid arrived. He handed the bills back to Nick. 'You don't have to pay, dinner's my treat tonight, Nick,' he joked. 'Those bills are so good I could pass them off in here.' He slipped a tiny squid into his mouth. 'The paper is good; can you keep the quality?'

'Yes.'

'It's always the paper, Nick, that's where people go wrong.'

'The paper will be fine,' Nick said, not really knowing if it would be fine, parroting what Books had told him.

138

'That's nice, Nick. Show me some when it is.'

'There's not a lot of time.'

The Don looked up, dipping a small piece of garlic bread into the last of the scungilli sauce. He paused, daubing his lips with the bottom of his napkin. He let a moment pass before he spoke. 'There is always time, Nick, and you will have to make time if you want to deal with me. What is your proposition?'

'The product is for sale for twenty-five cents on the dollar.' Nick paused as the veal Marsala was delivered to the table.

'Best veal Marsala in the USA. My grandfather was from Marsala, Sicily, Nick. He arrived on Ellis Island with nothing but my grandmother. Those were some days. I'm happy they are restoring Ellis Island. I made a modest contribution to the fund, for my grandfather.' The Don raised his fork, signalling that it was time to eat. He was also signalling for quiet. He did not like to speak while he was eating his main course. Nick ate respectfully in silence. It was a personal quirk of the Don's that everyone observed.

When the main course was totally consumed, the Don spoke. 'Twenty-five cents on the dollar is high.'

'Not for this quality.' Nick paused for a second. 'And it must be paid in gold.'

'Nick, you want gold? Go to a jeweler, or to a dentist. We don't deal in gold.'

'These bills will be perfect, sequential numbers of existing series with no duplications, denominations of twenty, fifty and a hundred, unlimited quantities.'

'Unlimited quantities? That's a big promise. Be careful here.' The Don paused, staring at Nick, concentrating as if he were trying to see right through him. 'If there was real size it would involve all the major families. To pass off big numbers we require all our resources, the casinos, the drugs, the loan-sharking, legitimate loans, stocks and bonds purchased through our brokerages, complicated offshore laundering. How do we know that you can deliver? And believe me, accumulating gold in big quantities will be a problem.'

'There's plenty of street gold. Clean it up, buy from the jewelry wholesalers and the open market.'

'How would we take delivery?'

'On the high seas, the same basic procedures as narcotics.'

'Nick, we have done some good business together in the past. I will mention it to the families and see. Samples will be needed if we are to proceed; samples on the same paper you will be using.'

Nick reached into his pocket and handed the envelope with the five counterfeit bills back to Don Saverese.

'You're going to pay for dinner after all, Nick,' the Don smiled. 'These are the best, I'll admit. The engraving is perfect. What procedure are you using?'

'High technology.' Nick smiled.

'That's the American way, isn't it, Nick.' The Don held up his wine glass for a toast. 'To the American way, to free enterprise and high technology. Perhaps we can do some business.'

The glasses made a resounding clink as they met. No one in the club looked up or over at Nick and the Don, but many of the club members knew that a deal was being born.

After espresso, the Don nodded toward the next table and the man he had been shooting with. The man wiped his lips with his napkin and came over to join them. This time the Don introduced him. 'This is Bruno Pugliese. Nick, when you speak to him it is like speaking to me.' The man bowed his head to the Don. The Don did not respond to the gesture. 'You know our way, Nick, the way we do business. I will communicate to you through Bruno.'

Nick got the feeling that Bruno hadn't laughed in the last twenty years. There was no expression in the eyes. They were bottomless and dead.

The Don normally had only one meeting to approve a deal, and then appointed an intermediary. It created a layer between him and whoever he was dealing with, a legal veil that was difficult to penetrate. Nick felt encouraged that the Don had appointed a man so quickly.

The introduction of Bruno Pugliese ended the meeting.

'Bruno and I are going back to the range to finish our practice. I know you will excuse us.' The Don slipped the envelope with the fifties into his pocket, but remained seated, waiting for Nick to leave.

'Of course, Don Saverese,' Nick said. 'Nice to meet you, Bruno; always good to see you, Don Saverese.'

Nick and Bruno rose; Bruno slipped a business card into Nick's palm. It would have the contact phone numbers written on it. The Don stayed seated and extended his hand. 'We will move quickly. Give me a few days. It was good to see you as well, Nick; don't be a stranger,' he added, withdrawing his small hand. It was like a little cat's paw, Nick thought to himself, a little paw with big claws. Bruno did not offer his hand.

Nick walked down Bleeker then over to Sixth Avenue and grabbed a cab. He thought about asking the cabbie to go up Park Avenue but realized it ran in the wrong direction. He wanted to drive by the St John penthouse, to make contact with the Duchess, to tell her to embrace her son, to forgive him for that afternoon off New Providence Island, and to tell him to stop his foolish scheme.

Instead, Nick asked the cab driver to put out his smelly cigar. The cabbie ignored him, slamming the plexiglass protective window shut with a thud as he sped off into the dark Manhattan night.

141

Heather looked west into the descending sun for Books'
chartered plane. She saw the bright flash from the wing tips
as the plane dropped out of the sun and descended towards
the island. A tug was straining on the horizon, pulling a fuel
barge against the current. Heather wondered if it was the
Belcher fuel barge that Books had ordered from Miami.

Books had stopped at a warehouse in the Miami airport
on his return from Ottawa to pick up thirty gallons of black,
blue, and green ink. The ink had been sent to Miami from
Boston, per order from the Greater Miami Art Institute's non-
existent cover company, for their new method of 'video-
graphics'. The ink was the same as the Mint used, indelible,
colorfast, and magnetic to enable automatic teller machines
to read the denomination of the bills.

The pilot circled and approached the Cay Sal Bank from
the south, flying low, into the wind.

The Butler construction crew had arrived on the island
from Miami, and were busy digging holes in the coral rock
to plant the steel posts that would hold the buildings' iron
framework in place.

Books and Heather walked the tiny atoll, inspecting the
construction work that had been completed.

'Any word from Nick?' Heather asked.

'Not a peep.'

'Do you really think the government will attack us?'

'No, but they must consider it as one of their options, an
option they can't exercise. They must consider the publicity.
Remember, we haven't done anything wrong yet. What's on
your mind, Heather? Why do you ask?'

'How much currency will we make and sell before we stop?'

'We haven't even begun and you're asking when we will

stop; we're only getting twenty-five cents on the dollar. We have a lot of costs to cover, start-up costs,' Books answered.

She continued, 'I see these buildings going up and Nick in New York with the Mafia, then flying to France to meet with the Corsican Brotherhood; it's heavy stuff, Books. So, I need to know. How much? How much are we going to print? How long will we be here?'

'Not long. We'll print only as much as it takes, then we're gone,' Books answered, slightly annoyed. He noticed the tug on the horizon pulling the Belcher Oil barge. He pointed. She ignored his arm in the air.

'Our tug!' he said.

'Books!'

'A billion, maybe two. Relax, Heather.' He dropped his arm and eased it round her shoulders.

'There's a big difference between a billion and two. Let's stop when we have enough, Books.'

'We will.'

'I hope so,' she said. But something inside her didn't believe Books.

'Where is the Black Box?' she asked.

'It's safe.'

'Where is it?'

'I'll get it when the time is right, don't worry.'

'You'll produce it when the time is right. Thanks a lot!' She removed his arm from round her shoulder.

The tug and barge were clearly visible now on the horizon, threading their way across the flats. She turned and walked back toward the concrete pads that had been poured for the Butler buildings. Books didn't follow.

She rounded the first concrete pad and burst into tears, looking to see if anyone was watching as she wiped the tears away. She did an abrupt turn and ran toward the Whaler, jumped in and headed for Nick's boat, where she wouldn't be disturbed.

She plopped down on Nick's couch in the salon and cried

uncontrollably, in racking sobs, and she didn't know why. Why the hell was she crying?

It was all different now, and changing every second. It was out of her control, and she had a deep instinctive feeling that someone was going to get hurt.

She cried silently for herself and for her father. Her father, driven mad by cruel reality and his inability to cope with the demands of real life.

Heather had vowed to use the system against itself, to bide her time and get her revenge.

And then Books walked into her life and suggested a plan that was so logical and concise that she wondered why she had never thought of it. At first they had discussed blackmail; steal the copier and ransom it back to the Zed Corporation. Then Books explained to her how easy it would be actually to manufacture money, turn paper into gold, using his contacts and expertise. He said he could supply the paper. It was almost as if her prayers had been answered.

But things were changing; she could feel it and it scared her. She missed her father. Their minds had been so tightly united that in many instances they could communicate without speaking.

Heather was a child prodigy, the light in her father's eyes. She was able to absorb and understand advanced mathematical concepts, complicated concepts of physics and chemistry at first reading, and never forget what she had absorbed.

But she paid for it. She advanced quickly through school leaving her peer group in her wake and with it her social life. She never missed what she never had, not until Books appeared and showed her a side of life that was exhilarating. She had learned to take action; now she needed to learn to follow through.

Heather walked forward to the galley and took a beer from the refrigerator. The top popped open with a hiss. The can felt cold and damp in her hand as it started to sweat in the hot air. It brought her back to reality. She wasn't going to falter now or weaken as her father might have. She must be resolute.

She went into the head in Nick's stateroom and looked in the mirror as she washed her face with a wet cloth, trying to purge the tears and redness from her eyes. She took several deep breaths and felt her heartbeat begin to slow and get back into rhythm with her body and the tropical world around her.

When she decided to steal the Black Box she had told herself that she was doing it for her father, to get even with Zed, and all the people like them. But was Books really just a means to that end?' Was that why she loved him, because he provided the means for her to live out her dream of revenge? She wasn't sure that she wasn't doing it for herself, for the rush, the excitement.

And where was the Black Box? Books had taken it for safekeeping. Who the hell did he think he was? And most importantly, what was the difference between Books taking it from her and the Zed Corporation taking it from her father? Was she just a victim, too, like her dad? Was she sitting down at a table to play a game against giants?

So many unanswered questions . . . She felt totally exposed – vulnerable.

Heather noticed Nick's Loran lying in pieces on the galley table. She sat down with a screwdriver and started to work. The smooth metal felt good in her hands; the small panels of transistors and wires were something she knew about, something real, something she could fix. And Nick would be pleased when he returned.

Wednesday night 9:00
BROOKLYN NAVY YARD, NEW YORK CITY

Nick crossed the Brooklyn Bridge and ten minutes later they were inside the Brooklyn Navy Yard.

Ernie Sands was waiting at the foot of Pier 22, his trench-coat collar pulled up against the night air, a black US Navy watch cap drawn down tight round his ears. He looked almost sinister, except for the taped temple of his horn-rimmed glasses that he kept pushing back up the bridge of his nose. He had left a pass for Nick and the cab at the security gate.

Ernie was a retired Navy commander who lived on the Chesapeake Bay and kept a small apartment in Manhattan. If you wanted something deadly or illegal that floated or exploded, you called Ernie. He had supplied Nick with six fifty-foot Uniflite patrol boats for an emerging African nation years ago. They were riverboats used in Vietnam. Ernie had bought them from the Republic of Vietnam at the auction after the war. He funneled them through the Philippines and Singapore, where they had been loaded on a freighter and shipped to West Africa.

Ernie was buying a coffee from the catering truck when Nick tapped him on the shoulder. He jumped, almost spilling his coffee. He flashed a big smile at the sight of Nick.

'I never thought I'd see you back in the business, Nick. Not after Nigeria, and Paris.' He shoved his coffee into Nick's hand, pushed his glasses back up his nose, and ordered a second cup. 'Don't worry, I won't ask where you been,' he said, winking.

'And you, Ernie. They haven't put you in jail yet?'

'No. They need me too much. It's nice; all these little nations think they invented me. I help them after I get the nod from Uncle Sam. We keep switching sides so much with

146

these little assholes that I never know what the hell is going on.' He hit the bridge of his glasses with the heel of his hand, driving them back up his nose as if he could plant them in his forehead. The right temple was taped to the frame with white surgical tape. It had been there since the first day they had met; it was his trademark.

'Ernie, after this job, why don't you treat yourself to a new pair of glasses?'

'Why?'

'No reason.' Nick smiled. 'Where's the hardware?'

'The liberty ship is on the end of this pier. There's a crew on board, doing what you requested, and the tug comes a week from today to take her away. The subs are packed in mothballs over on Pier Six. The General Services Administration still won't let them go, though.' They walked slowly down the dock, dodging the forklifts and boxes stacked along the route. Arc lights lit up the night as welders and pipefitters scurried about; sparks flew in the air as hot pinpoints of acetylene flame hit cold steel.

'The ordnance?' Nick asked, sipping his coffee.

'In a bonded warehouse at La Guardia: fifty fully auto stainless steel Ruger mini 14s, seventy Claymores, two M-60s on tripods, four SAM launchers and twenty Laws rockets, fifty handguns, plenty of ammo, and a complete defensive early-detection radar system that we're installing on the bridge of the liberty ship right now. Sound good?'

'Fine,' Nick said, stopping to look up at four hundred running feet of rust.

'She looks worse than she is, Nick; like us, you can't tell everything from the outside.'

'It's a wonder she still floats.'

'Don't be disrespectful. She's been in mothballs for forty years. We're refitting her like you asked, with a commissary, twenty decent cabins, self-contained sewage disposal, desalinization plant for fresh water, and the communications set-up you requested: phone, special radar, the works.'

'A real floating palace, Ernie,' Nick said, rubbing the rust from the handrails off his hands as they climbed to the bridge. Its glass had been tinted black. The main console was over twenty feet long. Instruments, dials, microphones, screens were being installed. There were three command seats anchored into the metal plates. It was strictly functional, military and spartan. It was designed to be the command post, the nerve center of the island.

The staterooms and commissary had the same gray military feel: utilitarian, bare, only the essentials permitted.

'A week, Ernie? You can have this completed in a week?'

'Yeah, with two shifts; pay double-time to these boys and they skip breaks, Nick. It'll be done.' Ernie stopped to talk to a few of the workmen on the walk over to the subs.

The subs were moored stern to, extending like gray torpedoes, sleek and dangerous. Nick was surprised at how small they were.

There were twenty subs in the line. The mothball domes sat perched on the conning towers with only the periscope showing through, needle spikes in the dark Brooklyn sky, giving the submarines a surreal quality, like sleeping insects with deadly stingers.

'Do they work?' Nick asked.

'Not all of them, but I'm sure we could get three seaworthy.'

The Staten Island ferry blasted a long shrill angry note in the distance as a garbage scow crossed her bow.

Nick reached into his jacket pocket and pulled out an envelope. It carried the seal of the Mako Marine Institute. Books had had the letterhead printed in Miami.

Ernie read the letter in silence. 'You think the GSA will believe that you need four subs for marine biology and mariculture experiments for the betterment of mankind?' He shrugged. 'Maybe. I've seen dumber things fly.'

'Thanks, Ernie.'

'No offense.' He waved the letter at the subs. 'These babies are headed for the scrap heap next year, and this is almost year end. I'll try.' Ernie smiled.

Nick reached in his jacket and pulled out a second slim envelope. He handed it to Ernie.

'One million six hundred thousand in a cashier's check drawn on the Chase Manhattan in your favor. That should do the job. I'll need submariners. Can you find them? I'll need the minimum crew to man three boats: captain, engineer, navigator, first mate. I'll pay well.'

Ernie put the envelope in his pocket without looking at the contents. 'You know why I've always liked you, Nick?' He didn't wait for an answer. '*Cojones*; you have the built-in confidence that money can't buy. If the GSA approves the sale, I can find the men. But there'll be a problem.'

'Yeah?'

'Your crew will look like the over-the-hill gang: the golden guys. There's no one under fifty who knows his way round one of these things.'

'So be it. We're an equal opportunity employer.'

'Nick, I'm available also, if I can be of help. I'd like to see some action.'

'Ernie, you have it made in the shade. You don't want to dodge torpedoes at this point in your life.'

'Well, maybe I do have it made in some ways, but I got some bad news from the sawbones up in Bethesda last month. I'm going to be shipping out soon. The big C, my lungs.' Ernie paused to light up a cigarette almost in defiance. 'I'd like to go out with a bang, not a whimper, preferably on the ocean. Think about it, will you?'

'Yes. I'll think about it. Meantime, get me those subs.'

'I'll try.'

Nick slid into the back seat of the cab. Ernie leaned over to shake hands, holding his loose-fitting glasses on his nose with his left hand.

'Don't forget me, Nick.'

'Never,' he smiled. 'You're like a bad dream, hard to shake!'

149

Nick stared straight ahead as the cab threaded its way back to the gate and directly off to Kennedy Airport. His next stop would be France.

The cab inched its way through the rush-hour traffic toward the airport. Nick was restless; he couldn't get the thought of Ernie Sands and death out of his mind.

And he was dreading his return to Paris.

Thursday morning 4:00
QUEBEC, CANADA

Cobb was nested in the Gatineau Hills, positioned directly above the Valjean paper mill. He adjusted his infrared binoculars until he could see the office and warehouse buildings clearly through the predawn blackness.

He sat alone in the darkness, waiting for 'Pyro', the CIA specialist, to do his job. Pyro had come highly recommended by the Company as a merchant of fire, and the human origin of hundreds of specialized blazes. He trained CIA operatives to set undetectable fires.

Cobb waited to see if the praise was justified.

Pyro approached the Valjean mill from the Gatineau River. He floated down with the current in a stolen aluminum canoe, quietly sure of his purpose. The current meandered lazily; the ice was only two weeks away from forming into clusters and finally blocking passage down the river. He could see his breath as he exhaled, a steady white mist.

He found a clump of birches just south of the pyramid of logs. He buried the nose of the canoe deep in the trees and took a few seconds to throw some loose branches over the gunnels.

150

It was midnight and there was no moon. Pyro had learned long ago, in the jungles of Asia and the bustling cities of the world, to take his time, not to rush. Fire was for ever.

It was cold and the earth scrunched under his heavy boots as he leaned forward into the bow to pull out the two five-gallon cans. Even though the tops were on tight he got a piercing whiff of gasoline from the first can. The second can, kerosene, gave off that sweet smell that he knew so well, almost like napalm jelly; but nothing smelled exactly like napalm. The odors were familiar and gave him pleasure. They made him feel safe and secure. They were old friends.

The trek up the bank to the mill was treacherous and slippery. He took his time, resting several times. He was careful to make sure the cans did not hit any trees or make any sound.

He reached the clearing. He had been warned about Charles, the security guard, by the Secret Service agent. Charles would be napping by now. He would be asleep in the small boathouse down by the pier and the conveyor belt where the log booms were anchored.

Pyro trundled towards the main warehouse and set the cans down under the building. He then crept over to the office building with the living quarters located in the rear, to see if they were occupied.

He edged along the rough unpainted clapboard until he was directly under the bedroom window. He pulled his black watch cap down tight against his head. It was a ritual with him to try to see his victims.

Slowly, he raised his eyes to the edge of the window sill and peered inside. The shade was torn, and hung loosely from the top of the window. Pyro's eyes edged higher over the sill. He saw the flickering of a single candle and heard the loud snoring of Percival Smathers, and then he saw Claudine, Smather's French-Canadian girl friend. Her long black hair flowed over Percival's chest. She was asleep, cradled in his arms. Her legs were spread wide apart, her pubic V a dark triangle in the glow from the small candle and coil heater in the wall across from the foot of the bed. The sheet had fallen aside and she was naked from the waist down.

Pyro stared at her for several minutes. He finally turned and slid down the rough boards into a heap outside their window. He buried his hands in his own genitals and fondled his pulsing erection until he was relieved. Seeing a woman naked was more than he had ever hoped to expect. He stumbled away, light-headed, almost crawling back to the warehouse and the two red cans that sat hidden in the gloom of the night, waiting for him.

His hands trembled slightly as he took the top off the gasoline can. Slowly, methodically, he circled the warehouse, pouring a ribbon of gasoline along the base, making sure it soaked into the weatherbeaten wood.

He stopped to look inside the warehouse windows. He was curious. His breathing was almost back to normal and he was fully operational now. There was a bare lightbulb hanging. Through the window he saw pallets stacked high and covered with tarpaulins.

He shrugged. He didn't really care what was in the warehouse. He took the top off the second can. He made a trail of kerosene a foot wide that reached from the warehouse into a clearing a hundred feet away. He did it twice to make sure it had soaked well into the grass and the frozen ground.

He followed the same procedure round the office. Pyro knew from experience that the kerosene would burn slowly and give him a chance to return to the canoe before it met and married with the gasoline and ignited. He built a tiny fire and poured the final foot of kerosene to join the fire to the soaking trails. It ignited immediately and started two blue-red serpentine trails; one trail led to the warehouse, the other trail led to the office building.

Pyro took off at a run, almost laughing with glee, his adrenaline high. He tripped, slipping, crashing through the branches on his way down the bank to the hidden canoe. The noise didn't matter to him now and he was enjoying himself. He yanked the canoe from the birch trees and jumped in, almost tipping it. He paddled quickly to the opposite river bank and found an overhanging maple tree that he could hide under. He boated his paddle and waited.

From his perch high above the mill, Ralph Cobb saw the night light up in a sudden flash, a crimson red burst illuminating the blackness. He saw the boathouse door spring open. Charles the nightwatchman stood there in his long johns, stunned, as he scanned the river bank with his lit flashlight.

He didn't need it. The entire camp was floodlit by the raging fire.

Pyro sat in the canoe under the maple tree on the farside bank. The fire was snaking red and orange spires of flame skyward to lick the heavens. For Pyro, fire was a dragon of magnificent evil, something that he knew exactly how to create and control. He, Pyro, knew the intimate secrets of the dragon. They had been together many times and many times he had loosed the red devil to do its earthly work.

That was Pyro's purpose on earth, to unleash the dragon.

He was both its servant and the master. Without him the dragon must stay contained, but once released, the dragon was all-powerful and became Pyro's master.

He coughed violently into his clenched fist as he got his first full whiff of the fire. The smell was new to him, like no smell he had ever known. He didn't wonder about it very long; he knew instinctively that it was dangerous. The dragon was warning him. He dug his paddle into the cold water and disappeared into the blackness of the river and the gloom of the Gatineau Hills.

Cobb watched the cloud rise and float down the river as the buildings burned out of control. There was no fire department that you could call out here in the wilderness. And the toxic black cloud hung over the mill like a shroud, keeping anyone from attempting to put out the fire.

Cobb watched a naked dark-haired woman streak out of the office and run for the river bank. She was followed by a bare-assed skinny blonde man who seemed to be disoriented, almost drunk. The man turned in a circle twice then finally followed her.

Cobb stayed in his position for over an hour, wanting to make sure the warehouse burned to the ground. When there was nothing but ashes left, he found his car and drove leisurely through the Gatineau Hills to Ottawa and the airport. As he drove, he thought carefully about how he would explain this to the President.

He had taken action and it had worked.

He smiled, pleased with himself. 'St John is finished; no paper, no currency. They are out of business. The President will be happy; even that asshole Phillip Sturges will be happy.'

Pyro and the Secret Service agent had already arrived and were waiting silently in the coffee shop. As Cobb sat down, Pyro turned and smiled, waiting for praise like a child. Cobb tried to smile back but couldn't. There was unrestrained evil in Pyro's dark eyes, a deep revolting sickness that Cobb recognized.

It made him turn away.

Thursday evening 6:00
PARIS, FRANCE

Nick's plane landed smoothly on the tarmac at Orly Airport. He cleared Customs and took a cab to the Ritz Hotel, napped for an hour, then showered, shaved and got into his evening clothes.

On his way out, he stopped at the dark, richly-panelled Ritz bar for a quiet drink. He wanted a private moment before his appointment with Colonel Le Clerc. He ordered a Scotch. For Nick, Scotch and Paris went together. Paris was a maelstrom of memories for him.

His first trip there had been sponsored by Books' mother. The Duchess was coming to the couturier showings and she had decided, on a whim, to bring the three boys with her for company.

Phillip, Nick and Books discovered Paris together, the beauty of the Louvre, the bleak, skeletal starkness of the Eiffel Tower, the sleaze of Place Pigalle, the opulence of the Palace of Versailles, the intellectual bohemianism of the Sorbonne, and the exotic decadence of the Latin Quarter.

In the evening the three boys would dress formally for dinner. The Duchess would take them in tow to the finest restaurants and nightclubs of Paris. It was at Maxim's that Nick saw Aristotle Onassis and Jackie together; he was amazed at how small a man Onassis was.

The Duchess was pleased to have the three boys as her escorts. They were all fit and handsome; heads turned whenever the four of them entered a room. The Duchess loved to teach the boys, fuss over them in her subtle ways. She would nod at the 'chosen one', the one who would order her meal for her; each night she would select a different one of her 'escorts' to do it for her. She watched them like a lioness, making sure they did things properly; she would gently remove the dinner fork from Nick's hand and slip a salad fork between his fingers. She would explain to them all about wines and how to order them, the proper way to select vintage champagne, how much to tip the maitre d', and when.

She would nudge them when they fell asleep at the ballet or the opera, and when her evening was over she would have them escort her to her room and say good night, like three young suitors. She knew perfectly well that they would go out on the town as only rich young men can do with their sap boiling and a fistful of cash. And she knew they would go to the roughest, sleaziest clubs of the Place Pigalle and explore the fleshpot that is Paris at night, and they did.

Nick swirled the ice cubes in a circle in his glass as he looked at the amber liquid. How different those early trips were from his last trip three years ago when he had to fix Sean O'Reilly. Was violence latent, asleep in his psyche, lying there waiting to be woken, a sleeping wildcat just under the surface?

'Ah,' Nick thought, 'these musings are carousel thoughts that go nowhere but round in circles in my brain and I always come back to where I started. The fact is that I shot the bastard, and I probably would again. I feel no remorse and maybe that's what really bothers me.' Nick plopped his empty drink onto the coaster, slipped a fifty franc note onto the check tray and left the hotel.

It was eight o'clock by the time he found his way to Le Dernier Legionnaire, a private club located near Montparnasse in the Latin Quarter.

Nick had been there many times before, dining or drinking with Colonel Le Clerc, a famous officer of the French Foreign Legion. The Colonel had lost his right hand at Dien Bien Phu. He had replaced the missing hand with a wooden black-gloved replica that he usually kept tucked inside the third button of his shirt when he was in public view.

No one knew what his real name was.

He was waiting at the center table for Nick. There were four working girls with him, drinking his wine and telling jokes. Le Clerc snapped the fingers of his good hand for the girls to leave as Nick approached. They walked away insolently, pouting, their fun over for a few minutes.

Le Clerc smiled. The smile tilted one side of his bushy moustache to an angle that almost made him look comical. His eyes were deep brown, and deceiving: they gave off false warmth. Nick had supplied the Colonel with a lot of hardware over the years, most of which had found its way down into the heart of Africa where the Colonel was known as 'Le Main Noir du Mort', the Black Hand of Death. He was retired now, but still his name carried power all over the world.

'Sit, sit!' The Colonel pointed at a chair. He offered Nick his good left hand without rising from the table. Nick shook it, sat down, and ordered a cognac.

The club was for mercenaries and arms dealers. It was owned by Le Clerc and had paid for itself in many ways. Nick and Le Clerc, at this very table, years ago, had made a deal for arms that had brought the Belgian Congo, finally and completely, to its knees. And Rhodesia's struggle for independence had made the Colonel a rich man.

Membership to the club was highly selective and allowed only after the most careful screening process, personally supervised by the Colonel.

It was in this club on a gray, rainy Paris night, years ago, that Nick had shot Sean O'Reilly to death.

Nick walked in and slipped off his raincoat, shook the rain off his London Fog, folded it precisely in long narrow panels, and hung the raincoat over his left arm. He felt the few beads of water that remained on the coat run down his suit jacket and onto his wrist. With his right hand he reached into his left armpit, eased the US Army Colt .45 out of its holster and quietly slipped the bolt back, popping a cartridge out of the magazine and into the chamber. It was a devastating weapon at close range and he was using soft-tipped bullets that spread like cream cheese when they hit a target, smashing bone and tearing flesh. Nick transferred the raincoat to his right hand, hiding the gun from sight.

He took a deep, cleansing breath and walked through the black beads that hung from the arched entranceway. He entered the main room of the club. Nick knew that Sean O'Reilly was in there; he had followed him through Paris all day. It was difficult to find Sean O'Reilly solo, without his usual retinue of bodyguards. The club was quiet; there were no other customers but Ernie Sands at a corner table with a woman. The Colonel was alone at his table, smoking, studying invoices. The evening had not yet begun. O'Reilly looked up over the shoulder of the pretty girl on his lap to see Nick enter. His glance took in the raincoat covering Nick's right hand.

O'Reilly pushed the squirming girl away and swept a second one out of her chair with the back of his arm. The girl landed hard on the floor and crabbed away towards the bar. These girls didn't need much explanation; they knew when danger was near. Sean O'Reilly started to reach inside his tweed jacket for his shoulder holster.

'No,' Nick said quietly. 'Sean, don't end your life sooner than you have to. Put your hands on the table, palms flat. Do it, Sean.'

Slowly, O'Reilly did as he was told. 'Nick, 'ave a bleedin' sense of humor, will ya.' O'Reilly had all the charm of the Irish and a heart as black as the coal in Wales. 'Forget Nigeria. We can work it out. I 'eard you were pissed, but for Christ's sake, mon, it's only bloody business. We've 'ad disputes in the past, ya know.'

Nick lifted the raincoat with his left hand and dropped it on the floor. He stood holding the .45. It was stainless steel and it flashed in the dim spotlights of the club. There was silence; the bartender had turned off the music.

The Colonel was sitting directly behind O'Reilly; he rose slowly from his chair, out of the line of fire. 'That's a good idea, Colonel; please join Ernie at his table.'

'*Oui*,' was all the Colonel said.

'If it's money that's botherin' ya, boy, I can tell ya, 'tis no problem. I can 'ave all the profit I made in Nigeria 'ere for you in cash tomorrow; it's over two million pounds. It was just business, ya know, Nick?' O'Reilly knew that if he was still talking he wasn't dead, and the longer he talked, the longer he breathed.

Nick heard the main door open behind him and the murmur of two voices. He hadn't much time.

'I got a message from Alf. Remember him?'

'Sure. 'E was workin' for me two years in the Congo before 'e went with you. Feisty little SAS fella.'

'He's not so feisty anymore; he only has one arm. Blackpool Brutus and Liverpool Larry, remember them?'

'Sure, they was all in my employ at one time or another. I heard they bought it in Nigeria.' O'Reilly shook his head from side to side in a gesture of sadness for the loss of those men. He knew he had run out of words; his time was up. Without looking up, he moved lightning fast. His left palm sped back, caught the lip of the table, and flipped it. His right hand flew to his shoulder holster. His gun had almost cleared his tweed lapel when the first slug tore into him. It hit him just above the bridge of his nose. The second one hit him in the throat. His blood sprayed everywhere.

The Colonel and Ernie Sands were on their feet before O'Reilly hit the floor. 'Lock the door!' the Colonel yelled at the bartender. He bent to check O'Reilly's pulse and found none. 'Lisette, you and the other girls work with the busboys and mop this blood up.' The Colonel looked over at the bouncer who had just come on duty and had walked in from the kitchen. 'Gaston, get the two cooks. Wrap him in garbage bags and carry him out back.'

The Colonel looked over at Nick who stood over O'Reilly's body with the gun still smoking. 'Don't stand there, Nick! I will have someone come by to pick up the body. You and Ernie come with me. Ernie! Let's go.'

The three of them headed for the back stairs that led up to the Colonel's apartment. The Colonel lived over the club in a lavish apartment. When they were inside, he locked the door behind them and rushed to the phone and dialed. It rang once, and was answered.

'Hello.'

'This is Colonel Le Clerc. Who is this?'

'René. It is good to hear from you, Colonel. You have a problem?'

'Yes, at my club. I have a mess.'

'You want it to disappear?'

'Yes.'

'Say no more. I will have two men there in five minutes. They will do what you need.'

'*Merci.*'

'Happy to be of service. *Bon soir.*'

The phone clicked dead in the Colonel's hand. That was Nick's first encounter with the Union Corse.

The Colonel spoke. 'Nick, you look, how do they say, fit as a violin?'

'Fiddle. Fit as a fiddle. And you, Colonel, you look like you are enjoying life.' He had put on at least twenty pounds since Nick had last seen him, but his vanity refused to let him buy new uniforms. His two hundred and fifty pounds were bursting out of the Legion khaki shirt buttoned round his six-foot-two frame. His starched shirt collar was so tight his eyeballs bulged.

'The tummy? You refer to my ample tummy? *Oui*, of course you are right, *mon ami*, but for me the real action is over, so now I get the other action.' The Colonel smiled over at the bar girls. He nodded his red beret to them and winked. They all bowed at the waist, almost in unison, like a chorus line, then went back to their chattering at the bar.

It wasn't quite nine yet. The club had not officially opened, but a few members had filtered in early. They went directly to the changing rooms and their private lockers. For some of the men, the lockers held uniforms. By midnight the armies of almost every nation on earth would be represented at the club, mingling with civilians who bought and sold the goods of war.

There was a stage show every night. It was usually a sex show of some kind. It was up to the members to suggest what they wanted to see. Tonight the Prince of Pigalle was visiting; the Prince billed himself as having the 'heaviest penis in Paris' and he had a taste for tiny Oriental girls. The first show was at eleven.

There was dancing provided for the patrons after the show. Nick thought of it as a macabre masquerade, the soldiers and the hookers, dancing a slow dreary dance of life. It gave him the shudders.

'Nick, I often think of that rainy night and O'Reilly; I have had people ask where he is. I tell them he has taken a long journey. You did us all a favor that night, *mon ami*. But you look serious! Nick, you have not come for fun?' the Colonel asked.

'For profit. I need to contact the Union Corse,' Nick said, sipping his brandy, watching a lieutenant commander from the Royal Navy enter in his full dress whites. The commander touched his visor in an informal salute to the Colonel.

The Colonel nodded back. 'The Union Corse. Nick, are you into something different?'

Nick knew that the Colonel had done a great deal of business with the Corsican Brotherhood over the years. They had transported almost all his arms into Africa; borders and Customs inspectors were no barriers to them. The Union Corse had ten thousand people on the streets of Europe and England distributing their drugs. Smuggling was their lifeblood. They controlled eighty per cent of the European drug business, and most of the heroin that flowed from India and the Golden Triangle into the hands of the Mafia in the USA passed first through the Corsican Brotherhood.

'Or is it arms, and you need the Brotherhood to help in the delivery? It is an arms deal, eh, Nick?'

'No. It's cash.' Nick slipped five fifties to the Colonel. 'These are newly made.' He then reached in his pocket and pulled out five new, real fifties. 'These were made by the US Mint.' The Colonel examined them in the candlelight. 'I need distribution,' Nick added.

'To my eye they all look good. But what do I know about the funny money?' He smiled, sliding all ten bills back to Nick. 'So you want me to act as the middleman? Save you time with troublesome introductions and reference checks?'

'Yes.'

Le Clerc studied Nick for a moment, then signalled for a bottle of champagne. The waiter came immediately and silently popped the cork. Nick knew the Colonel was stalling, thinking.

'I could use a new diversion. I will call René Descartes tonight. If he is in Nice he will see us, I'm sure. Do you want me to go with you?'

'Yes.' Nick knew that his loyalty and trust were valuable to the Colonel. They had never broken their word to each other. He knew this fact would be passed on to René Descartes.

Le Dernier Legionnaire was starting to come alive. Nick recognized several of the attending members. They nodded curt hellos, but no one bothered the Colonel while he was talking business. Many wore their formal dress uniform; even the girls dressed up for the occasion, wearing scanty short party dresses and extra make-up. None of the girls wore underpants, and they were not bashful about displaying what it was they had for sale. But still, formality and proper behavior was demanded, at least at the beginning of the evening.

'You will stay for the fun? The Prince of Pigalle is paying us a royal visit tonight,' the Colonel said.

'He's still at it?'

'It's all he has; his organ is his only asset. He has no brain.'

'Thank you, not tonight, Colonel. I'm jetlagged and I would like to have my wits about me tomorrow.' The room held strong images for Nick. It seemed like a lifetime ago, dealing with Sean O'Reilly . . . the Colonel . . . the blood on the floor . . . splattered on his raincoat. Nick remembered stopping to pick up his raincoat for some reason and carrying

162

it with him as they spirited him away from the club that night.

'A wise decision. You will need your wits,' the Colonel said. 'You are at the Ritz under your name?'

'Yes.'

'I'll see you at nine, then. We will drive, see a little of the countryside, chat about old times.' The Colonel smiled; he stood and snapped his fingers at the bar girls, giving the signal that his meeting was over. Three of the prettiest and youngest of the girls marched directly over to the table and sat down.

Nick said a fast hello to a few old friends dressed in Marine dress blues and hurried out. He breathed easier as he quietly closed the door behind him. The door was black with only the gold letters 'Le Dernier Legionnaire' visible from the street.

The streets were alive with the smells, sights and sounds of nighttime in the Latin Quarter as he strolled down the Boulevard Montparnasse looking for a cab. Every city had one, the tenderloin. Nick always found himself in the bowels of whatever city he visited. It was life, exaggerated life, that attracted him. He could never fully adjust to the facade of high society, the veneer that hid the indolence and decadence. He was always drawn to vivid characters: the Colonel, Don Saverese, even Sean O'Reilly. He thought of Books and Phillip in the old days, when they were relaxed and full of the wonder of life.

He spotted a cab and headed for the hotel.

At nine the next morning the Colonel was waiting in front of the hotel in a battered old Renault. He wanted no attention when he was on his way to visit the head of the Union Corse. The fenders were dented and covered in rust, but Nick knew the tires and engine would be in perfect condition. The doorman gingerly opened the door for Nick; when he slammed it shut he checked his white gloves for dirt.

On the ride down they discussed the Colonel's theories on politics and war.

'Wars, *mon ami*, are not won the way the public thinks they are won: by great generals. No. They are won by average generals who pay great attention to every detail, or they have a staff that pays attention to every detail and they pay attention to their staff. Eisenhower, Patton, Rommel, Bonaparte, Nelson, they didn't make a lot of mistakes. That's the key, Nick. Let the other guy make the slip-up.'

Nick agreed. He wondered how Books could keep all the details of this venture together, and whether he would ever print his first dollar.

Nick wondered why he was even thinking about printing the first dollar.

The French countryside flew by as the Colonel continued to ramble on about his theories and philosophies. Nick took the time to relax and plan; it was good to be with his old friend.

The gray Marseilles shipyards and the closed beaches of St Tropez appeared and disappeared. The stately Meridien Hotel of Cannes passed, and finally the two men entered Nice. There were still half a dozen of the world's largest private yachts anchored in the harbor.

René Descartes' villa stood on the shore. His property climbed halfway up the mountain. Nick could see the high stone fence as it snaked its way up the hill and outlined the borders. He noticed the elaborate and subtle alarm system of invisible beams and TV cameras that could see in the dark. Nick used to have the distributorship for the system in Africa.

Two black Dobermans sat on their haunches, poised and silent, behind the wrought-iron gates. A slight white mist pumped out of their nostrils as they began to emit an almost inaudible growl, their lips curling upwards, showing white fangs. The gatekeeper appeared and yelled, '*Allez!*' The dogs ran fifty feet to the side of the driveway and sat waiting for another command.

'I am Colonel Le Clerc.'

'*Oui, monsieur*,' the guard murmured, opening the gates,

nodding his head to the side for them to pass. Nick saw batteries of permanently placed cameras follow them as they passed through the gates and up the wide circular drive.

The house was immense, a converted stone farmhouse that seemed to go on for ever. They were led into the large foyer and greeted by a trim, petite brunette.

She smiled. 'Hello, Colonel. It has been a long time.'

'Too long, *mon chérie*. This is my friend Nick Sullivan. Nick, this is Michelle.' The Colonel offered no last name.

'Hello, Michelle.' Nick extended his hand.

They followed her to a small room with a large metal detector inside, exactly like in the airports.

'I'm sorry, but you must both pass through. If you have any weapons, please declare them now, and leave them with me.' They understood that if weapons were found beyond this point it would be interpreted as a threat on Descartes' life. 'There has been much trouble lately,' she shrugged.

On the trip down, Colonel Le Clerc had mentioned to Nick that there was dissension in the ranks of the Union Corse.

They passed across the metal-detector threshold. It was state-of-the-art and would display on the computer monitor any metal or plastic that they might be carrying.

Michelle read the screen, and then they followed her to the library. The library consisted of an entire wing of the house. Nick estimated the room was at least seventy feet long, with alarm-wired bay windows that overlooked the harbor. Nick's experienced eyes noticed that the glass bore the seal of bulletproof treatment.

René Descartes was barely visible at the end of the room, dwarfed by his Louis XIV desk. He didn't rise until they were at the edge of the desk.

Nick was shocked at how old Descartes was. He was bent and wrinkled; white hair covered his tanned head. His eyes were blue, the color of the Mediterranean Sea that glistened outside his window.

'Ah, Colonel Le Clerc,' he said affectionately.

The Colonel almost snapped to attention as he introduced Nick. 'An American friend of mine, Nick Sullivan.'

Nick shook his hand. They were looking about for seats when Descartes said, 'We will go aboard my yacht and talk there. I treated myself to a new toy. I don't have much time left on this planet, so I feel I must celebrate life while I can.' He smiled over at Nick, putting his hand on the Colonel's shoulder. 'Just to steady me a little on our walk.'

As they made their way towards the door, Colonel Le Clerc stopped and gazed up to admire a lifesize painting of Napoleon. Descartes winked at Nick as he walked on with the Colonel.

'Our most famous Corsican,' was all he said as he passed the painting.

An electric golf cart was waiting in front of the main entrance to take them down to the pier and the yacht.

The *Aigle Corse* stood gleaming in the noon sun, its one hundred and ninety foot Oceanfast aluminum hull, built in Australia, reflecting brilliant white off the blue Mediterranean Sea. Nick had seen the boats in the winter months in the West Indies, high-tech masterpieces of design powered by Mercedes MTU diesels and three Kamewa water jets that could take the *Aigle Corse* up to fifty knots. The boat did not use propellers.

Michelle was waiting on deck. She hurried down to help René Descartes up the gangplank. They settled into the main salon and took coffee.

'How may we be of service?' Descartes asked, after everyone had been served.

Nick hesitated before speaking, looking over at Michelle.

'Speak freely, Mr Sullivan,' Descartes said, sipping his coffee. 'Michelle is my brother's daughter. She is the best of us, and one day soon she will replace me. She is pure Corsican.'

'Not soon, I hope, Uncle,' she said, holding his hand.

Nick suddenly understood why there was a rumor of

166

dissension in the ranks. The Brotherhood would have a difficult time accepting a woman leader. He wondered if it would affect his deal.

'We would like you to distribute our money,' Nick said, reaching in his pocket and extracting the five bogus bills. He handed them to the Corsican, placing them on the coffee table. He reached into his other pocket and took out five real fifties, placing them next to the forgeries.

'These are yours?' Descartes asked, holding the five counterfeit bills in the air.

'Yes,' Nick answered as Michelle rose to leave the room. She re-entered seconds later with a magnifying glass and a fistful of US fifties from the boat safe. The two of them studied the bills for several minutes.

'They are impressive,' Descartes said. 'We have not done a great deal with counterfeit currency in the last few years because the quality has been poor, especially the paper, and the serial numbers were always limited, easily traced.' He handed the bills back to Nick.

'We can produce English pounds, French francs, German marks, Swiss francs, Italian lire, South African rand, and Japanese yen. And, of course, all the American dollars you want.'

'The cost? ' Michelle asked.

'Twenty-five per cent of face value, paid in gold.'

'Expensive!' Michelle said, looking over at her uncle.

'Hard currencies are always of value to us, Mr Sullivan, as you know.' Descartes was referring to the black market smuggling of hard currencies into East European nations. 'With the Iron Curtain crumbling, there is an even greater demand for hard currency as the Soviet bloc freely enters into world trade.'

Since the Second World War, the Union Corse had been a main source of hard currency for those countries. Yugoslavia, Albania, Poland, East Germany, Czechoslovakia and even Russia bartered arms and other black market exports for hard currency. They often smuggled gold over their borders in return for the paper currency of strong nations. Nick had bought arms on many occasions from Yugoslavia and paid for them in crisp, new US dollars.

'How would you deliver?' Descartes asked.

'We would hook up with your fleet at sea and make the transfer there.'

'What are the quantities?' the Colonel asked, thinking about his commission.

'The first delivery must be five hundred million in US funds at face value. After the first delivery, we will print any mixture of currencies that you like.'

'These are enormous quantities. How do we know the quality of your shipment will equal the samples – if we approve the samples,' Descartes asked.

'Take random samples at sea, on delivery. Send an expert on board to check the delivery before you hand over the gold. The bills will be as we represent,' Nick said.

'Colonel, will you stand ready to vouch for this transaction? Am I correct in assuming you are involved, and will request a percentage from us?' Descartes asked.

'Yes. Nick and I have a great deal of experience working together; I have no reason to doubt.'

'We will consider your proposal and await your next visit,' Descartes said. 'Would you like a tour of the boat?'

'*Merci*,' Nick said.

'Michelle will escort you. I must save my legs. I will stay and chat with the Colonel.' Descartes motioned for Le Clerc to join him on the couch. It was time to discuss the Colonel's end of the deal.

Nick followed Michelle up the stairway to the bridge. Her slim muscular calves flexed as she took the steps. Nick wondered how the Brotherhood would ever accept a woman in charge, but decided Descartes must have anticipated that problem.

They stood at the helm on the bridge looking out at the

harbor. The bridge resembled that of a modern warship. The consoles glistened with the dials and digital displays of highly sophisticated electronic gear.

Nick fingered the satellite phone receiver. He was tempted to call Books on the Cay Sal Bank, but an open line would be dangerous. He decided to wait until he got back to New York that afternoon.

As Michelle led Nick through the innards of the yacht, something gnawed at his brain, a sense that something was dreadfully wrong. It went right to the pit of his stomach and dug in. It was a familiar feeling; he knew there was trouble ahead.

Friday morning 9:00
CAY SAL BANK, BAHAMAS

Books was overseeing the installation of the GM 451 diesel generators. The connecting fuel line from the diesel barge was being buried by the construction crew as the mechanics fine-tuned the engines.

When he was finished, he walked into the main Butler building. Heather was dressed in shorts and a shirt, a black bandanna pulled tight across her forehead to keep the sweat out of her eyes as she installed the IBM PC/XT and the Zed 3600 copier onto the concrete pad. A marble pedestal stood alone and empty between the copier and the computer; it was where the Black Box would sit. A crew was installing the air-conditioning. They were running ducts across the roof to ensure a consistent ambient temperature for the sensitive machines. Dehumidifiers were also placed in both the main building and the warehouse, to keep the humidity at the proper level for the drying of the finished currency.

Books stood still in the doorway, watching Heather as she connected the wires and tubing. She sat in the lotus position, directly under the computer, crocheting wires, knitting red, green, yellow, blue, and orange threads. He marvelled at the speed and sureness of her hands as she reconstructed the complex wiring diagram imprinted in her mind. They had spent the last three days finalizing the main construction and supervising the location of the air-conditioners that had been ferried in by helicopter.

Books heard the soft whining of a muted siren. Heather had hooked up the siren to indicate that the satellite phone was ringing in the war room of *Desperado*. Books carried a hand-held remote phone receiver in his pocket. He flipped the mouthpiece out and answered the call.

'Mako Marine Institute.'

'It's Perce. I mean Alchem,' Percival Smathers added quickly, remembering his code name.

'Yes? What is it?'

'We got big trouble.'

'This line isn't secure,' Books warned, wishing Heather had installed the scrambler on the line. 'How severe?'

'A ballbreaker.' It was the code word for total disaster. Percival continued, his voice cracking with emotion, 'Fucking fire. It's all gone. Arson. I can't believe it, only cinders left now; not enough paper left to wipe your ass with.'

'Injuries?' Books asked.

'Yes. Claudine, a friend of mine. She's pretty bad, smoke inhalation. She's in the hospital in Hull. Those fumes are toxic, you know.'

'Don't say any more,' Books interrupted. 'Where are you?'

'In town, Hull.'

'Go to Ottawa. Now! Get out of there and get on the first flight to Des Moines.' Des Moines was the code name for Miami. 'Connect any way you can. Don't fly direct, and use Harry.' 'Harry' meant that Percival was to use a fictitious name. Books could picture Percival on the other end of the line, slightly drunk, as he fumbled through his tiny code book, frantically trying to figure out what the hell Books was talking about.

'Look, I can't come right away. I need to see Claudine and make sure –'

'Get on that plane, Perce; get on it today!' Books knew it was the wrong thing to say as the words slipped out of his mouth. He had to control his anger. Perce was always capable of doing the opposite of what he was ordered to do. It was his nature. There was silence on the line. Books persisted. 'Send her a get-well card and a check for all her hospital bills and a little extra for herself. I'll cover the cost. You've got to move now, Perce.'

'Des Moines?' Percival had found the code reference.

'Yes. Go directly to church; leave now.' 'Church' was the warehouse on the Miami River.

'Books, look, I'm real sorry, but it wasn't my fault. These people up here, they're so fucking crazy. It might have been jealousy over Claudine, who knows?'

'We'll talk about it in Des Moines.'

'Right, I'll be there tomorrow.' The line went dead.

Books stood on the beach, looking at *Desperado* anchored in the harbor. He thought of all the things that he could have done to prevent this from happening, how easy it would have been to avoid. He had been followed to the mill, there was no question. It wasn't jealousy. It was the Feds. They must be tapping the communications lines.

Heather stepped up beside him, stretching and slipping her black bandanna off her forehead, whipping her hair from side to side, letting the sun wash her face. She stood next to him, her eyes closed, her chin tilted up towards the sun. 'Hey, why so glum?' she asked, looking over at him. 'Anything wrong?'

'There's nothing the matter. I'm hungry, that's all,' Books snapped, 'and sometimes when I get hungry I get a little cranky. Sorry. How about a swim to the boat?' he offered, smiling, realizing he had been short with her.

'You swim. I'll take the Whaler. I'm not disrobing in front of all these construction types,' she said, still smarting from his curtness; she started walking over to the Whaler.

Books swam slowly to *Desperado*, hoping the exercise would help him to think. But it didn't.

Above the fluffy tropical clouds, orbiting in the heavens, a satellite had recorded the entire conversation between the two men and relayed it to CIA headquarters in Langley, Virginia. The conversation was, in turn, sent to the office of Ralph Cobb.

Friday morning 10:00
SECRET SERVICE, WASHINGTON, D.C.

'Not enough paper left to wipe your ass with. I like that!' Cobb said out loud to his empty office. He finished reading the transcript of the conversation between Percival Smathers and Books St John, stood, and slapped his desk hard with the flat sheaf of papers. 'Presumptuous assholes, to think they could bump heads with Uncle Sam and survive.'

The President would be at Camp David all weekend; Cobb decided to wait and tell him the good news on Monday. But first he would call Phillip Sturges and pull his chain a little. Cobb hated Princeton and the privileged pricks it produced.

He grinned as he placed the call.

Phillip was in the Federal Reserve subterranean Gold Room, buried nine stories below Manhattan Island, watching the transfer of one hundred million dollars in gold bullion from the French reserves to the German. The gold cart, piled high with gold bars, was pulled out of the cage marked 'France'. The steel-barred door was slammed shut behind the cart, shaking the wheels on Phillip's chair.

Phillip watched as the guards labored to place the dense gold bars on the giant circular disc of the scale, one at a time, until the entire pile was assembled. The weight was offset on the other disc by counterweights. It was primitive by today's standards, but totally accurate. The scale had been built in 1932; it was so precise that if a person placed a single piece of paper on one of the giant circular trays, removed it, signed his name and replaced the paper, the weight of his signature would be registered.

Phillip asked the Chief of Security to bring a gold bar to him. The Chief, in turn, nodded his approval to the official weigher who shuffled and scraped his way over, dragging his sluggish iron boots. The iron boots were worn for protection. Gold is so dense and heavy that if a bar, the size of a common brick, was dropped, it would crush a man's foot. The iron boots looked ominous, futuristic, like steel ski boots. They reached above the guard's ankles, halfway to the knees.

Phillip cradled the gold bar in his lap; it was trapezoid, indicating that it was minted in Europe. The American and Canadian bars were rectangles.

It shimmered in Phillip's lap. With his finger he traced the stamp of the Banque du Rothschild on the bar and calculated its worth at today's London gold opening: $160,000. Amazing what men put value in. At least gold was rare.

Phillip knew that the real power of paper money was faith, faith in the state. When the people lost faith, the power of panic took over. It nearly toppled the banking system in the Depression when people stampeded the banks to empty their accounts.

The bar was cold in his lap, pure and objective, unfeeling, unaffected by the vagaries and greed of man. Philip could feel his biceps bulge as he handed the bar back to the waiting man in the iron boots.

The attendant at the main vault lock-up gate yelled his name. 'Call for you, Mr Sturges.'

Phillip wheeled over to take the call. He muffled the receiver and asked the guard. 'Who is it?'

'Mr Cobb, Secret Service.'

'Hello, Ralph,' Phillip said.

'Your pal is out of business.' Cobb's voice was at an all-time high, a quivering tenor. He continued, 'Burned to the ground. I had his mill burned to the fucking ground. No paper, no currency.'

'Where was the mill?'

'Quebec, Canada.'

'You got it all?'

'Yes. Only ashes left. We intercepted a call from the mill foreman, some guy named "Perce". He called the island. He confirmed that they are OOB, out of business. To quote: "There's not enough paper left to wipe your ass." So, Phillip, you can rest easy for a while. It will give us the time we need to find the Black Box.'

'What kind of mill was it?'

'Jesus Christ, who cares what kind of mill it was? It was a fucking paper mill,' Cobb snapped back.

'Those are pulp mills in Quebec. I don't know of any mill up there capable of manufacturing ultra-fine linen cotton paper.'

'So?'

Phillip raised his voice. 'So how the hell did they have the capability to manufacture currency paper? Did you get a sample?'

'Hell, no. But I had two agents confirm it. The paper was there, stacked in a big warehouse on skids, ready to roll.'

'Was there any special equipment on the premises? Equipment capable of manufacturing currency paper?'

'Why all these technical questions? It was the main warehouse, and it's gone, and they're out of business.'

'How do you know? Maybe there's a second warehouse. How did they manufacture the paper without a factory full of sophisticated equipment? Ralph, did the President approve your action?'

There was a long tense silence on the line. The silence answered the question.

'Have you told him?' Phillip asked.

'Not yet.' The timbre of Cobb's voice had dropped. It was lower, by force of will.

'Big decision to make on your own, Ralph. I thought we were in this together. I thought we would confer.'

'I had to move fast. There was no time for committees.'

'The President isn't a committee, Ralph.'

'That's not what I mean, and you know it.'

'All I know is that you moved mighty fast.'

'I thought the news would cheer you up, for Christ's sake.'

'It does, Ralph. But maybe, just maybe, if you had moved a little slower, we might have rounded up some evidence; we could've shut them down for ever.'

'They're shut down for ever,' Cobb spat out.

'I hope so. Keep me posted.'

'Sure,' Cobb muttered, slamming the phone into the cradle. 'Goddammit!'

He stood and walked over to the wall map, a letter opener in his hand; seven tiny tacks glowed green across the United States. Cobb knew none of them mattered. He slipped the edge of the letter opener under each tack and popped them from the map. He did it rapidly and violently, letting the tacks fall where they might.

'Shit!' Why hadn't he thought to put a tail on Percival Smathers when he had the bastard. The RCMP could have easily picked up his trail in Quebec. He knew he had to confront the President now, not Monday.

He walked back to his desk and put a call through to the White House. As he waited, he said out loud, into the air, 'Hello, Mr President. Good morning, Mr President. How are you today, Mr President?' He was trying to get his voice under control, down an octave. He took several deep breaths to calm himself.

'Hello, Mr President,' Cobb said in a strained tenor as the President picked up the line.

Friday afternoon 2:00
NEW YORK CITY

Winter was creeping in on New York. Nick Sullivan stood in his room at the Plaza holding the phone to his ear, looking down on the fading green of Central Park, waiting for Books to finish.

The gods had made his decision for him. It was over. They were finished. The mill was burned to the ground and the paper was destroyed. Now he could go back to his quiet life.

But Books wasn't quitting.

'They are obviously monitoring our moves. I probably led them right to the mill. Do you think you were followed?'

'I know I was. But I gave them the slip.'

'Good. I want you to stay in New York. I'll find a way to shake them and meet you there.'

'How about this line?' Nick asked, concerned about the phone.

'We're secure. Heather has scrambled all transmissions from our end.'

'Books, why don't I just come down there?'

'No. I've got Percival coming into Miami tomorrow.'

'Percival Smathers?' Nick knew Percival from Princeton. 'Percival is involved?' Books was full of surprises.

'Yes.'

'How did Heather take the news?' Nick asked.

'She doesn't know.'

'Keeping her in the dark is a strange way to treat your partner,' Nick said, with an edge of sarcasm.

'She has plenty to do. She needs a clear mind, and besides, she can't change anything. Your trips were productive?' Books asked.

'Yes. But that's academic now.'

'Not necessarily. I need to meet Don Saverese for brunch tomorrow. Can you set it up?'

'Probably. What should I tell him it's about?'

'Paper,' Books answered curtly. 'I've got an idea. It may be our last chance.'

'Can you give me any clues?' Nick asked.

'Not now. I'll fill you in when I see you.' Books hung up without saying goodbye.

Nick stared down at the park and watched as two police cars, sirens screaming, lights flashing, sped past the slow-moving hansom cabs and into the Fifty-Seventh Street entrance to the park.

They were after somebody.

Heather wanted to keep her mind occupied. She put the IBM PC/XT computer through its factory paces. When she was satisfied, she slipped in her own software program. The output would be limited without the Black Box, but she wanted to test it, in order to anticipate any potential problems.

Someone who looked exactly like Books had flown out that noon, to throw any observers off. The real Books, disguised as a construction worker, took off two hours later in a thirty-eight-foot Scarab, capable of seventy miles an hour, headed for Marathon and a waiting chartered Learjet that would take him to New York.

He had been on edge all night, not speaking at dinner, gruff in his commands to the workers; unable to sleep, he paced the deck until he finally fell asleep at four. Heather had left the stateroom to check on him as he slept naked on the teak decks of *Desperado*: no pillow, no blanket. Almost like a monk, she thought punishing himself. She went below to get a sheet to cover him, but he kicked it off into the water in his fitful sleep. He was silent in the morning, barely remembering to give her a kiss goodbye as he stepped into the offshore racer.

It was a long way from the hours they used to spend making love in the morning in London. She knew something was wrong, very wrong, and he had not told her. He had not confided in her. It concerned the project and she was part of it, the biggest part, she invented the goddamn thing, she and her father. And now he wouldn't talk when they had a problem. She thumbed the edge of a floppy disk. It must be to do with the paper, she thought.

'Not to worry, just stay in the kitchen, stay in your place, let the men handle the big stuff like a good little girl,' she mumbled to herself as she moved from the computer to the copier, a shiny new Zed 3600.

She worked the copier hard, exercising all its options until she was satisfied that the machine was performing properly.

Beside the copier were two gurneys that looked like stretchers on wheels. Above the nearest gurney was a grid of twelve water-jet nozzles, pointing downward, each nozzle the size of a needle point and fed by its own hose. Fresh water was forced through the nozzles at fifty thousand pounds per square inch. The force was so great that a finger placed in the path of the water would be instantly severed from the hand. Heather had invented the 'hydro slicer' to cut the stacked paper sheets into individual piles of bills. The system was better than any guillotine-type cutter. It left no ragged edges, and could cut through five hundred sheets at a time, smoothly and evenly, just as a cloth cutter follows a dress pattern. While the water jets traced a pattern over one gurney, the second gurney would wait for the next sheets to come spitting out of the ZED 3600 copier.

Finished with her machine tests for the day, she strolled out onto the beach, realizing she had no home now, just this bleak island, broiling under the noonday sun.

And where was the Black Box?

Why had she put up with Books' secrecy, his not telling where her creation was hidden, his evasiveness and vagueness whenever she asked him? The thought solidified in her mind. Books was acting like the goddamn Zed Corporation had acted with her father. He was in possession of what was hers. He was in control. She collapsed onto the sand, folding into the lotus position, her knees suddenly weak. She was afraid. Why was she such a coward with him, afraid to confront him when he acted willfully, when he took charge and left her out?

'Goddammit!' she mumbled. 'I hate being a victim. My life should be in my own hands.'

She gazed out to sea watching a gang of seagulls slam into some bait on the edge of the flats. An idea slowly crept into her mind; at first it shocked and appalled her and she forced it away, but the more she relaxed and thought about it, the more acceptable the idea became until she finally allowed it to implant itself in her brain.

After all, the Black Box was really hers!

Friday evening 5:00
WHITE HOUSE, WASHINGTON,D.C.

'It just isn't right, Ralph,' the President said as he handed Cobb the surveillance photos of smoke and ashes, all that was left of the Valjean mill. 'Why the hell didn't you inform me – us. I could have persuaded the Canadian Government to move in on them, arrest them, or wait and set a trap. Jesus, to act on your own like that was damned impulsive. I just hope you're right, and that's the end of them.'

'What's the latest on their activities, Ralph, and why aren't we getting the CIA satellite surveillance reports of their communications?' Phillip asked.

'They've jammed the phone links by using scramblers, so we're cut off from their verbal transfers. And today we thought we had St John made, flying to Miami, but it was a lookalike. We assume he is still on the island.' Cobb was out of his seat pacing; his voice was quivering slightly. 'The construction activity on the island is still heavy. They have two large Butler buildings erected, and a fuel barge in place in the harbor. I can have the aerial recon photos sent over.'

'Why are they still working if they're out of paper?' the President asked.

'Not sure,' Cobb muttered.

'Wouldn't they have stopped construction if they were out of business?' Phillip asked.

'I don't know; it could be a bluff.'

'Why would they be bluffing?' the President demanded.

'Blackmail. Make us think they still have producing capability, and then hit us with a blackmail threat.'

'I don't like it. Ralph, you blew it. And for Christ's sake sit down, stop pacing.' The President got to his feet and went to the window to stare out at the rose garden. Several minutes went by before he spoke.

'No further moves are to be made without my approval. And I want regular reports on their activities, complete reports; do I make myself clear?'

'Yes, sir.'

'And Ralph, just so you know, if we didn't go back together so far, and if your Secret Service record weren't so outstanding, you would be looking for funny money in Alaska right now,' the President snarled.

'Yes, sir.'

'This other fella Nick Sullivan. What the hell has he been up to?'

'He's still missing. We lost him, and so far his trail is cold,' Cobb said apologetically. 'Phillip, he was a friend of yours, wasn't he?' he asked, trying to shift the spotlight.

'Yes. He was an arms dealer, one of the best in the business. He ran into trouble in Africa – lost a big shipment of arms and some men were killed. Nigeria, I think. He came to see me afterwards. He was badly shaken up, burned out, and had lost most of his money. He dropped out and bummed around the Caribbean after that.'

'Why is he with them?' Cobb asked.

'Money, adventure, who knows? He's a loner, hard person to figure.'

'Speculate on your own time, gentlemen. Unless there's something else concrete to discuss here, I have to move on.'

The President returned from the window and took his seat behind the desk, dismissing them.

'I don't get it,' Cobb said as he and Phillip went down the hall towards the elevators.

'What?'

'Every other time I've acted on my own he was happy. We've had plenty of dealings over the years.'

'No, you don't get it, Ralph. On this one I'd keep him informed.' Phillip punched the button for the elevator.

'Yeah. I already got the message!' Cobb said, taking the stairs, not waiting for the elevator. Phillip waited, locked in his wheelchair.

Saturday midday 11:30
NEW YORK CITY

'I appreciate the meeting on such short notice, Don Saverese,' Books said.

Don Saverese sat quietly, listening to Books and watching Nick. The three of them sat in the corner booth of the Club Siracusa, sipping Sambuca and Courvoisier. Books had not told Nick what he was going to say to Don Saverese.

Nick felt an uneasiness between the two men from the minute they were introduced. Books had a built-in confidence and crispness that bordered on arrogance. The Don did business slowly, easily, in a roundabout, subtle style. There was nothing that was so urgent that it couldn't be handled with finesse.

'You own the control block of Waste Control Corporation, correct?' Books asked.

'I own a few shares only.'

Nick wished Books had told him what was on his mind before the meeting began. The Don was talking to Books as though Books were wired. 'Books, just ask of the Don whatever it is you want, without questions,' Nick said.

Books looked at Nick; irritation flashed through his eyes. 'We need to obtain a large quantity of the shredded currency paper that Waste Control Corporation hauls from the Federal Reserve to the Jersey Meadowlands.'

'It is buried, used for landfill. I can give you the name of the man who heads up Waste Control. He will be glad to sell it to you. There is no law against selling it.' Nick could see a glimmer of understanding flash across the Don's eyes. The Don understood immediately how they were getting the paper. 'Have you already been purchasing from him?'

Books ignored the question. 'Our problem goes beyond the normal supply, and they may be cutting the supply off soon. We need two barge loads. Two big barges. You would have to dig up a large quantity.' Books knew it was only a matter of time before the Fed discovered that they had been recycling the shredded paper. They might already know.

'That would be difficult, like exhuming a body. Men would be needed, special construction equipment, and a lot of attention might be focused upon such an undertaking; there could be prying eyes.'

The Don was couching his words and talking cautiously to Books, skirting round the subject. If he did what Books wanted, it would be at a hell of a price.

'You could do it at night, with specialized equipment. It shouldn't take more than three nights. Restrict access to the area –'

'Please do not tell me details about such things. I am not in the landfill or the waste control business. And it is an expertise I have no interest in attaining.'

'Of course. My apologies.' Books was beginning to get the picture.

Nick spoke. 'Don Saverese, as you have already stated,

there is nothing illegal in selling the shredded currency paper, so all we are talking about is inconvenience, and perhaps some attention to an area where no one has looked closely. For this we would naturally expect to offer you compensation.'

'As I said, I have only a few shares in Waste Control Corporation, but perhaps I could discuss it with friends. I would have to be very specific.'

'We need two large barges loaded. I'll supply the barges; they will be waiting at a pier in Hoboken. My estimate is one hundred truckloads,' Books said.

'It might be possible. From what I have heard, the shredded paper is collected and disposed of all in one location to keep it clear of foreign matter and garbage.'

Nick wondered if the Don had his own future plans for the paper, or perhaps just felt that someday the paper would be a valuable commodity, a commodity worth saving, like gold.

The Don studied Books, raising an eyebrow over his Sambuca. Three coffee beans floated on the surface of the thick licorice liquid. He daintily lifted a bean from the surface with his thumb and forefinger and bit it in half with a hard crunching sound. He licked his finger and said: 'There is no going rate for such a thing as you ask. I will need a specific number, an offer to take with me for my inquiries.'

'I believe a hundred thousand would be fair,' Books offered hastily.

'For a hundred truckloads? I do not think the Waste Control management would consider such an offer.'

'You have a good feel for such matters, Don Saverese; what would you think was fair?' Nick interjected.

'Ten thousand dollars a truck,' the Don said quietly, signalling for another Sambuca.

'A million dollars? For a hundred truckloads?' Books was incredulous. 'For wastepaper that would cost twenty-five thousand dollars at the most, paper the Fed pays you to cart away?'

'The Fed pays me nothing. I am only a small shareholder

of Waste Control, as I have said. I suggest you go elsewhere if the price is too high.' The Don pushed his Sambuca away. 'Nick, always good to see you. I must go downstairs and join Bruno Pugliese on the range. Nice to have met you, Mr St John. Perhaps we can do business some other time.' He stood and signalled the waiter to take his drink downstairs to the shooting range.

Books stood and extended his hand which was shaking slightly. 'You have a deal, Don Saverese, at one million.'

The Don stared calmly at Books, not moving, almost teasing him. Finally, he smiled but still withheld his handshake. 'I can't promise. I'll do the best I can for you.'

'When will you get back to us?' Books asked.

'I won't,' he answered. He nodded at Nick. 'My associate Bruno Pugliese will be in touch with Nick. You remember Bruno, don't you, Nick?'

'He's hard to forget, Don Saverese.'

The remark brought a smile to the Don's lips. 'He's supposed to be.'

Saturday afternoon 3:00
BROOKLYN NAVY YARD, NEW YORK CITY

Ernie Sands stood smoking on the gangplank of the liberty ship, waiting for Nick and Books to arrive. He greeted them with a wave of the cigarette in his right hand; he used his left to push his glasses up the bridge of his nose. His eyes were pale; fear had crept into them, as it does with men and animals who know they are close to death. The cancer was creeping from his lungs into his soul.

Nick introduced Books.

They climbed to the liberty ship's bridge. The refurbishing job had been completed.

An ocean-going tug sat patiently waiting at the bow of the ship like a bulldog, scraping quietly against the hull. The tug swayed to the rhythm of the undulating currents of the murky East River, its mighty engine growling and spewing dirty black diesel clouds into the air. It was waiting for the final inspection to be completed, when the thick hawser would be attached to the bow of the liberty ship for the long pull down to the Cay Sal Bank.

The bridge of the liberty ship was spartan, utilitarian, but highly sophisticated with its radar equipment, a satellite communication system that made phone calls to anywhere on the planet possible, a firing panel to launch the ground-to-air missiles after they were installed, an intercom system that would provide communication anywhere on the small island, and special high-powered infrared binoculars mounted on a pivot.

They left the bridge and inspected the iron bunks in the twenty no-frills staterooms. They passed on to the center of the ship and the galley that was fully equipped with commercial restaurant equipment. Ernie had done the job well, and on time.

Books and Nick gave Ernie the nod to proceed. Ernie walked to the bow with a bull horn and shouted down at the tug: 'Haul away.'

They passed down the gangplank to the wharf. The sign painters had just completed the final lettering on the hull: 'Mako Marine Institute' stood out in giant white letters.

The three of them walked slowly over to Pier 6 and the long grey line of antique submarines. Ernie spoke. 'The bullshit letter you gave me for the Mako Marine Institute worked, Nick. We got three subs, and the price was cheap, a hundred grand for the three of them. I'll need two weeks to get them operational, and to find your crews. We'll use four men per boat and keep one crew in reserve.'

They stood looking down at the three cold grey cylinders that Ernie had selected.

'Great job, Ernie,' Books said as they walked back to the waiting Yellow cab.

'Did you ask your partner about me, Nick?' Ernie whispered.

'Not yet.'

'Ask me what?' Books smiled at Ernie.

'I got a little medical problem, a problem with my lungs, fatal problem. Nick knows about it. I want one last fling, some action. My wife's dead. Kids are gone. I got maybe a year left. There isn't much I don't know or can't fix when it comes to guns or boats. Nick will verify that.'

'It's Nick's call,' Books said, opening the cab door and getting in.

'So what do you say?'

'How's the ordnance?' Nick asked, changing the subject. Nick didn't want to be there when Ernie's lung cancer finally closed the curtain on his life. They had shared too much.

'It's sitting, waiting at La Guardia. So what do you say, Nick?' Ernie stared at his friend, making a glancing pass at his taped glasses with the heel of his hand, driving them upwards off the tip of his nose. He tilted his head back to keep them from sliding back down his nose. He smiled a sad smile.

Nick climbed into the cab beside Books. 'Sure, Ernie. We could use an experienced hand like yourself. Welcome aboard. Come down with the subs. I'll give you all the details when it's time.'

'Thanks,' Ernie said, gently closing the cab door. 'I won't let ya down, Nick.'

'You never have,' Nick answered, rolling up the cab window.

The driver headed back to Manhattan over the Brooklyn Bridge and up the East River Drive.

Nick broke the silence. 'Tell me, why the liberty ship, Books? We could have used a yacht or chartered a few houseboats.'

'I want them to think that's where we're storing the gold and maybe the paper.'

'That makes it a target, doesn't it?'

'I don't expect any violence. This is a mind game and the liberty ship is a diversion, that's all, Nick. Don't add anything to it; don't speculate, please,' Books said.

'I hope you're right. Ernie Sands and the people like him are only small players in this game; there's no point in putting them in danger.'

'They won't be in any danger,' Books asserted.

The battered cab rolled to a squeaky stop in front of the Plaza to let them out. Nick waited in the Oak Bar while Books checked for messages at the front desk.

'He's here,' Books said, flipping ten dollars on the counter to pay for Nick's unfinished drink.

'Who?'

'Bruno Pugliese. He's in the Palm Court of all places. Why would he choose there to meet?'

Bruno stood out in the elegant setting of the Palm Court like a Sumo wrestler at a tea party. He was sitting formally, upright in his chair, yet he managed to look as if he was squirming. Books and Nick shook Bruno's hand and sat.

'Glad I caught youse. I had some time to kill so I been waiting for a few minutes.' Books noted from the front desk message that Bruno had been waiting for over two hours. Bruno continued, 'Our mutual associate has sent me here to tell youse that he don't mind doing as requested but the expenses are heavy so there's goin' to be a slight extra charge.'

Bruno let his words hang as he clutched a Scotch on the rocks in his fist and looked around at the afternoon crowd of elegant shoppers that were assembling for high tea and chamber music. 'I ain't been here since I was a little kid. My aunt was a maid here for years. She used to look after that tray over there with them buns on it and the jelly and shit. Nice joint. I like comin' here now as a customer.'

Books glanced over at the silver tray of scones and the elegant spread of jams and jellies from around the world. 'How much of an extra charge?' he asked, his eyes now on Bruno, not blinking.

Bruno turned away from the shoppers, and stared back at Books. 'Two-five-o more. So da total is one-two-five-o. Half in advance and half when da barges are loaded. One hundred trucks just like ya asked for. And the product in question ain't too dirty. Our mutual associate and me, we had it checked for garbage and crap. It was buried in its own pile so it ain't too bad. It don't even stink.' Bruno smiled. 'So we on, or not?'

Books checked his watch. 'I'll have the cash tonight. Nick, would you please set up a meeting at nine tonight in my room?' Books rose, nodded at Bruno, and left.

Bruno frowned at Books' back as he went through the spinning brass doors out onto Fifth Avenue. 'Rude prick, your pal. I ain't meeting in no room, specially his. Bring the goods to the Club Siracusa tonight at nine. I'll be dere.' Bruno went to pay his bill.

'I've got the bill, Bruno. Put your money away.'

'Thanks. But I pay here. It's just a thing between me and my aunt, even though she's dead now. By the way, the Don says he did this favor for you, Nick. He don't like your pal much, and he sure as shit don't need the extra two-five-o. But he figures he'll take the vigorish for da ten minutes he was sitting, putting up with the asshole.'

'Tell the Don thanks for me,' Nick smiled, and shook Bruno's huge hand.

'So I'll see youse tonight.'

'We'll be there, Bruno.'

Bruno turned on his heel and slowly strolled through the

Palm Court, smiling at the splendidly dressed women as they sipped their tea. Nick could see them cringe and draw closer to each other as he passed. He smiled. Their instincts weren't wrong.

Then his smile disappeared. 'Thanks, Don Saverese. Thanks for nothing,' he thought to himself, knowing that he would now have to go on.

Saturday evening 5:00
SECRET SERVICE, WASHINGTON, D.C.

The new photos of the burned mill showed a desolate sight, wisps of smoke still rising days after the fire had burned itself out. Cobb had ordered the photography team back to the mill to take a final set of photos. He had sent them, along with samples, to the paper experts at the US Mint to evaluate and study. The report was on his desk.

It was negative. The people at the US Mint did not believe the Quebec mill had the capability to produce currency-quality paper. The normal equipment and chemicals required in the manufacturing process of currency paper were missing. The burned-out barrels had not contained chemicals normally used in the production of currency paper. They had contained common chemicals available to anyone with the money to buy them.

Cobb had read the report twice and found only one thing that was incongruous. A garbage truck with New Jersey, New York and Quebec license plates. It was a new truck, hardly burned at all. It had been parked in the bush on the edge of the mill property, out of the path of the flames.

He opened a sealed brown manila envelope marked for his

attention. He shook out a plastic bag containing paper shavings. There was a note enclosed, explaining that one of the more zealous Secret Service agents had climbed into the compacter of the garbage truck and done a 'dumpster dip'. The agent had found a handful of paper shred in the steel shell, and had carefully enclosed them in a zip-lock bag. Cobb fingered the bag as he stared down at the photo of the garbage truck.

In the centre of his desk was a small glass dome his wife had given him for his fortieth birthday, with the note: 'Your first million'. It was a million dollars of shredded and compacted currency. He pulled the dome towards him while he unsealed the zip-lock bag, letting the paper shavings spill out onto his desk.

'Motherfuckers!' he whispered. 'You motherfuckers; no wonder that paper was so good. It's recycled currency paper from the Fed!'

Cobb reached for the phone on the edge of his desk and punched in Phillip Sturges' private line. He stood with the receiver to his ear and started to pace. The phone carriage fell off the edge of the desk into the wastebasket just as Phillip answered. Cobb scrambled to place the phone unit back on his desk.

All Phillip could hear was noise. 'Who is this?' he asked into the receiver.

'Ralph Cobb here. Phillip, I know how they're doin' the paper.' Cobb let his statement hang.

'How?' Phillip asked.

'You're supplying them.' Cobb waited a beat before explaining. 'They're somehow getting hold of the shredded paper that the Fed produces, and recycling it. There was a garbage truck found at the mill site in Quebec, and my men found shreds of used currency paper in the hopper. We didn't know what it was at first, but I've got a jar sitting here on my desk with a million dollars in it. And it's the same damn paper, no doubt of it.'

'That's great. Shredded currency paper is easy to get; we don't restrict its sale. Souvenir people buy it by the ton.'

'Not any more, they won't; we have to get control of the supply. Today. This very instant. Where does the shredded paper go now? Who is the contractor?'

'It's hauled out of here by Waste Control Corporation and taken to the Jersey Meadowlands for landfill,' Phillip said calmly. He dialed the loading dock on his other phone as he talked to Cobb. It rang through to the security officer on duty. 'Just a minute, Ralph.'

'Phillip put the second phone to his mouth so Cobb could listen. 'Harold, that you?'

'Yes, sir.'

'Cancel all shipments of shredded paper until further notice. That includes everyone, no exceptions.'

Phillip hung up the second phone and resumed his conversation with Cobb. 'That should take care of it for the moment.'

'Good. Late, but good.'

'Well, if the mill hadn't burned . . .' Phillip waited for a second before continuing. 'I still haven't received any aerial recon photos of that little island they bought. What's the hold-up?'

'It's the CIA. I'll follow up and get them sent to you right away. Sometimes they drag their ass a little in releasing things.'

'Please do. The old man is upset. Our deal was that we would see all the pictures at the same time, and I haven't seen the first photo yet.'

'I'll get them over to you today. Promise.' Cobb said, thumbing the file of recon photos on his desk.

'Anything else?'

'Yes. I'm doing a full background check on your pal Nick Sullivan: FBI, Interpol, Internal Revenue, the works. He's been a pretty active boy. And there's a rumor he was involved in a murder in Paris, of some Irish arms dealer. I'm waiting for confirmation on a few details. I should have a full report in a few days.'

'Okay, Ralph, you've given me a lot to think about.'

The phone went dead in Phillip's hand. He placed the receiver gently into the cradle.

'Nick,' Phillip mumbled to himself, 'I never meant for them to get into your life, to unravel your secrets.' He snapped off the desk lamp, leaving himself in total darkness. There were no windows in his office. He thought best in the darkness. 'But what the hell is this murder of an Irishman in Paris all about?'

Sunday morning 9:00
MIAMI

Nick and Books stepped out of a chartered Gates-Learjet into a biting, blustery wind that was building up to gale force. A waiting cab took them to the Miami River. The cab followed a serpentine route up the winding river for about four miles.

Nick inhaled the pleasant smell of the river, a combination of creosote, salt water, dead fish, and cooking odors that came wafting off the decks of tired old freighters and shrimp boats that were waiting for a spruce-up, a refit, or a tow out to the Gulf Stream to be gutted and sunk. The men and women who lived along the river were hard at work scrambling along the decks, bulkheads, and sea walls, attaching lines to secure their boats against the angry wind.

The cab stopped abruptly, on Books' orders, in front of a solid concrete block warehouse that fronted on the river.

193

The window frames were filled in with bricks; the door was the only opening, and it was heavily barred. Tiny TV cameras moved in lazy harmony, surveying the entire perimeter.

Books paid the cab driver and buzzed the doorbell with three long grating rings. Finally, the door flew open, caught in the exhaling breath of a hot gust. Percival Smathers stood in the doorway, unshaven and needing a haircut. He was dressed in dirty denim cut-offs and a white Moosehead Beer T-shirt pressed tight against his skinny body. He held a long-necked Budweiser in his right hand. He smiled at them both, switched the bottle to his left hand, and tried to retrieve the flapping door with his right.

'Sorry about this damn door; there may be a hurricane coming. Jesus Christ, Nick! It's you! I don't believe it. Shit, it's great to see you. I've heard about you over the years but somehow I didn't think you were alive. It's great to see you.' Percival stuck his clammy right hand into Nick's, giving up any attempt to harness the door. He gave Nick a hug.

'Books always tells the minimum. I just found out you were involved in this wild scheme,' Nick said, looking over at Books.

'Let's get out of this wind,' Books said, grabbing the flapping door and closing it behind them.

Inside were a dozen pallets of currency paper that had been sent down days ago from the mill in Quebec, and thirty barrels of chemicals. Some of the barrels carried a skull and crossbones with the word POISON stamped across the skull in clear black letters.

Percival had been wrapping the pallets of paper with heavy-duty dark plastic film to protect it from salt water spray. A small electric forklift truck sat idly in the corner like a sleeping crab. Nick went over to the last pallet that remained to be shrink-wrapped and pulled off a sheet of paper. He rubbed the paper with his thumb and forefinger and held it up to the desk light. It was translucent, almost glowing.

'I thought you said . . .' Nick began.

'The currency paper wasn't all destroyed. This was the test batch to be used for our first experiments,' Books said calmly. 'We expect some waste, maybe one pallet, possibly two. This was sent down so we could get started. There's enough paper here to print about a billion dollars, maybe eight hundred million after waste.'

'Books, how much was burned at the mill? How much are you going to make?'

'Enough to make it worthwhile.'

'How much?' Nick asked.

'There was a warehouse full, enough sheets for seventy or eighty.' Books winked at Nick.

Nick stared, amazed at the full scope of what Books was planning.

'Don't get your balls in an uproar, Nick. Remember, we only get twenty-five per cent in gold, and that's the maximum amount. And the start-up costs have not been minimal,' Books added, trying to smooth the waters.

Their conversation was interrupted by a long shrill whistle. It came from directly behind the warehouse building.

Percival went over and pressed a series of switches that raised the heavy iron gate. The gate was about the size of a garage door. A small sleek freighter was fighting against the wind as it tried to slip into the mooring at the dock, its crane already creeping round in a slow arc to prepare to pick up the pallets of paper.

'Christ, either they're early or I'm late,' Percival said.

Books and Nick looked at each other and rolled their eyes. They knew Percival Smathers. 'I've got one more pallet to shrink-wrap. But I better put some pallets on the loading dock first,' he added, jumping onto the forklift, gulping his beer, and driving off towards the first pallet to be loaded. The wind blew his long blonde mane back like an outstretched yellow mop.

Both Nick and Books saw the black electric extension cord snap, like a broken umbilical cord, as he pulled away. Percival had forgotten to unplug the line used to charge the batteries. They smiled at the loud 'FUCK!' that resounded through the warehouse and walked over to check the thirty barrels of chemicals.

'So we make our own paper on the island, right?' Nick asked, idly tracing out a skull and crossbones with his finger on the top of a barrel, not looking at Books.

'Right as rain. When those barges arrive, we start to process our own paper. In the meantime, we begin with these nine pallets. That is if Percival doesn't drop them in the Miami River first.' They both looked over at Percival as he fought the wind and his own incompetence as a forklift driver. He set the first pallet down heavily onto the loading dock; it shuddered against the wind, only inches from the water's edge.

'How much do you think we can make with those barges, after the paper is processed?'

'I haven't figured it out exactly,' Books lied.

'Well, if nine pallets makes a billion . . .'

'Just drop it, okay, Nick?' Book stared at him. 'Please leave it alone. We have plenty to think about. I don't like the way this wind is making up,' he added.

Nick shrugged and went over to the forklift. 'Get down out of that seat, Perce, before you hurt yourself or some innocent pedestrian.' Percival was only too happy to turn the forklift over to Nick and go back to wrapping the last pallet of paper.

When they were finished, they locked the door behind them and jumped in the waiting cab that headed down the Miami River for Government Cut and Chalk's Airlines.

Nick asked the cab driver to stop at International Fisheries, the largest fish house on the river. Percival and Books waited in the cab while he went in.

The floor foreman nodded at him, barely taking his eyes

off the hundred Haitians and Bahamians who were sitting at long wooden tables gutting and filleting fish. Fishing boats were lined up unloading their catches from the Florida Keys, the Bahamas and Central America.

The facility was spotless. Men were constantly hosing down the fish blood and offal into the floor drains. Nick spoke to the foreman. He had to yell over the noise of the people and the machines.

'What do you do with the waste, the fish guts?' he asked.

'Fertilizer. We put it in barrels and some guy picks it up and turns it into fertilizer for the farmers in northern Florida. Why?'

'I want to buy some.'

'How much?' the foreman asked. He got a commission on every barrel he sold.

'Twenty barrels a week.'

'You got it, pal!' The foreman dropped his filleting knife on a table and signalled for Nick to come to his disheveled desk. He took out a pad and paper and handed it to Nick. 'Address?'

'No address. We'll pick it up. How much?' Nick asked.

'Twenty bucks a barrel. They're sealed nice and tight to keep the stink in.' The foreman laughed.

Nick peeled off five hundred dollars in cash, thought better of it, and gave the foreman a thousand dollars. 'I'll inform our freighter to dock here in about two hours. He'll take fifty barrels for the first load, and from then on he'll come by once a week.'

As Nick walked away the foreman yelled, 'What are you going to do with all that shit?'

'Feed the fish . . . mariculture project.'

The foreman shrugged his shoulders and mumbled, 'What next?' under his breath as he went to shut the main door that led to the dock; the wind had picked up. He waved and smiled as Nick climbed back in the cab.

'What was that all about, Nick?' Books asked.

197

'A surprise, Books, a little surprise for later.'

'Let's roll,' Books yelled at the cabbie. 'This wind is really brutal. I wonder what's going on,' he said to no one in particular.

'Hurricane Griselda,' the cabbie said in a thick Cuban accent. 'Griselda, she comin' to pay us a visit. November's late for a blow like this, but the TV says she's kissin' the coast of Cuba right now.'

'That's great. Just fucking great. A hurricane. Just what we need.' Books slipped an extra twenty to the cabbie and told him to hurry. 'Let's hope Chalk's is still flying in this weather.'

'I wonder how Heather is doing?' Nick said.

'Who's Heather?' Perce asked.

There was no response.

Sunday morning 10:00
CAY SAL BANK, BAHAMAS

Heather walked over to the stack of heavy white Bristol Board artist's paper she had ordered from Miami. She took twenty sheets over to the gurney that was positioned under the water nozzles. She laid a template pattern on the top sheet and drew rectangles with a pen; when she was finished, the top sheet had thirty-two perfect rectangles in the exact configuration and dimensions of dollar bills, the same pattern the US Mint used to print and cut currency sheets.

Next, she took a stepladder, climbed above the cluster of lines she had drawn, and aligned the nozzles to follow the pattern that she had drawn. Finally, she programmed their path into the computer, and locked it in.

She checked each of the twelve water lines that led directly to the needle-nosed nozzles; she nodded at the mechanic to start the compressor. It would take about five minutes for the compressor to build up enough back pressure to pump the water through the nozzles at fifty thousand pounds per square inch.

She sat down on the floor next to the gurney when she was through, to wait. She undid the black bandanna she had wrapped round her head and used it to wipe the sweat from her face. Tomorrow the air conditioning would be completed for both buildings.

She wrapped the bandanna tightly round her right wrist to keep the sweat from dripping onto her right hand as she worked the computer one-handed.

The computer, the copier, and the gurney with the high powered water system, all reminded her of her father.

She remembered the morning, sitting at breakfast before school, when he gave her the perfect color photocopy of the Van Gogh painting, with its bright blasting colors. The painting was of Van Gogh's own father slumped on a chair in front of a lagging fire in his humble cottage, dejected and alone.

Heather cradled her head in her arms and sighed.

'Okay, lady. It's all yours,' the mechanic said. 'You got fifty thousand PSI by the time the water comes through those nozzles. What are you going to use it for?' he asked.

'Mariculture research. New way to clean fish.' Heather smiled.

'Yeah, right,' he said, closing the door behind him as he left the building.

Heather sat at the computer and punched in orders for the hydro slicer. She wrote LOAD, hit the button and waited.

A hiss came first as the thin quarter-inch lines filled with water. The hiss stopped. She wrote GUILLOTINE, hit the button and turned to watch the result.

The water shot out in tiny needle-thin jets, slicing through the paper like a razor through flesh.

The nozzles started to travel in their pre-programmed pattern over the gurney that held the Bristol board. They made their pass over the sheets of paper, choreographed perfectly by the computer. In seconds the cross-cut was made, and the water jets stopped abruptly, all at the same instant.

Heather went over to the gurney. The Bristol board was sliced into thirty-two crisp piles of rectangular paper, each pile about the size of a brick.

She reached into her pocket and laid a fifty-dollar bill on top of one of the cut pieces. The bill fitted perfectly; the cut was exact to the millimeter.

Where the hell was Books? What was he doing? If there was a problem, why didn't he consult her? Here she was doing all the goddamn grunt work, all alone, again!

Angrily, she dumped the six hundred and forty cut Bristol Board pieces into the waste bin. Many of the pieces missed the lid, and scattered onto the floor.

She hurried off to see if the warehouse dehumidifier had been installed, cursing Books again for keeping the Black Box hidden from her.

It was only after she calmed down that she decided really to do it. To hell with Books, she was going to find where the Black Box was hidden; after all, it was her invention, her baby.

Sunday afternoon 2:00
NEW YORK CITY

Don Saverese was in his Manhattan office, located upstairs over the main showroom of his Alfa Romeo/Ferrari/Maserati dealership, idly spinning the wheels of a scale model Ferrari Testarossa.

He was listening on the phone to Sergio Lucci, the general manager of Waste Control Corporation. Sergio identified himself in an obscure Sicilian dialect; he spoke from a phone booth in Hackensack, New Jersey.

'The Secret Service swooped in on us like a fucking SWAT team, had to be over fifty men. They confiscated our records, wanted to know exactly where we buried the paper. Luckily, we've been burying it with the regular garbage like you told me. Remember that slaughterhouse contract? Well, the boys have been putting it in with that shit. Even my own men almost pass out when they work that fuckin' hill. The fuckin' flies get sick up there from the stink.' Sergio laughed.

The Don had to smile at Sergio's little joke.

After his conversation with Books St John, the Don had instructed Sergio to leave the clean mountain of shredded currency paper alone and incorporate the new shipments from the Federal Reserve with the regular garbage, just in case anyone started to nose around.

Sergio spoke again. 'They stayed for about an hour then took off in cars, and two vans that they used to carry off our records. There ain't shit in those records. They asked a lot of questions about the Valjean mill in Quebec. I told them we had hundreds of clients that bought shredded Fed paper for souvenirs and shit like that. They even brought a bunch of Secret Service spooks that spoke Italian, and they tried to get friendly with my boys. Waste of fucking time. My guys don't know shit.'

'You sure that no one spoke to them?' The Don thought of the hundred trucks and the two barges in Hoboken.

'Can't ever be sure.' Sergio was careful not to use the Don's name on the phone even though they both believed the lines to be secure. 'But those were my best men, and they all got greased real good for the midnight hours they put in.'

The Don knew what he had done was legal but he also knew how easily a conspiracy charge could be put together,

201

especially when it involved the paper products of the US Mint.

Sergio continued, 'The head Secret Service honcho told us to stop selling shredded Fed paper for souvenirs. And if we didn't do like they said; we'd spend twenty years in Sing-Sing. They were hot to trot, those boys, kicking ass and takin' names. They said they didn't have to explain shit to me, just do like I was told and everything would be okay. They weren't friendly.'

Don Saverese knew that Sergio Lucci would talk as long as anyone would listen. He was a good man, but not one of few words. The Don listened patiently for a few seconds more as Sergio started to repeat himself. He thanked him and cut him off, saying that he had a shipment of new cars coming in, which was true, and a lot of work to do.

'*Ciao, Sergio, bon giorno.*'

A smile was carved onto his tight lips. Things were going well. The fact that the Secret Service had raided Waste Control meant that the Feds were concerned; the fact that they had sent so many men and took the records meant they were 'very' concerned.

His office safe was hidden behind a picture of his mother. He took out the five fifty-dollar bills Nick had given him in the club as samples, and examined them carefully under the light, comparing them to five real ones. They were perfect. And Nick and this St John hadn't hesitated to pay the million and a quarter for those barges full of shredded paper.

He examined the bills one more time, then placed five long-distance phone calls personally. They were all taken immediately or returned within minutes. The Don's voice was recognized in each case. After saying hello, he explained that they would be visited by his envoy within forty-eight hours. They were to listen to this man and give him their answer. It was a formality that showed respect for the families, but it was a foregone conclusion that the answer would be yes to the Don's request.

He called down for his car, a brand-new four-door Maserati Quattraporte. It was waiting for him as he stepped out onto the bustle of Columbus Avenue. The Don's car was changed every week for security reasons, and also so he could enjoy the new-car leather smell he loved so much.

The chauffeur stood patiently waiting at the curbside. The Don smiled and nodded at his bodyguard who sat in the front seat. He instructed the driver to take him to the Club Siracusa. He was meeting Bruno Pugliese to do a little shooting and to give Bruno a few instructions for his next meeting with Nick.

The Don had stuffed the five loose fifties Nick had given him into his coat pocket. He idly rubbed the bills together with his thumb and forefinger as he drove south along Columbus Avenue, watching the army of Yuppies as it marched formally by in opposing directions. He noticed that those marching north all marched together in one solid file and those marching south also marched together in a solid phalanx in the opposite direction, like well-trained soldiers on parade. Orderly people, very orderly, and predictable, he thought to himself.

Sunday afternoon 4:00
CAY SAL BANK, BAHAMAS

As the chartered Chalk's plane took off from Miami, gale-force winds were starting to build up over the Gulf Stream.

Hurricane Griselda was spiraling her way over Cuba in a drunken, lurching swath. After Cuba, it was anyone's guess which way she would head. She could go east, west, or north; north would give her a heading for the Florida Keys. The eye of the hurricane was only one hundred and sixty miles to the east, but the outer tips of the grey swirling storm clouds, like probing fingers, already reached as far west as the Cay Sal Bank and the Straits of Florida.

The small plane wasted no time in disembarking its passengers in the tiny protected harbor of Anguila Cay and heading back to Miami.

Nick and Books jumped, one at a time, from the wallowing pontoon of the aircraft into the rolling Whaler. Percival was last. He stood with a large heavy black artist's case, struggling to hand it over to Books and Nick. When it was safely aboard, Percival finally jumped into the Whaler. The waves breaking over the bow caused the tiny bilge pump in the stern to whine and sputter as it worked non-stop. Heather yelled a hello and drove them to shore where they took refuge in the main building which had finally been completed.

They were alone. All the workmen had flown home to Miami at noon to protect their property against the whimsical attitudes of the hurricane. The freighter captain had left a message for Books: he was going to find shelter in the lee of the Miami River, and wait until the storm passed before bringing the paper.

'What next, for Christ's sake,' Books said, slapping the iron beams of the Butler building with the flat of his hand, making sure they were well-anchored to the concrete pads.

Heather stood watching Books as he angrily walked from post to post. He had barely said hello to her. A slight kiss on the cheek and a squeeze round the shoulders was all she had received from him. He stopped at the copier-computer, and idly fingered the empty marble monolith where the Black Box was to stand. He looked at Heather. She looked away.

Books broke the silence. 'We've got to make our boats secure, Nick. We'll tie a bow line round the two biggest palm trees and plant two anchors in the sand off each stern; better do it now while we have a chance.'

'I'm ready,' Nick said, using his shoulder against the heavy metal door and the wind.

Nick and Books ran for the palm trees with extra thick line to tie round the tree bases. When they were finished, they fought their way against the howling wind back to the Whaler and out to the boats.

Both boats had dragged their anchors in the shifting sand of the harbor bottom. They had drifted a hundred feet from their original anchorage. Books held up his arm and pointed toward Nick's boat, *Ubiquitous*. It was drifting dangerously close to the shore and a patch of jagged coral. The storm was intensifying.

They boarded *Ubiquitous* and Books fought his way to the bow holding the loose end of the long line they had secured to the palm tree. Nick fired up both engines and plowed his way against the wind and the breaking waves until he was in position to drop the stern anchors and secure the bow with the line that ran from the palm tree. Nick checked the stern lines to make sure the Danforth anchors had bitten into the sand. When all was secure he and Books jumped into the Whaler and headed for *Desperado*. It took twenty minutes of hard work to secure her. They were sweating under their jackets in the humid wind.

Books motioned to Nick that he was going below, and for Nick to follow. When Nick worked his way back from the bow and into the salon of *Desperado*, Books was nowhere to be seen.

Nick sat at the galley table and waited. He ignored the plates and condiments that had fallen off the table onto the floor. He watched the stove swing in short violent arcs on its gimbals.

Books came staggering through the passageway carrying a small square object hastily wrapped in green garbage bags to seal it from the weather. He cradled and caressed the green plastic as if it was a newborn child.

Nick knew what it was before Books spoke.

'The Black Box.' Books pointed at the package. 'We can't leave it on board; if *Desperado* goes down, so does our plan. The salt water will kill it,' he said.

Books climbed the steel stairs that led to the cockpit and the giant stainless steel helm. Holding the package tight against his jacket with one arm, he turned to see that Nick was right behind him. Nick boarded the Whaler first and cranked up the engine.

Books carefully handed the package over to Nick. For a flashing second Nick thought of dropping it into the harbor, pretending that it had slipped out of his hands. Instead, he gingerly placed it on the center seat, holding it until Books jumped aboard and cradled it again in his arms, protecting it from the jarring of the rough ride. The bow of the Whaler pushed slowly against the breaking waves as they made their way towards shore.

Nick used both hands to hold the warehouse door open against the blustering wind. Books passed quickly over the threshold, still cradling the green package close to his chest.

'Here it is,' he said, extending the bundle to Heather and Percival, like a proud father showing off his son.

'Here what is?'' Heather asked, already knowing what was in the bag before she asked the question.

'Black Beauty.' Books smiled. Percival approached to finger the green garbage bags. Books gingerly set the wrapped package on the marble monolith.

Heather turned her head to avoid Books' eyes.

Books was oblivious of everything except the package on the monolith. He tore at the green plastic garbage bags, shredding them as he ripped them from the square form they encased. Finally, he held it in his hands, shiny and black.

It glowed with a life of its own, an invisible power that could be felt, but not explained. It had everyone in the room in its grip except Heather, who had turned her back to them.

Books noticed Heather turn away. He raised and lowered

the Box as if he was trying to guess the weight. Slowly, a frown crossed his face as it dawned on him.

Silently, he sat down at the small card table with the spindly legs that they used to make coffee. He pushed the Mr Coffee machine aside and asked Perce to bring him a screwdriver and a set of Allen wrenches. Carefully and precisely, he unscrewed the first plate from the six-sided black box. It fell with a tiny metallic sound as it rattled against a couple of spoons that lay on the table.

Heather turned as the panel fell so she could see the reaction on Books' face. The Black Box was hollow, empty, eviscerated.

Books and Heather stared at each other with a fierce anger; the fire from their eyes seemed to illuminate the dark room, which was cast in grayness from the storm. The silence hung heavy like a dark shroud of death.

Books spoke. 'Where is it, Heather?'

'It's safe! Isn't that what you always told me, Books, when I asked you? It's safe. Well, that's what I'm telling you now. It's safe.'

'This isn't amusing.'

'It's not supposed to be.'

'You've gone too far with this, Heather.'

'You went too far, you bastard! You think I loved assembling all this machinery, alone on this island, with you gone and the Black Box, the keystone, hidden only five hundred feet from me, on your goddamn boat? You kept its location a secret from me. My own invention! You thought of my creation as yours and when you were goddamn good and ready, when you thought it was time, then you would bring it forward and present it to me, like it was a gift from you! Well, guess again.'

The room was nearly dark, filled with the gloom of the storm. The 451 GM diesel generator coughed into life, sputtering and wheezing over the noise of the tropical storm. The swirling storm clouds had covered the sun entirely now, stealing the light, deceiving the sensor into thinking it was nightfall. The interior of the Butler building was suddenly illuminated by the strings of fluorescent tubing on the ceiling, glowing bright white, as electricity filled the power lines.

Heather watched Books. He rested his head in his hands for a second in anger and frustration. It had no effect on Heather. The overhead lights flickered and sputtered as the generator skipped a beat. They could hear the diesel coughing in the wind outside the building as it warmed up.

Books just sat there looking at Heather with no expression on his face. 'Okay,' he said at last. 'You've made your point.'

She reached into the cupboard where they kept the coffee and related supplies and rummaged through packages of paper towels and napkins, way into the back. She pulled out a coffee can and a cereal box. She carefully removed wrapped items from the containers, separating the working parts, wiring junctions, circuit board, and wires from each other. Perce came to help her. He carried items to the marble monolith that stood waiting. 'We'll try it,' Heather said. 'See if it still works.'

'Good. It'll keep our mind off the storm,' Books said, trying to lighten the tension. 'The general contractor assured me that this building can sustain two-hundred-mile-an-hour winds and the generator won't quit; it's anchored in concrete.'

'This will take about twenty minutes to hook up. What about paper?' Heather asked.

'Perce?' Books said. Percival went over to the case he had carried from Miami and took out a package of one hundred sheets of currency paper. He put it on a table near the copier.

Heather smoothed back her ash-blonde hair and tied her black bandanna round her forehead to keep her hair slicked back. Nick watched her. She looked like a pirate, an elegant pirate queen, in her simple white designer shirt and khaki shorts.

'Why don't you boys amuse yourselves while I do some women's work here. Like maybe go back to the boats and get some groceries and a Coleman stove to cook on, and some ice for drinks. I don't think we're going to go outside for a while, and Griselda seems to be building up a real head of steam.'

She walked over to the marble monolith and put aside the first panel on the Black Box. They watched as she pieced together a labyrinth of brightly-colored wires, solid-state boards, and one long old-fashioned selenium glass tube. It looked out of place among all the high-tech boards and circuitry, but it was the key that tied it all together. She studied the pattern and made a few adjustments, then plopped down onto the floor and sat in her favorite position, opening her small kit of delicate tools. She started to weave the loose wires from the computer and the copier into a new complex pattern. She looked up and caught the three men staring down at her. They stood in a small semi-circle round her, mesmerized by the speed of her fingers and the depth of her concentration.

' 'Bye, boys. It doesn't do me a lot of good to have you three apes staring at me. How about the chores?' She smiled. She was in charge now.

The three of them dispersed.

Books and Nick left Percival behind to set up a small area with a table and four chairs and to clear a space for the Coleman stove and the Igloo ice chest. Thirty minutes later they were back with the supplies and a print-out from the weather fax machine.

The machine was located in the war room aboard *Desperado*. It hooked into a series of weather satellites that gave a clear thermal paper picture of the weather anywhere along the eastern seaboard; the picture Books was studying was of the Straits of Florida between Key West and Havana. Nick and Percival looked over his shoulder. The print-out showed an angry swirling mass, spinning like a ragged ball of gray yarn with a hole in the center. Books used a ruler to measure the distance from the eye to their location in the

Cay Sal Bank. 'One hundred and twenty nautical miles,' he whispered. There was a notation on the bottom of the weather fax readout that indicated winds of over a hundred miles an hour near the eye.

Heather was carefully filling the ink wells with the special magnetic ink. Next, she filled a larger well with clear thinner. The thinner would be fed into the ink lines automatically and in the right proportions as directed by the Black Box. The computer would instruct the Black Box to ensure that the thinner lines flowed freely, and that the ink was always the right consistency.

Heather finished and screwed the four black panels together into the metal frame. There was a core of wires and tubes leading into and out of the Black Box. She stood back and admired her handiwork.

She was ready.

The moment had come. Heather took the band off the hundred currency sheets and laid them in the self-feeder, making sure the edges were set perfectly to allow a free flow of paper on demand. Next, she checked all the water lines that led into the hydro slicer and the pressure level on the compressor. Finally, she sat down at the IBM PC/XT and called up the computer.

'It's time?' Books asked, looking down at her.

'It's time,' Heather answered, not looking up. She typed in her password and waited for the okay. Her fingers started to fly on the keyboard, issuing commands: US FUNDS . . . HUNDRED DOLLAR BILLS . . . FULL COLORS . . . PRINT BOTH SIDES . . . RANDOM SEQUENTIAL NUMBERS . . . GUILLOTINE WITH HYDRO-SLICER . . . DO A NICE JOB . . . THAT'S ALL FOR NOW . . . BYE.

I ALWAYS DO A NICE JOB, the computer answered. THANK YOU HEATHER . . . YOU HAVE A NICE DAY. BYE. The monitor screen flashed solid black as the green letters disappeared.

The three men stood around her, fascinated.

The copier came to life with a low hum and then a whirling sound as all the lights on the console showed green . . . ready. Heather took one more stroll round the Black Box and the copier to check the readouts. When she was satisfied, she sat back down at the computer and held up two hands with crossed fingers high in the air. The three men smiled and gave her the thumbs up sign.

She hit P for PRINT, took a deep breath and closed her eyes.

The automatic feeder on the copier ZINGGED and made a sharp snapping sound as it snatched the first sheet of paper and fed it by forced air to the copier. Less than two seconds later the sheet popped out.

Heather hit the U button to abandon the print command. She walked over to examine the first sheet. The bills were dark grey, with Ben Franklin's face smudged to a black mass. Heather examined the sheet carefully with a magnifying glass. She said nothing.

Percival shook his head, disappointed; he began to speak, but Books put his finger to his lips. Percival shrugged, threw his hands up in the air and walked over to the Igloo cooler to dig for a cold beer.

The air suddenly rang with a tremendous, resonant boom that rattled the steel walls, leaving an indentation in the beach-side wall about the size of a human head.

Nick ran to look out of the single window in the building. It was one-way glass; they could see out, but no one could see in. It was also bulletproof. The wind was strong and steady. The few palm trees that were on the island were bent over so far that the fronds were sweeping the beach.

All eyes were on him as he spoke. 'Coconut blew off a palm tree.' No one commented. Heather returned to what she was doing.

Nick looked back out of the window. The boats were wallowing heavily in the sheltered bay, but the lines seemed to be holding well. 'Maybe the damn thing won't work,' Nick mumbled at the glass panes. But deep down, for reasons he didn't understand, he wanted the Black Box to work.

Nick saw Heather's reflection in the window glass as she sat down again at the computer. He walked over. She sat straight and intent, the black bandanna encircling her ash blonde hair, her startling crystal-blue eyes concentrating on what she was doing. She looked up and locked Nick in her gaze. Their eyes met for the first time since that night on the bridge of his boat. He could feel his face redden and his ears tingle, but he couldn't look away. Neither could she.

Books watched them both for a second. He finally broke their stare. 'Show time?' he asked.

'I hope so. The first few sheets are always bad proofs. So don't you boys worry your pretty little heads.' She smiled, still looking at Nick, talking to Nick. 'We should do better this time.'

It took Heather less than two minutes to enter into the computer the changes she wanted. She typed in the final instructions, hit the PRINT button, and the machine snatched a second sheet of paper. As soon as the printed sheet of paper flew out onto the gurney under the hydro slicer, Heather was up to examine it.

Again they all gathered round. Heather pulled a real hundred out of her shorts and placed it on the center of the sheet. She examined the newly-printed bills carefully with a magnifying glass and compared them with the real bill. She took notes on a clipboard. When she was finished she opened the copier cabinet and adjusted the black ink flow so that the black would become blacker.

'That should do it this time,' Heather said, getting everyone's attention as she stood. She sat down and hit RP for Resume Printing.

The copier came to life again, pulling a sheet of paper into its bowels, printing both sides and ejecting it within two seconds. Heather had it on half speed. At half speed it was capable of printing over six million dollars an hour. Heather stopped the computer and walked round to examine her work. Before she got there Books snatched the last printed sheet off the top. Nick saw Heather stop dead in her tracks. She placed her hand at the corner of the sheet and looked him in the eye, challenging him again.

Books released the sheet, no emotion showing in his face.

Nick walked over to join them. He looked over Heather's shoulder as she held the sheet out at arm's length. 'Ben Franklin never looked better. Even his little granny glasses are perfect,' he said, smiling.

'He looks good, but not great yet,' Heather said. 'A thousand proof sheets and he will look perfect. It takes that many to get the machines fully checked out. But after that we'll be great.' She returned to the computer and instructed it to print all the ninety-eight sheets that remained ready to go.

'Books, I thought you said you had to scrap at least two pallets before the machine checks out,' Nick said.

'I guess my calculations were off. Just means we'll have more money to sell.' He smiled.

'How much is here?' Nick asked Heather, indicating the pile of paper.

'A hundred sheets with thirty-two bills to the sheet. That makes it three hundred and twenty thousand dollars.'

'In less than three minutes?'

'Yes, and that's at half speed,' Heather said, rubbing the palm of her hand lovingly on the smooth surface of the copier, proud of herself. 'I could use a beer right now.' Perce served her a cold one with a flourish. They watched the sheets fly onto the gurney as they exited the printer.

'Let's try the hydro slicer,' she said, sitting back down at the console. She typed in GUILLOTINE – HYDRO SLICER then hit control HS and spun round to watch the action.

Jets of water streamed down, needle-thin waterlasers that sliced through the paper like a wire through butter. The

213

twelve nozzles moved in their tight pre-planned pattern, hissing and spitting like snakes as they cut out piles of hundred-dollar bills. The water was collected in the drain below which ran back to the holding tank to be filtered and re-used for the next batch.

'How many sheets can it cut?' Percival asked, over the hiss of the water jets.

'Up to five hundred at a time.' Heather smiled. For the first time, she looked closely at Percival's face. It was lined, tired. He smiled back at her. She wondered what his story was. He had that dissipated lost look about him that she knew a lot of women liked: women who liked to mother their men, pamper them like babies. Percival looked harmless enough, kind and gentle, she thought.

The hiss ended abruptly. She examined the thirty-two piles of perfectly cut bills. She handed a stack to each of the three men.

Silence prevailed as they examined the bills, lost in their thoughts.

Books broke the silence with a mighty war whoop. He threw his stack of bills high in the air, the paper almost reaching the twenty-foot ceiling. They all watched the bills flutter back down, like rectangular green leaves resting on the stark white concrete floor.

Percival, Heather and Nick all followed Books' lead and threw their stacks of money high in the air.

'Goddammit, there's something about cash . . . nothing like it in the fucking world . . . stocks, bonds, mortgages are shit compared to cash,' Books said, dancing a jig in the pile of cash that had collected on the floor. 'Three hundred and twenty thousand dollars. More money in one place than most people ever see in a lifetime; created in less than three minutes. I love it!' He ran over and placed a kiss on the shiny Black Box, patting it approvingly as if it was a child.

Nick and Heather watched him, while Percival went to get two bottles of Cristal champagne. Heather fully understood now why Books gave the Black Box a hug and not her. He loved the Black Box and all it could do for him. Nick looked at her, guessing what she was thinking.

He took her by the arm and walked her over to the table where Percival was standing, put his arm round Perce's shoulder and said, 'Perce, did you ever think you would be standing right in the middle of the Gulf Stream on a tiny island, making money?'

'No, I never did.' Perce grinned from ear to ear. 'This is the most fun I've had since I dropped out of Princeton.'

'Thrown out is more like it,' Books added, joining them, taking a glass from Perce.

'Thrown? Dropped? Out is out. Who gives a shit.'

'Nobody here!' Nick grinned.

They all held their glasses high in the air. Books made the toast. 'Here's to doing the impossible. Thanks, Heather.' He made a slight awkward bow to her.

Heather bowed back and said, 'And friendship, here's to friendship.' Friendship if not love! she thought to herself. I hope we can still be friends!

They celebrated into the night, and when they were done they slept in sleeping bags on the concrete floor, lost in their dreams, oblivious of Griselda as she raged outside, like a wild deranged woman.

Hours later, while they were deep in sleep, Griselda crashed into two tugs hauling two barges of shredded Federal Reserve paper. She collided with them off Cape Hatteras, the graveyard of the Atlantic.

Just before dawn the telex on *Desperado* sputtered into life. The message was: 'Two tugs and one barge lost at sea. One barge missing. Thanks to Griselda. Sorry. Life's a bitch. I'll keep you posted. Ernie Sands.'

Sunday evening 8:00
FEDERAL RESERVE, NEW YORK CITY

The edges of the hurricane were lashing at the tip of Manhattan Island. The East River and the Hudson River were boiling at the Battery where they converged on their way to the Veranzano Narrows, Sandy Hook, and finally the Atlantic.

Griselda's fury was being felt in the long hollow canyons of Manhattan as her winds whistled through empty, narrow streets, shaking the tall glass, granite and concrete edifices until they swayed to her will.

Phillip wasn't worried about Griselda; he felt safe, ensconced in his top-floor apartment, secure in the knowledge that the strong granite frame of the Federal Reserve had thumbed its nose at mother nature's past hurricanes, natural disasters and calamities.

The Fed had also survived the frailties, foibles and greed of men. It sat at the head of Wall Street and the financial district like an impassive herald, forewarning the uninitiated that they were entering the land of Money, where the gifted and exceptional are chewed up for cannon fodder before they get a chance to play the game, where the rule is that there are no rules, only traps, and where greed and avarice, like death and desire, always collect their markers.

Phillip watched Veronica. She moved slowly like a sleek cat. She was preparing to leave.

'Next week sometime?'

'Yes,' he said, trailing her to the door in his chair. She had increased her visits to at least three, sometimes four a week on Phillip's request.

'You know, Phillip, this thing,' she leaned over and stroked the chrome wheel of his chair, 'bothers you more than it does me. If you ever want to get real and talk about it, I'm here

216

for you. I think I could even go straight for you, give up the biz, you know? I've always been a sucker for brains.' She kissed him gently on each temple and stroked his cheek, her long black hair cascading into both their faces. 'And I love your face, Phillip, so primitive and untamed.'

When their faces separated, there was a light film of tears in her eyes. She blinked them away and bolted out of the door, slamming it behind her.

Phillip sat in the chair looking at the closed door and wondered if it was Academy Award time or if she really meant it.

But the wheelchair and his mangled useless legs were always there, graphic and real, like a living photo that was imprinted on his mind. He judged people by the way they reacted to his affliction; less fuss was better.

Why had it been him, on that day, at that moment? In seconds his life was unalterably changed. But he should be thankful to be alive, he had so many other gifts. Somehow, it was his destiny, his karma. Perhaps he was trying too hard now to overcompensate, to over-achieve . . .

In the final analysis, he wrote the accident off to random action. There was no reason. And it was a waste of time to think about the goddamn thing. It was just that seeing Veronica always sparked the way it could have been in his mind: her long slim legs, the smooth dark hair that framed her face, her firm breasts, her flat stomach with just the hint of stomach muscles above the pubic mound; they could have danced, could have run, could have played. Didn't she need that?

He shook his head and wheeled quickly into his office, parked his wheelchair in the wide slot in the center of his desk, and opened the CIA recon photo file that Cobb had finally sent. He checked the dates and noted that pictures of the island came in every twenty-four hours. Cobb had been holding some of them for several days.

Phillip slipped the latest photo under his green-shaded

goose-necked lamp, examining it with a magnifying glass. The construction of the two buildings was basically completed and the two yachts sat at quiet anchor. Phillip absently circled the big sailboat with his finger; the reality of actually seeing Books' maxi racer sent a cold chill over all his skin.

He compared the latest photo to the earlier three photos. He noted progress every day. They weren't slowing construction. Ralph Cobb may have thought he had shut them down, but it didn't look like they were stopping the project. As far as Phillip could see, this game hadn't even begun yet. And Cobb was playing with a handicap: he continually underestimated Books and Nick.

What was Nick up to?

Nick, the quiet one, the one with the easy smile and the natural power. Nick, the Princeton charity case, no money, no family, yet he always seemed to be wherever he wanted to be: the Connecticut estates, the Palm Beach mansion, the Manhattan penthouses, crewing on the Sound during race week, and he always did it as if he had been born to it. They may have forgotten to give him the birth certificate, the pedigree, but he just proceeded without it.

Nonchalant Nick, and his easy way with women. Even the deadly Duchess had a crush on him. She fussed over Nick more than she did Books, always touching him, putting her hand on his arm or actually holding his hand on occasion, introducing him first to guests. She knew Nick's story, and he became her cause, her own private charity, except she funneled the money through Books and Big Books. Nick never knew where the Oberson scholarship funds were really coming from. He thought they came from Books and his father.

Phillip wasn't so sure that Books didn't finance Nick into the arms business as a ploy to get rid of him, to send Nick into the bowels of Europe and Africa. No one was more surprised than Books when the investment in Nick turned out to be a success.

But Nick had changed with the years, something had got to him, maybe it was connected to that murder in Paris. Certainly, he had never mentioned it, never spoken of it at all.

Phillip hadn't heard from Nick now for a long time, too long. He knew that Nick would not play out his role much longer; the deceit would be too much for him. He would either join Books for real or disappear into the Caribbean.

Phillip needed Nick to hang around; he was an important part of the overall plan.

Maybe there was a way to keep him in the game, maybe the leverage was this murder in Paris, if he had the information, the full story; all the details.

Phillip decided to check it out. He placed a call to Ralph Cobb.

WEEK THREE

WEEK THREE

Monday dawn 6:00
BROOKLYN NAVY YARD, NEW YORK CITY

Ernie Sands sat under *Tigershark*'s con, fingering the periscope, thinking about the lost tugs and barges and what they might have been carrying.

He had friends in the Coast Guard who had put a tracer on the tugs and garbage scows for him after the tug captains had called in their maydays. They had no news for him yet, they were still looking. They had their hands full; Griselda had left a long trail of broken toys in her wake. She was just hitting the Great Lakes now and every facility of the Coast Guard was stretched to its limits.

As the workmen around him continued to spot-weld old tired seams and fit new electronics and creature comforts on board, Ernie took a stroll through the iron hull. It reminded him of being inside a long, fat cigar; it didn't smell much better.

He took out a cigarette and examined it closely. Cigarettes had been his pals for a long time. He squeezed the cigarette slightly in the center, and rolled it in his fingers, then rolled it under his nose. 'What the hell,' he said out loud to the empty torpedo tubes. He had been told that an operation was out of the question and chemotherapy would only hold off the inevitable. 'Fuck them. I'm not going out that way, whimpering and whining, breathing oxygen through a plastic tube in some VA hospital bed, dreaming of a final puff.'

Ernie saluted the air with his cigarette. 'Thanks, thanks for sending Nick to me, with one more chance for some fun.'

He lit his cigarette and took a long slow drag, then made his way back to the conning tower. The smoke felt good, safe. He held his cigarette out in front of his face, watching the smoke curl upwards like a pig's tail; he wondered if it felt good enough to die for. Shit, too late for thoughts like that now. Nick was always where the action was, and Ernie needed a swan song to go out in style. Yeah, that was it, go in style.

As he exhaled his second long drag, the telex lit up and started to chatter. The Carolina Coast Guard station in Cape Hatteras had news about the missing barge.

Monday morning 6:30
SECRET SERVICE, NEW YORK CITY

'Sergio Lucci,' Cobb said out loud to his empty New York office, his words reverberating off the walls. 'Everyone knows you work for Don Saverese.' Cobb was reading the report that his lead agent had written on the surprise raid of Waste Control Corporation of Bayonne, New Jersey. He was sure that whatever shredded currency paper Books St John had was all he was getting. The report informed him that the shredded paper was being buried on a mountain of blood and guts; the paper was tainted beyond use. And all further Federal Reserve shipments to Waste Control Corporation had been cut off. But how much paper did Books St John already have, and was this Mafia chieftain, Don Saverese, involved?

Prostitution, gambling, extortion, drugs, even murder was all right under certain circumstances as far as Cobb was concerned. But counterfeiting? That was a different story.

Cobb finished reading the report for the third time and fed it into the shredder, page by page. He listened to the grinding noise of the shredder and watched the powerful machine strip the pages into long thin shreds. High tech violence made him feel better.

All he could do now was sit and wait.

Maybe he had destroyed most of the precious paper they needed, but somehow he didn't believe it. They were better than he thought, more resourceful, brighter; these weren't your standard criminals, terrorists or weirdos. He had to come up with a better contingency plan if he was going to beat them. He looked down on the slick, wet hurricane-swept streets of Manhattan.

Monday morning 11:00
CAY SAL BANK, BAHAMAS

Percival was taking a break; he sat on a driftwood stump the hurricane had blown in to shore, a cold can of Budweiser in his hand, patiently waiting for his chemicals and cauldrons to be unloaded and placed in a corner of the warehouse.

'No news is no news,' Books said, standing on the dock, looking down at Percival as he helped offload pallets of paper from the freighter that had arrived from Miami. Books was referring to the missing barges of shredded paper. 'Don't add a lot to it, Perce. We'll hear the minute Ernie Sands has news. In the meantime let's proceed as planned; you get the blanching process ready, I'll get the paper.'

'Whatever you say, Books.'

Heather stood at the main door to the warehouse. Nick

drove the forklift while she supervised the unloading in the warehouse.

She shouted to Nick, 'Bring the last six pallets into the main building.' She pointed at the building that housed the Black Box. Nick nodded and waved.

Each building was one hundred feet by seventy-five feet of simple construction: a poured concrete floor with steel beams implanted every fifteen feet. The beams ran the seventy-five-foot width, with several support columns positioned in the center and at either end. The long-running spans of steel and sixteen-foot ceilings gave Heather the feeling of being in a large empty hangar, or a quiet bowling alley.

The two steel buildings occupied almost one-third of the entire coral atoll. A covered causeway between the two structures was partially built, and would be the last item for the construction crew to complete. It was prefabricated and could be assembled in one day.

Heather was waiting for Nick in the main building which he had dubbed the 'C' building, for cash/control/center. He placed a pallet close to the Black Box as Heather paced off the other locations for the remaining five pallets.

Nick sat in the forklift and watched her as she squatted to place duct tape Xs on the floor to mark exactly where the other pallets should be placed. The hurricane had shaken the building to its foundations; the massive steel shingles had come loose in certain areas, but no major damage had been sustained. The four of them had felt only the edge of Griselda's fury as they slept on the concrete floor in sleeping bags.

Nick's sleeping bag was next to Heather's, only a foot away. During the night, he heard her soft breathing and fitful moaning as she dreamed. Nick saw her face clearly in the reflection of the one Coleman lamp they had lit. He wondered about her dreams and whether they were connected to the fact that they were finally into production. The illusion was over, the fantasy ended. It was going to be the real thing from now on.

Nick sat there, the forklift truck idling, watching her. She rose after she taped the last X, and spotted him watching her.

'Something wrong?' she asked.

'No. How about a dive this afternoon? Should be good after the hurricane. All work and no play, you know how that goes.'

'What time?'

'Two.' Nick backed the forklift round in a tight little circle and disappeared out of the front door to get the rest of the pallets and to invite Books along on the dive.

Nick drove directly over to the dock where Books was standing talking to Percival. He wanted Books to say he was too busy to go with them. He wanted to be alone with Heather.

But instead of asking Books, Nick drove past him. He picked up the remaining pallets of paper stacked on the docks and took them to the main building. Next, he unloaded the chemicals, vats, and cauldrons for Percival and placed them in the far corner of the warehouse. Finally, he unloaded the barrels from International Fisheries.

'What the hell is that stink?' Books asked, pinching his nostrils closed.

'Jesus Christ.' Percival gagged. Don't tell me what's in those fucking barrels.' He backed away from the dock, retreating down the beach. 'I don't want to know. Pheww!'

'Just a little mariculture experiment for later,' Nick said, placing the last barrel on the dock. Books was halfway to 'C' building when Nick caught up with him in the fork lift. 'Want to go diving this afternoon? It's got to be an interesting bottom after Griselda's visit. I've already asked Heather,' Nick added, feeling self-conscious.

'Can't,' Books answered. For an instant Nick thought he saw the evil cat, jealousy, dart through Books' eyes. 'Got to work with Percival, help him get his magic potions together to bleach the paper.'

'I'd be glad to stay and help too,' Nick said, not meaning it.

'No need. And Heather deserves a break. She's been working non-stop. Do her good. Do you both good.' Books smiled an enigmatic smile, placing his arm on Nick's shoulder. He looked him straight in the eye, gave his shoulder a squeeze, and departed, saying, 'Catch us dinner if you can. I have to keep Percival the mad scientist out of the goddamn Budweiser, keep his hand steady, concentrating on his work so he doesn't blow us all up.'

Two hours later, Nick was waiting at the stern of *Desperado* in the Whaler, the engine running, the scuba tanks filled with air.

'Aren't we using the hookah rig today?' Heather asked, stepping off the diving platform into the bow of the Whaler. She wore a thin black Lycra one-piece bathing suit and a black visor that said 'It's Miller Time'. She stuffed a folded long T-shirt inside the Igloo cooler and noticed the bottle of chilled Meursault and small lunch he had packed. She didn't mention it, closing the lid.

'No,' Nick answered, releasing the line from the stern of *Desperado*. 'The tanks will give us more flexibility and range. I'd like to cover a lot of ground today. We should see a big change in the ocean bottom after Griselda's visit.'

Fifteen minutes later they both had their diving gear on and were sitting on the gunnel of the Whaler. 'Stay close to me, okay?'

Heather nodded, and disappeared over the side.

Once in the water, Nick took his time, following his normal ritual of checking the anchor line and double-checking his gear; when that was completed, he headed for the first coral head. There was a cluster of heads, over a dozen, that sat nestled together like a vanguard on the furthest edge of the wall, a sheer cliff that fell off in a straight drop down two hundred fathoms, twelve hundred feet. Anguila Cay was surrounded by long miles of sandy flats and coral patches that ended in a wall, forming a perfect natural circle round the entire key, like a moat surrounding a castle.

The coral heads rose from depths of forty feet to within three feet of the surface. Heather and Nick started on the bottom and made a series of slow circles, climbing to the surface. Nick pointed out some of the better camouflaged inhabitants of the head, like the anemones, brittle star fish and calico crabs that were able to blend in with their environment.

They went along the line of coral heads until their tanks were down to eight hundred pounds. Nick was about to signal that they should return to the Whaler for the second tank when he saw the hole. It was at the base of the last coral head. The sand had been washed aside by the hurricane, and an opening had been left, about the size of a small manhole cover.

Nick stuck his head in the hole. It stretched into a cave. The cave was too small to slide into with the tank strapped to his back, so he slipped it off and pulled it behind him. He disappeared into the cave for about the length of his body, and immediately came back out. He signalled to Heather and they returned to the Whaler to get their second tanks.

'Put it out of your mind, Nick. Don't even ask. I'm not going in there,' Heather said, holding on to the gunnel of the Whaler, resting, her mask perched on the top of her head. 'Where the hell does that hole lead anyway? It looks spooky.'

'A blue hole. A natural cave formed in the shape of a bell. Probably one side is bottomless. They usually are.'

'They sound like hell holes. You've been in them before?'

'Only twice. There's one off Bimini and one in Belize that I've been inside. They're something to see, a very rare natural phenomenon. Give it a try; just follow my lead. I'll get some safety line so we can find our way back. We'll secure the line outside and use it to make sure we remember where the entrance is. Come on, what do you say? It's the chance of a lifetime.'

'Like Hansel and Gretel leaving the bread crumbs, we leave a lifeline. No thanks. I'll wait for you. Take the camera! Pictures will be fine for me.'

Nick just smiled at her and climbed into the Whaler to get the coil of extra anchor line that lay in the bow. He eased back into the water and helped her attach the second tank to her back. He checked their pressure gauges. They read three thousand pounds, enough for almost an hour if they kept their breathing quiet.

They returned to the entrance of the blue hole. She watched him as he secured one end of the safety line to a half-buried rock of dead coral. The line was bright yellow nylon, easy to see. He slipped the remaining coil of rope under his arm, then squirmed out of his tank harness so he could drag it behind him through the opening.

Heather swam up to him at the last moment, her face mask only inches from his. Their bubbles rose to the surface together in easy harmony; both of them were trying to keep their breathing calm. She studied him for a long minute then nodded, 'Me too!' Nick smiled and gave her the okay sign with his right hand, almost dropping his tank. He waited while she unstrapped her tank and backpack, then handed her the yellow safety line. He swam ahead as they entered the coral tunnel, a dark cylinder that ran for about fifteen feet. Nick guided himself along the walls with his hands. He could feel them tremble. He didn't want to come face to face with anything unfriendly in these tight quarters. There was a gray light that permeated the narrow cave, like the eerie light that comes at dawn on a sunless day. The light improved as he progressed. Nick could see the mouth of the cave now. It was glowing iridescent blue. He slid out of the coral tunnel into the blue hole; Heather followed.

She was dazzled. The light inside the hole had a deep azure hue. She looked at Nick. He appeared surrealistic, like he was drifting in a blue dream. He reached over and gently touched her shoulder. It sent a shudder down her body.

Nick's hand slipped down her arm until they interlocked fingers. Together they floated lazily towards the center. The hole was like a giant cathedral in the shape of a bell with an elliptical ceiling. They floated together on their backs, looking up at the dome and the thousands of pin pricks of blue light.

It was as if they were both dead, in an immortal dream, preserved together for ever on the most intimate plane that two humans could reach.

One side was shallow and ended just below the cave opening where they had entered, to form a hard bottom, while the other side had no floor, and seemed to fall off into a void, into nothingness.

The fish life was teeming; there were groupers, yellowtail snappers, even tuna that had found their way through the hole and could not find their way out. The fish were doomed to swim in endless circles, living in a giant carousel, eating each other.

Barracuda lurked in the shadows, waiting until their hunger aroused them enough to snap their jaws shut on a passing fish.

Heather was mesmerized by the holes in the dome of the bell, a myriad of small openings, like a cheese grater, none big enough to form an entrance for any but the tiniest angelfish or wandering crab. The thousands of holes caused the blue light to fragment and criss-cross in diagonal lines like laser swords of liquid blue light.

Heather shivered to think of how black it must be in that hole at night, like deepest darkest death.

It was at that moment she saw a gray shape appear like a thick cloud; then it disappeared with a flick of its tail. She squeezed Nick's hand with all her strength and pointed. But the form had disappeared into the blackness like a ghost. She moved as close to Nick as she could, holding onto his arm.

She sensed a presence behind her, and was afraid to look. But slowly she turned her head and there it was: two black bottomless eyes that were separated by a long thin strip of cartilage; underneath the eyes was a cavernous gaping maw

231

that opened and closed to pump water over the gills as it moved.

Nick heard the bubbles escape from Heather's mouthpiece, almost an audible gasp. He turned. They were face to face with a hammerhead shark, the biggest Nick had ever seen, fourteen feet long, with battle scars running like scabs along the top of its head, extending to the dorsal fin.

The shark hung suspended and checked them over for only a second before cruising past, almost rubbing its rough body against them. Heather pulled on Nick's arm and pointed to the yellow safety rope that marked the opening. Nick pulled her close and gave her a hand signal to tell her to slow down, breathe easily, calm herself. He knew sharks acted out of instinct; panic was a weakness they responded to. He put his arm round her and held her close against his body for a second as the shark disappeared into the black murk of the deep side. It had obviously found its way through the opening years ago when it was smaller, probably chasing prey, and had been trapped inside ever since.

Slowly, Nick started to descend towards the opening; he paused at the entrance to help Heather take off her tank backpack so she could squeeze through the passage. He watched her flippers and tank disappear into the cave as she pulled herself along the tunnel.

Nick waited a few long minutes, soaking up the natural light show and studying the grandeur of the dome that had been created thousands of years ago, perhaps when the great land mass of earth had buckled and broken into five continents, or when the earth had trembled and the magical empire of Atlantis was destroyed. He wondered how long the shark had been trapped, to grow that big. Even with plenty of food, it must be frustrated; the hammerhead needed to roam the oceans.

Heather was waiting for him at the entrance and signalled that she would like to return to the Whaler. After they were aboard, Nick opened the Meursault that he had stashed in the Igloo. He handed a cupful to Heather.

232

'Sorry,' Nick said. 'I had no idea we would run into that old grizzly in there.'

'I don't think I've ever been so scared. What an ugly creature, but beautiful at the same time – primeval. He didn't seem very interested in us.'

'He wasn't. He has plenty to eat. You did good.' Nick held up his glass to toast Heather.

'Wrong. I did awful. I almost dropped my mouthpiece.' She smiled.

'Yeah, but you didn't,' Nick said, squeezing her hand. He leaned forward and kissed her on the cheek. She was startled, but didn't move. Their faces were only inches apart. She reached up and touched his cheek gently with the tips of her fingers, letting them slide down his face.

'Thanks.'

'For what?'

'For giving me courage.' She withdrew her hand. Nick sat back down on his seat.

'It's nice here, in complete privacy, surrounded by the wonders of nature, and no laws, at least no laws until you make some.'

'There's always a law, a natural law.' Heather smiled.

'I suppose. Speaking of laws, why did the Bahamians sell the sovereign rights? Pretty drastic, isn't it?' Nick asked, trying to change the subject, ease the tension.

'They all owed Books a favor, a big favor.'

'Who's they?'

'The Prime Minister and his corrupt lackey Cabinet. And a lot of other people tucked away in the Bahamian upper crust.'

'What was the favor?'

'Books arranged for a famous American lawyer to come and defend Chandler and his cronies from serious criminal indictments. It was after a Miami newspaper exposed their deep drug connections, and how they acted as a conduit, funneling drugs into the USA.'

'How did the lawyer get them off?'

'He had great influence in Washington. He arranged for a trade-off. The charges would be quietly forgotten in return for granting the US Coast Guard free reign in the Bahamas. It was a serious charge. If the lawyer hadn't been successful, there's a good chance they would all have gone to jail. The evidence was clear, strong and damning.'

'So they repaid Books with the sovereign rights?'

'Yes, along with some cash he gave them. It's only for three years, so what do they care? They got paid handsomely for a worthless piece of coral and they get it back in three years.'

'Interesting,' Nick said. 'Now, how about us heading home?'

'You're the captain,' she said, moving to the bow to retrieve the anchor.

Twenty minutes later they were in the salon of *Desperado* having vodka and tonics with Books. Heather was excitedly repeating the story of their adventure in the blue hole to Books and Percival as they sipped their cocktails.

Books noticed the flush in her cheeks and the warm glow in her eyes. He recognized the look; it was the same look she had on her face that night they stole the Black Box in London, when they had made love in the Learjet. He rose to refill his drink.

'Anyone ready?' he asked pointing at his glass.

'I wouldn't say no.' Percival smiled, handing his glass to Books.

'No, you wouldn't, Perce. Heather?' Books asked with his back to the three of them as he made the drinks. 'Make a great natural vault, wouldn't it?' he commented as he turned and handed Percival his drink. 'I mean use the blue hole as a vault for the gold. We would have our own watchdog in the hammerhead. Can you see any problems with the idea?' Books sat down, looking directly at Nick, taking no more interest in Heather's story.

'There'd be a slight problem getting the gold down that

narrow tunnel but that could be solved with a stainless steel conveyor belt system. The ground is hard coral on that side; the mud is at the deep end, so we won't have any silt to deal with. Could work.' Nick looked over at Heather.

'Nature provides,' Books said. 'The gold comes out of the ground in South Africa, Canada, Russia, the good old USA, and we put it back. For a while, anyway.'

Again, Heather imagined that hole at night, bottomless black gloom; it gave her the willies. She took a fast gulp of her drink. 'How's our mad chemist doing?' she asked, smiling.

'Lovely. Just effin' lovely, and thanks for asking.' Percival tipped his glass to Heather. 'I should be ready to bleach something in forty-eight hours. Anybody need their pants bleached, maybe a shirt or two, underwear? I may specialize in undies,' Percival said, giving Heather a lecherous wink.

Books was still excited about the discovery; he turned to Nick. 'Let's try it. The blue hole as a vault, I mean. I'll order the conveyor to be fabricated in Miami.'

'It's worth a try,' Nick answered.

'When do we get to see your mariculture experiment, Nick?' Percival asked.

'After dinner. Let's eat!'

Two hours later they were standing on the dock watching Nick as he loaded the three barrels of fish offal onto the stern of a Magnum ocean racer. He was using one of the hydraulic davits that had been installed on the edge of the dock. He tied the chains round the barrels carefully and lowered them onto the stern. The weight caused the stern to sink about six inches into the water, almost filling the exhaust pipes with salt water.

Nick started the Magnum. The exhausts gurgled and spluttered as the powerful diesel engines spat salt water out of the pipes.

'Anyone for a ride?' Nick asked.

Percival held his nose. 'I get seasick on the goddamn dock.

And that stink! Whew, no thanks! I'd rather go play with my stink chemicals.'

'I'll go,' Heather said. 'I want to see what you're up to.'

'Ready when you are, Nick,' Books said, checking his watch as he undid the lines.

'Put this on,' Nick said, handing Books a yellow slicker to keep the fish guts from splattering his clothes. 'And hold onto this.' He shoved a fireman's ax into Books' hands.

Nick used the channel to get the Magnum up on a plane. The diesel engines strained with the extra weight on the stern. He had to take the boat to three thousand RPMs before it settled down to slide effortlessly along the surface. Racing at forty-five knots, it drew only eighteen inches of water. Nick swung the wheel hard over, leaping out of the channel, skimming along the great expanse of calm flats that surrounded the island. Heather stood next to him, holding onto the dashboard.

'Now,' he yelled at Books.

'Now what?'

'Smack one barrel with the pointed side of the ax; try for about a four-inch hole as near to the bottom of the barrel as you can.'

Books steadied himself on the bouncing deck and took a full roundhouse swing with the ax. He had to twist the handle to remove the point from the steel barrel. The offal started to squirt out behind the boat in a steady dirty stream. It left a thin wake of red and brown mucus that blended in with the churning white wake of the Magnum.

The stench remained behind them except when Nick turned into the breeze. He made an elongated S Pattern, working his way out to the Gulf Stream current where the water reached depths of three hundred fathoms. He saved one last barrel for the final run up the channel to the harbor. He signaled Books to crack it open. The setting sun reflected the oil slick that the fish guts made on the flats as they roared down the channel. It was almost high tide; the tide was still coming in. As the tide receded the chum slick would ease its way out into the Gulf Stream, tempting any large predatory sharks in the stream, drawing them onto the flats.

'Nature provides!' Books yelled over the roar of the engines. 'First a vault, and now a moat of live sharks. I love it! Nick, this is a great idea!'

Nick kept the boat at full speed right up to the edge of the dock. He backed off on the throttle at the last minute and the boat settled down in its own wake with a smooth whoosh, rocking from side to side as the waves it had created unfolded and caught up with them.

Books pulled off his smelly yellow slicker. 'I'll go see how Percival's doing,' he said and made his way to the warehouse.

Heather climbed out last; she sat on the dock watching Nick. 'When do you think they'll come?' She asked, referring to the sharks, fascinated by the experiment to lure them onto the flats.

'In a couple of days.'

'Well, I think I'll go make some money. It's still a little stinky around here.' She smiled and stood up.

Nick shucked off his clothes and dove off the end of the dock and swam to his boat. The warm tropical water felt soothing. He hung on the teak diving platform, letting the water relax his body.

His mind wandered back to that afternoon and the blue hole: the natural light show that mother nature had provided for them, and the shark – prehistoric beast – living there as evidence to show them that they were but small parts of what eternity was made of.

And Heather, what a wonderful creature of nature. The way her fingertips felt on his face as they slid down his cheek . . .

There had been women, plenty of women, but love was tough. Every time it had cost him: his sweet mother whom he never got the chance to know; his proud father taken away, shot by some drunken asshole. Big Books swept from the

237

deck and out of his life for ever that fateful day off Nassau. And the Duchess, Books' mother, had wanted nothing more to do with them after the accident.

Nick heard the clickity-click of the telex on *Desperado*. He swam over and climbed aboard, snatching a towel to dry himself against the cooling evening trade winds. He went below decks to the telex and read the message.

'Bad news first. One barge, one tug, sunk off Cape Hatteras, total loss. Good news. One barge saved, tug disabled. Salvage company sent two tugs to the scene. One tug to retrieve disabled tug. One tug to pull barge to you. Barge is on the way. My final project is coming along well, should be ready in a week. See you soon. Your pal, Captain Nemo.'

Nick read the telex twice, then swam over to his own boat, holding the message in the air to keep it dry. He dressed, and took the Zodiac ashore.

Nick heard the hum of the machines working inside the Butler building. He opened the door and walked in. Percival, Books and Heather stood in silence as the hydro slicer tore through a hundred sheets of the Miami currency paper.

The three of them looked up in unison as Nick walked in, then they looked down again, as one, all fascinated by the power of the Black Box.

While the hydro slicer was doing its job, the copier was ejecting a hundred more sheets of finished currency onto the second gurney, to be cut into bills as soon as the hydro slicer was ready to be fed.

When the machine stopped hissing, Percival walked over to the gurney and slid the finished hundred dollar bills onto a third table where Heather had set up an automatic wrapper. Percival lifted the stacks of bills and jammed them into the stainless steel holder. The machine took over, automatically wrapping, compacting and stacking the bills one hundred to the pack. Nick walked over to the finished side and lifted one pack of shrink-wrapped finished bills; ten thousand dollars, less than a half-inch thick, and they were perfect.

Nick handed the telex to Books. Books studied the message, reading it twice. 'All right!' he yelled. 'That ain't so bad.' He handed the telex to Heather. Percival walked over and read it, looking over her shoulder. Heather handed the telex to him. 'I guess you're in business in a day or so, Perce,' she said.

'That's fine with me. What the hell else is there to do in your kingdom?' He made a slight bow to Books, and a small curtsy to Heather. 'I need a fucking drink.' He smiled, walking over to the Igloo cooler. 'Anyone else for a libation?'

Everyone nodded. Percival handed a chilled, dripping bottle of Budweiser to each of them.

They held the bottles up in a silent toast.

After a short while, Nick wandered out and sat on the husk of a palm tree trunk that hurricane Griselda had ripped out of the ground. Ten minutes later Heather joined him, taking a break from the machinery.

She sat down next to him. 'Not fascinated like the rest of us?'

'Yeah, I'm fascinated. Who wouldn't be?' Nick took a sip from his beer.

'Books says you're not as money-oriented as we are.'

'Books isn't always right.'

'That's true. But he's never wrong. Just ask him.' She smiled and clinked bottles with Nick. 'Amazing, isn't it? The power of paper.'

'The faith people place in governments, and in the law, is unqualified and unquestioned, more faith than they have in themselves. It's easier that way, works better.'

Heather just stared at him.

'I'm sorry, that sounded bitter, or jaded. I'm not either.'

'I know,' she said. 'Who's Captain Nemo?'

'Ernie Sands, an old friend of mine. He's getting us the ordnance we need to secure the island: M-16 rifles, land mines, SAMs, radar, M-60s, stuff like that. He's ex-Navy, a good guy. The last part of that telex means that the subs will be down here shortly.'

The subs flashed through Heather's mind, cold gray steel cylinders; they reminded her of the hammerhead in the blue hole.

'What's that?'

'Where?'

'On the horizon.' She pointed at the mouth of the channel, the edge of the Gulf Stream. There was a huge black form about five miles off being pulled by a tug.

'I'll bet it's our new home.'

'Home?'

'Yeah, the liberty ship that Captain Nemo sent down from the Brooklyn Navy Yard.'

'That's nice,' she smiled. 'No one tells me anything around here!'

'I'll go and get Books; we'll take the Whaler out to pilot them through the channel. They'll never make it in the dark.'

He went to get up. She grabbed his hand and pulled him back down to the palm tree. 'It's real now, isn't it?' she asked. 'It'll be all right, won't it, Nick? No one will get hurt or anything?'

'Sure,' he said, not meaning it.

'No. Please, Nick, I really mean it. What do you think? All that military stuff and everything, will there be trouble?'

'You like poetry?'

'Love it.'

'Remember Omar Khayyam?' Nick asked.

'The Rubaiyat?' Heather remembered seeing a copy in the library on Nick's boat.

Nick quoted:

> 'The moving finger writes
> And having writ, moves on
> Nor all your piety or your wit
> Can change a line of it

Or your tears wash away a single word.

'The die is cast now, Heather; so be it.' He held a finger to his lips, kissed it, and placed the tip against her cheek.

Monday evening 7:00
NEW YORK CITY

Phillip gently closed the Interpol file and tapped his fingers on the red cover in a steady rhythm. He never would have believed that Nick was capable of murder – if it could be called murder to kill this Sean O'Reilly.

Sean O'Reilly was a bad Irishman. He used the IRA cause as a slim excuse to wheel and deal with the arms dealers, killers, and thieves that he associated with. He was a sociopath with a bloodlust; a long list of deaths could be traced directly to his doorstep.

The report was thorough, and included a large section on Sean O'Reilly. Ralph Cobb's formal request to Interpol for the dossier had been headed: 'Nick Sullivan – Suspected Terrorist'.

The report was drawn from confidential informants and police undercover agents who were buried deep in the crime cancer of Europe. There was no physical evidence, only rumors and conjecture. The Corsican Brotherhood had allegedly disposed of Sean O'Reilly's body on the direct orders of a mercenary ex-Legionnaire who called himself Colonel Le Clerc. No gun was ever found and the few eye-witnesses that were available all had checkered backgrounds: their testimony wouldn't hold up in court, in the unlikely event that they could be persuaded to testify.

Still, Philip thought, Nick didn't know what evidence was out there against him, and sometimes conscience is the hardest judge and jury of all. Phillip knew Nick had a strong conscience; maybe there was a way to use it against him.

He hadn't heard from Nick in over two weeks, and he needed to know what was happening on that island. He needed leverage to get Nick back in line.

He made a mental checklist of all the ramifications if a flood of counterfeit currency hit the world monetary markets, especially US dollars.

Word trade was built on the foundation of confidence in American money. There wasn't any other currency that was acceptable worldwide. No one wanted English pounds, Russian rubles, or French francs, and there weren't enough Swiss francs to supply the demand; even the mighty Japanese yen and German mark did not elicit the confidence of the US dollar.

Gold, silver, and all the metals, precious and otherwise, were quoted in US dollars. And oil was quoted in US dollars; what would the Arabs take for payment if they lost confidence in American dollars? Gold was no substitute; there wasn't enough of it.

There were massive changes ahead in the world of finance. With the introduction of the Euro dollar there would be one currency for the Common Market; the German mark would become more powerful as East and West Germany united; a new 'hard' ruble would be born as the USSR finally got its economic act together; and finally the empire of the rising sun and its mighty yen would have to be dealt with as it rose to challenge the dollar. But still standing alone, sacrosanct, was the US dollar, and Phillip was committed to keeping it that way.

He would have to squeeze Nick a little.

BROOKLYN NAVY YARD, NEW YORK CITY

'Come on now, you old whore. Let me hear you crank when I hit the button or you're going to become an unnatural reef!' Barney O'Brien was an ex-Navy chief engineer in his late sixties. He had been on subs all his working life and was an expert on diesel-driven, pre-nuclear models. He had fought in them in both the great oceans. He was a florid man, overweight, close to three hundred pounds. He moved slowly, breathing heavily, almost wheezing as he spoke. He went over to the console and the ignition switch. This was the *Batfish*, and she was the last of the two subs to be refitted.

The engine labored as the batteries strained to turn the mighty pistons. Finally, there was a strong boom-boom-boom as the first cylinders burst into life, then a constant throbbing as all the cylinders caught. Barney turned and smiled at the other workers; his large red nose seemed to glow with pleasure. The men all held out their fists, thumbs up.

Ernie Sands pushed his taped glasses up the bridge of his nose and went over to shake Barney's hand. It was like shaking a large wet ham.

'Good work, Chief. That's three.' Ernie slapped him on his beefy shoulders.

'Let's hope she stays together under pressure. I wouldn't go too deep with these suckers. No offense, honey.' Barney patted the engine in apology. 'The pressure may pop the outside structural rivets. I would stay above twenty fathoms. But it's your party, and they made things right when they made these babies. Know what I mean?' Barney winked, as if the engines were listening.

'Yeah,' Ernie answered, taking a deep breath. He loved

the sweet acrid smell of bilges and diesel fuel. 'You going to join us later, down south?'

'Hell, yeah. What have I got to do up here? I'm living on the Jersey shore, bored shitless, just me and the wife sittin' around watching paint dry.' He smiled at Ernie and patted the periscope. 'Besides, these were the real thing, know what I mean?' He didn't wait for Ernie to answer. 'Those nuclear jobs are like flying a fucking rocket, just sit around watching screens and pushing buttons. But these, these babies are a different story. When you had sea duty in one of these and it was war time, it was a real trip. You had to have your shit together to make it through a tour as a submariner then, 'specially against the Japs and the Germans. Four hours of straight sleep was a luxury, and you didn't have no space to be arguing with your shipmates. You got your arguments over in a hurry.' Barney took a deep wheezy breath, and spun the arms of the periscope.

Ernie knew he was going to lose a few hours listening to his stories, but what the hell, Barney had worked hard, and Ernie's job was done now. Tomorrow the three submarines would leave for their journey down the East coast and into the Bahamas.

Barney carried on with his stories as the other workmen and crew wandered over and joined them at the galley table for coffee. Ernie nodded as the Chief spoke, but his mind was on cancer and death. Occasionally, these thoughts slipped into his brain without his consent. He was going to die, to be no more, to disappear into dust for ever.

Why were we here? What was the point? To live our paltry lives trying to figure out the riddles and then disappear like gas into the air?

Barney's booming laugh brought him back to reality and the present. The diesel was humming now like a sewing machine. 'She sounds good, don't she?' the Chief asked Ernie, tilting his head toward the engine. 'Like she's been sleeping for thirty-five years and is ready to go after a good rest. Yeah, she's a good girl, ain't ya, honey?' Barney stood, gave the purring diesel a pat and poured himself a coffee. He sat, and continued to regale the men with his stories.

Ernie wondered what life on an island in the Cay Sal Bank would be like, and exactly how much time he had left. He lit a cigarette, inhaled deeply, waiting for the nicotine to hit. He leaned back on his chair, sipped his coffee, and listened to Barney talk about the role of his submarine during the battle of Midway.

Tuesday afternoon 2:00
CAY SAL BANK, BAHAMAS

Printed sheets of currency paper cascaded out of the entrails of the copier onto the gurney. Heather didn't notice Nick standing nearby. She sat at the console of the computer, occasionally changing or modifying orders.

In front of her were three large steel strongboxes. She opened the center box and took out the top bill. The strongbox was packed with fifties.

She carefully scratched notes on a legal pad after she examined the bill. She completed her notes and slashed both sides of the bill with a yellow highlighter, then placed the bill in a shoe box.

'Pretty sophisticated,' Nick said, pointing at the shoe box.

She looked up and stared at him, her concentration broken, eyes not quite focusing on his face. Finally, she smiled. 'Sorry, I was lost in this fifty.' Nick was still pointing at the shoe box. Heather looked down at it. 'Does the job; we're too sophisticated as it is.'

'What are you doing?' Nick asked, lifting up the marked fifty and studying it in the light.

'You really want to know? It's a bit complicated.'

'Try me. I'll let you know if you get too technical.'

Heather ripped off the top page of her yellow legal pad and took her pencil in hand. 'We use the same numbering system that the US Mint uses. It's one of the hardest things for counterfeiters to deal with. The numbers have to be a current live sequence, still in circulation, and all our bills have to be in the proper series.' She reached up and took the fifty out of Nick's hand. As she did, their fingers touched. She let them linger there a fraction of a second longer than she had to.

'See how the serial numbers match, the top right hand corner and the bottom left, on the face of the bill?' She pointed them out to Nick. 'Well, ours do also, and they must match up with a current series or they're a dead giveaway.'

'But that means there will be two bills in circulation with the same numbers.'

'Yes. Better than having an invalid serial number on the bill when the Fed matches ours with theirs, if they ever do. The way we are doing it, with live series, the Feds will have to decide which one is real and which one is the counterfeit. If the paper's good, I defy anyone to tell the difference.'

'How do the numbers work?'

'Serial numbers consist of eight numerals, preceded and ended by a letter of the alphabet, making a total of ten designators. The only letter of the alphabet never used is O because it can easily be mistaken for a zero. This is the way a numbering series is begun. The first note is numbered A00000001A, and sequentially thereafter through to A99999999A.

'At this point, the 1000 millionth note, we see a star instead of a letter. Then the suffix changes to B, and we do it all over again. This system, if used in its entirety, allows us to print sixty-two billion notes without duplicating any serial number.'

246

'But you don't use the entire series.'

'No. That would make it too easy for them, they would know what series to identify and then just pull the entire series and declare all of ours counterfeit.'

'Therefore the strongboxes,' Nick said, walking over to them and opening the other two lids. The boxes were filled with twenties, fifties, and hundreds.

'Yes, we use the real thing to find an actual series.' Heather took out a handful of twenties. 'All I need is one real bill, and I can run the whole series, but as I said, we limit each series.'

'To what?' Nick reached into the steel box and snatched a fistful of hundreds.

'Each denomination has a different limit. We follow the same ratio as the US Mint: for twenties, it's a twenty million dollar limit, for fifties, it's thirty million, and for hundreds, it's fifty million. We reach a total of one hundred million, then we change the series.'

Nick glanced over at the hydro slicer and the automatic wrapping machine. Percival was busy sealing the stacked and wrapped new currency in bundles of clear shrink-wrapped plastic.

'Each one of those shrink-wrapped packets are worth a quarter of a million dollars,' Heather explained, 'no matter what the denomination we are using.'

Books entered the building and smiled at Nick and Heather. 'We'll be able to make our first American delivery in two days, Nick. How do you feel about going to New York and informing our distributor that we are ready?' Not waiting for an answer, Books switched his attention to Percival. 'Perce, I'll take over for a while. Maybe you could get back to being a mad chemist. We're going to need more paper.'

There were eight pallets of paper left. Books was planning on mass production, and soon.

Perce nodded. 'Yassir, boss.' He smiled. 'I's be goin to de paper mill jus lak use sez, and mix dem kem-e-kals.' He tipped his peaked baseball cap and shuffled past Nick and Heather; he gave them both a broad wink.

'Heather, I'll take over if you have the programming completed.' Books sat down at the console. 'You've been at it since dawn.'

'The programing is done, just punch in STOP or START. We're making fifties,' Heather said.

'When do you want me to leave for New York?' Nick asked. 'Tomorrow?'

Books looked up from the console. 'Sooner the better.'

'Let me try for tonight, then.'

'Great. Give my regards to your pals.' Books smiled. 'I think we'll get their undivided attention this time; take some samples.'

'Right.'

Books lowered his head, quickly absorbed in the screen of the computer, only looking up to listen to the hiss of the hydro slicer.

Nick and Heather walked out into the blazing late afternoon sun. The raw heat almost bowled them over. The liberty ship looked incongruous, anchored in the tiny harbor, almost filling the anchorage with its great bulk. The two yachts stood like beautifully finished jewels against its huge dark hull.

The heat was oppressive and stifling, with nowhere to go to find shade. The hum of the diesel engines filled the air like a Buddhist chant.

'I still think about it, you know,' Heather said, as she stepped into the beached Whaler. 'Yesterday in the blue hole. It was fascinating, very scary at the same time.'

Nick started the engine to take them to the liberty ship. 'Want to go back?'

'Maybe sometime, but not for a while. You didn't seem to be afraid; were you?'

'Nervous. Fear is a pretty rare thing with me now. I guess I've been scared so many times it's scared some of the fear out of me. When things are totally out of my control and I can't see any way out, that's when I start to worry.'

Nick nudged the Whaler up against the gangplank of the liberty ship and tied it off. They made their way to the galley. It was air conditioned and fully stocked. They poured coffee and sat at the galley table.

'You getting scared?' Nick asked.

'Yes. Maybe it's like you say; I feel it's all beginning to get out of control.'

'What did you expect?'

'I don't know what I expected. I didn't give it a lot of thought. I just did it.'

'You want out?' Nick asked, his mind racing: maybe if Heather would give it up now they could stop. He could tell Phillip and . . .

'No. I've thought about it and there have been moments when I wanted to run as fast as I could, but I'll see it through.'

'Why?'

'Personal reasons,' Heather said, rising to get more coffee.

'Sorry, I didn't mean to pry.'

'Coffee?' Heather asked. Nick nodded. 'You're not prying. It has to do with my father and the Zed Corporation. They did him wrong, real wrong.'

'Well, you've certainly devised a major payback scheme for them!'

'Nick, can I ask you something personal?'

'Sure, I just might not answer it. I might change the subject, like you do when I get personal.' He smiled.

'Is there a woman in your life?'

'No. There hasn't been a woman in my life for a couple of years. Something happened a few years ago that's taken me a long time to get over.'

'Bad love affair?'

'No. It had nothing to do with love. It was an incident in Africa that took away my interest in things for a while. But my interest is coming back,' he added lightly.

249

'I think you love Books, and that's why you're here.'

'Naw, it's just business. I'm out of dough and I don't want to get a straight job. I want to get rich quick.' He winked. 'That's what we're doing, isn't it, getting rich quick?'

'Who the hell knows what we're doing? I had no idea this operation was going to be on such a grand scale. I thought we'd just print a million or two.' Her hand shook slightly as she set her cup down on the galley table. 'Do you think Books is changing?' Heather turned her head away slightly so that Nick could not see the tears welling up in her eyes.

'Maybe. Maybe he's changing, but then again maybe he's just falling more into character, into his genetic pattern, his breeding.' Nick sighed. 'You never met the Duchess, did you? Now there's a piece of work.'

'Books' mother?'

'Yeah. I was there when she found out her husband was missing and presumed dead. It was in Miami, a wet stormy day, years ago; there had been two bad accidents on board their sailing yacht. She wanted all the details, the facts. It was an accident partially caused by human error, Books' error. But he was young, inexperienced; it could have happened to anyone.

'After she interviewed the crew she came back to Books and just looked at him with that cold stare, banker's blood we used to call it – comes from turning people down all the time. Anyway, she just stood there staring at Books, didn't put her arms round him or cry or say one goddamn word, just stood there looking at him as if to say . . .' Nick got up. 'Shit, I could use a drink.' He walked over to the liquor cabinet. 'You look like you could use one, too.'

'Yes, thanks,' she said. 'As if to say what, Nick?'

'Nothing. I'm way out of line here; I have no business even discussing these things with you. They're very personal. Books should be telling you, not me.' He dug out a lime and cut it into quarters in two strokes.

'Please tell me. What was her message to him?'

'Well, you have to know the family. The Duchess really loved her husband and maybe she couldn't love anyone else. She's not very maternal. I think she only had a child to please Big Books and when Big Books was taken away she blamed . . . oh shit. I don't know, let's drop it.' He handed her a vodka with tonic and lime.

'Tell me how she looked at Books that day. What was she trying to tell him?' Heather persisted.

Nick stared at her for a second, sipped his drink and looked away out through the porthole at a flock of circling seagulls. They were waiting for the nighttime offal that would draw the sharks. In the meantime, they were dining off a school of trapped bait in the harbor.

Nick remembered the Duchess standing outside of Phillip's hospital room, her hands on her hips, her eyes dead, her lips tight with anger.

Nick spoke to Heather without turning his head from the porthole: 'She looked at Books as if to say: why wasn't it you, why wasn't it you who got swept off the deck!'

Tuesday night 9:00
NEW YORK CITY

Don Saverese sat at his highly-polished mahogany desk. He looked diminutive in the large high-backed desk chair, his white hair contrasting against the smooth black leather. But his eyes were never still; they watched every move that Nick made as he carefully unwrapped three shrink-wrapped packages of crisp new bills: twenties, fifties, and hundreds – five hundred individual bills of each denomination; a total of eighty-five thousand dollars.

251

High-intensity bulbs had been placed in swing-arm lamps that were secured to the Don's desk, and magnifying glasses were laid out under the lights.

The Don stood and walked over to the one-way dark glass that allowed him to look down at the showroom. The cars glistened in the lights below. The dealership had closed two hours before. He checked to make sure that his men were stationed in every important corner of the dealership; additional men had been placed outside on the street.

The Don had agreed to examine the money personally, after he had spoken at length to Bruno Pugliese. Bruno had informed him that the money was so good that he wasn't sure it wasn't real, a trick perhaps, to get them to think that the remainder of the shipment would be as good, a trick to steal the gold. But the Don said he had known Nick a long time and did not think him foolish enough to try such a stupid thing.

The Don let his eyes caress the Ferraris, Maseratis, and Alfa Romeos for a moment. Then he turned and walked back to his desk and Carmine Calabrese, who was waiting.

The Don had brought Carmine Calabrese in from Detroit. He was a retired counterfeiter who had spent ten years in Leavenworth on a fifty-year sentence for counterfeiting US Savings bonds and corporate bearer bonds. During his imprisonment, all the families had taken care of him. Carmine's currency and bond counterfeits had made them over ten million dollars in five short years: two million dollars had been laid aside for Carmine in trust. Don Saverese had held the money and invested it wisely. Carmine received three million in cash the day after he left Leavenworth prison.

He was in his late sixties, and had hated prison. He would have preferred the ten years of freedom to the three million dollars the Don had presented him with, but he had never mentioned that to anyone.

Carmine turned on the high-intensity lamps and picked up a magnifying glass. He examined more than fifty bills, comparing them to real bills that the Don had provided.

After twenty minutes Carmine put the glass down and finally spoke.

' 'Scuse me for being so long but I had to be sure,' he said to Nick. Smiling, he picked up a hundred-dollar bill and waved it at the Don. '*Multo bene, multo bene. Bellissimo.* The very best I have ever seen. They are perfect.' Carmine shrugged at the Don. 'I can say no more. The paper is *perfecto.* I don't know how they achieved the paper, but it is excellent.'

Carmine put the bills down on the desk, placed his hand on Nick's arm and looked into his eyes. 'You have done well. I do not know how you got the plates so perfect and the number sequences – each bill different. If it is you who built these plates then you are a real smart boy; I tip my hat to you.'

Nick thought of Heather, sitting with her black bandanna wrapped round her forehead, concentrating on the keyboard of the computer, lost in her own world of microchips; talking to the computer in a language that was totally foreign to him; talking as if she and the computer were of one mind. He wondered what Carmine Calabrese would have thought if he knew the genius behind these bills was a woman.

Carmine continued, 'The Federal people, they will be very upset. They hate it most of all when people try to make their puny paper money. And they have much power.' Carmine turned to bow at Don Saverese, who remained seated. 'With respect, Don Saverese, you also have great power, but this will incense them beyond what has ever happened before.' Then he took one of Nick's hands in both of his. 'You look like a nice young man, and you should know that life is precious and the money is not what gives us the life; we give the money life – it is only paper before we bless it with life. *Capisce?*'

Nick smiled at the old man, squeezed his hands, and said, '*Grazie.*'

'I know you are being polite, humoring an old man. Young

men and women do not listen. But you will see I'm right. There is evil in the money, it triggers greed: too much money and men will do their worst, not their best. I know.'

The Don rose from his seat and stood facing Carmine. It ended all further conversation. He placed the miniature Ferrari car he had been holding in his hand on top of the desk and flicked it with his fingertip; it sped over the twenties, fifties and hundreds. Nick caught it in the palm of his hand as it shot off the edge of the desk.

'Nice catch, Nick,' the Don said as he circled the desk to put his arm round the shoulders of Carmine Calabrese and walk him to the office door. Two family members who were guarding the door stepped aside to let the Don pass. '*Grazie*, Carmine, your opinion is most valued. The favor you have done us today will not be forgotten.'

'It is nothing, Don Saverese, a trifle. If there is anything further I can do, please call.' One of the bodyguards reached over and opened the door to let Carmine pass. He stopped, turned, and looked at Nick. 'I hope you heed me, young man. You are entering a dangerous land in what you are trying to do; you stand on shaky ground.'

After Carmine had left, the Don turned to the bodyguards. 'You men will please excuse us,' he said in Sicilian. 'Bruno, not you, you will please stay and join us.' Bruno Pugliese sat down in a chair in front of the Don's desk.

'These bills look good. The paper looks good. The money comes from the shredded paper that you bought from us, doesn't it? Those barges that we loaded for you, they had a successful journey? No problem with Griselda? Griselda, she hit us hard in New Jersey.'

The Don doesn't miss a trick, Nick thought. 'We did fine. We'll be ready to ship by Monday of next week.'

'How much?' Bruno asked.

'Five hundred million in hundreds, fifties and twenties.'

'That makes a hundred and twenty-five million in gold payment from us,' the Don said from his high-backed chair.

'We must lay out a lot of money for the gold, a lot of our own cash.'

'You should only have to do it once. You don't have to discount our paper to pass it,' Nick countered.

The Don spun the wheels on his miniature Ferrari. He knew that he could pass off the money, dollar for dollar, in his many legitimate businesses: the casinos, the car dealerships, the laundries where cash could disappear into the purchase of capital equipment or for inventory. The five hundred million would go right into equity in the many businesses he controlled – not to mention the street action. The street would be a bonanza: loan-sharking, gambling, drugs, the numbers, necessary bribes and payoffs. The Don's mind whirled with the possibilities that this beautiful crisp new money presented. But he showed no emotion; he must be careful how he involved the other families, how he explained the source of this money, if he explained it at all. 'Nick, you put a great strain on my cash to buy the gold. It will mean I take a lot of my reserve and commit it.'

Nick knew the Don was just whining a little, telling him how hard he was working for his end of the deal.

'How youse planning to swap the cash for da gold?' Bruno asked.

'At sea next Monday.'

'Where?' the Don asked.

'Smith Shoals, just west of Key West. You'll need two shrimp boats. We'll be in fifty-foot Magnums. We can make the transfer in twenty minutes.'

'Won't it look too obvious?' Bruno asked.

'No. Smith Shoals is where the shrimpers anchor every morning after a night's trawl in the Dry Tortugas. Have your people pack ice and shrimp in the hold on top of the gold, then the money, to throw the Customs heat lasers off the track. The money will be shrink-wrapped to protect it from the elements.'

'Sounds too easy,' Bruno mumbled. 'They got lotsa drug

gadgets down there to pick up the dopers. We know that for a fact, don't we, Don Saverese?'

'Yes, Bruno,' the Don confirmed, looking over at Nick. 'Drugs, yes; cash, no.' Nick smiled. 'Sniffer dogs, low-level radar, laser beams to check on the holds of the shrimp boats to see if they are loaded with ice. I know how all that works. I used to sell a lot of that high-tech hardware, but no one is looking for paper.'

'How do we check da cash, see if it's da real thing?' Bruno asked.

'Random samples, from any part of the load, as many as you want. The money will be packed in quarter-million-dollar lots, no matter what the denomination. Bring experts like Mr Calabrese. But it must be done quickly. We don't want those Magnums hanging around the shrimp boats for more than twenty minutes; that would cause suspicion.'

'We don't want no rush job. Dis is a lot of gold we're talkin' here,' Bruno said.

'And our cash,' Nick snapped. 'Each load of cash you take out of the Magnums, you return a load of gold. The knife cuts both ways, Bruno, so don't give me a lot of shit here. This is a good deal for both of us.'

'Please, Nick,' the Don intervened. 'Bruno is only concerned about the family's best interest. He means nothing personal.'

Nick looked at Bruno. He wasn't so sure. He turned to the Don. 'Well, are we on?'

'Yes. We will try it just as you say.' The Don nodded. 'By the way, Nick, how much does one hundred and twenty-five million in gold weigh?'

Nick paused for a second as he made the calculation in his head. 'Fifteen thousand six hundred and twenty-five pounds at the current price of five hundred dollars an ounce.'

'Seven and a half tons,' the Don said, trying to imagine that much gold in one pile. 'So, if there is no more business, perhaps we can all go to the club for some dinner.'

'That would be nice,' Nick said.

'Good, we will have a fine dinner. We deserve it after this meeting.' The Don reached into his desk and extracted a full bottle of Sambuca and three aperitif glasses. He carefully filled each glass with the sweet clear liquid. He had a small white sack filled with coffee beans in his top drawer. He plopped three beans into each glass. 'Three beans for good luck, a week tomorrow.' The Don raised his glass. 'Let's hope we all get what we want.'

The Don locked his desk, leaving the Sambuca bottle and three glasses on his credenza. He walked over to the one-way glass overlooking the showroom and looked down on the shiny cars below, motioning for Nick to join him.

'Beauties, no?'

'Yes. They are beautiful.'

'Nick, you are a clever fellow. I think in the long run you will come out better than me on this business.'

'How so?'

'Well, you get the gold and we get the cash.'

'Yes.'

'Well, the more gold we collect off the streets, the scarcer it becomes, so the price will rise, and the gold you have received from us will become increasingly more valuable. Is this not so?'

'Yes. I think that's how it works, but you get instant use of the cash and will wind up buying back the gold you give us with our own money. Is this not so?'

'This is possible; everyone benefits. That is the basis of a good deal. But somehow, I like the idea of the gold better than the paper.' The Don smiled a benign smile at Nick and flipped off the lights on the showroom floor, casting the Ferraris, Maseratis and Alfa Romeos into a black void.

Wednesday evening 5:00
CAY SAL BANK, BAHAMAS

Heather sat on the end of the dock peering through the infrared scope of an M-16 automatic rifle. The scope gave her twenty times normal night-vision, but she felt uncomfortable with the weapon. She laid the rifle down on the wooden planks and rubbed her eyes with the palms of her hands.

She cradled her head in her knees and rocked back and forth, trying to relax, trying to rock away her fear. She wished that Nick was back from New York, back on the island; she needed someone to talk to, and Books wasn't interested in anything except the Black Box and the money they were producing. They had gone out together to feed the sharks at twilight, saying nothing of consequence to each other during the entire operation. She felt like a stranger to him, someone to whom he showed perfect manners, no more. She couldn't talk to him about what was on her mind.

The boards of the dock creaked and Heather turned round expecting to see Books, but it was Percival. He was carrying two long-necked Budweiser beer bottles. He sat down next to her, letting his spidery legs dangle over the end of the dock, his feet splashing in the water.

'Real fragrant, ain't it? Phewww!' Percival held his nose and handed her a beer. He wiggled his toes in the warm water.

'Percival, I wouldn't dangle my toes in there.'

'Oh shit, I forgot. They don't come in this close, do they?' he asked, raising his feet out of the water and pulling the rifle toward him.

'Not yet. But Nick says they will, after they get to feel comfortable.'

'Well, if Nick says it, it's probably true.' Percival clinked

258

the neck of his beer bottle against hers and smiled. 'One thing about Nick, he's di-fucking-rect and usually right.'

'You've known them both a long time, haven't you, Perce?'

'Yeah, since school. Nick came into the school on an athletic scholarship; he wasn't born to the high life like most of the boys in that joint, but everyone liked him. Something about him gets people to trust him.'

'Maybe because he's trustworthy. What about you, Perce? Were you born to the manor?'

'Yeah, sort of, a family full of chemicals and paper. Can you believe it? And now look what I'm doing: I'm a professional black sheep; I could've written the black sheep manual. My folks still love me, take all my calls, tell me I can stay with them, tell me what great potential I have. But they won't let me work in any of the fucking plants or mills, and they won't lend me one thin dollar. So I guess I'll have to make my own dollars, won't I? I mean make your dollars,' he winked.

'Tell me about them, Books and Nick, when they were young,' Heather said.

'The three of them were thicker than bullshit at a sales convention, until that accident.'

'The three of them?'

'Yeah, Nick, Books, and Phillip Sturges, thick as thieves.'

'Phillip Sturges? The Phillip Sturges who's head of the Fed?'

'Yeah, the very same; they fell apart after the accident on the boat. Phillip got hurt bad and the rumor was that he blamed it on Books, that it was because Books had fucked up at the controls, or something like that. I don't sail, so I can't say for sure. They didn't talk much about it, but they drifted apart after the accident. It was their last year of school anyway.'

Heather needed a distraction; she leaned over and picked up the rifle and tried to unscrew the infrared scope. She noticed that her hands were shaking. She dropped the rifle and supported her hands on her knees and closed both her eyes. So Phillip was the other 'accident' that day, the day Nick had told her about. Poor Books! Poor all of them.

'Look, I'm sorry. I thought you knew about Phillip Sturges. Shit, I've said too much, I guess. I'm real sorry. It was such a big thing in their lives, I thought for sure Books would have said something. Shit, I can't do anything right, can I?'

Heather patted Percival on the knee. 'It's fine, Perce, it really is. Books keeps a lot to himself. It's his business, anyway.'

'Yeah, well I've already fucked things up enough. Story of my life. I think I'll hit the road before I do any more damage.' Percival stood up.

'No, Perce, please sit down. I like the company. It's okay, it really is,' Heather said, and began to cry, her face in her hands, her back shaking with the sobs.

'Jesus, I'm sorry, Heather. I had no idea this business about Phillip Sturges would –'

'It has nothing to do with Phillip Sturges,' Heather managed between sobs, wiping her nose with the back of her hand, and, at the same time, brushing away the tears. 'It's the whole thing, Perce. I'm scared. It keeps escalating, and I don't like being trapped here all the time, not being able to go anywhere.'

'Well, maybe we could build a mall or something, and then you could go shopping,' he said, smiling. 'It works with all the women in my family. When they get depressed, they go shopping.'

'Jesus, Perce, you're weird, but I like you,' Heather screwed up one side of her full mouth in an attempt to smile.

'What's not to like?' He gave her a hug. 'I know how powerful Books is; shit, look at what he's done so far. He's got you, me, and Nick to follow him in this preposterous plan of his. He's always been able to get people to do what he wanted them to do, but he's never been exactly right, not since that accident. That was when he lost his father. And they were close.'

'Nick told me about Books' father,' Heather said, and looked out to sea, realizing how little Books had ever confided in her. She only knew what he wanted to tell her. But she knew what it felt like to lose your father.

Percival pointed out to sea. 'What's that?'

She stared at the blackness in silence for a minute and said nothing. She saw a ripple on the surface, then it disappeared.

'It's them, I think,' she said, checking her watch. She picked up the M-16 and looked through the night scope. 'They come every night about the same time.'

Percival yanked his feet up onto the dock. 'No shit, really?'

'Time for hors d'oeuvres,' Heather whispered as she picked up the first dorsal fin in the cross-hairs of the scope. The fin was about four hundred yards away, a tiny triangular black sail cutting the water as the shark skimmed through the offal floating on the surface. A second fin appeared, then a third and fourth, until there were dozens of dorsal fins criss-crossing, all swimming at the same speed as they quietly ate what had been offered to them.

'A gruesome ballet going on out there; wanna see, Perce?'

'No. I'll have bad enough dreams as it is. Can you shoot that thing?' he asked, pointing at the rifle.

'Yes, but it scares me.'

'This gives me the creeps,' Perce said. The sharks were gliding, moving together now in a large, ever-increasing circle, getting nearer to the dock. Perce stood up. 'I have to go and check on my alchemy. I'm over watching these beasts. I'm bleaching some paper. Wanna come?'

'No. No, thanks,' Heather said, still looking through the nightscope, fascinated by the sharks. 'Maybe later.'

'I'll be there.' Perce walked down the dock. Heather continued to stare at the schooling sharks. She spotted the surfacing head of one of them in the cross-hairs of the sight as it straggled in close to the pier, less than twenty feet away.

261

On impulse, she pulled the trigger. The safety was on; nothing happened. She slipped the safety off and pulled again. She heard the dry click of the firing pin. It startled her back to reality. What if there had been a bullet in the chamber?

She began to shake. She placed the rifle on the dock. 'All this crying and trembling, I must get a grip on myself,' she mumbled. But it didn't stop her tears. 'God, I miss you, Dad!'

Wednesday night 8:30
NEW YORK CITY

Nick stood in the alley across from the Federal Reserve building, waiting in the darkness, staring up at the single light in the fourth-floor corner office, Phillip's apartment.

The floor below was fully lit. Nick could see the forms of the nightshift people as they scurried about, counting money, shredding defective bills, doing their part to keep the country's cash supply up to date.

Nick pulled up his collar as he stepped out of the shadows and under a street light to a public phone.

'Hello,' Phillip said into the red phone.

'I need to see you.'

'Where?' Phillip recognized the voice.

'Pier 48, right next to the Seaport, in thirty minutes.'

'Okay.' The line went dead.

Nick eased back into the shadows and watched the office, thinking about what he wanted to say to Phillip. A picture of Heather flashed through his mind, and with that he thought that he might not see her again, ever, depending on the outcome of his conversation with Phillip.

Nick didn't wait for Phillip's office light to go dark. He started to walk to the Seaport. It would take him less than five minutes at a good pace. The financial district was deserted and quiet. The only sound was the echo of his footsteps reverberating off the monolithic glass and concrete structures, structures that seemed to rise out of the bedrock as if they had been propelled from the center of the earth. He craned his neck to the side so he could let his eyes travel up the tall spires of office towers. There was no moon. It made the buildings look as if there was no end to them; they were one with the dark sky.

The Seaport was bustling with life; the restaurants and bars were packed with trendy Manhattanites and tardy stockbrokers who had missed their early trains to Connecticut and Long Island.

He checked his watch as the Seaport lights disappeared behind him, and the Fulton Fish Market came into view. There was plenty of time; he slowed to a stroll. Men and women were cleaning and setting up for business, which would start to happen around one in the morning when the buyers would arrive from the restaurants and supermarkets to choose the best fish.

An old Chinese woman stood in a doorway, a limp cigarette hanging out of her wrinkled mouth, broom in her hands. A single bare bulb above her head shone on her smooth grey hair and wrinkled face. She gave Nick a weary, toothless grin and a slight wave with her cigarette, the ash dropping as she took it from her mouth. Nick nodded back and smiled.

Pier 48 loomed up directly ahead of him. It was one of the last piers to be renovated. Still under construction, it was covered with scaffolding and heavy tarpaulins. Nick found the darkest corner and eased into the blackness. Out of habit, he checked his escape route and possible positions where anyone could observe him or cut him off.

He saw the armored truck waddling down Fulton Street toward him like a sluggish beetle. It was the same vehicle that had brought Phillip to meet him at the Staten Island ferry. Nick watched from the darkness as it pulled to a creaking halt and two men in the front seat got out to open the back door and monitor the lowering of the hydraulic gate. Nick could see Phillip's silhouette clearly in the street light, the sturdy upper body compacted and contained in the squat steel wheelchair. He saw him wave the men back to their seats in the front of the truck as he started to propel himself down the lonely sidewalk toward Pier 48.

When Phillip got to the pier, he spun his chair round in a circle, bewildered, looking for Nick.

Nick stepped out of his corner but stayed in the shadows.

'Phillip,' he said quietly, 'over here. Watch the loose boards.'

'You pick the weirdest goddamn places to meet,' Phillip said, extending his hand. Nick shook it. 'It's good to see you, Nick. You're sure a man of few words. I thought you were going to stay in touch?'

'I'm in touch now,' Nick said, tugging on his collar, leaning against a wooden railing. Phillip wheeled closer.

'Don't get crusty, Nick, please.'

'Phillip, I want out of this thing. I told you before, I won't be an informer. I don't care what the justification is; a spy is a spy. I lose on both sides. I'm disloyal to Books, and how can I ever look you in the eye again after being a Judas. I'm fucked. I just want out, and I want out now.'

Phillip said nothing. He looked over Nick's shoulder as the East River rolled by on its way to the ocean. The water was black and glossy, broken only by the odd piece of debris being carried by the strong current to an unknown destination.

'Nick, I'm sorry you're boxed in, but so am I, and so is Books. You know what's happening and I need you to keep me informed. Does he have any paper? Is he still in business? How is the island armed? How does he plan to distribute the paper? The Secret Service thinks he's out of business because

264

they burned the mill. I'm not so sure. I need information, Nick.'

'I'm sure you do, but it ain't coming from me. I'm sorry, but that's my final decision. I'm telling Books the same thing.'

'I'm afraid not, Nick. I need your help. We're not going to let him distribute that paper.' Phillip wheeled even closer, almost touching Nick's shin with the foot of his chair, crowding him. His voice was just audible over the quiet rush of the river. 'There's something that's come up on you, Nick, in the Secret Service investigation. It concerns a file from two years ago.'

'What are you talking about?'

'Paris. Sean O'Reilly. A scene between you and him in The Last Legionnaire private club in Paris. It concerns murder, Nick.'

Nick spun round and kicked the center board out of the railing he was leaning on, sending it flying into the East River. The doors of the armoured car swung open and two men leaped out.

Nick hissed at his old friend, 'You motherfucker! You think you can use that to get me to do what you want! Go fuck yourself, Phillip. There wouldn't have been any investigation of a murder in Paris if I wasn't involved in this thing trying to help you. Fuck you!' Nick put his foot on Phillip's footrest and pushed, sending him wheeling backwards, straight at the two running security men.

They stopped to catch the reeling wheelchair and to secure Phillip as Nick took off down the wharf. They looked at each other and at Phillip as if to ask him what to do.

'One of you stay here, the other go get him,' Phillip said, pointing at Nick's disappearing figure in the darkness. 'Bring him back, but no shooting. I don't want him hurt. For Christ's sake, move!'

Nick looked back. One guard was coming after him. Nick

spotted a Dempsey Dumpster and ran for it, hiding in the shadows behind the steel container.

As the Federal Reserve guard flashed by the dumpster, Nick called out, 'Hey!' The man stopped and spun. Nick hit him with the side of his hand. The man flew, tumbling, along the wooden planks onto Pier 47. Nick was on him with both knees in the man's chest. He clipped him once in the chin. It dazed the guard. Nick searched the man and found a police .38 and a leather sap filled with shot. He tapped the man on the temple with the sap and felt him go limp. He threw the sap and the pistol into the river and took off again, crossing Fulton Street into the canyons of Manhattan, where he felt safe and at home.

An hour later Don Saverese had sent a private car for him that took him over the George Washington Bridge to Teterborough Airport in New Jersey and a waiting chartered Learjet that was routed and cleared for Miami.

Nick sat alone in the salon of the Lear as it soared out over the New Jersey Meadowlands, drinking a Scotch on the rocks, thinking. 'How could he have found out about Paris? How could he misread me so badly and expect that I would yield to a form of blackmail? Phillip isn't stupid; why would he use such tactics? What fucking next?'

Thursday morning 10:00
ATLANTIC OCEAN

Ernie Sands was in the lead sub only eight miles from the Cay Sal Bank. They had been travelling in convoy on the surface for most of their trip, cruising at a steady twenty knots, only occasionally doing test dives to depths of no more than one hundred feet. The original batteries had been completely overhauled and were operational on all three subs; if necessary, they would be able to stay underwater for up to twenty-four hours.

Ernie stood in the conning tower and wondered how they looked from the air, all in a chain. Each sub had been painted black with mako shark insignias on the conning towers, large white letters on the side said: Mako Marine Institute.

Ernie felt better than he had in five years; the salt air was balm to his cancer-ridden lungs. He could almost take a series of long deep breaths without coughing.

He pulled his black watch cap down tight over his ears and shoved his taped glasses up the bridge of his nose. He had been instructed not to make any radio contact with the island, just to follow the chart and the hand-drawn map of the channel that Nick had given to him.

Ernie called his crew the 'over-the-hill gang'. There were twelve men to crew the three subs, not one of them under sixty. But all of them had seen action and had proven themselves in battle against the Germans or the Japanese. To a man, they were anxious for some excitement in their lives, and the chance to make a last whack of dough. Each had received a ten-thousand-dollar bonus for signing, in addition to their salary of ten thousand dollars a month and a promise of one hundred thousand dollars in cash when their mission was completed. Ernie had hand-picked every man and interviewed them in depth before accepting them.

They had been told that they would have no further contact with friends or family for at least ninety days from the time they set sail. And each man had manufactured a plausible story for his absence; every story had been personally approved by Ernie.

They were on the far side of the Gulf Stream, staying just clear of the shallows of the Great Bahama Bank.

Ernie turned and looked at the two following subs as they knifed through the water, the black bows disappearing in the sea only to rise again like porpoises. He waved at the other men in the trailing submarines and they waved back. These men were proven warriors, reactivated, recycled warriors, with a new sense of their own worth.

Ernie felt the steady smooth hum of the diesel engines through the steel floor of the conning tower; he put his hand on the shoulder of Barney O'Brien, the 68-year-old chief engineer, and gave his shoulder a hard squeeze, nodding his approval. Barney smiled, and nodded back.

Nick had explained what they would be doing: transporting counterfeit money and trading it for gold on the high seas. Ernie had to be very careful with the selection of the men; he had to make sure that no crew member had any deep-seated moral objection with the selling and transporting of counterfeit money, notably US money.

Ernie slipped below, sliding easily down the steel ladder. He walked towards the bow. Nick would be happy with the way they had redesigned the subs. Now they were just hollow tubes that were capable of moving below the surface. The welders had sealed the torpedo tubes against the sea, and torched out the cylinders that held the torpedoes, leaving the hull clear, the ribs exposed; the crew bunks had also been removed, except for the four that were required by the current crew.

Ernie stood in the bow, his arms outstretched, holding on to the steel ribs to support himself, as the boat plunged through the waves in a steady rhythm. He was facing the stern and could see along the entire length of the sub. The exposed pipes and tubing gave the boat a surreal look, like a skeletal, underwater spaceship.

Ernie pondered about what might have happened on the *Pilotfish* during the war and the ten years it was in active service.

'Land ho, Captain! Cay Sal Bank dead ahead,' Barney called, his head sticking below the conning tower.

His words echoed off the steel walls, sending a chill down

Ernie's back. 'I'm on my way, Barney,' he yelled, his own words reverberating in his ears. 'This would make one hell of a big casket,' he mumbled to himself as he took one last look before he climbed the steel ladder to the conning tower.

Thursday midday 11:30 UNITED STATES

Don Saverese was talking in a thick Sicilian dialect on the phone. He completed the phone call and hung up. It was the last of five calls he had made that morning to the heads of the families in Detroit, Chicago, Los Angeles, Miami, and Newark. He had given very specific instructions on how they were to gather gold for him. Each family was to acquire twenty million dollars' worth at current market prices.

It was a practice run, and if the currency supplied was as good as the samples he had seen, it could be the biggest score of his life, a bigger profit than the dope, the gambling and the vice all put together.

Carefully, he wrote out a checklist of details on his desk pad. He had completed them all, except a few minor things that he would take care of in the morning. But something was gnawing away inside him about this deal, and he didn't know what it was. The Don had learned long ago not to dispel these feelings, but to follow them. He knew he had a fine intellect, but it was his ability to recognize and follow his instincts and feelings that had kept him alive and prosperous. He disliked this Books St John, but it was more than that; there was something essential, something innate in the deal itself that upset him.

He dropped the tiny Ferrari on his desktop and sat in his

office with only the desk lamp on. He absently twirled his wedding ring in small circles and thought of Angela, his wife of forty years. He looked at his finger. It was the same plain gold band that he had worn since Father Giorgio had married them in St Anthony's Church on Thompson Street forty years ago.

Then it hit him why he didn't like the deal. It was the gold. There was something unnatural about giving gold for paper, giving this precious metal and receiving paper in return.

He squeezed his ring tightly and closed his eyes. Men trusted gold. Something about its color, its timelessness, and its scarcity made it the only medium of barter that had been acceptable to all civilizations over the centuries. Even the murderous barbarians took the yellow metal for trade or plunder: Jean La Fitte the pirate, Gengis Khan, Attila the Hun. The evil Hitler had it extracted from the teeth of the prisoners he killed, and then hoarded the barbarous metal deep in the belly of South America.

It was probably the same gold used over and over, since so little of it had been mined over the centuries. His little wedding band could have once been part of a queen's chalice, inset with jewels. Gold, loved and hoarded the world over. He did not want to give up the precious metal, but what could he do? There was honor involved here. The Family kept its word.

The Don turned out the light on his desk and sat quietly in the darkness, thinking. If he was patient, the solution would come to him.

He turned the desk lamp back on and smiled to himself. He was calmer now; a plan was forming in his head that would satisfy his instincts and not dishonor the family.

He picked up the tiny Ferrari and gently spun the ball-bearing wheels, one at a time, until they were all humming.

Nick wiped the back of his hand on the window to clear the condensation. It felt cool on his warm skin. The Chalk's plane from Miami was having trouble with the cabin air-conditioning unit, but Nick had accepted the plane as it was in his haste to get back to the island. He had spent the day at a motel on Miami Beach, thinking. Now it was time to tell them.

He looked through the plane's porthole, down at the completed buildings; the covered canopy joining the warehouse to the main building had been erected. The liberty ship sat serenely at anchor in the tiny harbor like the hulk of a tired tramp steamer that belonged in some romantic port in the South Pacific. Three submarines were moored to its stern in a daisy chain that shifted with the tide.

Nick smiled to himself when he saw that Ernie Sands had made it. It was the first time he had smiled since he left New York.

Nick banged on the pilot's door and asked him to circle the island once more. He needed a little extra time before he saw Books and Heather. The pilot started a second wide, sweeping circle round the island, one wing dipped lower than the other so Nick could see better.

But he saw Phillip, barreling backwards, rolling away from him, helpless, as he kicked the wheelchair; a look of shock was in Phillip's eyes as he groped for the brake handle. How could he have done that to Phillip? What was happening to him?

Phillip! What the hell are you doing to me? What is really going on? Nick gripped the arm rests and squeezed the well-worn padding. He hated to be trapped, cornered, and that's just what Phillip had done. He was snookered, boxed in from every angle, with Phillip threatening to use Sean O'Reilly's death. Even so, how could he kick the wheelchair like that? He could have hurt Phillip. But Phillip was using him like a pawn, with no care for anything except stopping Books.

And Books was changing. The money was consuming his spirit, driving Heather away, maybe right into Nick's arms. And Nick was promoting it – falling in love with his best friend's girl. He had never admitted to himself until now that he might be falling in love with Heather.

'Fuck it all,' he said out loud. His life had been so simple: cruising the West Indies, living off the fish he caught, having only to haul the anchor to find a new home with no complications, no vulnerability. He put his head in his hands and squeezed the bridge of his nose, shaking his head from side to side.

He looked out of the window. He thought he saw lightning bolts of brown streaking across the white sandy bottom of the flats that surrounded the island, and wondered if the sharks were waiting for their dinner.

A school of leopard rays were cruising along in an extended V pattern, feeding off the bottom, heading up the channel to the harbor; they scattered like scared birds as the plane hit the water, skimming along on its pontoons into the harbor.

Percival was in the harbor doing small circles in the Whaler as he waited for the plane to land. He had one hand on the engine throttle, the other choking the long neck of a bottle of Budweiser.

Nick was disappointed that Heather had not come out to meet the plane.

He stepped off the pontoon into the Whaler and heard the voice of Ernie Sands calling to him from above, 'Hey, Nick! Whaddya think?' Ernie was standing in the conning tower of his sub, twenty yards away. He made a sweeping gesture towards the other two subs and smiled.

'Looking good! Do they work?'

'Is the Pope Polish?' Ernie yelled. 'Of course they work;

we're here, ain't we?' He flung his arms out to embrace the harbor.

'I'll see you in an hour in the galley of the liberty ship,' Nick yelled over the motors of the Chalk's plane, pointing at the liberty ship and signaling one hour with a finger up, then pointing to his watch.

'I'll see ya then.' Ernie gave a final wave and disappeared belowdecks.

'Perce, how are ya?'

'Overworked and overpaid! I'm good,' Percival said, stowing Nick's bag. 'Books is anxious to see you. He's been working like a Trojan. They've been in there night and day, knocking out the cash; still gives me the fucking goosebump willies to see all that legal tender. It might as well be stacks of toilet paper, it's coming out so fast and easy now.'

Percival twisted the throttle in his hand hard, causing the Whaler to rear up in the water like a wild stallion. Nick had to grab his bag to keep it from falling overboard.

'Sorry, Nick, I'm still having a little problem with this throttle.'

'No shit, Perce. I would never have guessed.' Nick smiled. 'At least you stay consistent.'

When they hit the beach, Nick left Percival to secure the Whaler and walked alone into the main building; he saw three pallets stacked high with shrink-wrapped packets of currency. Heather had her head down at the computer console and didn't notice him walk in.

'Seven hundred and fifty million and growing,' Books yelled at Nick from the far end of the warehouse where he had just stacked a freshly-cut two hundred and fifty thousand dollar packet of cash on a pallet. 'That's what we're up to. How was the trip?'

'Fine. They're ready when you are. Hello, Heather.' Nick approached the console; she looked up almost dreamy-eyed, in a trance.

'Nick.' She leaped up and planted a kiss on his cheek and

gave him a squeeze. 'Missed you,' she whispered in his ear.

'Me, too.'

'So what do you think, Nick?' Books asked, coming up to Nick and putting an arm round his shoulders.

'Looks fine,' Nick said, taking a fast glance around the room. The serpent-hiss of the hydro slicer broke the silence as it suddenly came to life, spitting water down at the sheets of currency, slicing smoothly through the one hundred sheets of paper that were stacked on the gurney.

'Not bad, huh?' Books said, grinning as he slid a second gurney in to replace the one he was taking. He pushed the full gurney over to the shrink-wrapper and loaded the machine. 'I love this work, Nick. I'm inspired.' He winked, moving to the other end of the wrapping machine and collecting the finished packets. 'I like hundreds the best, the packets are a lot smaller. The work goes faster – more satisfying.'

Percival came banging into the building, letting the door slam against the outside wall before he shut it. He moved over to the shrink-wrapping assembly line.

Books left the packets and turned to Nick. 'So tell me all. How'd you get along with the wise guys?'

'The wise guys are ready. They send their best to you.'

'I'll bet they do.' Books rolled his eyes.

Heather turned and went back to work at the console. She wanted to know nothing of 'wise guys'.

'Their shipment will be ready by tomorrow,' Books added.

'I need to talk to you both,' Nick said. 'In private.'

'Trouble?' Books asked.

Heather looked up from the computer console, staring at Nick.

'Trouble,' Nick answered, nodding his head.

'No time like the present. Let's go talk on *Desperado*. Hey, Perce, how about looking after things while we're gone. If you have any problems just shut things off and call us.'

'If you can find your way around this machinery I can find mine, for sure. See ya. Besides, if it's trouble Nick's talkin' about, I don't wanna hear it.' He smiled, picking up finished packets of money and stacking them in a wheelbarrow.

They rode out to *Desperado* in silence. Books poured everyone a drink, and they sat down at the galley table, waiting for Nick.

Nick took a deep breath and began. 'I didn't just come to La Fitte Cove because you sent me a telegram, Books; I was sent.' Nick paused to let his words sink in and continued, 'Phillip came to see me in Martinique and told me what you had done, that you had stolen the Black Box.'

'Phillip Sturges?' Heather asked.

'Yes,' Nick answered. 'Phillip asked me to come and join you, to try to persuade you to stop.'

'And to keep him informed,' Books added.

'Yes. I told him I couldn't do it, but he convinced me you were in lethal danger, and I could maybe keep you from being hurt real bad, work out some kind of a deal.'

'Nick, please get to the bottom line.'

'The bottom line is that I saw Phillip in New York yesterday and I told him I was out. I couldn't carry on any more with the double-dealing. He tried to blackmail me with something in my past to keep me in your camp, keep the information coming.'

'I don't believe this,' Heather blurted.

'Let him finish. Go on, Nick. Tell us everything.'

'We got into quite a scene. I told him to fuck off. I was out and that was all there was to it. You know Phillip; he doesn't take no for an answer. Anyway, I'm screwed from both sides.'

'How much did you tell him?'

'Not much; I think he knew most of it through his own sources anyway.'

'Did you tell him about the mill?'

'How could I? You never told me.'

'I thought maybe I might have slipped up, and let something out.'

'You never mentioned it, Books.'

'Did you tell Phillip how we were going to distribute the money?'

'No. I was close to telling him, but I never did. I really told him very little; there wasn't much to tell him. You didn't tell me much until just recently.'

'The subs, the ordnance we purchased to defend the island, the Brotherhood or the Mafia, Percival doing the paper. Did you tell him any of that, Nick?'

'Don't cross-examine me, Books. The answer is *no*, I didn't tell him anything of importance. And don't ask me anything else. I didn't betray your operation. I'm not staying, Books. I just came back to tell you both. I'm going to leave tomorrow; I've had enough.'

Heather spoke, 'Christ, Nick, I thought . . . I thought we could depend on you. Oh shit, I don't know what I thought.' She got up and went to the porthole, looking out at nothing.

'Me neither,' Nick said. 'I don't know what I must have been thinking of when I saw Phillip and let him talk me into coming after you. They were still negotiable then.'

'They were negotiable? The Feds! That's a joke. They're going to be even more negotiable when this paper hits the street.'

'You may be right, Books. I hope so for your sake, for both your sakes.' Nick walked over and stood beside Heather. She had her back to both of them.

'I feel so stupid,' Heather said. 'Confused. You, of all people, Nick, I believed you were on our side.'

'He was. He certainly wasn't on their side.' Books went over and placed his arm round Nick's shoulders. 'Nick, I believe you when you say you told Phillip very little about our operation.'

'Honest people are honest all the time,' Heather blurted. 'Where does it end?' She looked out to sea, not expecting an answer.

Books went on, 'We're all tense. Let's calm down, and

think this through. Nick, tell us about the meeting with Don Saverese.'

'They accepted the samples, and only need forty-eight hours to assemble the gold. They have the exact co-ordinates of where to rendezvous, and the time; all that's required is one further brief message of confirmation and the date when you can deliver.'

A silence filled the room as they all pondered the magnitude of the first transaction: five hundred million in currency, one hundred and twenty-five million in gold; a king's ransom.

After a few seconds, Books spoke. 'Since they can be ready in forty-eight hours, we can move the rendezvous up. We'll do it from ninety-six hours from now. Nick, I need to say something to you and for you to listen without getting upset. Please don't respond, just think about it. It's shark feeding time in about ten minutes; why don't you think about what I'm going to say while you're feeding our watchdogs. Then we'll talk again.'

'Go ahead.'

'I heard what happened in Nigeria. Five million was what I heard you lost, almost your whole stash after you finished paying me off for your original stake. I heard it was a set-up and you got fucked by one of your competitors. You had just enough left to buy the boat and wander around the islands if you watched your pennies.'

Nick shifted his shoulders, uneasy.

'Nick, I'm sorry I have to go into this, but please hear me out. I'm satisfied that you did what you did out of friendship and not out of some venal motive. I'm also satisfied that you didn't give us up. Phillip would have tracked down most of the information on his own anyway, in time. I want you to stay. We need you, and I think you need us, especially now if you've managed to piss Phillip off.

'So I have an offer for you: two million in gold bullion in ninety days. You can leave any time you want after that with no hard feelings.'

Nick started to speak.

'No, Nick, please just think about it. I know that money has never been your prime motivation, but please just think about it. Go feed your sharks and give it some thought. Heather, do you agree?' Books asked.

'I do.'

Nick rose in silence and finished his drink. He stepped out on the deck of *Desperado* and into the final glow of the sun's rays before it sunk into the sea. He saw Ernie Sands with two of his old-timers on the bow of the *Pilotfish*. They were examining the anchor chain. Nick yelled at Ernie. 'I'm going to be late, meet me in two hours.'

'See ya then,' Ernie yelled back. He put an arm round the two men that were with him on the bow. 'I'm going to bring these two all-stars with me. They wanna meet you. I told them we were friends in the old days.'

'See ya.' Nick had to smile as they waved and dropped their heads back down again to examine the thick iron links of anchor chain.

The barrels of offal had already been loaded onto the back of a Magnum racer. Books and Percival, with advice from Barney, had modified the boat and built a proper cradle for the barrels so they would sit on the stern. All that was necessary was to push the barrel, and it swung out on a cantilever over the transom. With the lid removed, it could be tipped on its side to empty its smelly contents into the wake.

Nick started both engines and waited for them to warm up. The deep-throated noise and gurgling of the engines vibrated throughout the entire boat. He went to the stern and made sure that each of the four straight pipes that extended through the transom was emitting salt water, so critical to these high-powered engines.

Nick saw Heather running down the dock, slipping on her jacket as she ran. 'Nick, can I come? I'd like to talk, and I need a boat ride. I'd like to go out every night to feed the sharks. Can I come?'

'Jump in. We've only got about ten minutes before the sun sets.'

Heather released the dock lines and jumped in. She positioned herself in the navigator's chair. 'Whew, that stuff stinks! I think it's getting higher and higher.'

Nick eased the throttle into forward and they crept into the channel until they were positioned in the center. Then Nick pushed both throttles full forward. The bow jumped skyward for a second then settled down until they were finally on a plane. Halfway down the channel they swung left onto the flats. They were less than a mile onto them when Nick gave her the signal to dump the first barrel.

The roar of the engines and the work involved made it impossible to talk. Nick ran a continuous flat S pattern.

When all three barrels were empty, he slipped off the flats into the deep water of the Gulf Stream, where he released the barrels from the cradle. He watched them sink into the azure water; maybe they would make a habitat for the lobsters, he thought. He cut the engines and let the boat drift in the current.

The fast boat ride had cleared his mind and somehow lessened his anger. Heather sat on the engine box, her knees curled up under her chin, looking out off the now-empty stern.

The sun had set but the sky was still vibrant with the afterglow: iridescent pink, powder blue, purple, and red streaks filled the sky in a constantly changing pattern.

Nick had his arms folded on the top of the windshield as he looked across the bow, his mind awhirl with thoughts.

The boat was drifting in the Gulf Stream on the edge of the flats. Nick cupped his hands above his eyes to eliminate the afterglow that was still in the sky. The water was flat-calm with only a slight chop from the prevailing northeast trade winds that gently rocked the boat from side to side. He saw the first dorsal fin appear out of the corner of his eye as it slipped out of the Gulf Stream and up onto the flats.

The fin was followed closely by four more, the bold ones, from the school of hungry sharks that now waited every night in the Stream to come in and be fed at sunset.

Once the leaders moved, more sharks came pouring in out of the depths of the Gulf Stream; they reminded Nick of the rats he had seen running in packs in Africa, often fighting and killing each other.

'They scare me and fascinate me at the same time,' Heather said. She was standing in the bow with him now, also leaning with her arms folded on the windshield. 'I want to come out to see them whenever I can.' She pointed off about a hundred yards at eight more dorsal fins as they crossed over onto the flats. 'Do you think I'm perverse?'

'No. We're all fascinated by sharks.'

'Can we run up to the north, raise the outdrives, and just drift back right over them?'

Nick reached down and fired up both engines. Heather's ash-blonde hair flew straight back from the pressure of the wind. She looked like one of the wooden maidens that used to ride the bowsprit of sailing vessels. She didn't move, facing seaward, taking in the night air. He headed due north in the Stream, until he was about a mile above their previous position. He veered hard to the left and skimmed over onto the flats, plowing over a feeding school of sharks, surprising them, sending them scattering like a starburst. Nick cut both engines and the boat suddenly stopped and sank down to the painted waterline, giving them about a foot of clearance over the sandy bottom.

They drifted.

There were hundreds of dorsal fins cutting the surface, setting up an almost audible hiss as they cruised along, with occasional loud slurping noises as a single shark raised his mouth to the surface to engulf a fish head or the entire carcass of a filleted fish.

Heather moved closer beside Nick as the flats started to fill with hungry sharks. They heard a grating sound as one of the sharks scraped against the side of the drifting boat.

'Nick, do you think we can succeed with what we're planning?'

'Maybe. But you're going to make a lot of people angry; important, powerful people who have lots of resources at their fingertips.'

'I know, and I'm scared. But it's almost like it is with these sharks: I'm scared and fascinated at the same time. I never in my wildest dreams thought I'd be . . . Look!' Heather pointed at three sharks that had turned on each other, fighting over food; the water was boiling as they snapped and bit like a pack of wild dogs. Other sharks approached and circled the fighters, watching for weakness, but the fight ended as quickly as it had begun when two of them disappeared, their tails beating the shallow water. The flats were alive with cruising dorsal fins.

The boat came to an abrupt halt as it wedged onto a small sandbar. Nick went forward to the V locker and took out a paddle. He stuck its shovel end into the sand and pushed the stern free.

There was a sudden crack and Nick was jerked forward.

'Nick!' Heather yelled.

Nick flipped what was left of the paddle into the water; it was nothing but a jagged pole. A shark had bitten it in two.

Heather was shaking. Nick put his arm round her to calm her down.

'Violence is swift and final, Heather. You're in deep with this thing.'

'I know.' Heather replied, as her brain tried to comprehend everything. 'Nick, stay and help us. I don't care about what you just told us. I trust you. Please stay.'

Nick didn't answer. He turned his attention back to the swarming sharks. He could see the broken paddle in the moonlight floating on the surface of the water. They drifted in silence until they came to the thin channel that led to the harbor.

WEEK FOUR

WEEK FOUR

Monday dawn 6:00
SMITH SHOALS, GULF OF MEXICO

Nick was in the lead Magnum, pounding over the slight swell of the Northwest Channel. Ernie Sands followed in the second boat, Books in the third. Each of them had brought along a mate from the over-the-hill gang to help with the exchange. The Magnums were in a tight single file, riding in each other's wake where it was the smoothest. They had picked up the Sand Key light first, and followed the green triangles into the Northwest Channel.

Smith Shoals was located seven miles beyond the channel in the Gulf of Mexico. It was a safe haven for the Key West shrimp fleet when they returned from their nightly drags around the Dry Tortugas. Over eighty per cent of the entire United States shrimping fleet was based in Key West during October to May; seven to eight hundred shrimp boats all clustered in one small area made it difficult to pick out the *Laura B*.

After a night of trawling for the 'roach of the deep', the shrimpers pulled into the shelter of Smith Shoals to sort out their catch and to sleep. The early dawn hours were spent separating the mountain of sea life that had been collected in the trawl nets and then dumped on the rear decks. The shrimp were saved and everything else was jettisoned over the stern: junk sea life of all kinds, fish, crabs, urchins and thousands of pink shrimp heads that the crews pinched off tiny bodies.

This brought hungry fish in from the Gulf of Mexico, and the fish brought the commercial fishermen and the game fishermen, who circled the shrimp fleet every morning like condors over carrion. It was not unusual to see them approach the shrimpers and trade a six-pack of beer for a bucket of bait or five pounds of fresh shrimp, so no one paid any special attention to slick, high-tech sport fishermen rafted alongside anchored shrimpers.

The three Magnum ocean racers came at Smith Shoals from the east going full bore. The noise of their high-powered engines defiled the quiet dawn. They sped past Smith Shoals in a blur and ran for another two miles, looking for the *Laura B*.

The *Laura B*, out of Mobile, Alabama, was one mile from the designated co-ordinates, her diesel engine straining, chugging along at a slow eight knots. She was wallowing deep in the water with her cargo of gold.

The Magnums were fifty-three-footers, the galleys and berths ripped out: hollow-shelled fiberglass bullets, each powered by two five-hundred-horsepower turbo-charged diesels. Each racer was carrying one hundred and sixty-five million dollars of freshly printed United States currency under its cowling.

The *Laura B* had been on Nick's radar scope for twenty minutes as she plodded along on her course. Nick dropped the throttles down as soon as he made visual contact with the trawler. The two other Magnums did the same.

The first thing he saw was Bruno Pugliese vomiting over the rail towards the stern on the port side. The slow steady rhythm of the shrimp boat, combined with the rotting fish stench from the afterdeck and hold and the heavy smell of diesel fuel, was too much for Bruno.

He turned a green face towards Nick and offered a weak wave then went back to his original position. Carmine Calabrese stood on the bridge of the shrimp boat with the Captain of the *Laura B*. The Captain yelled at the Magnums with his bullhorn to raft up on either side of the shrimp boat. The net booms would be used as cranes to lift the gold.

Everyone was armed. Nick carried an Uzi on a leather strap round his neck and a Colt .45 on his hip. The crew of the *Laura B* all carried stainless steel Ruger Mini-14s and .357 Magnums with speedloaders in their belts.

The *Laura B* cut her engine dead and waited patiently as the ocean racers nestled in against her wooden ribs, like cubs to their mother. They were lashed to her hull, and rocked gently with the slight swell. Nick's boat was first to start to unload.

The shrink-wrapped packets of freshly printed money were stashed in heavy-duty green garbage bags. Nick's mate hauled the bags out of the bow and passed them to Nick, who slung them up over the gunnels of the *Laura B* from his position on the cowling cover. The *Laura B* crew caught them and piled them neatly on the deck, waiting for the gold to be removed and room to be made in the hold.

Carmine Calabrese clamored down the steel steps from the bridge and walked over to the stack of garbage bags, only stopping to pat Bruno on the back and to tell him: 'Inhale deeply; take deep breaths.'

Bruno managed to pant, 'I'm lucky to breathe at all,' but tried to follow Carmine's advice, taking gulping bites of air.

Carmine turned away from him. He carried a pearl-handled switchblade that he popped open. He slit the side of one green garbage bag and extracted two packets of money; he did the same to two other bags, checking to be sure he had two samples of all three currencies, and took the six shrink-wrapped packets into the galley where his magnifying glass and chemicals were neatly assembled. As he passed into the galley he motioned for the crew to wait for his sign before they started to offload any gold onto Nick's boat. There was no time to lose, but they had agreed to wait for Carmine's sign of approval. Books had climbed into Nick's boat to speed up the unloading process.

Carmine heard the creaking of the booms as the winches were set in preparation for lifting the gold out of the hold. He knew how anxious the men were. He gently closed the door behind him and sat down to examine the money. First, he set out a real hundred, a fifty, and a twenty; next, he opened the first package and took out ten bills at random. He did the same with the other five shrink-wrapped packages.

Next, he took a vial of premixed chemicals and poured small drops of the clear solution on five of the new bills, all picked from separate batches, all three denominations. If the spots turned dark blue within sixty seconds, he would know that the bill was made of the right composition of paper and cloth.

He examined the bills, checking the sequence of serial numbers against a book he had in his pocket to see if the numbers were current. They were. He picked up his magnifying glass and studied the finely-engraved pattern round the borders of the pictures of Ben Franklin, Ulysses S. Grant and Andrew Jackson. They were perfect. He looked for blue and red threads: they were there. He compared the cut of the bills with the real ones and wondered how they guillotined the edges of the bills so perfectly. Finally, he checked the chemical spots he had made on the six bills. They were all dark blue.

He rose and opened the galley door and came face to face with Nick.

'The first boat is unloaded and ready to receive the gold,' Nick said.

Carmine gently patted Nick on the shoulder and eased him aside. 'You may start the unloading,' he said to the Captain. Bruno was still at his position, head over the rail, only occasionally looking up and round to check the action.

The booms of the shrimp boat started slowly to lift the gold out of the hold. It was in open boxes in the cargo nets and the tops glistened bright yellow in the morning sun. Everyone stopped what they were doing as the gold emerged; they seemed to stop breathing as it was hoisted over to the first Magnum and lowered into the cockpit. Books and a mate started stacking the gold bars in an orderly fashion in the bow.

As this was happening, the Magnum on the port side, driven by Ernie Sands, started to unload its cargo. The men of the *Laura B* were ripping open the green bags and counting the shrink-wrapped packages. Carmine walked over and grabbed four packets at random. He took them into the galley. Nick walked in with him, taking a seat within view of the open door.

Carmine sat down, and repeated his careful examination of the bills, only this time he turned on the two counting machines that were planted securely on the galley table. He stacked the bills in the automatic counters and waited. The hundreds were done first, twenty-five hundred bills in all. The twenties took a few minutes more. Carmine loaded a full pack of fifties into the other counter; he smiled at Nick. 'Nice work.' He waved a bill at Nick. 'Wanna talk about how you're making these?'

'Maybe some other time.' Nick smiled.

'That's what I thought.' The counter that was spinning through the twenties suddenly stopped. Carmine noted the count on his clipboard. There were twelve thousand, five hundred bills.

'Bulky, these twenties,' he said, stuffing the loose bills into a box in handfuls.

'Yes. Fifteen per cent of the load is twenties, thirty five per cent is fifties and half the load is hundreds, just like we agreed,' Nick said, watching Bruno stagger down the deck, heading towards them. He entered just as the fifties were being tallied by the counter. Carmine noted that there were five thousand fifties. He checked serial numbers and repeated the entire process, using new stacks of money.

'Well, how's it lookin'?' Bruno asked Carmine, ignoring Nick.

'They look good so far. I'll need four packets of money out of the last boat when they start to unload it.'

'They're unloadin' now,' Bruno said, rubbing the back of his hand across his mouth, wiping away some spittle. 'It's too tight for me in here, I can't fuckin' breathe. I'll go and get ya dem packets ya want.' He bolted out of the door.

'Poor man. He's in great pain.' Carmine winked, walking over and closing the door. 'A landlubber!' He smiled. 'So, you're still ignoring my advice, you continue to make this money.' Carmine pointed at the galley table piled high now with money. He patted it. There was over five million dollars on the table. 'I always felt it was anti-climactic; the money itself, I mean. The fun was in the making, not the selling and spending. The challenge! You have achieved the challenge, so why don't you quit now? I could have quit many times and I never would have had to do time in Leavenworth Prison. It ruined my life, you know?'

'I hear.' Nick studied the old man's face. The skin was smooth, almost without wrinkles. He wondered why the old man took such an interest in him. Nick was about to ask him when Bruno burst in, his arms full of shrink-wrapped packages of currency. He spilled them onto the table; three packages cascaded onto the floor. Nick bent down to pick them up; seven hundred and fifty thousand dollars, he thought, fingering the three packets as he put them back on the galley table.

'Sorry; I ain't myself today, I hate dis fuckin' boat. I brought plenty of packages 'cause I can't tell if dey are hundreds or twenties, ya know? So it looks all right to ya, Carmine?'

'Yes. It's as good as the samples. The Don should be pleased.' Carmine filled two more counting machines with fifties and hundreds. 'And how is the loading going?'

'Da gold is all outta da hole; dey should be done any minute. But who da fuck knows, I've had my head over da side for da last two hours.'

'They're loading a hundred and twenty-five million dollars

worth of gold onto those boats, thirteen tons. The Don is going to expect you to know what's goin' on.'

Bruno nodded, and left the galley.

'Why the interest in my welfare, whether I carry on making these bills or not?' Nick asked.

'Because no one ever did that for me. No one gave a shit, and as a result my son never got to know his father. You and I are strangers, I know this, but you remind me of myself when I was a young man.'

Nick studied Carmine. He put his hand on the older man's shoulder.

The door burst open and Books was standing there, a big grin on his mouth. 'Let's roll. We're loaded, engines running, ready to cast off. We've already been here for twenty eight minutes and we don't know what kind of surveillance we're under.'

'Thanks for your words. They haven't fallen on deaf ears,' Nick said to Carmine.

'Words? What were you guys talking about?' Books asked as they walked to the gunnel of the shrimp boat.

'Nothing important, Books, just some fatherly advice.' Nick pointed towards the stern where Bruno's bulk was hunched over the railing. He coughed and sputtered when the Captain of the shrimp boat hit the start button on the diesel engine and a billowing dirty black cloud of diesel fumes climbed up over the stern to envelop him. He ran towards the bow, passing them without even a nod.

'Have a nice day, Bruno,' Books said as he flew past.

'Fuck you,' was Bruno's reply.

Nick looked at the boats below him and was shocked to see how low in the water the bows of the Magnums had sunk with the weight of the gold. The sterns were raised so high that the propellers almost showed. He looked at Books.

'I know,' Books said. 'We miscalculated the weight. We put what we could in the stern, under the tarps, but we didn't want to bury the back end, either. It's going to be a bitch to get the boats up on a plane, and our top end is going to be a lot slower.'

The engines were gurgling, bubbling exhaust and hot water through the sterns. Each ocean racer was carrying about fifty-two hundred pounds of dead weight in the bow under the cowling.

The lines were cast off, and the shrimp boat eased away, leaving the three speedboats alone on the ocean like three lost children. Carmine stood motionless in the stern of the shrimp boat, watching.

Books and Nick both knew what the problem was: if they weren't careful and they pushed too hard, the engines would burn out with these heavy loads. 'Nick, you go first. Ease her up slow, we'll follow.' Ernie Sands had pulled up next to Nick and heard what Books said. He acknowledged with a casual salute.

'We'll travel in the same order,' Books said.

Nick eased the black knobs of both throttles forward. He felt the vibrations of the straining engines through the soles of his Topsiders. The noise from the straight-pipe exhausts filled the morning air, high-pitched plaintive wails.

The bow of the boat cut deep into the water as waves washed over the cowling. The bow dug deeper as Nick pushed the throttles forward, raising the speed two hundred RPMs at a time.

Finally, the bow slowly started to rise as the tachometer approached fifteen hundred. At three thousand RPMs, with the trembling RPM needle just below the red line, the bow finally cleared the water and the boat planed out. Nick left it there. It gave him a speed of close to thirty knots. He kept his eye on the temperature gauge. The two following boats matched his performance and climbed at the same rate, hovering in his wake.

The three boats made their way due west, travelling in the Northwest Channel until Nick spotted Key West, where they turned and headed northeast towards the Sambos and the Gulf Stream.

The wind was up to twenty knots, but still there was only a slight chop on the water inside the reef line, less than three feet.

But when they hit the Gulf Stream it was a different story.

They were met by whitecaps and sloppy breaking seas; a heavy cross-chop slapped into them. It was caused by the northeast wind bearing down directly against the creeping Gulf Stream as it headed north. Nick cursed himself for not having personally checked the way they had loaded the gold into the bow. He felt it shift slightly as he crashed headlong into a six-foot breaking wave. He eased off the throttle slightly, and turned to see Ernie and Books trailing, the strong Kevlar hulls of their boats disappearing in the white water, resurfacing, only to slam down into the curling waves and disappear again into the angry seas.

A screaming high-pitched whine rose above the wind.

'Shit'' Nick yelled. He knew what it was before he turned round.

A propeller was out of the water, spinning wildly like the blade of a saw, spraying a fine mist into the air. It was Ernie's boat. The gold had shifted, and she was listing on her side with one outdrive submerged and the other one fully out of the water. Ernie and the mate were scrambling, climbing over the gunnel of the sinking craft, staying clear of the slicing prop, their bright lifejackets contrasting orange against the white hull as they leapt into the sea.

Books was there first, standing off, his boat wallowing in the heavy seas, engines idling, as he threw a life ring to the men in the water. The high-pitched scream suddenly turned into a death-rattle as the ocean swallowed the powerful diesel engine.

Ernie and the mate clung to the life ring until they were pulled against the hull of Books' boat. They were helped over the side and flopped into the cockpit.

Nick eased his Magnum next to Books and yelled: 'Any injuries?'

'Just my fucking pride,' Ernie yelled back, standing, pushing his glasses up the bridge of his nose. The glasses had survived the ordeal, tape and all. 'Bad seamanship. I caught a big green one off center and the whole fucking load shifted to one side and flipped us.' He motioned with his hand.

Nick watched as the white Magnum hull of Ernie's boat disappeared finally and for ever into the blue ever-grinding Gulf Stream. Forty million in gold lost, to sit evermore on the ocean bottom. They were in five hundred fathoms of water, too deep for salvage.

Nick picked up the VHF radio microphone and held up a fistful of fingers signalling that he wanted Books to turn to channel five.

'I'm going to keep it down to around fifteen hundred RPMs for the duration. We'll take a beating but we'll make it. Over.' Nick said.

'I read you. I'll follow.'

'Bad luck.'

'Not bad luck. It's no luck at all,' Books snarled.

'Hell, you still got eighty-five million left in gold for some worthless paper; that ain't all bad!' Nick said to the microphone.

But Books wasn't listening.

Monday night 10:00
NEW YORK CITY

Don Saverese watched from his darkened office window as the eighteen-wheeler backed into the service bay. Only

294

his most trusted men were on the premises tonight.

He descended his private stairway into the service area and made his way past the racks of sports cars and sedans. He reached the truck, took a key out of his pocket, and ceremoniously opened the heavy padlock. He stepped back as the men swung the doors open. The truck was half-filled with green garbage bags. Two men jumped up into the trailer and started to hand out the bags. The Don watched as the bags were tossed out onto the floor.

Men started to carry them to long banquet tables that had been set up at the far end of the service area. Rows of flat corrugated boxes had been stacked behind the tables for packing. The Don watched as the bags were cut open and the shrink-wrapped packets of money were spread out upon the long tables.

Carmine Calabrese came over to the Don. 'I counted twenty packets of money on the boat, all from different bags, and each time they were perfect bills in exactly the correct amount, two hundred and fifty thousand dollars.'

The Don nodded at him, but said nothing; he continued to watch the men pile up the banquet tables with the shrink-wrapped packets of cash as other men unloaded the trailer, making a mountain of green bags.

The packing crew started to assemble the corrugated boxes, using heavy-duty tape to seal the seams. Five hundred boxes would be filled and sealed tonight. The Don was going to retain one hundred million, and send the remaining four hundred million to the five families he had previously contacted – eighty million to each family.

The trailer was to be reloaded, and driven with the boxes to a trucking depot in Hoboken that was owned by the Don. From there, the boxes would be transferred to trucks and delivered to the families, labeled as advertising material.

'You have done well, Carmine,' the Don finally said, as he signalled for one of his men to come over. The man came and bowed his head slightly in respect.

'Take the next bag, and bring it up to my office.' The Don patted Carmine's shoulder and smiled, then walked back to his office alone.

The man followed the Don into the office, carrying the green bag. The Don pointed at the coffee table. 'Leave it there, please. You may rejoin the men downstairs.'

The Don took his letter opener, slit the bag down the center and arranged the packets of money in orderly stacks on the table. The bag he had picked at random contained ten packets of fifty-dollar bills. He selected the packet on the top right-hand side of the pile and took it over to his desk. He peeled the shrink-wrapping off the currency and flipped through the money. He stacked the loose bills up on his desk in eight neat piles; eight was his lucky number.

Next, he took a single bill, and held it up for examination under the light. He rubbed it between his thumb and forefinger and lifted it directly under the single glowing magnifying light.

This money would alter the lives of many people when it hit the streets: as advances to desperate people by loan sharks, as money used to buy drugs from smugglers, as currency handed through the cages of family-owned casinos to buy back chips and pay off winners, as laundered cash to bolster inventories or buy capital equipment for his legitimate businesses. And real estate – it would buy shopping malls, office towers and raw land.

The Don stood, sighed, and walked over to the wall safe located behind the photograph of his mother. He swung the picture out and deposited the two hundred and fifty thousand in the safe in eight neat piles. 'A little spending money, petty cash for emergencies,' he said to himself.

He rose, flicked off the light, and looked down through the one-way glass into the service area below, watching his people as they unloaded the truck and repacked the money.

He was uneasy. He walked back to the couch and sat down,

staring at the two and a quarter million in cash that was lying on the coffee table in front of him.

He should feel happy, elated. But he felt nothing, nothing at all.

He knew what was wrong. He had made the mistake of going to look at the gold that had been collected by the families before it had been placed on the *Laura B*. It had been stacked four feet high on wooden pallets, and glistened bright yellow under the overhead lights of the warehouse they had used. When he touched the gold it felt cool to his fingers, yet hot at the same time.

He wanted the gold back. He felt better now, better in knowing that he had possession of the money, and that it was only a matter of time until he had the gold, too.

He would find a way.

Tuesday morning 9:00
CAY SAL BANK, BAHAMAS

Heather watched the two of them below her as they worked methodically at the mouth of the blue hole. She hovered ten feet above them, tiny air bubbles escaping from her mouth like a long string of clear pearls. She was watching for any stray sharks or approaching boats.

Books and Nick each wore an extra weight belt so they could hug the sandy bottom. Together they eased the stainless steel conveyor belt into the mouth of the blue hole. Once it was in place, Nick removed his backpack and tank. He slid along the metal rollers on his stomach into the blue hole, dragging his scuba tank behind him; the rollers tickled his stomach through the wetsuit as they spun under his weight.

After the pickup of the gold, Books had insisted that the three of them stay with the Magnums, sleep on board, and leave for the blue hole at sunrise.

Books had been in a foul mood, refusing to talk to anyone. He blamed the loss of the gold directly on Ernie Sands.

Nick waited inside the giant bell for the first gold bar to appear. The enormous cavern had a ceiling that would rival any cathedral in the world, a giant domed structure that transported him back to St Patrick's Cathedral in New York and the times he had gone there to early Mass with his father before their Sundays on the city.

Books and Heather ascended to the Magnums to start unloading the gold. The bars were dropped into a waiting wire basket that hung on a guide rope a few feet below the surface. The basket was lowered down the guide rope to the mouth of the blue hole. After the first load, Heather would be in charge of dropping the bars into the basket by herself, Books would load the conveyor belt, then swim the basket back up to the boat.

Fingers of filtered blue light poured through hundreds of tiny holes in the dome, coloring everything blue. Nick watched his blue hands and fingers glide through the water as he made his way up towards the center of the ceiling, wondering where the hammerhead was hiding.

He treaded in the apex of the dome, watching the sea creatures move in their never-ending circular parade. His eyes followed the curve of the bell to the far side where it disappeared into bottomless darkness.

He looked down to see the first gold bar shooting along the stainless steel rollers and through the opening. It landed with a puff on the sand.

The bar was blue-green in the distorted light, glistening with its magic.

Nick swam down to the opening and began to stack the bars of gold against the cave wall as Books propelled them along the belt.

After the first basket had been emptied and stacked, Nick had time to relax. He sat on the gold stack and idly stroked one of the rectangular bars.

Somehow, he felt as trapped as the poor creatures inside the blue hole.

Tuesday morning 10:00
WASHINGTON, D.C.

Cobb had snitches planted in most Government agencies, as well as hundreds on the street. He had a three million-dollar slush fund, for buying information, under his control.

The Secret Service was responsible for the safety of the President and visiting dignitaries of the highest rank. The Secret Service never got public credit for ninety per cent of their deeds; because of their successful intervention, they were usually able to get to the perpetrators before an act could be committed. And these successful interventions stemmed from good information – from informants.

Cobb had set up four information analysts in a small office in the basement of the Secret Service building. They read and filtered all the information that flowed in from every source.

If anything looked at all interesting or valid, it was forwarded to Cobb. As a result, his desk was always piled high with files that read PRIORITY – SECRET. They were all read by Cobb personally, and shredded; only one out of hundreds ever proved to be of value, but he had found out long ago that unlimited information gave him his intuition and famous good instincts.

He had just finished a classified file on the 'Hundred

Richest Lebanese citizens in the United States'. He was looking for terrorists. The report was from the IRS and analyzed all bank withdrawals and foreign transfers made by these men in the last six months. He fed it into the shredder and considered it a waste of time.

The next file was from a snitch in Las Vegas that was highly placed in the accounting department of the Versailles Casino and Hotel. The report stated that the casino, acting as a middleman, had used part of its large cash reserve to purchase five million in gold bullion. The casino stored the gold temporarily, then shipped it out within two weeks. The gold buyer paid for it with a thirty-day note from a small, practically unknown bank in the Midwest. The casino received payment in cash in fourteen days.

The accountant suspected something and actually did a physical count of the money in the vault and found that there was ten million in cash, not five million as reported. He mentioned it to his superiors and the next day he noticed that the extra five million had been removed. All the bills were brand new and looked fine, but somehow it disturbed him. He had written 'Smells Funny' on the bottom of the report.

Cobb wondered why the report had found its way to his desk; it looked more like an IRS problem than Secret Service. He slipped it into the shredder, then grabbed it back just before the sharp teeth could chew it up.

He set it aside on his pile of ACTION files, not knowing why. His secretary was always complaining that he saved too much useless information.

But she wasn't the head of the Secret Service, he was.

Almost in dread of her nagging, he took the file off the pile and put it in his top drawer, locking it. This was his lucky drawer: almost everything he had ever put in that drawer had paid off later.

Tuesday evening 6:00
NEW YORK CITY

Don Saverese had sent Carmine Calabrese to visit the head of each family with specific suggestions on how to feed the four hundred million in cash into the system.

The families were to loosen up the pressure on street activities. Loan sharks were to receive larger cash reserves to work with. Drug dealers were to pay slightly higher prices for fast delivery and better quality drugs. The illegal books for sporting events should offer bonuses for higher bets. Family-owned casinos were directed to redeem their chips with crisp new twenty-, fifty-, and hundred-dollar bills and stash the used money in the vault. Pornography was to be expanded: more production money was available for films and magazines, with larger advertising budgets to promote sales.

Existing family-owned legitimate businesses were encouraged to make capital expenditures and acquisitions with easily obtained low-interest loans secured by laundered cash. New legitimate companies were capitalized with large cash injections: import/export businesses, car dealerships, real estate acquisitions, any type of activity where the cash could be turned into hard assets and back into laundered cash. The families were expert at laundering money. They had been doing it for years.

The families were also requested by Carmine Calabrese to continue collecting gold from the street. The Don had scheduled the next delivery to take place in only two weeks.

Two billion a month was what they planned to feed into the system, once they had ironed out all the problems of distribution. And most of the money would find its way into legitimate enterprises, to strengthen their business base.

'How would it end? How could it end?' the Don pondered.

He then made a list of all the ways it could go awry, and when he was finished with the list he studied it for a moment.

He took his pen, stroked two lines through everything he had just written and wrote '*No importa!*' in big letters across the center of the page. He tore the sheet into tiny squares which he sprinkled into the wastebasket, watching the scraps of paper descend like confetti.

'Even if they discover and stop the flow of this money, they will never publicly prosecute; the possibility of monetary panic would be too great.'

The Don broke into a whistle. He was whistling the melody of 'Funiculi, Funicula' as he pulled the small replica of the Ferrari Testarossa out of his desk drawer. He would just have to ensure that he stayed removed from the actual operations. And that was easy for him; he always stayed removed.

Wednesday night 10:00
PARIS, FRANCE

The doorman of Le Dernier Legionnaire snapped the bolt into the deadlock with a loud click. Nick handed his raincoat to the coat-check girl and entered the main room.

It was ten o'clock and the first show was just starting. Tonight it was a dog show.

Nick could see the black and yellow fur rippling down the Alsatian's back as he worked over a naked girl; she had her arms round his thick neck, her hands tearing at his fur. About twenty men, most in uniform, were on their feet in a semi-circle in front of the stage, yelling and laughing.

Nick paid little attention to them and went directly to Colonel Le Clerc's upstairs apartment. He remembered the

302

dark stairway by the smell, a combination of stale beer and carbolic acid.

He had flown to Paris that morning. He carried only an overnight bag with him, and a money belt that contained fifty thousand dollars of freshly-printed US currency.

The Colonel stood as Nick entered, and offered his good hand and a large smile. He seemed to be stuffed into his starched shirt. The Colonel nodded towards Michelle Descartes, René Descartes' niece. Nick smiled a hello at her and then sat down on the leather couch next to her. It was a large, well-appointed apartment located directly over the club, with one-way glass on the street side that overlooked the Place Pigalle and Montmartre.

'So, you have been a busy boy?' the Colonel asked, handing Nick a snifter of VSOP cognac. 'You must try this; it is a special blend I have casked for me. I get a barrel a year. It's forty years old and getting better every year. Like us. No?'

'*Oui*.' Nick smiled and offered his glass as a toast to them both. 'I hope so. And Michelle, you and your uncle have been well?'

'My uncle grows weaker every day. But I have been fine.' She left the couch to look out of the window at the churning street life below them on the Place Pigalle. 'He sends his regards. He is very interested in your project, but he is too weak to come himself. In any event, I speak for him,' she said, turning to face Nick.

Her slender body was sheathed in a loose-fitting black Chanel dress, modest, in the best of taste.

Nick studied her calves; he remembered following her up the circular steel ladder in René Descartes' yacht and watching her calves pulse with each rung she climbed. They were curved, slightly muscular. He wondered if she was the type who worked out regularly or just walked a lot; and what kind of a love life she had, as the hand-picked heir to the Union Corse. He also wondered if she had passed through the club to get to the apartment when the dog show was being performed on the stage, and what had gone through her mind.

There was a strong murmur, then a cheer from the crowd below that vibrated through the hardwood floors of the apartment like a muted ocean wave. The dog must have consummated the act, Nick thought.

'So, you have samples?' Michelle asked.

'Yes.' Nick slipped off his blue blazer and opened his loosely-fitting shirt. He pulled apart the two Velcro tabs that held the belt tightly to his stomach like a girdle. The belt was nine inches wide and spanned his waist. He pulled it through the opening in the shirt and laid it on the coffee table, motioning for Colonel Le Clerc to do the honors of opening it while he finished buttoning his shirt.

The Colonel ran his finger down the Velcro seam of the money belt. It made a sound like a dry crackling fire. He flipped the top open, pulled out the sheaves of bills, and laid them out on the polished mahogany table: fifty thousand US dollars in twenties, fifties and hundreds.

Michelle opened her purse and withdrew a magnifying glass, and twenty newly-minted bills that she had picked up that same day at the Chase Manhattan Bank branch office in Paris. She dealt the real money out directly below the counterfeit, then snapped the paper wrapper of the first stack, fanned the bills, and began to examine them.

As she did this, Nick walked over to the window. He watched the street action below, the girls in the doorways, the doormen trying to lure tourists into the flashy nightclubs and sex shows, drugs being secretly handed from fist to fist, beggars trying to be as pitiful as possible.

'They're very good,' Michelle said, not stopping in her examination of the bills. 'I had the best men in your business come to Nice for two days last week. They gave me a course in detecting forgeries. I can see none of the faults that they told me to look for. But how do we know that you simply haven't just provided us with real bills as samples, to deceive us? Then you will take our gold on the high seas and leave us with nothing of value.'

Nick turned to face her. 'Because I say they are real samples, Michelle. I've seen them made with my own eyes, and I don't do business by ripping people off. The Colonel knows how I operate.'

The Colonel was about to speak when she interrupted.

'People can change. And for one hundred and twenty million in gold bullion you can have great control over people's moral fiber.'

The Colonel did not like being interrupted, especially by a woman. He persisted. 'Nick and I have done many deals together. He is a man of honor.'

'We have already made a delivery in the United States, a delivery as big as this one. It was made to clients of yours in New York; a client who buys your goods from India and the Golden Triangle. They are satisfied with the product. We would prefer that you do not contact them, since there is no point in letting them know what we are doing in Europe, but if you doubt us, you have my permission to contact them.'

'I do not need your permission. But I appreciate what you have said. How else can we be sure?' Michelle asked.

'Keep the fifty thousand in front of you for further study and send an expert, come yourself, when the transfer is made at sea; take random samples while we unload the boats and satisfy yourself. Our plan is not to make one delivery and rip you off. Our plan is to set up regular deliveries, increasing the ante, until we are doing five hundred million in gold every two weeks. That means we deliver two billion in cash to you.'

'How long do you think we can do this? That is a lot of gold to take out of circulation, and a lot of cash to inject into the monetary system,' Michelle commented.

'As long as you can get the gold, we can supply the currency.'

'You are serious, aren't you?'

'I'm deadly serious.' Nick sat down next to her and held

305

his empty glass out to Colonel Le Clerc. 'Any more of that delightful cognac?'

'That's better! Everyone is getting too serious and I'm getting too old to be so serious for so long.' The Colonel knew that this was the first big deal for Michelle Descartes and she was being overly cautious. If she failed here, it would for ever ruin her chances to become head of the Union Corse.

The Colonel handed Nick his refilled glass.

'So, where do we make the transfer?' Nick asked, looking at Michelle.

'The Bay of Biscay, near the Ile d'Oleron. From there we can get to Bordeaux with no problem.'

'The boat?' Nick asked.

'A tramp freighter of Panamanian registry. We will give you her name at the last moment and the exact time and co-ordinates. And you?' she asked.

'Submarines. Two of them. World War Two vintage.'

'Wheee!' The Colonel whistled through his teeth. 'You are very creative! *Très bien, mon ami.*'

'They are in perfect working order, restored for the job.'

'You will call me twenty-four hours before they are to arrive in the Bay of Biscay; I will have the freighter standing by, and give you the co-ordinates at that time,' Michelle said.

Nick said nothing; he smiled at her and nodded. She seemed to wilt a little under his gaze, and imperceptibly to return to being a woman. He wondered what kind of a lover she would be; probably fierce. His mind unconsciously drifted back to Heather. He had never allowed himself to think of Heather in bed; why was he doing it now? Michelle stared at him, and finally cracked a smile at the corner of her mouth, as if she knew what he was thinking.

A roar from the club below startled them. It was a deeper, heavier sound, more raucous, more people.

'Maybe a donkey this time,' she smiled.

'Or a Clydesdale,' Nick said.

'Now, a Clydesdale I might want to see for myself.'
Michelle laughed.

'Shall we go to the Legionnaire for a nightcap?' the Colonel
offered them both.

'No, *merci*, Colonel, I must get back to my uncle. He does
not have much longer to be with us.'

'I'm very sorry.'

'I also have to pass,' Nick said. 'I must return and make
some money.'

Michelle smiled. 'Perhaps next time, Nick, you will come
to Nice and spend the weekend with us. And we will drink
champagne instead of this excellent cognac.'

'I would like that,' Nick said, as he left.

He slipped into his raincoat and walked out into the
drizzling rain and the buzzing of the Place Pigalle. The
streetwalkers were all in their designated spots, all holding
umbrellas, wearing transparent raincoats; the whims of nature
would not keep them from their profession.

He pulled his collar up against the rain. He decided to walk
along the Place Pigalle for a while and watch the hustlers.

Thursday afternoon 4:00
NEW YORK CITY

The Commissioner of the New York City Police Department
sat silently listening to Chief of Detectives O'Hara and the
five borough chiefs. They had asked for the special meeting
with the Commissioner to brief him, bring him up to date
on what was going on in the streets.

Chief O'Hara explained. 'You see, sir, it's nothing that any
of us can put a finger on, but something's definitely

happening. It's creeping across the boroughs of this city like a slimy fog. The mob is cash rich and they don't know what the hell to do with their money. You tell him, Arnie.'

Arnold Schwartz was the only Jewish borough chief. He was Chief of the Bronx. 'In my borough, it's drugs and loan sharking with the blacks. It's like they are willing to lend the money out almost at bank rates, and the drugs! Shit, the price on the street for grass and coke has dropped twenty per cent.'

'In the garment district it's gambling and big-time loan-sharking,' John Herlihy of the Manhattan Borough spoke up. 'The loans are almost at legitimate factor rates and there's an unlimited supply of dough. One dressmaker I know, a small-time guy, was about to go under. The mob advanced him a cool million. The wise guys do better financial analysis than the Chemical Bank. Why would they lend so much on a shaky deal?'

'In Queens, it's the dirty movies,' Jake Howard of the Queens Borough said. 'The boys bought an entire block of apartments, over fifty units, and evicted all the tenants. Now they're making skin flicks like a regular Hollywood studio. They must be churning out three, four movies a day. And they got a security system that you can't believe. We raid, but by the time we hit them they all have their clothes on and the film hidden.

The Borough Chief of Brooklyn was next. 'Real estate. The mob is buying all the real estate they can get their hands on, no matter what the price; anything in the Heights, anything within five miles of the Bridge that comes up, they grab. That's Yuppie heaven in there, and all of a sudden the mob is becoming a major landlord. They're doing it perfectly legit, of course, and they're doing it in a big way.'

'I know,' the Commissioner interrupted. 'Chief O'Hara has told me a little of this already, and I've heard it from other sources: bankers, Wall Street people, the garment district, the diamond district, even the Chinatown gamblers;

they've been burning up my phone and door. They wanna know what's happening. It's like the mob has a well of money all of a sudden, a deep well. Has anyone got any evidence on where this money is coming from?'

'No, Commissioner,' Chief O'Hara said. 'But they can't keep it hidden for long.'

'I have a little something.' It was Chief John Herlihy of the Manhattan Borough who spoke. 'It's in the jewelry district. The mob has a standing order for gold at five per cent above the London quote. They pay cash and take physical delivery.'

'That's almost twenty-five dollars an ounce premium. A jeweler could make a good living just supplying them at those prices,' the Commissioner offered.

'Yes, and plenty are, sir. It's an open order, twenty-four hours a day. They'll take delivery night or day.'

'I don't get it. Why gold? Where the hell is the fucking money coming from?' O'Hara asked.

No one answered.

'And why so much gold?' the Commissioner asked.

Chief O'Hara shrugged. 'So, what do we do, Commissioner?'

'Not a fucking thing we can do, but something will break, and when it does, I want to know. And I don't want conjecture, hearsay, or gossip. I want to know definitively: that means with prima-facie evidence, real stuff. You boys know the drill. Put this on the top of your list. It disturbs my beauty sleep knowing this is going on.' The Chief smiled the broad smile that he was famous for, the smile that indicated that the meeting was over.

Chief O'Hara left One Police Plaza and decided to go for a stroll to think. He told his driver to keep the four-door black Buick about fifty feet behind him so he couldn't hear the wheels churning in the snow. It was the first snowfall of the year in New York, and O'Hara enjoyed the noise his shoes made as they squashed the snow underfoot. The cold blast of air felt good and it gave him a chance to light up one of his fat Cuban cigars that he only smoked at home. He got the cigars from a friend of his in the garment district who smuggled them in with imported clothes from Colombia. He lit the cigar with a thick flame from his Zippo lighter and inhaled deeply. He loved his job. He had three thousand detectives working for him. That was more men than many armies were made of. He exhaled a large puff from his cigar that evaporated into the night. 'This is big. It involves big money. Real big money.' He signalled his car forward, jumped into the back seat, and punched out Phillip Sturges' phone number on impulse.

'Phillip? It's Chief O'Hara. How are you?'

'I'm good, Chief, and you?'

'Never better. How's Veronica?'

'She's with me now. She's fine, says hello. What's up?'

'We got a big problem in the city that has to do with money. Thought maybe you could help.'

'I'll try.'

'The mob has all of a sudden got a lot of cash, and they're making a lot of moves, buying and lending. We can't figure it out. And since it has to do with money, I thought you might have some thoughts. Maybe they hit it big somewhere.'

'Not that I know of. What else?' Phillip asked.

'They're buying gold, all they can get at five per cent above the London quote.'

'No one can make a profit like that, Chief.'

'So why are they doing it?'

'Don't know,' Phillip said.

'Well, put it in your inventory of mental notes, will you? You never know.'

'No, you don't, Chief. You never do know. I'll keep it in mind.'

O'Hara slid the mobile phone back in the holder, sorry that he had bothered Philip while Veronica was visiting. He was proud of the match he had made there. When Phillip had told him once over after-dinner drinks that he needed some companionship and didn't know how to go about filling his needs, Chief O'Hara had been more than glad to introduce Phillip to Veronica a couple of days later.

The head of the Federal Reserve was almost innocent in the way he handled her payments, routing them through O'Hara so it wouldn't seem like a paid service. They had liked each other a lot, though, and the relationship had lasted years now. Still, they weren't any normal couple; their time together was limited, and O'Hara didn't like to get in the way. He barked at the driver to take him home.

Minutes later Veronica was hurriedly dressed and also on her way home in a limo.

The next day when O'Hara arrived in his office at nine thirty, he had an urgent message to call Ralph Cobb at Secret Service headquarters in Washington.

Cobb told O'Hara that he had talked to Phillip Sturges first thing this morning, and he wanted the Chief to repeat everything that he had told Phillip, and anything else that he could think of relating to the mob's new wealth.

'Why in hell does the Secret Service want to get involved in this?' O'Hara wondered.

The answer wasn't difficult to work out. There could be only one reason. Funny money.

Friday morning 10:00
WASHINGTON, D.C.

'It stinks, sir,' Cobb said. 'And you, Phillip, what do you think?'

'The same. I don't like it, but we don't know for sure yet.'

'What the hell do we need? I got the same report from Los Angeles, Chicago, Detroit, Vegas and Atlantic City: plenty of cash available all of a sudden,' Cobb said.

'I don't like it either.' The President rose and walked to the picture of Harry Truman that hung over his credenza. 'I admire this man above all the others because he had to drop the Big One. His philosophy was: spend a great deal of time making the decision, but once made, never think about it again, just act. He was right. It's how you keep your sanity in this job. But in this case, there's no decision to make yet.

'So far, all we know is that St John and his gang have the capacity to print currency, and as a result, counterfeit bills may be coming into circulation and they may be using organized crime as their means of distribution. Have I left anything out?'

'Yes, sir,' Phillip offered. 'Gold! Gold is involved somehow. Either the mob is hoarding it, or they are paying for the paper with gold.'

'I agree,' the President acknowledged as he sat down behind his desk. 'Ralph, you're responsible for this investigation. You will contact Alvin Marks of the FBI and instruct him that he is to use all his resources to penetrate the veil of organized crime; his objective is to determine the size and scope of the distribution.

'Next, brief the head of the CIA, and ask him to do the same as the FBI, but have them do it in Europe to see if there is an influx of US dollars or any other currency flooding the European market.

'Also, the National Security Council should investigate any out of the ordinary transactions in gold, silver, and diamonds – any hoarding. Tell them to check hard assets also, like oil contracts and real estate. Tell them to use their judgement. They are to look for any unusual transactions.'

'Won't the FBI figure out what's going on? Do we need all these departments knowing? The press might find a leak;

can you imagine if the six o'clock news ever got their claws into this?'

'Yes, Ralph, I can imagine, and that's why you're going to have to think of a solid cover story for the agencies involved; they are to know only one piece of the puzzle, no more. And we will hold no general meetings for information sharing until we have put more of the pieces together.'

'Yes, sir,' Cobb said.

'Finally, get hold of the Treasury Department, the Drug Enforcement Administration, and the Coast Guard; position your investigation as a drug-money laundering and counterfeiting problem; tell them to look for counterfeit money along with their drug searches – money belts, attaché cases full of cash.

'Contact Admiral Longstreet of the Coast Guard, and have him increase all coastline surveillance; we know they are located off the coast of Florida, so maybe that's where they are delivering the money. Let's increase the surveillance on freighters, tankers, cruise ships and fishing boats in those waters.'

Cobb was feverishly taking notes, his head bent over his yellow legal pad. The President paused to let him catch up.

'Ralph, do you have someone in your department who can operate a computer, someone you can totally trust?'

'Yes.'

'Co-ordinate and assimilate the information you receive from every source. Keep the data discs locked up under the tightest security, and make no print-outs, except at the request of Phillip or myself. And no memos. I'll provide you with a carefully-worded letter of authorization for the other department heads, giving you the authority to get what you need. Anything else?'

'Suppose our worst fears are true, and they are flooding the country with bad paper. What the hell do we do then? They are a sovereign country. If we go after them on their turf and miss, they can use the media to destroy confidence in paper money.'

'What would you suggest, Ralph? Destroy their island based on our fears, the way you burned down the paper mill?' Phillip asked.

Cobb rose from his seat. 'It was your brilliant idea to use this method to print currency in the first place. And Books St John is your best friend.'

'Ralph, Books St John put me in this chair.'

The President broke in. 'Cut the crap. You two gentlemen are working together on this case, and will co-operate fully with one another; do I make myself clear?'

'Yes, sir,' they both said, almost in unison.

'All right, that's better. We need to build a case. We need more facts. Will it take too long? Will we be too late? Who knows? But we can't take action now, with nothing concrete, no evidence. Let's just get on with it.'

The meeting was over.

Phillip's hand shook as he reached upward to press the elevator button. Cobb had taken the stairs. Phillip was angry, but not with Ralph Cobb. He was angry at himself.

It was the first time ever in public that he had blamed Books for the accident.

Friday midday 12:00
CAY SAL BANK, BAHAMAS

Nick stood silently watching Percival Smathers as he worked. They were in the storage warehouse, the larger of the two buildings on the island. Percival had set up his vats, rolling machine, and mixers in the far corner of the building, where he had installed heavy-duty fans and ventilation ducts to expel the heavy toxic fumes from the acid washes and the chemical baths.

It was here that Percival took the shredded paper from the barge and processed it into slurry, a gooey mass of grey oatmeal. The slurry was pressed back into sheets of paper on the rolling machine. The sheets were then cut into the desired size. The smell from the chemicals was like dirty unwashed socks left in a gymnasium locker for months.

Ten pallets stacked high with freshly-made paper were waiting, ready to be printed. Nick walked over and stood next to Percival, who didn't notice him.

Percival was singing a tuneless version of 'I Heard It Through the Grapevine.' Nick watched, fascinated, as he moved from vat to vat, oblivious of everything else.

'Not much longer would you be mine . . . because I heard it through the grapevine . . .' Percival cut off in mid-chorus when he saw Nick standing there. 'Jesus, Nick, you scared me! How long you been standing there?'

'All day.' Nick smiled.

'Bullshit.'

'Might as well have been, you wouldn't have noticed.'

'It's true I get caught up in my work, but I'm not that bad.' Perce polished off the last of his Budweiser. 'Want one?' he asked, walking over to the refrigerator.

'Sure. So what's new?' Nick sat down on the floor leaning his back against the refrigerator.

'New York, New Jersey, New Haven . . .' Perce laughed, sitting down beside Nick.

'Cut the jokes.'

'Sorry. I have to do that one once a year; it's out of my system now.'

'Good. How have things been while I was away?' Nick wiped the sweat off the bottle before he drank.

'Okay. Books is using brand-new high-powered Bertram yachts with the interiors torn out instead of the Magnums.'

'I saw them in the harbor. What else?'

'Books is getting stranger every day. Hard to talk to, you know what I mean?'

'No.'

'Well, you'll find out. All this cash and gold is getting to him, I think. And being stuck on this little postage stamp island ain't helping either. Does he know you're here?'

'Yes. And Heather?'

'She's getting squirrelly too. But I think maybe with her it's something else. Something personal that's bothering her.'

'Like?' Nick asked.

'Like maybe the fact that Books treats her like shit. Or maybe she has island fever. Do you know much about her?'

'No. No more than you do. And you, Perce, how are you doing?'

'Fine. Shit, you know me, Nick, I take it as it comes, usually right on the fucking chin.' Percival rose. 'Gotta get back to work now, make my quota for today. I got a tough boss.'

'Looks like you're ahead of the game, Nick said, pointing at the ten pallets.

'Just a tiny pittance of my quota, I'm afraid, a mere drop in the bucket. Books wants at least a hundred pallets within two weeks.'

'A hundred pallets? Shit, how much will that make?'

'More than the annual gross national product of most of the nations on the face of the earth. Let's hope the gold supply holds out. It's really starting to give me the willies.'

'What?'

'All this money has no value to me anymore.'

'It only has value if other people believe it has value. See ya, Perce.'

'See ya. Stinks in here, doesn't it? The stink that comes from making money.'

'The stink of greed,' Nick said as he closed the door behind him, walking into the bright sunlight, then under the canopied walk that stretched overhead from the warehouse building to the factory building. Nick strolled slowly along the shaded pathway, wondering about the magnitude of what they were doing, and its effect on the natural monetary balance. With love, sex, crime, violence, even war, there was a natural balance that had developed over thousands of years. The balance was dynamic, changing with each generation, the wealth of nations, the whims of nature, the fortunes of war, and the perversities of man. On this little island, they were tampering with that balance, tilting at the fiscal scales.

The temperature inside the factory was sixty-eight, ten degrees cooler than the outside afternoon air. It took Nick's breath away as he stepped inside.

Heather stood ready to remove the gurney underneath the hydro slicer as the water jets hissed their way through the hundred stacked sheets of finished bills.

Her profile was towards him as she stood there in her khaki shorts, a black bandanna wrapped round her head holding her ash-blonde hair in place.

Heather looked up and smiled at him as she wheeled the gurney over to the compacting machine where the bills would be stacked and wrapped. Books waved for Nick to come to the computer, not wanting to stop what he was doing.

'So, things went well in France?' Books asked, as he hit the final order to print into the console keyboard.

'Yes, things went well.'

Heather joined them, giving Nick a kiss on the cheek. 'Welcome back,' she said.

'The Union Corse? They're in?' Books asked.

'Yes, ready when you are; they will take delivery in the Bay of Biscay off the coast of Spain. There will be a freighter waiting for the subs. You ready to make another delivery to the boys?'

'Two days from now, off Sombrero light.'

'Marathon?'

'Yes, we'll meet them in the middle of the Gulf Stream and make the switch.'

'How much?'

'A billion cash. And we can go ahead with the European delivery. Ernie Sands is ready with the subs; all we have to do is load them. We'll load two subs but send three, in case one of them breaks down on the journey.'

'Sounds all right. I'll make the call. And you guys, how've you been?' Nick asked.

'Great,' Heather said with forced enthusiasm. 'Just great; couldn't be better.'

Nick watched her as she walked back to her gurney to wait for the next stack of sheets to be cut.

'Maybe it's that time of the month,' Books said quietly without being asked. 'I can't take time for her moods. I'm about to load Ernie Sands and his boys up.'

'Right. I'll call France, then I'm taking a nap. Wake me in time to say goodbye to Ernie. I'm jetlagged and exhausted.'

'Sure, Nick, I'll see you later.' Books smiled up at him, then looked back down at the computer console.

Nick walked out, taking a second to look at Heather before he closed the door. She looked up at him and shrugged her shoulders; her face was sullen. She turned her head back to what she was doing.

Nick was awakened at sunset out of a deep sleep by Books shaking his shoulder. 'They're leaving. Ernie and his gang are ready to pull out. He wants to see you.'

'Right. Just let me grab my shirt.'

Ernie stood on the dock with the waiting Whaler tied to a piling, nervously fingering the tape on his glasses. 'Nick. I just wanted to say goodbye. I'm a little skittish, ya know? I've never seen a billion dollars before. We loaded five hundred million on each of the two boats and left the escort sub empty. High tide is here and the boys are all chomping at the bit to get going. They told me to tell ya goodbye for them.'

'Give them my best,' Nick said, squeezing Ernie's shoulder.

'There's one thing, Nick. One thing that is bothering me; do you mind?'

'Spit it out, Ernie.'

'It's Books. He's still pissed at me for capsizing that boat in the Stream, losing the gold.'

'No, he's not, Ernie,' Nick lied, 'but the way to put it right is to have a successful trip now. Bring back the Union Corse gold, and he'll be happy.'

'Who wouldn't?' Ernie smiled, and shook Nick's hand as he headed for his waiting sub.

Nick watched from the pier as the subs glided slowly down the channel, the blood-red sun slipping into the ocean for the night. The propellers churned the sandy bottom, leaving a trail of brown silt as the subs eased into the Gulf Stream. The conning towers and the black topskin of the hulls was all that was visible as they slid through the water like fat, steel needles, purposeful and deadly.

Nick answered Ernie's final wave before Ernie left the conning tower and slipped into the iron fish. 'Rather him than me,' Nick said out loud, wondering how they could stand the close quarters and breathe the claustrophobic air.

'Me too,' Heather said; it startled Nick. 'Thought you were alone, huh? They put people away for talking to themselves, you know.'

'Well, you can't blame me; talking to myself is a small matter when you consider that I've got to be nuts to be here in the first place.' They started to walk back to C building and the Black Box. 'I don't envy them that trip in those old clunkers.'

'Nick, I need to talk to you,' Heather said, suddenly stopping. 'Books has gone out to feed the sharks, and Perce is operating the computer.'

'Let's go back to the dock and sit there.' They walked in silence to the end of the dock.

'I'm sorry. I just get the jitters so often these days. I've had enough. I'd like to wrap it up.'

'Talk to Books. It's all right with me. I'll quit any time. The sooner the better.' Nick suddenly jerked his arm from her shoulders as he heard the whine of the powerful outboard engines of the Magnum racer as it spread the fish effluvium on the surface of the water. He was embarrassed. He didn't want Books to catch him with his arm round Heather. She understood.

'Thanks. I needed to talk to someone, someone who . . .' She shook her head, not finishing her thought. 'I guess I'm just a weak woman.'

'Don't try that line on me.' Nick smiled. 'There's nothing weak about you.'

She squeezed his hand and left him sitting there.

Saturday morning 9:00
BAY OF BISCAY

The three subs plowed through the surface waves easily. There were three men in each conning tower with binoculars, all looking for a tramp steamer that would be waiting off the Ile d'Oleron.

The wind was less than ten knots, but it was bitterly cold. Ernie Sands had his eyeglasses sitting on the top of his black watch cap as he tried to focus his binoculars on a rusty hulk that seemed to be drifting aimlessly at their co-ordinates, rocking gently from side to side with the waves.

Ernie finally made out the name on the stern: *Penelope*. He raked the steamer with his glasses and saw someone looking back at him with binoculars. He waved a greeting and shouted to his men to look alive. Smoke billowed out of her stack as the freighter came to life; men moved swiftly like ants on her decks.

Ernie ordered the subs to move in.

The men on the freighter were all dressed in black, wearing turtleneck sweaters. No effort was made to conceal their sidearms or automatic weapons.

Michelle stood on the bridge as the cargo net was hoisted over the side and slowly lowered to the waiting sub; large rubber fenders were dropped on ropes to keep the subs from rubbing against the hull of the freighter.

'You first,' Michelle yelled from the deck.

Ernie Sands acknowledged her with a salute. The deck hatch of the sub popped open and the first of the green plastic bags was thrown out onto the wet deck. The bags were quickly tossed into the cargo net. When half the cash cargo was in the net, the freighter raised it.

Michelle saluted Ernie from the bridge and disappeared with samples of the cash. She went to the galley and spread the money in front of two expert counterfeiters, a Swiss and a Frenchman, and waited. In less than five minutes she reappeared on deck. '*Très bien,*' she yelled, and gave the okay for him to unload the rest of the cash.

Five hundred million in cash against one hundred and twenty-five million in gold. Each crate was weighed as Ernie computed with his hand calculator. There were two and a half tons of gold; it took thirty minutes to load it.

Michelle used the time to examine more samples of the money. She stood in the center hold with six men as they emptied the cargo net. She had them slit open the bags and sort the stacks by denomination, taking random packets to inspect.

Her uncle would be proud of her for today's work.

Ernie laid off as the second sub was unloaded. They followed the same procedure. Finally, they were done. The fenders were pulled up, and the second sub veered off to join the first.

Gently, like diving porpoises, they disappeared, the bows dipping into the water, followed by the bubbling sterns, and at last the conning towers slipped under as all three subs sank into the cold dark belly of the Bay of Biscay.

Michelle climbed to the bridge of the old freighter. The rusty, apparent disrepair belied the ship's ultra-modern steering and communications center, a nest of high-tech computers, dials and screens. She nodded at the Captain as she flipped on the TV cameras that filmed the center hold. The cameras slowly scanned the hillocks of stacked twenties, fifties, and hundreds in an endless pattern.

The Captain called the engine room and ordered three quarters full ahead. The freighter lurched as the high-powered engines revved into life, bringing the freighter up to twenty knots.

Michelle walked outside and was hit by a cold blast of Brittany air. It felt good on her face. It was easy to get euphoric and sloppy when things went well.

Her mind traveled back to the hold in the center of the ship, and the fact that in there was five hundred million in hard US dollars; dollars with no debt against them, dollars that had been paid for in full with gold. The thought of all that money made her shiver and smile.

Her smile turned into a frown as she remembered what her uncle had said: 'You will one day be the head of the Union Corse. You must be wary when everyone is confident, and you must be confident when everyone is scared. And you must always, always be suspicious when things go too well.'

And things had gone well tonight.

She went back onto the warm bridge and told the Captain to head up the Gironde River, directly to their warehouse in Bordeaux.

'Billion,' Don Saverese whispered to himself, letting the word form slowly on his lips, savoring it like his wife's pasta. He said it again, even more slowly. 'Billion. One thousand million.' Not an easy concept to get his mind round when he had started business thirty years ago with three hundred dollars and a Smith and Wesson .38.

Why not a billion? He was big business, so were the other families, and big business thought of assets in billions, not millions. But a billion in cash, that was a different story.

He had received his second shipment of currency, a billion dollars, that very evening, and had distributed it to the four families.

Don Saverese was very careful in keeping the source of this money secret from the other families; they knew nothing. And with each load the Don had increased his percentage of the cash. He had kept five hundred million of the current shipment, for which he had paid one hundred and twenty-five million in gold.

There was a soft knock on his door. 'Enter!'

Carmine Calabrese entered the office with two shrink-wrapped packets of fifties. He placed the parcel on the desk respectfully and sat down.

'So, Carmine, these are as good as always?'

'Yes. It is beyond my comprehension how they can produce such consistent quality, the paper with the blue and red threads, the numbering systems, the quality of the engraving – *bellissimo*.' Carmine pulled a bill out of a broken stack and looked at it under the light, as if to reassure himself that what he had just said was true. He snapped the corner of the bill in the air with his forefinger. It made a loud cracking sound in the silent showroom office. '*Bellissimo*,' he repeated, and replaced the bill in the stack.

'Carmine, you know I keep my own counsel. I have no *consigliore* any more.'

Carmine nodded silently.

'I wish for you to be my *consigliore* for tonight, on two matters that are of grave concern to me.'

'Anything, Don Saverese.' Carmine bowed his head slightly, in deference.

'Thank you, my friend. First, I want you to take over the buying of the gold from Bruno Pugliese. You will work from a fund of cash that I will supply.'

'I see,' Carmine said. 'We will use their own money to buy the gold.'

'Exactly so. If the money is perfect, why launder it? We have tested it enough; there is no question that it passes every test.'

'The other families?'

'No more. They are out. We tell them the source has dried up; there is no more paper for them.'

'Don't we need them for the gold purchases?'

'No. We will pay seven per cent above the market price.

'The other families will hear that we are still buying the gold.'

'What do we care?'

'We will drive the price of gold up quickly if we have a standing order for gold at seven per cent above the London quote.'

'Once again, what do we care? We pay for the paper money based on the market value of the gold on the day of delivery. We just give them less gold as the price increases; it's always good for us.'

Carmine sat in silence thinking about what Don Saverese had said.

The Don broke the silence. 'What we are doing will not go on for ever, something will snap. In the meantime we want to increase the position of this family, the strength of this family over the others.

'There is nothing we do, not even the drugs, that can yield this kind of instant profit in cash. We have no one to collect from, we do not have to wait for our investment to pay off, and we can leverage our profits almost instantly.'

The Don rose, and picked up his miniature Ferrari. He spun the little spoked wheels with his finger as he walked over to the one-way glass window that looked down on the showroom below. He hit the light switch; the spotlights flared into life, illuminating the shiny cars below. He stared at them for several minutes, thinking.

'There is one more thing,' the Don said, walking back to his desk. 'It concerns the gold that we hand over to these people.' He sent the red Ferrari across the top of his desk with a flick of his finger. The tiny car crashed into the stack of newly-printed money, spun three times and stopped. 'I want you to arrange to have a signal transmitter concealed in the gold. It must be done by an expert. Pay whatever you have to, but use the best person we know for the job. The signal must be powerful; they are no doubt placing the gold in some kind of vault.'

Carmine sat upright in his chair. The Don was going to go after the gold.

A thousand thoughts raced through his mind. He did not think it was right to take the gold, but it was not for him to think such thoughts. He was on the wrong side of the desk. The Don had risen to power because he had made the right decisions. And Carmine had wound up in prison because he had made the wrong decisions.

'Bruno Pugliese will handle all the other details. He will follow the signal and find where they are producing this money, and where they are hiding the gold. Do you have any questions, Carmine?'

'No.'

'Good. Start buying the gold tomorrow.' The Don stood, indicating that the meeting was over.

Carmine walked to the door.

'Carmine! I almost forgot. This is for you.'

The Don was holding out a shrink-wrapped packet of fifties. Carmine walked back and took the money from the Don's hand. 'There will be more,' the Don said.

'Thank you.'

As Carmine walked through the fully lit showroom to the back door and his waiting car, he stopped to look back, up at the one-way glass of the Don's office, and knew that the Don was watching him. The showroom lights went black as he reached the door.

Carmine opened his car trunk and carelessly threw in the packet of cash. He got behind the wheel and waited for the car to warm up in the cold night air. He gripped the cold steering wheel and spoke out loud.

'It wasn't the money. It was never the money!'

WEEK FIVE

Monday sunrise 6:00
CAY SAL BANK, BAHAMAS

At dawn the next morning, Books, Heather, and Nick stood on the dock watching the sunrise. The gold from the last exchange had been loaded into one of the fifty-foot Bertram yachts; the vessel was packed with two hundred and fifty million dollars in gold bullion. Slowly, laboriously, it eased its way down the channel towards the blue hole. Books took the helm as Nick checked out the diving gear.

'Rip off the tarp,' Books yelled as they cleared the channel.

Nick went to the bow and pulled back the tarpaulin covers one at a time until all the gold was exposed. It was piled in bars of twenty pounds, each rectangle worth one hundred and sixty thousand dollars.

The interior glowed luminescent yellow in the rising sun. The water was waveless, the wind less than five knots. Books stopped the engines and slid down the stairs from the flying bridge. They all stood in the cockpit looking at the gold. Everything was still as they drifted on the edge of the flats. All that was audible was their breathing.

'It's an amazing metal,' Heather said, stroking a bar with the palm of her hand. It felt warm to the touch.

'This soft yellow metal has an ultimate power over men.' Books held up a bar. 'If you possess it, as we do, then you have power, ultimate power.'

Nick hit the lower station starter button; the engines roared into life, shattering the calm, pacific morning. 'Let's get on with it. We can dream in bed,' he said. He climbed the stainless steel steps to the flying bridge.

Thirty minutes later he was inside the blue hole catching the gold bars as Books or Heather slid them down the rollers. Nick had taken two extra air tanks. They rested against the sheer wall inside the blue hole that rose straight to the almost perfect natural dome.

In two hours of hard work Nick managed to build a ten foot-square pile, four feet high. Hard to believe three hundred and thirty million dollars could occupy such a small space. He hoisted himself to the top of the gold square, carrying the last gold rectangle. He put it in place and sat on the edge of the pile and marvelled at the ceiling; the whole bell was still, lit softly.

Heather's head emerged below him through the opening as she slid down the conveyor belt. He motioned for her to swim up to him. She nodded, and lazily, almost dream-like, she ascended, floating upwards until she was sitting next to him. She signalled that Books had gone back to the boat.

Nick knew that part of the reason she came to see him was to quell her fear of the bell and the shark. And part of the reason was to be with him.

She sat close to him, her hand sliding across the top of the gold rectangles until her fingers intertwined with his. He looked at her; her eyes were wider than normal through the glass mask, bubbles rose from her mouth in bursts. He reached over and placed his hand on her shoulder, then caressed her neck until his fingers were on her mouthpiece. Slowly, he removed her mouthpiece and with his other hand he removed his own. Gently he kissed her. As their lips met air bubbles escaped. The bubbles danced, interweaving as they rose slowly to the surface.

Just as gently as he had kissed her, he replaced the mouthpiece. She took a deep breath, smiled and exhaled. He removed his hand from hers to check his pressure gauge; less than six hundred pounds. He showed the gauge to her, and signalled that they had to leave.

While Heather climbed the anchor line to the boat, Nick covered the entrance of the blue hole and secured his extra empty tanks to the crab line, giving it a tug as a signal for Books to raise them to the surface.

As he watched the air tanks rise through the crystal-clear blue-green water, he thought about Ernie Sands, and wondered where he was at that exact moment.

He didn't want to think about Books, and what he had just done with Heather, and how fast things got complicated.

He started his ascent to the surface, drifting upwards at exactly the same speed as his bubbles. His pressure gauge showed only one hundred pounds remaining.

It should have read three hundred pounds. His breathing rate was twice as fast as normal.

Monday morning 9:00 WASHINGTON, D.C.

Ralph Cobb, Phillip Sturges and the President were studying the M1 and M2 reports to determine how much cash was floating in the monetary system of the United States.

'Not good,' Phillip said, tossing the reports onto the coffee table. 'Even though we don't know for sure, I feel that there's cash coming into the system that isn't being printed by us.'

The President asked, 'What do you think, Ralph?'

'No doubt about it.' Cobb waved the pages of the reports. 'There're several billion dollars more in the system than normal.'

'There's a constant flow of dollars out of the United States,'

Phillip added, 'from criminal activities, hoarders, nations in need of hard currency, and blackmarketeers, which means that the amount of money we have printed in the past has never been a real inflationary problem. But now I see a blip on these M1 and M2 charts, an increase of several billion dollars in the domestic cash river; that's not drastic, but it could be an unhealthy trend that might lead to extreme inflation.'

'My thoughts exactly.' The President tossed his report on top of Phillip's. 'What do we do?'

'Shoot the pricks!' Cobb smiled, looking up at them, flipping his copy on top of the other two reports.

'Would that we could, Ralph. But we still have no real evidence. In the meantime, how much progress have you made since our last meeting?' the President asked.

'The mob is cash rich, there's no question about it; their street action is way up, and so is their legit stuff. They're acquiring every fucking thing that they can get their hands on; they're even doing big leveraged buy-out deals with legit companies, financing junk bonds. I have a mountain of information from Alvin Marks and the FBI's organized crime strike-force division.

'The CIA reports a glut of US dollars in Europe. The money is in the hands of the Union Corse, same pattern as the mob: more street action, and more legit business dealings.

'Finally, the National Security Council says there are powerful open-to-buy orders for immediate delivery hanging over the cash gold market; the bids stay constant at five to seven per cent above the London price. The problem is that the buy orders come from about twenty different sources and middlemen, so we don't know exactly who it is yet that's buying the shit.'

'Ralph's right,' Phillip said. 'I called Handy and Harmon, the precious metal dealers in New York an hour ago, and they confirmed that there is a permanent 'buy' order for gold. And the buyers take physical delivery in every case. It's brought chaos to the futures market. The price of gold keeps rising; the London close today was six hundred and ten dollars an ounce.'

'The foreign action, this Union Corse business, worries me. Maybe we should inform our allies,' the President said.

'No!' Cobb responded. 'They're too self-serving. If they get wind of this they'll panic and stop taking dollars, or let the word leak out to the media. Who the hell knows what else they're capable of.'

'Phillip, what do you think?' the President asked.

'I'm not sure. It's inevitable that they will have to be told, unless we can stop the counterfeit cash supply at the source. But the question is, when should they be told, and how much? We also know that Ralph is right: the minute they get word someone is printing money on a large scale, they will concentrate only on what is in their own best interest.'

'Phillip, I'm the politician here, not you.' The President smiled. 'Just tell me yes or no. Should I contact the Europeans?'

'Yes, inform them on a limited basis.'

'I disagree,' Cobb stood up in his agitation. 'They can't help us even if they know. What can they do for us?'

'Ralph, please be seated. I hear what you're saying.' The President leant back in his chair. 'It's a real Catch-22. If we tell the Europeans, there is a chance that they will leak it to the media, or do something reckless. If we don't tell them and they find out that we knew what was going on then they are going to call us irresponsible bastards whom they can't trust.'

'They call us that now, sir,' Cobb said. 'And they don't co-operate with us; just look at the NATO Alliance. Anyway, we can always stretch the truth, tell them we just found out about it too. We've done it before.'

'How exactly does the gold tie in with all this?' the President asked Phillip, changing the subject.

'We don't know for sure if the buying is connected to the

mob. It could be a whole other set of circumstances, a different group. But if it is the mob buying the gold, then they must be using it somehow to exchange precious metal for counterfeit paper,' Phillip responded.

'So, sir, if we do tell the other nations, our allies, who do we tell, and how much do we tell?' Cobb asked, finally sitting down.

'Let's ease the information out. You are going to have to tell them, Ralph; I want to stay out of it until it gets further along. Speak to the heads of each police force in the next forty-eight hours and schedule a meeting. Contact MI5 in London, the French Sûreté, the Italian Carabinieri, the Canadian RCMP, the German and Swiss Secret Police, the Japanese, and the Chief of Interpol.

'You will inform them that a device developed for us was stolen several months ago, and that this device, the Black Box, has the capacity to print money, not only dollars, but also the currency of each of their nations. Tell them that as far as we know, only dollars are being produced at this time, because they are acceptable world-wide as currency.

'Ask for their assistance, but each of them will have to make up a detailed believable cover story for their police groups; they are not to reveal the existence of the Black Box.

'Do not disclose the location of the island, the names of the perpetrators, or how big the potential problem might become. Let's see what they come up with. We want information from them on any out of the ordinary cash movements or organized crime activities in their countries. Present it as almost hypothetical, and as a potential problem that must be nipped in the bud.'

'Some fucking bud,' Cobb mumbled.

'Ralph, I'm counting on you for this. I want it handled exactly as I say, with no embellishments, no extra little clues.'

'And there's more,' Phillip added.

'You might as well tell him,' the President said, nodding at Phillip to continue.

'Yeah, you might as well,' Cobb muttered, his feelings hurt that they had talked in secret, without him.

'We want a contingency plan of attack.'

'Attack?' Cobb perked up. ' 'Bout time we did something.'

'We know that you have favored something like this from the beginning, but it is only a contingency plan, Ralph, and you are to carry it no further without consulting me,' the President interjected.

Phillip continued. 'We would like a basic plan to assault and destroy the island, using any service or agency you like – Rangers, Seals, Marine Recons, Delta Force, whatever. But it is only an exercise at this point.'

'How much time do I have to put it together?'

'Seven days from today.'

'Okay,' Cobb nodded. He broke into a grin, unable to keep the smile off his face. Finally they were taking some action.

Tuesday midday 12:00
CAY SAL BANK, BAHAMAS

Heather turned off the Whaler's motor. She hugged her shoulders and sobbed. Her sobs turned to anger and frustration as she remembered all the recent nights of tossing and turning. They slept in different beds, in different state-rooms. Books hadn't touched her in weeks. It was as if now that he had her, and she was doing what he wanted, he didn't want her anymore.

She never knew her sex life could mean so much to her until now. It was the touching, the intimacy, not just the sex. All she knew was that she was missing something.

And now Nick had entered her thoughts.

Was her attraction to Nick just to spite Books, to heal her wounded ego? And where could her feelings for Nick lead?

'To disaster, that's where!' she answered her own question, yanking the black bandanna from her forehead and using it to wipe the tears from her eyes.

'Hi,' Percival said, startling her.

'Hello,' she said, trying to hide her face from him, looking down as she stepped onto the beach. She turned her back to tie the Whaler to the dock.

'Something wrong?' he asked.

'Allergies,' she answered.

'Me, too,' Perce said, looking away. 'Allergic to greed. You checked the warehouse lately?'

'No,' Heather sniffled.

'Come with me. It'll help you to forget your allergies.' He smiled.

Percival opened the warehouse door to let Heather pass. It was almost half full of stacked pallets. Heather walked among the pallets and slid her palms along the columns of shrink-wrapped, shiny new money. She had been concentrating on the Black Box and the computer, and hadn't been in the warehouse in days.

'I know the inventory figures, Perce, ten billion in US dollars, but it's different when you see it all piled up like this. Is it stinkier in here than normal?' Heather asked, holding her nose.

'It's the slurry I'm bleaching right now, using a little extra hydrochloric acid.' Percival pointed at the paper-making equipment in the far corner of the warehouse. 'I'm preparing paper for English pounds. It's easier paper than dollars, almost the same formula, but, for pounds, I have to bleach out the red and blue fibers in the leftover dollar slurry.' Percival headed over to the far corner and picked up some finished blank pound-note paper. 'Did you know Hitler tried to counterfeit the pound during the war?' Percival examined the paper sheets. 'Our boy Adolph was going to drop pound notes, fivers, from the air like falling leaves on a struggling Britain. The flood of counterfeit currency was to ruin their internal economy, destroy confidence in English currency, and make it unacceptable anywhere else in the world.'

'And?' Heather asked.

'Hitler lost air superiority over England. Good old RAF whacked him so badly over the Channel that he never got the chance to drop the paper. But there were rumors that a lot of SS and Gestapo officers left Germany for Argentina with suitcases full of perfect pound notes which they fed back into the world monetary system through Switzerland, Argentina, Brazil and the Bahamas after the war. You like the history lesson?'

Heather smiled at him. 'So we're printing pound notes tonight; tens, twenties and fifties,' she said. 'I knew this moment would come. Books had different inks delivered yesterday, beautiful red and yellow and more blue.'

'You don't seem thrilled,' Percival said, probing. He reached into the refrigerator and pulled out two long-necked bottles of Budweiser. He waved one at her and she nodded.

'Pounds, French francs, Swiss francs, German marks. I just think we're getting a little excessive,' Heather said, retying her black bandanna round her head. She took a sip of beer from the sweat-beaded bottle.

'It's weird being here doing this,' Percival said. 'You never get to see what the net results are, what effect you're having on anyone else.'

'Like making ammunition,' Heather said. 'You never know where or how the bullets wind up being used.'

'In our case you have to know the product we are making is being spent,' Percival smiled. 'As fast as we can make it.'

'Yeah. Makes his gold stash worth more every day,' Heather added. 'Perce, I think I know why I'm in this, but I can't figure why you're here. I hope you don't mind me saying this but you're jaded in a nice way. You don't seem driven by money, so why are you here?'

337

'Good question. I was at rock bottom when Books came to me with this scheme; I was huddled in a corner of some flophouse in a permanent fetal position, with no options. He never explained the whole thing to me, only a little bit at a time; I never asked.'

'You could have gone to your family.'

'Maybe, but I'd done it so many times before I couldn't stand facing them again. See, I'm an inveterate coward with no real ambition. All my ambition has come from someone else; now it's Books who supplies me with the drive.' He tilted his bottle up and drank deeply.

'Perce, come on.'

'No, I speak the truth. I had come to a major personal conclusion just life-moments before Books found me, and I was pondering the logical next step based on the conclusion.'

'Perce, stop talking in riddles; what are you trying to say?'

'I had squandered my life, totally squandered it. So, I was examining ways to end it.'

'Perce! Nick and Books both love you.' Heather moved closer and patted his knee.

'Maybe Nick has some affection for me, but Books? Naw, Books is a cold fish. But he offered me a last chance, a chance to do what I really want to do.'

'What's that?'

'Nothing.' Percival stood, and took another beer out of the refrigerator. He sat back down. 'No joke. I'm going to take the money from this job, stash it somewhere, and just live in my own tiny paradise somewhere in the South Pacific and fiddle around with my chemicals, maybe discover something.'

'Kind of like a combination of Gauguin and Du Pont.'

'Kind of! You know, everyone has something that they do well. With me it's chemistry. Understanding chemistry has always been easy for me. Must be in the genes.' Percival smiled. 'Thanks, Gramps, for the genes.' He saluted, tipping the long neck of his beer bottle in the air.

338

'You'll look great in a grass skirt!' Heather said, lightly punching his shoulder. 'Let's get out of here, it's too stinky.'

They left the building and walked down to the dock. The sun was high in the clear afternoon sky. There were no clouds.

'What's that?' Heather asked, pointing at three black specks on the horizon.

'Looks like Ernie Sands and his over-the-hill-gang coming back from another delivery to our French friends. That makes it two deliveries so far.'

'Those subs look weird,' Heather said, and an involuntary shudder ran through her body. 'They give me the creeps, always have.'

'Steel coffins.'

'Let's hope not,' Heather said, knocking on the base of a palm tree for luck and pulling on Percival's arm to lead him into the main building.

WEEK SIX

Monday morning 9:00
WASHINGTON, D.C.

The seven days the President had given him were up. Cobb thumbed the thick assault action document in front of him as he hummed a tuneless song.

He was happy. Happy with the plan and with his good luck.

It was time for action. They would have to do something, and do it soon. He traced out the title of the document with his forefinger, slowly running over each letter, 'Operation Bogus'.

The bogus bills were spreading across the world like a creeping virus that was gaining speed every day. Cobb had contacted the heads of the major police forces of Europe, and they each had the same response: the Union Corse was cash rich, spreading the money around in street activities and increasing action in legitimate enterprises. But the police didn't know why or how the Union Corse was being funded.

And there was one more piece of very bad news. It made Ralph Cobb grin and he didn't know why.

A package had arrived from Scotland Yard that morning. The English police had raided an illegal gambling club in Soho the night before, and found one million pounds in the safe in new, unused bills. The money was perfect except for one inconsistency. The bills were new, but the series was old, and about to be taken out of circulation. The Yard felt the money was counterfeit, and they had asked the Bank of England to try to match notes with the same serial numbers.

The packet that was sent to Cobb contained samples of the confiscated English money. Cobb examined the bills carefully. If they were phonies, they were terrific, including the thin metallic threads. Only they weren't the conventional metallic threads, they were silver lasered lines that looked like threads.

Cobb went to his office door and checked to see if anyone was in the main office area. It was six in the morning. He looked around; the office was empty. He walked back in and closed the door behind him. It was a worldwide problem now; the Secret Service would be off the hook, and he knew more about it than anyone. Everyone would have to come to him.

'Those bastards have balls as big as watermelons,' Cobb said to his empty office as he sat down.

He split the English pounds into three packets. One for himself, one for the President, and one packet for Phillip Sturges. He scribbled a short note to accompany Phillip's packet and called for the Secret Service courier who was on duty twenty-four hours a day.

His note said: 'Let's hammer these bastards! They've invaded England. The Continent will be next.'

Monday noon 12:00
CAY SAL BANK, BAHAMAS

When the sun was at its zenith, the light pattern inside the blue hole formed vertical beams that stretched from the ceiling to the floor in thin sticks of blue light. The gold stash had increased to an area almost twenty feet square. Nick slid the last bar into place.

Again, Nick had brought food for the shark.

He hadn't seen it since the first time he had been in the dome with Heather, but he knew it was in there somewhere, because the food he had been bringing for it always disappeared before he left. He always left the food in the dark corner of the bell, where the bottomless side began to sink into an endless black hole.

Books emerged through the entrance of the blue hole, head first. A puff of sand surrounded his body as he slid off the stainless steel rollers. He landed on his chest, dragging his scuba tank behind him.

Books carried a clipboard and an underwater pen that he used to mark down the new inventory figures. He held up the clipboard so Nick could see it. It said: '$4,000,000,000 at current prices.' Too many zeroes to keep track of, Nick thought as he sat in the sand at the base of the gold pile and rested, his back against the yellow bricks. He watched Books complete his inventory.

It dawned on Nick, 'Maybe he thinks I'm hiding some of the bars in a corner of the dome somewhere, or swimming out with the bars stuffed in my wetsuit. I wonder.' The gold glowed like a solid square incandescent yellow mound as the light rays bounced directly off the top of the stacked pile. Nick idly swam over to where he had left the shark food on some rocks. Once again, the food had disappeared into the blackness of the bottomless side.

Books signalled that he was done, and together, lazily, they pulled themselves up the anchor line to Heather and the waiting boat.

'Very impressive, that pile of glowing gold in that strange light. Made me feel like King Midas. You should go down next time,' Books said to Heather.

'Next time I may,' Heather said, avoiding both men's eyes, remembering sitting on that same pile of gold, kissing Nick. 'I haven't seen the gold for a long time,' she added.

'There is four billion down there at seven hundred dollars an ounce.'

345

'Isn't that enough, Books?' Heather asked.

'Not quite.' Books forced a smile. 'Those French francs and German marks are works of art; they're too pretty to leave unspent. They're just hitting the monetary markets.'

'Well, if we have four billion in gold, that means there's close to sixteen billion of our funny money floating out there,' Nick said. 'The impact of that extra cash on the monetary system will be evident by now.'

'So?'

'So? Books, you know as well as I do that sooner or later they're going to shut us down.'

'Try to shut us down, Nick. There's a big difference.'

'God, you amaze me. Try to shut us down? You have guts, I'll certainly attest to that.' Nick slammed his scuba tank into the built-in holder.

'No guts, no glory,' Books commented.

'I just don't want it to be our guts and your glory,' Heather snapped.

Books said nothing. He just stood there and stared at her, anger lashing in his eyes. Finally, he shook his head from side to side and walked forward to start the engines. 'Get the anchor line, will you, Nick?'

'Sure,' Nick said, glad to have something to do to relieve the tension.

Books hit the starter buttons, and both powerful diesel engines roared into life.

Monday afternoon 3:00
WASHINGTON, D.C.

The President gently tossed the thick assault action document titled 'Operation Bogus' onto the coffee table in front of him.

'Looks all right to me, Ralph. But we still have to wait for a while.'

'While we wait, they print more currency,' Cobb said, looking at Phillip. 'You received the English money I couriered?'

'Yes.' Phillip waved the pound notes in the air.

'They're doing German marks and French francs also. I just heard through the CIA that the French Sûreté and the German Secret Police feel positive that a large-scale counterfeit ring is in operation. The ring is somehow connected to the Union Corse.'

'How do they know?' the President asked.

'Snitches, and raids that have turned up a lot of cash accidently, like the Scotland Yard bust in Soho.'

'We have to speak personally with the other nations involved,' Phillip said.

The President looked at Ralph. 'We can we do it by satellite transmission. All the down links are completed. The countries involved are plugged into the system. We could set the meeting for tonight at five; it would be eleven their time. Who do you want notified?'

'England, France, Germany, Italy and Switzerland. Japan, too. I want to talk to the heads of state, and the heads of their federal police forces.'

'The Russians?' Phillip asked.

'Not yet,' the President said. 'They'll hear about it soon enough.'

'The Russians?' Cobb asked. 'Why the Russians?'

'Some of their border states trade heavily in dollars on the black market, under the direction of the KGB. The Russians trade goods and precious metals for US dollars,' Phillip told him.

'So, what do we care?'

'They store American dollars in their Federal Bank and use them to support the ruble and finance certain other international trade, like buying wheat from us and oil from the Arabs. They have done this for years. Now, with the fall of the Iron Curtain, they will somehow have to create a hard ruble that will be accepted internationally.

'So, if the Russians get wind of what is happening from someone else, they will dump their hoarded US dollars into the world monetary markets, and they have a lot of greenbacks, a lot more than anyone thinks they have. They'll pound the hell out of us. They pass millions of ounces of gold over the Yugoslavian border for hard currency every year. And I'm sure if the Union Corse is involved, their people are on the Soviet borders right now, feeding the Russians phony dollars for gold.'

'Shit!' Cobb spat out.

'My sentiments exactly, Ralph,' the President said. 'That's why we have to move carefully, and be sure there are no surprises.'

'Meantime, those pricks keep the presses rolling.'

'We're aware of that,' the President said gently. 'We won't pussyfoot around this anymore, Ralph.' A flicker of anger flashed through the President's eyes.

'Yes, sir.' He buried his head in his copy of Operation Bogus. 'Any comments on the plan?'

'Yes,' Phillip said. 'I've thought about it, and I don't like the idea of using US Navy Seals to assault the island.'

'Why?' the President asked.

'If anything were to go wrong we would have no excuse. It would be a totally American exercise. If the media got hold of it we would have no way out.'

'Nothing is going to go wrong,' Cobb said. 'And what the hell difference does it make?'

'If we use the British SAS or French Frogmen, we can always say that it was a NATO exercise that went haywire, that we were on military maneuvers, and something went wrong.'

'I think we should use our own guys. I don't trust anyone else,' Cobb said.

348

'It also commits our allies to us,' the President added.

'I'll modify the plan accordingly, sir,' Cobb reluctantly acquiesced. 'Who do you prefer, Mr President, the English or the French?'

'The English. They've always been our best allies.'

'Done,' Cobb said, slamming his assault plan book shut, smiling.

Monday afternoon 4:00
NEW YORK CITY

Don Saverese had spent his life dedicated to the importance of small details; he had won his position by attention to minutiae and careful planning. But this time the Don had overlooked an important detail. He hadn't realized how big the counterfeit operation was going to become.

He sat behind his massive desk and listened to Carmine Calabrese. 'The other families are ready to turn on you, Don Saverese. There is going to be too much heat coming down from the Feds, and since the other families are not profiting from the counterfeit money anymore, they will turn on you. They will not risk losing their assets. They will give information to the Feds that will tear your family apart.'

'*Omerta*. They are bound to it by oath.'

'No. They are not bound to the pledge of silence to you because you are not their direct family, and because they can say your actions are jeopardizing the existence of their families. So, if it is either them or you who suffers, it's going to be you.'

'Perhaps there is something in what you say.'

Carmine continued: 'The Federal agencies are starting to

apply the pressure now because they are just beginning to realize the magnitude of the counterfeiting. They have many resources to work with, the FBI, the DEA, the Secret Service, the Treasury Department, the IRS –'

'Enough! I know their power and what they can do when they wish to. What are you recommending?'

'Include the other families or stop.'

'Is there anything that you haven't told me? I get the feeling there may be something else.'

'Perhaps. Perhaps there is one other thing, but I am reluctant to tell you.'

'Carmine, I know that if you tell me you are only the messenger, and that you have my best interest at heart. I do not hurt the messenger that bears me bad news; you of all people know that.'

'The other families are worried about you, Don Saverese, they say you have changed.'

'How? How have I changed?'

'They say you are overcome by greed because of this counterfeit money; that you will not share with them, and that you will use your good fortune, these counterfeit bills, to increase your family until theirs are all dwarfed. Yours will be the richest family by so large a margin that you will dominate all of them. And they are right. Fortunately for you, Don Saverese, they do not know how much false money you have already smuggled in and distributed; they can only guess.' Carmine let his words hang in the air while he tried to anticipate how his benefactor would respond.

'Continue! Is there more I should hear?'

'The families know about the law, and criminal justice. There are only two crimes mentioned in the Constitution of the United States: treason and counterfeiting. There will be much heat from this enterprise, no relenting. The Federal Government will go to the furthest limits to protect the dollar.

'Greed is a strong word, Don Saverese, but it is a word I have heard them use against you. They feel that there is plenty of profit to go around, and if all the families get to share in the gains, they will share in the risk; there is strength in unity, in solidarity.'

They were sitting in the Don's office. The Don rose and went to the picture of his mother; he swung it aside, opened the safe, and extracted two shrink-wrapped packages of money; five hundred thousand dollars in newly printed bills. He stacked the money in front of Carmine. 'For you, with my thanks.'

Carmine knew it was a reward for good counsel and was offered in good faith. Rejection of the money would be an insult to the Don. '*Grazie*,' Carmine mumbled, bowing his head.

'You are a brave man to tell me this. Is there anything else?'

'Yes. They wonder, with the quantities of money so large, and flooding into the monetary system every day, what will happen if the public ever finds out. If, in the end, confidence in paper money is lost, we all suffer. There may be inflation, and a run on the banks. And the gold market – the price of gold will skyrocket. No one will want to buy or own government bonds . . . all monetary paper may be abandoned in favor of precious metals, diamonds, oil, real estate. It could mean going back to the barter system. It is a concern they all share. They have much to lose.'

'Rightfully so. It is something I have asked myself. I would like to be alone now.'

The Don rose and went to the closet door in the corner of the office. He pulled out a large brown paper bag that had 'Gristede's' printed in bold letters across the center. Gristede's was the Don's favorite supermarket; they sold the best fresh pasta. He stood holding the bag open. Carmine dropped the two packets of shrink-wrapped bills into the paper bag and took it from the Don. They shook hands in silence, and Carmine walked out through the showroom of Ferraris and Maseratis to his waiting gray Chevy sedan.

The Don walked over to the safe and closed it. He carefully

351

swung the picture of his beloved dead mother into place. He studied the portrait for a minute, running his fingers down her face, feeling the rough canvas against his fingertips. He sat down, opened his top desk drawer, and withdrew the red Ferrari Testarossa. He placed the tiny car on his clear desktop and flicked it across his desk, using his forefinger.

He knew that what Carmine had said was the truth and that he would have to share.

'*Fongule!*' he said out loud and flicked the Ferrari sharply, so hard that it jumped the inkwell, tumbled down off the desk, and rolled end over end on the plush white carpet.

Carmine fought the traffic with his gray Chevy and pushed his way onto Columbus Avenue. He didn't like the upper west side of New York, too damned many Yuppies. He wondered if he should have told the Don there was still one more thing: the other major families had already decided to stop Don Saverese if he did not share his largesse with them. His greed was unacceptable. Carmine wondered if the Don would understand this from their conversation.

He looked down at the brown Gristede's shopping bag that was lying on the front seat with the half-million in cash. He patted the bag like he would a good dog.

He shook his head and sighed, wondering what he would do with the money. There was nothing he wanted to buy.

Monday evening 5:00
WASHINGTON, D.C.

The television down-link system was the brainchild of the National Security Council. It was a satellite hook-up designed to send and receive signals only with other countries that had the system. The President dubbed it his private television network.

But it was much more than a hotline: it provided the means for an instant summit meeting that excluded the press, that could take place in total secrecy.

To hook into the system, a receiving country needed special equipment plus an elaborate set of frequency keys, programmed by computer in advance. This made it impossible for unwanted ears to listen, unless they decoded the frequency. In addition to the NATO allies, the Japanese and Chinese had each received a 'PBS', *President's Broadcasting System*, as it was called by the NSC.

At the last moment, the President had told Ralph Cobb to use Proposition 'R'. Proposition 'R' was a built in 'flaw' that had been planted in the system by the CIA.

The CIA knew the Russians would attempt to tap into the system after it was installed, to eavesdrop. So the CIA made it easy; they created a puzzle they knew the Russians would decipher. They fed the Soviets a few key clues that were carefully worked into the signals, similar codes to other series used openly by the US. The Russians could listen in whenever the United States transmitted using Proposition 'R'.

Cobb thought it was contradictory of the President to allow the Russians to 'listen in' after what he had said about their possibly dumping dollars, but he did what he was told; he included Proposition 'R' without comment.

Cobb, Phillip and the President sat in the small White House basement 'PBS' room waiting for the giant screen in front of them to light up. The screen filled the entire wall, which was ten feet by twelve feet. The screen came into focus at five o'clock exactly. The heads of state of Britain, France, Germany, Switzerland, Canada, and Japan filled the screen one at a time, each projected into a section by the PBS computer. There were small red and green lights in front of each head of state.

At one minute after five the little green light in front of the President of the United States lit up, and he began to speak.

'Thank you for being available at such short notice. We have a grave problem in this country, which we feel may be spreading to each of your countries. The problem either exists now or soon will.'

The President waited, taking the measure of each person who faced him. His eyes moved from screen to screen, pausing at each face. Each head of state had been asked to bring their most important government police representative to the meeting. These men sat on the righthand sides of their country's leaders. They were serious men.

The President spoke. 'About three months ago, a small Black Box was stolen in London.' The President continued his briefing, speaking uninterrupted, for three minutes. The only thing he left out was the exact location of the counterfeiting operation.

When he was finished he flicked off the microphone in front of him. There was a pause of about thirty seconds and then eight green lights sparked into life. The US President acknowledged Germany first. 'Mr Chancellor?'

'They have the capacity to print marks, you say, but we have not seen any yet,' he announced. 'Only extra US dollars are circulating at the moment.'

The French President was next. 'What are we to do with the dollar? If we refuse to take dollars, it will cause incredible complications in the world monetary markets.'

'That's why we called this meeting, to warn you,' Cobb said, leaning forward. 'You cannot either refuse to take dollars or dump dollars on the world markets. It would seriously hurt us all. Above all, we cannot let this leak out to the media.'

The President acknowledged the green light in front of the British Prime Minister. 'I am assuming that you know the location from which these men operate, and for reasons of your own have not disclosed it. I'm also assuming that you have looked at all your legal remedies. I can only assure you that if these people are operating out of the United Kingdom, we have means to take care of them, and would be happy to do so.'

'Thank you,' the President said, 'but they are not operating from the United Kingdom. And yes, we have exhausted all legal avenues. We may have to use other means, and if we do, we may be calling on one or more of you privately to help us.'

The Japanese Prime Minister spoke. 'My nation survives on imported oil. If any of the Arab nations find out about this theft, they will be very upset, since they take dollars in payment for oil. There is no other currency that could be substituted at the moment, not even yen. How may we be of service to help eliminate this threat?'

'We are here to determine that,' the US President replied, signalling for Switzerland to speak next.

'Is the United States planning any covert action?' the Swiss President asked.

'We have a contingency plan, but we have not made a decision; if we should proceed we may be asking for all of your support.'

The Commissioner of the French Sûreté spoke up. 'Does the United States take any responsibility here, since it was your Federal Reserve that commissioned this Black Box in the first place?'

'No,' the President answered evenly. 'The Black Box was stolen from English soil and it is the United States that is suffering the most. We have called this meeting as a courtesy to our allies. I think we have said all that is necessary for the moment. I would like to see our police forces co-operating. I suggest Interpol be kept out of this, for the time being, and all information be filtered through our Secret Service. Ralph Cobb will handle this; please communicate through him. He will be available twenty-four hours a day.

'Unless there is anything of vital importance, this meeting

is closed. Thank you.' The President hit the 'OFF' button and watched the faces wash away, disappearing in a green haze.

'That should set them into motion.' The President smiled, draining his coffee. He rose and walked to the door, halting when Cobb spoke.

'Sir, why did we go with Proposition 'R'? We know the Russians are going to listen in. I thought we had decided to –'

'Ralph, I just had a hunch, a feeling, that we should leak the information to them. You know, fellas, there are really very few things that are good about this job, but one of them is that once in a while you get to follow your instincts, and no one can say or do a damn thing about it.' He opened the door, then turned and added, 'I think they're more likely to believe what they hear if they eavesdrop.'

Tuesday sunrise 6:00
YUGOSLAVIA

Michelle stood warm and comfortable, safe in the wheelhouse of the *Aigle Corse* with the Captain, listening to the autumn winds whistle through the rigging. Her uncle's yacht was cruising the Dubrovnik-Trieste pleasure coast. Luxury yachts were common in the Adriatic as they cruised the Yugoslavian coast, but not many were seen in the late fall or winter. Michelle had decided to use the *Aigle Corse* for this delivery.

She was carrying counterfeit Swiss francs, German marks and US dollars to be traded for Russian gold and Kalashnikov AK-47 automatic rifles. Yugoslavia was their main smuggling conduit for gold and arms out of the Soviet Union. Her uncle had taught her early in life that the Soviet Union was the world's largest miner of gold; no one knew how many ounces came out of that rich country every year.

Michelle and the Corsican Brotherhood had been trading the precious metal for dollars, francs, and marks for many years; hard currencies were essential to the Soviet Union's underground economy and their balance of trade payments. In most cases the Union Corse dealt with smugglers who were thinly disguised undercover agents: card-carrying members of the KGB. It was an unspoken trading understanding, a natural balance that had been established over a long period of time. Michelle had so far passed off over two billion dollars in counterfeit hard currencies through this conduit, in return for gold and arms. The smuggling on the Yugoslavian coast was under the auspices and watchful eye of the Soviet Union, one way or another.

The Captain had navigated the boat behind the island of Hvar, just nine miles off the coast of Yugoslavia. The boat was cruising at four knots; they were waiting for a familiar Yugoslavian trawler.

Suddenly four dots crept onto the radar screen like four tiny white insects. The dots were approaching from the island of Brac, moving quickly towards them.

The Captain's hand immediately went to the throttles. He looked at Michelle. The Captain had been a smuggler for thirty years; he had the best instincts of any man in the Union Corse fleet. Michelle put her hand on top of his, and held it.

They watched as two of the clustered white dots separated on the radar screen and broke away; they were advancing at great speed. 'Soviet helicopter gunships,' Michelle said, pushing the Captain's hand, and the throttles, down – full forward.

'Two high-speed patrol boats and two helicopters. They were waiting for us! Bastards!' Michelle said.

The Captain said nothing; they had to make it into international waters. The pleasure yacht was more than an ocean-going toy. The hull was aluminium reinforced with double ribs, and the engines were powerful MTUs, Mercedes diesels, turbo-charged and fully blown. The hull shook like a wet dog as the engines kicked in and ran immediately up to the red line – four thousand RPM. The bow lurched up out of the water. The yacht was jet-powered, no propellers; it used water like a jet plane used air: water was inhaled at the bow and spat out through three underwater exhausts, leaving a high roostertail of water behind them. The *Aigle Corse* leapt to thirty knots, then forty knots.

The patrol boats were still four miles away, but the helicopters were coming fast, less than a mile off.

The radar screen lit up again as eight more dots popped into life: four blips off the island of Vis, and four off Korcula.

They were trapped in the center of a deadly triangle; no chance to reach the open sea.

Michelle heard the whump, whump, whump of the first two helicopter gunships as they hovered above them. They were talking on their loudspeakers in bad French. She and the Captain both knew the Russians would shoot if they didn't stop.

Michelle placed her hand on the Captain's and pulled the throttles back to idle.

The boat lurched, and stopped dead in the water. They were trapped with a billion dollars of counterfeit currency aboard, in Soviet waters.

Tuesday morning 7:00
CAY SAL BANK, BAHAMAS

It was one hour past dawn. The light was still magic and the air was cool. Nick was jogging round the coral island before the hot sun blistered the air and melted his will for exercise. The thin rim of white coral sand ran round the island, stretching a little under a mile.

None of them swam anymore. The sharks were getting very bold.

On Nick's second lap, he noticed Heather sitting on the end of the dock, nibbling on some breakfast that had been made in the liberty ship galley. The currency delivery crews were leaving that evening for the Florida Keys and the Bay of Biscay. They were delivering money regularly now.

After the third lap, Nick joined her. She smiled as he sat beside her and said, 'I notice you don't dangle your toes in the water anymore.'

'No. Although I've never seen any of those toothy monsters in this close.' She squirmed, tucking her toes in even tighter under her thighs. 'I don't see your toes in the water either, Mr Macho.' Nick sat with his knees tucked under his chin.

'So,' he said. 'There are twenty-four days left on this adventure, but who's counting. Think you can stand it?'

'Yeah, probably. There's something else happening here, you know.' Heather looked at him, shading her eyes from the rising sun with the flat of her hand.

'Explain, please,' Nick said, already knowing what was on her mind.

'Do I have to?' Heather smiled. 'The only clue you get is that it involves you and me. Enough?'

'Yes. He's my best friend.'

'And my ex-lover.'

'Ex?'

'Yes. And we'll never be lovers again. It's gone, totally gone. I don't understand where all that passion goes, and how fast it can disappear, like it was never there, as if we were never lovers. That's how it is now.'

'And me?' Nick asked. 'How do you feel about me?'

'Confused. But I'm pulled to you, Nick, strongly, in a

different way than I was drawn to Books. Oh shit, I can't explain it, not even a little bit. Except . . .'

'Yes?' Nick prompted.

'Except I feel better when I'm around you than . . .' Heather scraped the remaining food off her plate into the clear blue-green water. A school of small mangrove snappers came up to the surface and started to nibble on the floating powdered scrambled eggs. It made Heather smile. 'Than when I'm not.'

She reached over and held his fingers in her hand. She admired his fingers for a second. They were long and graceful, almost feminine, sensitive fingers, but strong and sinewy at the same time. They could caress or crush with equal ease. She gently placed his hand on the dock.

'I understand,' Nick said. 'I feel the same. But Books and I go back a long time, almost twenty years, and he was always there for me during that time. There are things in my past . . .' Nick looked up into her eyes.

'No!' Heather's hands flew to her face. She rubbed the palms of her hands into her eye sockets, smoothed her forehead and ran her hands through her flowing hair. 'No more words, please.' She dropped one of her hands and without looking at Nick she placed it on his shoulder. 'I want it to be good between us. Maybe someday when we're a long way from here you will tell me about your past, but I can't bear it now, and besides . . .' She smiled, and took her hand off his shoulder so she could rise and begin her day.

'Besides, what?' Nick asked.

'Besides, in twenty-four days I'm going to qualify as a person with a weird past myself. And you know what I think about the past?'

'No,' Nick said.

'I think it should stay in the past. I like you right here in the present, no ghosts.'

'Right,' Nick said, smiling as he walked her to the factory. He wished it were that simple.

Michelle sat on the bridge of a Russian nuclear-powered frigate, in handcuffs. They were drifting in the Adriatic Sea off the island of Hvar with the *Aigle Corse* in tow.

The Russian KGB Colonel in charge had commandeered large samples of the counterfeit money for examination; he sealed off the frigate's galley to examine the money in secrecy.

The KGB had sent the chief of their currency department to assist the Colonel in evaluating the confiscated money. The money was stacked high on the galley tables; the shrink-wrapped packs glistened under the fluorescent lights.

'Amazing; this is an amazing duplication.' The currency expert handed a fistful of Swiss francs to the KGB Colonel. 'The truth is that I see no imperfections – dollars, marks, and francs, these notes appear to be perfect.' He smiled as the magnifying eyepiece dropped from his eye. It dangled on a black cord that hung round his neck, swinging in slow pendulum rhythm. 'In fact, if I had not already been warned that these may be counterfeit, I would have concluded they were real, and that this was some sort of a test for me. The serial numbers are all active, they are numbered in sequence, the definition and configuration in every area is perfect. These would pass anywhere.'

'Will you say exactly that in your report?'

'Yes, Colonel; it is the truth.'

'Thank you.' The KGB Colonel had already received his orders. He was only to get confirmation of the quality of the confiscated money.

He made his way to the bridge, where he dismissed everyone except the frigate Captain and Michelle. 'I am notifying you that your boat and all the contents have been seized by the USSR.' The Colonel was in full uniform. He stood in front of her, stiffly, his hands at his sides. 'You have violated Soviet territory by entering our waters. You are carrying over two thousand dollars in foreign currency and therefore have broken our currency laws. Under these laws it is within my power to seize all your property and imprison you for the illegal transport of foreign currency into the Soviet Union.' The Colonel stopped speaking, and stared at Michelle. He let his words fill the air, hovering over her like black clouds.

She stared back at him, her Corsican blood pounding through her veins. The Russians needed the trade that was smuggled in over their borders by the Union Corse. She knew the Russian charade, the bluster, was part of the procedure. She didn't know what was really on their minds, so she remained still, her dark eyes blazing.

The Colonel ignored her stare. He opened his briefcase, took out a single typed page, and resumed his position in front of her. He held the sheet of paper at his side.

'The Soviet Union, in its mercy, has empowered me to propose a compromise. If you and your crew will sign this full confession, the Soviet Union will accept it. The confession states that you and your men are guilty of the currency violations cited, and that you agree willingly to give up your vessel and all its contents. If you ever enter Soviet territory again you may be arrested and subjected to fifteen years' hard labor in prison. Do you so agree?' The Colonel thrust the single sheet of paper in her face with one hand, and reached into a pocket for the key to her handcuffs with the other.

The confession was written in careful French. But why this? Were they trying to rip her off, or did they somehow know that she was dealing in counterfeit, trading gold and arms with the Soviet Union and feeding them counterfeit cash? Was that other high-ranking official brought on board the frigate to examine the currency? Michelle shrugged and scratched her signature on the confession. She tossed the pen on top of the paper. The Colonel handcuffed her again and gently picked up the pen. 'Now, we will bring your crew up to the bridge, one at a time; they are to sign the confession. We have their passports, so make sure they sign their proper names.'

Four hours later, Michelle and her crew were on a train, a train that once was called the Orient Express. They boarded it in Trieste. They were given their passports, a final warning never to return to the Soviet Union, and a one-way ticket to Paris. The handcuffs were removed just as the train started to creep out of the station. The KGB Colonel and four men stayed with them until they crossed the border into France.

Michelle sat in silence for the entire journey to Paris. She wondered what the Russians knew, and what she was going to say to her uncle. She had lost one billion dollars in currency that had cost the Union Corse two hundred and fifty million in gold, and her uncle's favorite toy, the *Aigle Corse*.

Most important, she may have lost her chance to become queen of the Union Corse.

Tuesday night 1:00
FEDERAL RESERVE, NEW YORK CITY

It was one hour after midnight. Veronica sat alone in Phillip's living room in the Federal Reserve building, looking out at the dark, dead-quiet financial district, the sleeping heart of the American financial colossus.

'Why am I so attracted to Phillip Sturges?' she asked herself. He was powerful and rich, but she had been with many powerful rich men. Some had even asked her to marry, but she had never considered their proposals.

And what could she give him? He seemed to have everything.

He purchased her services. He always kept part of himself in reserve. And tonight he had been totally preoccupied. A call had come through from the Secret Service, something that involved Russia. She had heard him say: 'The Russians will no doubt feed it back to us.'

It had taken all her love skills to soothe him with pleasure into sleep. She knew he would be waking soon, calling her name, and asking her to go home.

She eased into bed beside him and held him in her arms, kissing him gently awake.

'Darling,' she whispered. 'I think I'm falling for you.'

'No! Now's not the time.'

'Yes,' she said, kissing him hard on the lips. 'Now is the time; there is no other time.'

His arms enveloped her. And she knew what it was that she could give him.

Wednesday morning 9:00
WASHINGTON, D.C.

'You're sure of this?' the President asked Ralph Cobb. They were in the Oval Office of the White House. Phillip sat on Cobb's left.

'Yes, we got the information from the French Sûreté. They have an informant inside the Union Corse. The number was one billion dollars in assorted currencies. They were caught off the Yugoslavian coast.'

'So, the Russians will be feeding this confiscated counterfeit back into the monetary system of Europe,' the President said.

'Not just into the monetary system of Europe; it can be

fed back into the United States, South America, or Asia,' Phillip stated flatly.

'Is there any new information besides this Russian news?' the President asked.

'No, sir,' Cobb answered.

'Let's vote, then,' the President said. 'Ralph, you for going in? Hitting them?'

'Yes.'

'Phillip?'

'Yes. But I think we should enlist the aid of one of our allies, perhaps an SAS team as we discussed. They are supposed to be the best, and the Bahamas used to be a British possession.'

'Okay,' the President said. 'We'll follow your assault plan, Ralph. You brief the British commander.'

'Yes, sir. When?'

'Your decision. The sooner the better. I'll make the call to the PM and tell him we're going in; from then on it's yours.'

'Consider it done,' Cobb said.

Friday night 11:30
GULF STREAM

The US nuclear submarine *Key Largo* lay submerged on the edge of the Gulf Stream, a one-mile swim to the sand flats that formed the Cay Sal Bank. The weather was good, the wind less than ten knots, and the moon was only halfway through its cycle.

'You and your men must cross half a mile of flats before you reach this channel. Cobb held an aerial photo in a file on his lap. He passed the photo among the twelve SAS men who were sitting loosely round the table.

The SAS team was dressed in wetsuits of skin-tight one-eighth-inch black Lycra, the same material the astronauts wore when they took a walk on the moon. Their faces were blackened. All that stood out was the whites of their eyes and the flash of teeth as they spoke.

The SAS Commander addressed his men. 'We know they have sophisticated low-level radar on the island, so we are not surfacing. The sub will rise to within ten feet of the surface and expel us through the lock-out tubes. We'll use the rebreathers all the way in to the island. You got a problem, Shamus?' Shamus Flannery was a red-headed blue-eyed Irishman from Dublin.

'Just this bloody rebreather. The exhaust-scrubber-filter is focked.' It was lying in pieces on the table. The rebreathers were military versions of scuba tanks, with one difference: the exhaled air was recycled and purified in a second small tank, then returned to the original tank to be inhaled once again. The rebreathers provided the SAS team with up to thirty-six hours of good air without changing tanks; most importantly, there were no bubbles to be seen on the surface. Unlike scuba gear which used a mouthpiece, the rebreathers required full face masks; each mask had a microphone and a transmitter so the men could communicate with each other underwater.

'We have extra units. Just take a new unit, Shamus, and don't fuck this one up.'

'It wasn't me, sir, just bad luck. My luck's been very bad lately.'

'Stow it, Shamus. Don't talk to me about luck. I don't believe in it,' the Commander said. 'In less than thirty minutes we're out of here, so listen hard. Mr Cobb wants to say something.' The Commander looked at each one of his men. They were trained tighter than piano wire. They shifted their eyes from their Commander to Ralph Cobb, and waited.

Cobb began, 'One of the perpetrators involved in this scheme used to be an arms dealer, and he has access to just about whatever he wants: Claymore mines, rockets, SAMs, all kinds of small arms, military radar, infrared night vision systems, the works.'

Cobb paused and maneuvered to stand over the men, but even sitting, their bearing seemed to raise them to Cobb's height. 'For all we know, the beaches may be mined or trip-wired, and with their night-vision capability it could get hot as hell. So don't think you're just going to stroll in there and clobber these assholes. Once you're inside, you are to destroy everything except this.' Cobb held up a picture of the Black Box. 'This little item is to be saved and returned.' He dropped small packets of dollars, English pound notes, and German marks onto the table, and sat back down in his chair. 'You're going to see a lot of these, once you're inside. Destroy all the currency you find!'

The team glanced at each other but showed no expression. They were trained to expect the unexpected, and react. 'Deal with it!' was their credo. Each man was a specialist and a back-up specialist in at least one other area.

'They're printing money, using advanced technology.' The men sat poker-faced listening to Cobb. 'There's more. We also think there may be a stash of gold somewhere. We have a US Navy Seal team waiting. They will come in later for clean-up. You locate it and they'll come and get it.'

'As usual, we do the work and someone else gets the focking glory.'

'Flannery, put a sock in it,' the Commander said.

Cobb continued, 'With regard to casualties, we will take prisoners, but if anyone should get injured badly, we feel it would be better if the injury were terminal.'

The SAS team understood: no matter how bad the bad guys acted, terrorists or criminals, if they were wounded they could eventually elicit sympathy with the press; they would always scream excessive brutality. Dead men don't file legal suits or write biographies. The world has a short memory for unpleasantness and a fondness for swift retribution, especially if it's final.

'There are two buildings, as you can see from the maps and photos. We want these reduced to rubble, after you secure the Black Box and locate the gold,' Cobb said. 'Any questions?'

There was silence.

'Okay,' the Commander said. 'The dive master will be in charge from this point. We take our orders from him, until we reach the beach.'

Twenty minutes later the team was in the lock-out cylinder in the bow of the sub, sitting six abreast, waiting for the steel room to fill up with warm Gulf Stream water.

The water came pouring in as the pet-cocks were opened. The indigo blue current turned clear as it swirled around their flippers and up their Lycra-covered ankles; in less than a minute the water had climbed to their chests and shoulders, circling in little rivulets as it snaked past their chins and up their full face masks until the small steel room was full.

As the water pressed against the ceiling, a hatch popped open, and they were one with the sea. The Commander was first out, followed by Shamus Flannery. The dive master was last. They swam in single file for two hundred yards, checking their gear and getting oriented.

'Double up,' the dive master said, and six men kicked harder, filling up ranks until there were six two-man teams. They had a fifteen-minute swim ahead of them before they reached the edge of the flats.

Each man carried a backpack filled with his ordnance. They would unstrap the rebreathers and backpacks in the final few seconds before they emerged from the water. Once on shore they would take less than twenty seconds to cast off their flippers and face masks, extract their weapons and be ready to follow the Commander.

They were swimming towards the island at a depth of thirty

feet. The Commander hit the Cay Sal wall first. He stopped at twenty-five feet and waited as the other men gathered against the coral cliff. When they were all assembled, they climbed it hand over hand, finally easing over onto the flats in a fan formation, a loose V, with the dive master in the center, in the lead. Like a flock of birds, they followed the leader. Their formation allowed them all to see the dive master, and ensured they would all land together on the island at the same time, in the same spot.

The flats were shallow, only four to six feet in depth. The team crossed over the white sand and patches of sea grass; they moved together, deadly dark animals from the deep.

'Fock'n bloody hell!' Shamus Flannery whispered into his face mask. It was picked up by the other men. 'What the fock are they?'

Then the entire team saw them: dark blotches, dusky spots in the moonlight, flashes of white underbellies, long thin tails that whipped wildly, stirring up the sand into fine white crystals in the half-moonlight, like an under water dust storm.

'Easy, men!' the dive master said calmly. 'It's only a school of leopard rays having their dinner of crabs and grass shrimp.' He let a full minute pass until he heard everyone's breathing return to normal, then he spoke. 'No more talking unless it's me.' He waited thirty more seconds so each man could settle down before he began to swim. 'Okay, let's go. Tighten up a little, keep about one meter between each of you.'

The men could feel the warmth of the tropical water on their hands and necks, areas the Lycra suits didn't cover. The sun heated the flats every day, and the temperature remained higher than the Gulf Stream current throughout the night. They were sweating inside their suits; beads of perspiration formed on their foreheads and under their armpits. They swam using only their fins, arms tight to their sides, like twelve black bullets.

'Hold it,' the dive master said in almost a whisper.

The twelve men stopped as one and closed ranks. They

could all feel it, but they didn't know what it was. A deep eerie silence prevailed over the flats, an almost primeval calm.

They weren't alone.

These men were warriors with the best survival instincts of the race, trained to the highest physical degree. They knew danger was lurking in the darkness that surrounded them.

'There's something weird in this focking water,' Shamus Flannery said.

'Zip it, Shamus,' the dive master said, his throat tight; he thought he knew what was in the water with them. 'Form a circle with your heads facing –'

The dive master never finished his sentence. He was bounced like a kicked top, hit by a blur. A charging animal had rubbed its own abrasive body up against the Lycra suit, scraping like sandpaper on wood to see what was in the water, and whether it was edible.

No one spoke. They all knew now what it was.

Sharks!

The dive master broke silence as he tried frantically to swim back into the safety of the human circle. He held his face mask like a microphone as he blew out the water and secured the straps. The mask had fallen off his head from the blow he had taken. 'Get your bang sticks; take off the safeties.'

Each man carried a twelve-inch stainless steel rod on his calf. It was a tube with three twelve-gauge shotgun shells in the clip. The shells fired on contact, exploding when pushed against soft flesh or cartilage. They were designed to kill sharks.

They waited in silence, a circle of heads, all facing outward, all holding loaded bang sticks.

'It may have only been a stray shark, everyone stay calm,' the dive master said.

After another two minutes the dive master signalled the men to go back into formation. Slowly, the circle opened round him into a flat V; a small flutter of flippers, and they were moving again, hands at their sides still clutching the

370

bang sticks. Twelve men, six to a side, three feet apart, made the formation almost twenty feet from one end to the other. The last man on the southern tip of the formation was Oliver Cromwell, the Cockney radio operator. They all called him Ollie.

The attack came from the east, Ollie's blind side, left leg, Lycra suit and all. The shark bit twice, shook Ollie and the leg like a cat with a rat and dragged him out of the formation. The man next to Ollie saw it happen out of the corner of his eye and by the time he turned his head Ollie was being dragged away. The man broke formation to follow Ollie and saw a second shark charging towards him. He pushed his bang stick into the incoming shark's eye and heard the thump as the firing pin hit the twelve-gauge shotgun shell; the cartridge exploded underwater, blowing out the shark's other eye as the pellets passed through the animal's tiny brain, sending it into a wild convulsing spin.

The shallow water, only four feet deep, was churning with sand and blood, a combination of Ollie's blood and the blood of the blasted shark. The trailing SAS man stood upright in the shallows to find Ollie. His head broke water and what he saw made his heart sink; the breath left his body. The dive master was also standing. The flats were covered with fins, hundreds of cruising dorsal fins all moving in a slow grinding circle round them. Ollie floated on the surface only a few feet away from the standing man. He moved to help Ollie, who was thrashing the water, minus his left leg.

'Leave him! Our only chance is to stay together,' the dive master yelled into his microphone, cursing himself for not standing to observe the surface before he ordered them to break the protective circle. Three sharks were heading for Ollie's thrashing form. His bleeding body would divert the sharks.

'Form a circle; we'll work our way off these flats, back into deeper water, back to the sub,' the dive master shouted. The shark that had received the head shot was floating now, on the surface. Six dorsal fins were heading towards the inert lump as the men submerged.

'Ehhhhhh. Oh my God. Ehhhhhh, please help me, boys, mother of God help me,' Ollie screamed, ripping off his face mask, shouting into the microphone. The sound shattered the ear drums of the men who were all back underwater now. They could hear and feel the thumps through the water as the sharks pounded Ollie's body. The dive master spoke. 'We have to move now while they are preoccupied and confused. We have only seconds.'

Shamus Flannery was the next victim, but he was ready. He turned at the exact moment of impact. The open mouth of the shark missed. Flannery jerked away; the bottom jaw slipped up his leg, making a grating sound. Shamus hit the shark a glancing blow with the bangstick just behind the dorsal fin; the explosion took out the fin and a piece of flesh the size of a football. Two cruising sharks immediately hit the wounded shark, carrying it to the surface, shaking it, tearing it open.

The men understood what to do. No words were necessary. Kill the sharks!

They had to take the initiative, be aggressive, if they were to survive. Each man had three shots in the bangstick magazine. They had to make them all count.

The men broke the circle and formed a tight V with the last two men on each side swimming backwards to protect the rear of the formation. The sharks got bolder and closed on the men; the SAS team signalled to each other, indicating who was to take the shot, who was to use their powerhead. One by one, the men used up their three shots. Shamus Flannery lost his bang stick as he stuck it into the mouth of a passing shark; the explosion caused the shark to snap its jaws shut, and spin away in its death throes carrying the bang stick with it. The flats were churning with sand and blood as attacking sharks pounded away on the dead carcasses of other sharks.

They finally made it to the wall and the edge of the Gulf Stream. They left the shallows of the Cay Sal Bank and entered the deep water of the Great Bahama Bank, a trough that dropped into a canyon of water two miles deep. They hoped the fighting sharks would remain on the flats.

But they had guessed wrong; things got worse in the open water.

New, bigger sharks moved in: hammerheads, bullsharks, blacktips, lemon sharks – the roamers, the nomads that travel the currents of the world on a never-ending, never-stopping journey, drawn in by the frantic sounds and vibrations combined with the smell of fresh blood and ground-up fish guts wafting from the stinking offal that had been poured fresh on the surface that very night to seduce the big sharks in from the Stream.

'Sweet Jesus,' the dive master sighed. 'These are big bastards.'

The men regrouped into a circle and drifted. While they were on the flats they had been safe from attack above and below; now they were vulnerable from every angle. And these sharks were big; the smallest one was six feet and some of them ranged up to fourteen feet in length.

'How many rounds left? Shout it out!' the dive master said.

'One.'

'Two.'

'Two.'

'One.'

'That's it?' the dive master asked. There was a silence. 'Six shots? All right, so be it. We're aborting this mission. I want us all to ease up to the surface. Ollie's gone and so is the radio. We'll have to use the underwater beeper, code red, and pray the sub hears it. Flannery, yours work?'

'Yes, sir.'

'Let it go. Commander?'

'Yes?'

'Let's shoot some flares.' The Commander and the dive master were the only ones that carried flares.

'Roger,' the Commander mumbled. It was a humiliation to call for help, not to be able to fight their way out and complete the mission.

A thick lumbering hammerhead made an aggressive pass at one of the men. The dive master heard two pops; the shark convulsed into spasms and veered off, spinning, dropping into the bottomless canyon.

Shamus Flannery engaged the rescue beeper and set it floating on a line tied to his belt, while the Commander sent three red flares arcing off into the night.

They waited, floating near the surface, cutting off attack from above and staying within earshot of an outboard motor. They remained clustered in a tight circle. Two lemon sharks came up from directly below on a straight line. The circle exploded like a starburst as the two sharks came through the center, almost jumping out of the water.

'Get back in the bloody circle,' the dive master yelled. 'Come together! We'll float on the surface.' He heard two more powerhead pops and watched the two lemon sharks twist and turn, spinning downward. The death spin ended suddenly when they were hit hard by two heavy bull sharks that had been circling the human cluster like outriders herding cattle.

The men knew they were down to only two shots, and there was a chance that the sub had not heard the SOS.

They remained welded together, each with his own thoughts. Visibility was less than twenty feet in the jet-black Gulf Stream water. They had given up swimming and were just drifting on the surface in the two-knot current of the Stream.

They heard it off in the distance. At first it was only a light whine but they knew the sound. It got louder until they could feel the churning of the propeller.

Shamus Flannery popped his head out of the water and

saw the black form of the twenty-man Zodiac. It was an inflatable launched from the submarine. Two men in wetsuits were silhouetted in the light of the half-moon. They were honing in on the constant sound of the beeper. They slowed down as the signal got stronger. Flannery broke the silence.

'Over here! For Christ's sake, we're over here!' Shamus Flannery had his fist raised in the air, a signal of emergency, a signal to retrieve as soon as possible. The boat was manned by two US Navy Seals. They knew the signal. To use it meant that you had failed.

They cut the engine and slid right up to Flannery and stopped. The stern man slipped a metal ring the size of a basketball hoop over Flannery's arm, caught him at the elbow and flung him on board. One by one, the SAS team was pulled on board the Zodiac. Not a word was spoken. The dive master and another man with one remaining bang-stick cartridge came out of the water last.

The Zodiac's outboard engine was cranked up and the inflatable headed back to the submarine at full speed.

The submarine had surfaced and was waiting for the SAS team. It had had to surface to launch the Zodiac. The Captain had made the decision when the watch had advised him of the flares lighting up the dark sky through his periscope.

The team was dispersed to the debriefing room, where Cobb sat waiting impatiently. The Commander broke the silence.

'Sorry, sir. It all went bad the minute we hit those flats. There was a smell on the water, the stink of fish guts. I think they've been feeding the sharks in there for a long time.'

'Bastards!'

'We lost Ollie Cromwell. He was hit early, before we knew what was going on. A water attack is out of the question, unless you want to just charge in there in boats.'

'We don't,' Cobb answered. 'So that's it?'

'Yes. That's it,' the dive master blurted acidly.

Cobb left the debriefing room. A sad silence filled the room.

'Well, I was wrong, Commander, about what I said before.'

'What was that, Shamus?'

'About luck, that my luck was bad. It ain't bad.'

'You talking about Ollie Cromwell?'

'Yes, sir.'

The eleven men of the SAS team looked from one man to another and thought of Ollie Cromwell, and his bad luck.

Saturday morning 7:00
CAY SAL BANK, BAHAMAS

The tranquil morning air on Cay Sal Bank was cut by a scream, a wild gut-wrenching scream. Heather stood on the shore near the dock staring at the remains of a human leg wrapped in black Lycra. The leg had been severed at the hip, torn from the torso by gaping saw-tooth bites with bone and gristle showing red in the morning sun. Crabs swarmed and crawled on top of each other, snipping and cutting at the flesh. Heather dropped to her knees and retched over an aloe plant. Nothing came out of her mouth. The dry heaves shook her entire body. Her scream had turned into one long uncontrollable sob.

Nick and Perce were the first on the scene. They saw the leg, half on the shore and half floating in the shallow water.

'My God!' Perce gasped.

'Get that damn thing out of here,' Nick said as he scooped Heather up in his arms and started up the beach.

'How?' Perce asked, too shocked to think.

'Use the goddamn Whaler, or the Zodiac; tie a line on the ankle and pull it out to sea; just get the damn thing out of here, and make sure it doesn't float back in with the tide and wind.'

Books ran past Nick down to the shore, took one look at Perce and the leg, and ran back to the Butler building, catching them at the entrance to the factory. He opened the door for Nick. Heather was still sobbing. She sat down on a couch in the small lounge area. Nick and Books walked over to the coffee machine.

Books had awakened Nick during the night. He had taken the watch that night, and just before midnight had noticed a bleep on the radar that he suspected might be an invader. They stayed on alert for several hours, ready to activate the defenses, but nothing had happened. Now they realized what had taken place.

'Let's take a walk round the island and then a cruise over the flats,' Books said softly.

'And Heather?' Nick asked, looking over at her.

'She needs to work this out alone. There's nothing we can do.'

Books and Nick began at the dock and walked along the narrow beach that Nick used as a jogging trail. They were only two hundred yards down the beach when they saw the first dead shark. The carcass was mostly head and tail. Everything in between was ripped away. The gulls were pecking away at the decaying frame.

'What happened to him?' Books asked.

'Whoever tried the assault last night was armed for sharks. See the bullet hole in the head? Looks like twelve gauge, probably from a bang stick. We should double up the watches and activate everything we've got. The next time they aren't going to be so subtle.'

As they walked along the thin strip of sand they saw three flocks of gulls moving in circles ahead of them, working over the bodies of three more sharks.

'Do you think that leg belonged to one of our own military?' Books asked.

'Possibly.' Nick thought a minute. 'We should keep this to ourselves. Ernie and his gang are all ex-Navy veterans. They're not going to like some of their own going down like this. We'll have to tell Perce and Heather to keep it quiet. We'll tell the rest of the crew that these dead shark carcasses are what upset Heather. And Heather, what do we tell her?' he asked. 'She's pretty upset.'

'I know she is. She'll just have to live with it.'

'That dot on the screen last night was probably a sub and a full assault team. They couldn't get through the sharks; but they'll be back, in one form or another.'

They walked back to the dock and started up the Magnum ocean racer they used to spread the offal. Nick eased it out of the channel up onto a plane and out onto the flats. They spotted more carcasses and clusters of birds orbiting the dead shark bodies. In some cases the gulls had landed and were actually floating with the sharks, heads bobbing, pecking away at the rotting flesh.

Nick counted a dozen carcasses in the small area around the mouth of the channel. 'The assault team must have killed a few sharks and then the sharks started to feed on each other.'

At the mouth of the channel on the edge of the flats, floating towards the Gulf Stream, they saw what remained of Oliver Cromwell. A torso with no head, arms, or legs, just a trunk with gaping jagged holes where toothy maws had ripped the flesh away; entire sections of the rib cage were missing. The shredded wetsuit fluttered in the wind and the moving current, like the black rags of a scarecrow.

'Jesus Christ, what a sight,' Nick said as he idled up next to the torso. Books looped a line and slipped it over the remains then tied it off on the stern cleat. He retrieved the trunk with the line so that it rubbed up against the idling hull of the Magnum. Nick reached over and fingered the two small airtanks that were strapped to the back of the torso. 'These tanks are part of a rebreather system, US Navy issue.

But that doesn't mean too much. We supply all our allies with this equipment if they want it. You can stay under a long time with these, up to thirty-six hours, and there are no bubbles.' Nick pushed the carcass away from the waterline of the Magnum. Both men watched as the body floated off, lazily bobbing up and down; the line gradually got taut as the torso snapped into the wake behind the boat and Books increased the engine speed.

They pulled the shredded form several miles out to sea into the Stream and finally cut it loose. They did it in silence.

'We better cruise the entire area; if anything floats up on shore, Ernie and his men may see it. We can't take that chance,' Books said.

For the next hour they patrolled the flats. They found nothing.

When they returned, Heather was working. All the side plates were off the copier. She was lubricating and wiping down the interior parts. She did not look up when they walked in.

Nick knelt down in front of her. 'Feeling better?'

'Not feeling at all is more like it; numb.'

'We had some visitors last night, probably an attack team. Some form of special forces. Books saw a pretty good sized bleep on the radar screen last night and called me. We stood watch all night. Nothing could have come close without our knowing it.'

Heather stared at him for a minute and looked over at Books before speaking. 'Suppose . . .' her voice quivered. 'Suppose they had made it to shore?'

'Let's not suppose, Heather,' Books said. 'They didn't.'

Heather shivered involuntarily, and rose to her feet.

Books continued, 'This was a hostile act. They've obviously discarded any legal remedy or solution and have decided to come after us with force. We must make a counter move now or they'll come right back. We were lucky with the sharks.'

'You have a plan, Books?' Nick asked.

'Yes. I'm going to hit them with their greatest fear.'
'Which is?'
'The media. We'll use the power of the press against them.'

Saturday midday 11:30 NEW YORK CITY

Don Saverese was on a scrambled conference call to the Dons of Los Angeles and Miami. He didn't like what he was hearing. He spun the tiny wheels of the Testarossa so fast that they made a faint humming sound in his empty office.

'There's so much of that funny money in circulation by now that the Feds have got to know, and they're goin' to come down on us like a ton of bricks. They've got plenty of stunts they can pull, including that RICO racketeering bullshit they like so much.' The Miami Don was excited, puffing heavily on his Cuban cigar.

'And the price of gold,' the Los Angeles Don interjected, 'is sky-fuckin'-high now, twelve hundred and twenty-two dollars an ounce on the London Exchange this morning. And climbing. The street gold is drying up.'

'So, is it your counsel to stop this enterprise?' Don Saverese asked.

There was a long silence on the other end of the line.

Don Saverese had relented after the advice from Carmine and had brought the other four families back into the distribution network. But he deeply resented having to give them eighty per cent of the action.

'Since we began this recent phase,' he continued, 'each of the five families has received two billion dollars in cash. We are expecting another two billion in this week, which will bring the total to twelve billion dollars. Most of this money has been leveraged by investment into legitimate enterprises.

'I agree with you that there is a limit before all this good fortune reverses and becomes a liability; this will occur when the Government understands what is happening. It is then that they will come down on us, hard. I recommend that we take delivery of the next shipment and talk again at that time.'

'*Si*,' the two voices chorused in agreement, and the line went dead.

As Don Saverese hung the receiver back in the cradle it rang again, and the small red light on the special scrambler attachment began to blink.

'Don Saverese, I have news.' Carmine waited for permission to continue.

'This line is secure, go ahead.'

'Our people have planted the signal on the last load; the one that was delivered yesterday.'

'And they have the means to follow the signal?'

'Yes, a plane will follow at first, then three high-speed boats will close in to triangulate the signal, once it stops.'

'Do these men have any idea what they are looking for?'

'No. They will think it is drugs, and I have taken the precaution of using our own men. We brought our people down to Miami from New York. Each man involved in the operation is a made man, loyal to you, Don Saverese.'

'Very good, Carmine. There is another load scheduled to be delivered at the end of next week. You should stay, enjoy the sun, until this business is completed.'

'Of course. *Ciao*.'

'*Ciao*, Carmine.'

The Don had to smile to himself as he hung up; it was working well for him. The stage was set for the other families to stop their activities, and this would have to be soon. The Feds would be the cause. The families, in anticipation of the inevitable heat from the Feds, would easily acquiesce and agree to quit after the next load.

In the meantime, Don Saverese would have found St John's base of operations and where the gold was hidden. He would destroy the base and take the gold as his reward. That would ease the pain of sharing the cash with the other families.

Saturday noon 12:00
WASHINGTON, D.C.

'So we failed. That's the bottom line, Ralph. With all our exotic military technology, including a nuclear sub and a crack SAS unit, we didn't knock them out. Thanks to Mother Nature and a school of sharks that we never observed, they're still printing money and we're sitting around having a meeting.'

'Yes, sir. I'm afraid so, sir,' Cobb mumbled.

'And there's more bad news, I'm afraid, sir.' Phillip handed the President a copy of the London *Times*. 'I've circled the article in red, from this morning's paper.' It was a small article on the second page:

INTERPOL WORRIED ABOUT FUNNY MONEY
MAJOR COUNTERFEITING RING FEARED

International Police are very concerned that a major international counterfeiting ring may be in operation. Reliable sources indicate that this ring began in the United States and has spread its paper tentacles into Europe and parts of Asia. The group may be gradually putting a stranglehold on the international money markets by feeding bogus banknotes into the monetary bloodstream of several major nations. Their base of operations is unknown at this time as is the full scope of their operation. The situation is being investigated.

'That's lovely, just lovely,' the President said, handing the article to Cobb. 'How did the London *Times* get this?'

'Anonymous source.'

'Of course. Can we get to the publisher?'

'We can't, but James probably can.' Phillip was on a first-name basis with the British Prime Minister.

'Have him do it!'

'I've already asked,' Phillip replied.

'This changes things. We'll need to talk to our friends on the down-link transmission. Let's do it tonight. Ralph, will you set it up for us?'

'You want Proposition 'R' in or out?'

'In.'

Cobb wondered why the President would want the Russians to eavesdrop on the transmission again, but said nothing. 'Yes, sir.'

Cobb left the meeting and drove over to the National Security Council building to set up the down-link transmission for that evening.

'So what? The water assault failed. There are plenty of other ways to take out that island, but sitting around in meetings ain't one of them,' he said to himself. 'It's time I did something.'

NICE, FRANCE

Michelle Descartes sat in front of her uncle's desk in the huge office library that overlooked the Mediterranean Sea. Her uncle was standing looking out at his dock and the empty space where the *Aigle Corse* used to berth.

She had told him the story of their capture, every detail. Descartes had also interviewed the Captain of the vessel. He stood at the window trying to understand what had really happened.

René Descartes and his brother Henri had risen from common stevedores on the docks of Marseilles to become two of the most powerful men in Europe because they believed in the future, and the power of the white powder. They were once known only as the French Connection, but in time became the World Connection. They supplied the Western World with heroin. This gave the Union Corse the resources to deal in guns, gambling, white slavery, loan-sharking, kidnapping and murder. But it all came from the powder of the poppy, grown in the rich soil of India and the Golden Triangle. It was carried hidden in the guts of freighters, tankers, pleasure boats, airplanes, trains, automobiles, and humans, dropped in ports from Istanbul to Calais, where the men of the Corsican Brotherhood stood ready to receive it, warehouse it, and distribute it to the tenderloin districts of the teeming, desperate cities of the world.

There were many reasons why René Descartes came to be chief of the Union Corse, but the main reason was his basic conservatism. He led a gang of men who could garrote a victim at five and sit down with their own families at six for a pleasant meal. But the Descartes brothers were different; they were thinkers. They analyzed situations for as long as it took, then moved with sudden and ferocious speed. It was this skill that René wanted to pass on to his niece. There was no question in his mind that the female was the more deadly of the species; it was just a matter of training. Michelle Descartes was the last of their strain, the only child produced by the two brothers.

And there was one more thing: René Descartes loved his niece. She was the last living soul that he did love, and he wanted the best for her; and the best was to become the head of the Union Corse. It was ultimate power. And ultimate power was ultimate pleasure.

He turned to speak to her. 'For years now the Russians have known that we trade hard currencies on the Yugoslavian coast for gold, arms, and anything else of value. And we know the KGB is the mastermind of much of what goes on; now they all of a sudden lie in wait for us and trap us. They take the money and our ship and threaten you and your crew. Why?'

Michelle knew the old man was testing her. 'Because they know we have fed them counterfeit money and taken their gold, and Kalashnikov rifles. They are punishing us for breaking an unwritten agreement, for cheating them.' Michelle paused.

'And what else?' Descartes asked, looking back at the dock where the *Aigle Corse*, his pride and joy, used to sit awaiting his pleasure.

'They are angry that we are upsetting the world monetary markets, because the Russians need them stable, just as the rest of the world needs them stable, especially now that they plan to enter the global economy.'

'Yes, and that is their real concern; very good. So what is your conclusion?'

'That we are walking on thin ice.' Michelle lit a cigarette and took a long drag. 'With the powder it is only a tiny per cent of the population that is involved, the weak and unproductive part of society. But the counterfeit money threatens the foundation of the entire society.'

'So?'

'If it becomes known by the populations of the countries involved that perfect counterfeit currency paper is filtering into the money channels at a great rate, then all paper becomes valueless, and confidence is eroded to the point that trade stops. If it stops in the Western countries, it also affects Russia, which is trying to join the twentieth century.'

'So?'

'So we should stop distributing the paper before all the resources of these countries are turned against us.'

Descartes turned and smiled as he walked over to Michelle. He sat in the chair next to her. 'Almost perfect, but there is one thing, one very important thing, that you have not thought of, Michelle. Take your time, think some more.'

He stood and returned to the window. He looked over his shoulder at his protégé and felt warm inside, comfortable. The Descartes dynasty was passing into the right hands, although Michelle would have an enormous battle to wage in assuming control of the Brotherhood after he died. Many deaths and much pain would follow René Descartes' death before she sat solidly in his chair, behind his desk; but there was no question in his mind that she would sit in that chair.

'Uncle!'

He turned to look at her.

'I was wrong. We must carry on distributing the money.'

'Yes, but why?'

'Because only then will we have something to trade, and there is still great profit left in the venture. When they come for us, that is the time, and the only time, that we agree to stop, because we will still have much leverage. And the leverage is in stopping, discontinuing our distribution for a price. Perhaps we will even assist these countries in the capture or death of the counterfeiters. In return they could give us amnesty and we would carry on with our normal business.'

'And would anyone be excepted from this action?'

'Yes. Colonel Le Clerc, since he has been of great help to us and very loyal over the many years we have done business; he is almost one of us.'

'Anyone else?'

Michelle thought for a second about Nick Sullivan; she liked him very much. 'No. No, there is no one else who would be spared.'

Descartes walked over to his niece and kissed her cheek. He put his hand on her shoulder and squeezed the base of her neck gently, nodding his approval.

'Anything else, Uncle?'

'Yes, there is one more thing: order a new *Aigle Corse*. We will call it *Aigle Corse II*. Order the same hull and engines. And Michelle.'

'Yes, Uncle?'

'You design the interior, since you will be the one using it.' Descartes put his forefinger to his own lips to forestall her automatic protest. He let go of her shoulder and left the room, passing under the giant portrait of Napoleon.

Saturday evening 6:00
WASHINGTON, D.C.

The down-link transmission was completed and the screen filled with faces; France, Britain, Germany, Switzerland, Canada and Japan were represented.

All the faces washed away and the screen was filled with words; the London *Times* article flashed on each video receiver at the same time.

The President gave everyone time to translate and read the article, then spoke. 'Thank you all for your personal attention

387

to this matter. We consider it to be of the highest priority.'

The words were swept away and the screen came to life once again with the faces of some of the most powerful people in the world. The President continued, 'The London *Times* article was, we believe, planted by the very counterfeiters we are after. The British Government is attempting to confirm the origin of the article from the publisher.

'We assaulted their base of operations yesterday and we failed. It is our belief that they intend to use the media to initiate a subtle form of economic blackmail.'

'Where is their base of operations?' the Canadian Prime Minister asked.

'A tiny atoll in the middle of the Gulf Stream called the Cay Sal Bank; the island used to belong to the Bahamas. The counterfeiters acquired the sovereign rights to the island for three years. We believe they are selling the cash for gold.'

'Why did the assault fail?' the German Chancellor asked.

'It failed because the assault team was intercepted before it could get to the island.'

'So the attack angered these people, this gang of counterfeiters, and they planted the story,' the German Chancellor continued.

'Yes, that is our conclusion.'

The Japanese Prime Minister spoke next. 'How do they obtain currency paper in such enormous quantities?'

'They are using recycled shredded paper that was discarded by the United States Federal Reserve, and modifying it slightly for each of your countries. We have stopped the source of this paper, but they have large stocks in reserve. That was one of the reasons we decided to assault the island and destroy their operation.'

'How big is the operation?' the French President asked.

'Our current estimates are that they are feeding a minimum of two billion dollars a week into Europe and Asia; and the same amount into the economy of the United States. It could be twice this amount; we don't know for sure.'

A silence settled over the leaders as they each contemplated what it meant to their countries.

The President said, 'We have a contingency plan to go back and attack the island from the air. But on this venture we will want to discuss the details with all of you, the way we did before we hit Libya in 1987, the Iranian oil platforms in 1988, and Panama in 1989. We will finalize our assault plan and submit it to you for consideration.'

'And in the meantime?' the British Prime Minister asked.

'We must discover exactly how this counterfeit money is being fed into circulation, and we must stop it. We have some theories and some clues, all of which Ralph Cobb, the head of our Secret Service, will share with the heads of your police departments. This must take first priority; if we know how it is being filtered into our monetary systems, we can stop it.'

The Swiss President gave a nod of agreement. 'What is the time frame?'

'Three days. We will meet three days from now. Thank you, once again, for attending this meeting.' The transmission ended.

'Why wait?' Cobb asked. 'I can have an air-assault plan together in twenty-four hours.'

'No, Ralph, a lot can happen in three days. We can always go in there and zap them then if that's the only alternative.' The President looked at Phillip, who nodded in agreement. The President turned back to Cobb. 'Now please put together all the information and evidence on the distributors and send it to the people we promised it to.' He stood to leave. 'I've had enough of this for today.'

The three men rose in the elevator out of the basement and back to the lobby of the National Security Council headquarters. They all got into their waiting limousines and disappeared into the dark Washington night.

Cobb instructed his driver to take him to his office. He closed the window between himself and the chauffeur and opened the one beside him. The glass hummed as it slid down into the door. A cold blast of fresh air hit him square in the face, rejuvenating him. He leaned back in his seat and stared out of the open window.

It was going to be a long three days.

Sunday morning 7:00
CAY SAL BANK, BAHAMAS

She was swimming easily, the full moon glowing soft-yellow on her back. The salt water felt warm, almost too warm, like bathtub water.

Heather was naked; the water was a velvet blanket that caressed her body as she swam, soothing her, gently massaging, seeping in through her skin, calming her heart-beat and pulse until she drifted in a languid cloud of contentment. She turned and floated on her back; she could see her nipples jutting up towards the dark clouds that took turns filtering the moon. She lifted her head slightly out of the water. She could see her pubic hair rise in a mound between her legs; a clustered clump of wet curly dark hair that reflected in the moonlight.

Her floating hand went to that dark mysterious spot involuntarily, as if being pulled by a magnet, a natural magnet buried between her legs. She gently rubbed her mound and parted the lips slightly as her finger found that little place that gave so much pleasure. Her finger rotated round her tiny pink pearl. The finger moved faster and faster as her excitement rose. Her desire had the power to take her over, almost against her own will, and transport her.

Her knees rose slightly with her pleasure so that her heels fell deeper into the water, toes pointed, and her buttocks sank up to her waist. Her head moved slightly as her lips parted and she moaned, moving her head from side to side, the water brushing each cheek like a gentle loving hand. Finally, she threw her head back and arched her back; her eyes open wide, she stared up at the full glowing moon overhead as she writhed in pleasure, her body finally sinking slowly back down until it was flat with the sea, and she was floating, drifting again.

The first searing pain began at her ankle, as if a ferocious dog had sunk its canine teeth deep into her Achilles heel and wouldn't let go; the piercing mouth shook her leg from side to side as it tried to dislodge her ankle from her foot. The next pain shot up from her waist and the small of her back as a chunk of her body was torn away. Her soft midriff was being pummeled and peeled, disappearing into the deep. She was lifted two feet out of the water as a giant set of razor-sharp teeth drove her into the air and ripped out the rib cage on the left side of her body. She flopped back into the water like a limp rag doll as she watched her rib cage disappear into the deep.

She raised her head to look; they were everywhere. She was surrounded by dorsal fins, and like a pack of wild jackals they were moving in for the kill.

An enormous pain shot up from in between her thighs like lightning as sharp teeth bit into petal soft flesh, tearing her female bouquet from her.

She screamed, baying at the moon in incredible pain and agony.

How could this be happening to her?

She was going to die!

'Heather, it's all right, come on now, snap out of it.'

'Nick, oh God!' She threw her arms round his neck and buried her head on his shoulder. She licked salty tears from her lips with the tip of her tongue. 'They came from every direction and there were so many of them. Sharks. That poor man – that leg that we saw – oh God, it must have been dreadful for him. Death must be so awful; you're so alone and so frightened.'

'It was only a dream, Heather.' Nick knelt beside her cot and smoothed her ash-blonde hair back against her temples. 'It's all right now. You're under great stress. It'll be over soon.'

'No. It won't. It won't be over soon. I'm afraid it will never be over. Nick, I never thought it would be like this. It's so . . . so ugly and depressing. I thought it would be fun and exciting, but it isn't.'

Heather struggled to sit up. She swung her legs over the side of the canvas army cot and set her bare feet on the floor. She was wearing a white cotton T-shirt and white panties. She pulled the sheet across her waist and reached for a Kleenex sticking out of a box on top of the two-drawer steel file cabinet and dabbed her eyes.

'I must be a mess,' she said, wiping her eyes.

She had been sleeping alone in the factory for the last two weeks. Books slept on *Desperado*. They had dropped any pretense of sleeping together.

Nick had been on his morning jog round the island when he heard moaning coming from within the factory building. He had burst in to see Heather writhing and twisting on her cot.

'I'm over this, Nick. Really over it.'

'What are you over, Heather, and why are you telling Nick?' Books stood in the doorway. They didn't know how long he had been standing there, watching.

A silence settled over them. Nick got off his knees and stood, looking away.

'Answer me, Heather. I deserve an answer.'

Heather rose and faced Books, the sheet dropping away from her body, exposing her long slim legs.

'You heard me right, Books, I'm over this whole goddamn thing. I never thought anyone would die because of it, and for what? Some money.'

'It isn't some money. It's a huge amount of money, and when the stakes get this high, people sometimes die.'

'Well, not this people. I'm not dying or going to be the cause of anyone's death. Do you hear me, Books? I'll say it again. Count me out of this whole fucking deal.'

Heather stormed off to look out of the only window in the factory. She saw the relentless sun rising to bake the island in tropical heat for another day.

'Heather, I've already agreed to stop in twenty-three more days, and –'

She didn't let him finish his statement. She spun to face him, her hands on her hips.

'I've decided that it's not yours to decide, Books. My life belongs to me, and you don't decide what happens to me.' Heather strode to the entrance.

'I thought we were all in this together,' Books said, looking over at Nick.

'Well, you thought wrong, you cold-hearted bastard!' Heather left, slamming the metal door shut behind her.

Sunday afternoon 3:00
NEW YORK CITY

'We have a location.' Carmine's voice was strong, almost too strong; the voice had a timbre that rang discordant in the Don's ear. He couldn't put his finger on it, but it was there.

'The line is good, please continue.'

'It is on a small group of islands called the Cay Sal Bank which is located in the Gulf Stream off the Florida Keys.'

'Who owns this island? The Bahamas?'

'No. They used to, but now it is privately owned and has been made independent of the Bahamas for three years.'

'How can that be?'

'These people, Nick and St John, have obtained the sovereign rights. They have total legal control of the island.'

There was silence as the Don digested the news. He felt inordinate anger rising within him. Then he realized it wasn't anger, it was jealousy. He was jealous of Books St John, who would dare to own a country.

'So, Carmine, the gold is stored right there on their little island?'

'For the moment, but I believe it probable they will move it. I have arranged for one of our radio-equipped commercial fishing boats to work in the Gulf Stream off the island for a few days. And I have instructed two speedboats to stand by in case the item is moved.'

'Carmine, arrange for a plane to photograph the island thoroughly. I would like to see what security measures they have taken.'

'I will have it done right away.' Carmine's voice was definitely strained; the Don was sure of it. He had an ear for tiny inflections or omissions.

'Is everything well with you, Carmine? Is there anything bothering you?'

'Everything is good with me.'

'We have known each other too long. I hear it in your voice, Carmine. Tell me what it is that bothers you.'

'Perhaps there is something . . . I have to say, in all respect, that I doubt the wisdom of this action.'

'Explain.'

'I feel we have an arrangement with these people and they have lived up to their end. That is all, Don Saverese.'

'And we should live up to our end of the bargain. Is that what you are saying?'

'I mean no disrespect.'

'Carmine, this is not a matter with which you have to concern yourself.'

The Don spun the wheels of his tiny Ferrari until they hummed.

Carmine was telling him that he was being dishonourable and breaking the business code of the Cosa Nostra.

In his own way, Carmine was commiting the worst sin of all against the Don. He was being disrespectful, no matter what he said, and questioning orders. The Don pondered recalling him to New York immediately. He decided against it because there was not enough time to replace him with another trusted man. There was a cash-for-gold swap scheduled within the next twenty-four hours, and he needed the aerial pictures he had requested on the defense of the island.

'Carmine, please, no thoughts in this direction. You must assume that I have thought all this out and that I am doing what is best for the family, for your family as well.'

'I do, Don Saverese.' It was back: that falseness in his voice.

'Good. We will talk about it when you return to New York.'

'When do you want me to return?'

'As soon as the delivery is made and you have the pictures in your hand. Bring them to me personally.'

'I will do as you ask.'

'Good, I will expect to see you shortly.'

The call ended. The Don sat thinking, then abruptly flicked the Ferrari across the documents on his desk. The tiny wheels made a barely audible crackling sound on the paper.

Don Saverese's mind was made up. Carmine Calabrese would be retired. He would never again do any work for the family.

WEEK SEVEN

Monday night 10:00
STRAITS OF FLORIDA

Nick was on board one of the specially-built Bertram yachts that they had ordered. The hull was hollow, stripped of beds, furniture and fancy fixtures; only a microwave oven in the galley remained. The boat was fifty-four feet long, and powered by two turbo-charged twelve-cylinder GM diesel engines. It could carry a big payload and still cruise along at twenty knots. There were three yachts in convoy that night; they were carrying two billion dollars in cash.

Was he going to lose it all? Both his friends and perhaps the one woman he could really love? For what? They already had an enormous fortune stored in the blue hole. Maybe he and Heather could leave together when he got back. Forget the money and the gold. He didn't need much to get by. Yes, that's what he would do if Heather would go with him. As soon as he got back to the island, they could take off in his boat. Let Books see it through to the end on his own.

Nick's reverie was broken by two blips that appeared on the radar screen. The blips would be the two vessels they were to rendezvous with. The boats were one to two miles due north of them, and were converging at 24 degrees latitude and 81 degrees longitude, just off the Nicholas Channel, halfway between Cuba and the Florida Keys.

Nick jumped on board the first shrimp boat and headed for the wheelhouse. He knew Carmine Calabrese would be in there, ready to spot-check the bills as they came on board.

Nick enjoyed Carmine; he had a wisdom that Nick identified but couldn't define.

'Ah, Nick! How are you?'

'Good, Carmine. You look well.' They shook hands. Carmine put his left hand on top of their hands and gave an extra shake.

'Here. Sit with me while I wait to count all this dirty money.' Carmine smiled. 'You OK?'

'Sure. Why?'

'You look bothered. You're upset about something.' Just then the door to the wheelhouse banged open and a sailor placed an armful of different thicknesses of packaged bills on the chart table. Carmine dismissed the man with a nod and a slight wave. He slit open the first pack of two hundred and fifty thousand; they were twenties. He moved his double-channeled microscope under the swing-arm light and rotated a bill slowly beneath the lenses. He looked up suddenly at Nick. 'I can talk and still do my job here.' He put his head down and locked his eyes into the microscope sockets.

'Just some philosophical problems; not worth talking about.'

'I'm a great jailhouse philosopher, the Aristotle of Leavenworth. I had lots of time to think while I was in Federal prison.' Carmine looked up and winked, opening a second packet of bills, fifties. They spilled out on the table among the twenties. He took three fifties out of the center at random and with his forearm swept the rest into a plastic shrimp basket on the floor.

His head darted back to the microscope eyepieces to examine the bill. He spoke as he adjusted the focus. 'You're wondering whether it's worth it. You see danger on the horizon, or rather you feel danger, you cannot see it, yet you can't seem to quit. Perhaps that is it?'

'Maybe.'

'Maybe? Maybe yes! I knew it the day I met you.' Carmine slipped out the fifty he was examining and placed another one onto the glass plate without looking up. 'You are too sensitive for this business; maybe you were too sensitive for your prior business too. Maybe you think about things too much, like the "artiste". Eh? Am I not right? I have long jailhouse ears; I know your prior occupation, and I know you quit. I hear things.' He took the third fifty and slipped it onto the glass, still not looking up at Nick.

'I never saw myself as being too sensitive.'

'A person never sees the truth in the mirror; they only see what they want to see. We are all the same that way.'

Carmine dropped the three fifties into the shrimp basket and watched them flutter downwards as the boat rocked gently from side to side.

'Ask me, Nick, go ahead, it's okay.' Carmine slit open a third packet of money. This time they were hundreds.

'Can't really explain it, because I don't really understand it. I seem to be living out someone else's dream, doing someone else's bidding.'

Carmine thought of his own situation, of Don Saverese and the power the Don had over him. Carmine had done the Don's bidding now for over forty years, since they had been boys in New York on Mott Street in Little Italy. Ten of those years had been spent in Federal prison eating shit-on-a-shingle and beans while the Don sipped Sambuca and dined on veal Marsala and fetuccine. And Carmine was still doing his bidding. Why?

'Family,' Carmine said, almost to himself. 'That's why you do it. You look on your friend as family and for family you do whatever is asked of you. But there is a limit. There is always a limit.' Carmine raised his head and stared at Nick, feeling for the bill under the microscope with his hand and pulling it out. He waved the bill in the air. 'But that is not entirely fair. See this paper?' He handed the bill to Nick. 'This is not paper. No no no. It is power, and we know the men we work for are obsessed with it. But we also are fascinated and dominated by the paper and the men we work for, or we wouldn't be here doing these things. Would we?'

The conversation was interrupted by a man in a black turtleneck sweater and black watch cap. He started to speak in Italian.

'Speak English. Don't be rude. We have nothing to hide.'

'We're almost through, Signore Calabrese; you got five more minutes and we'll be pullin' outta here.'

'*Ciao.*' Carmine waved the man away with the back of his hand and looked through the microscope. 'You know these bills are so good it still gives me a thrill. They are better than anything I ever did.'

'Better technology, that's all, Carmine.'

'You are a gentleman, Nick. A real gentleman.' Carmine switched off the light underneath his microscope. 'That's it, I don't need to see any more. You deliver good merchandise, never try to pull any fast ones.' Carmine rose, and walked outside the wheelhouse. Nick followed. Together they watched as the last load of gold was lowered by boom onto the waiting Bertram.

'Five hundred million in gold would be a big temptation to any man, wouldn't you say?' Carmine said, smiling.

'I would say yes, it is a big temptation for any man.'

'And the temptation to covet the gold rises as the amount rises, wouldn't you say?'

What was Carmine trying to get at? 'Yes, I would say that was true of normal men.'

'Lust is a hard thing to control in anyone, Nick. And honor can always be rationalized. You are still a young man; I like you, probably because you remind me so much of myself at your age. We both even suffer from the same tragic flaw. We are naive, dreamers.'

'Lust?' Nick asked, wanting to know what Carmine was trying to project. 'What do you mean, lust?'

'Some men lust after women, some after food, some strong drink, some power, or approval, or wealth, and there are some men who lust after gold. That elusive, captivating shiny

metal that has fascinated men and women for time eternal.'
Carmine put his arm round Nick's shoulders. 'I have already
said too much; pay no mind, it is just the ramblings of an
old man who will soon be facing his maker for a final
accounting.'

Nick walked to the rope ladder that hung over the side of
the shrimp boat. He swung one leg over the gunnel and
prepared to board the yacht. 'Why? Why always the
fascination with gold?'

Carmine held the rope steady as Nick swung his other leg
over the railing. 'Because it is eternal, and by possessing it,
men think that they also will be bathed in the glow, and they
also will be eternal, never wanting for anything.'

Nick stared at Carmine and asked, 'Is there anything else?
I get the feeling there is something you are trying to tell me.'

'I like you, Nick, and wish you well. You have a lot of life
ahead of you. I hope you get to enjoy it.'

'And?' Nick said. 'Please, Carmine!'

'Leave! Leave that island! Leave it as soon as you can.'
Carmine had raised his voice only slightly but it was
equivalent to a person shouting. 'Goodbye, Nick.' He shook
Nick's hand.

'*Ciao*, Carmine.' Nick took two steps down the dangling
rope ladder, timing the steps with the rocking of the shrimp
boat. He stopped. Carmine stood above him, watching him
descend into the Hatteras. 'Carmine, *grazie*.' He smiled.

'*Prego*.' Carmine smiled sadly back, waving, and walked
away from the rail.

Thirty minutes later, sitting in the navigator's chair on the
bridge of the Bertram it came to Nick.

'How the hell does he know we have an island? Christ, he
was telling me to leave; those bastards are going to come after
the gold!'

Phillip sat at his word processor, laboring over the speech he was writing. Tomorrow, the Fed was raising the prime rate by half a point. Philip had to explain why to the entire financial community at a press conference tomorrow morning. He had to invent plausible reasons. He knew why the economy was booming and inflation was beginning to escalate: all that fresh cash flooding into the monetary system. But that was not what he was going to tell the financial world; he had to fabricate a believable story.

Veronica was lying on the bed waiting for him. She had cancelled all her other clients a week ago when she decided that she was in love with Phillip. Last year a Wall Street corporate raider client had given her three insider tips in a row, and she had invested her money on his advice. It had paid off, so she would never have to work again if she was moderate in her living expenses. This was the final factor in her decision to concentrate on making Phillip fall in love with her. She knew he already loved her, but not enough. His first love was his job and the world he lived in. And he was never far from his memory of the accident.

But she was patient, she knew what men wanted: sex and love together. To capture a woman, but always doubt whether that woman could ever be truly possessed; to live in a field of ever-present electricity, fueled by desire and romance. Passion.

Fifteen minutes later she saw the light change as Phillip flicked off the desk lamp and entered the bedroom. He wheeled over to her side of the bed.

He took her hand and kissed it. 'Don't go anywhere, I'll be right back.' He spun his chair in a semi-circle and headed for the bathroom.

Just as he got to the bathroom door the red phone on his desk rang. He knew it by the special ring, like someone tapping a spoon against a bell at a constant rapid rate. He looked over at Veronica and shrugged his shoulders. She had only heard that sound once before, and it had upset Phillip enough to send her home early, without making love. She watched him disappear into his office and tried to listen. But all she could hear was the murmur of his voice.

It was Ralph Cobb on the other end of the phone. 'We got another fucking problem: Colonel Gaddafi.'

'Gaddafi?'

'The President of France called two hours ago. Almost half their oil comes from Libya. Well, it seems that someone on Gaddafi's staff read that article in the London *Times* and they called the French President to ask how extensive the problem was. Gaddafi's man said he didn't want to give his precious oil to France for worthless American paper; paper that was being printed by outlaws somewhere in the decadent West.'

'Not good!' Phillip said.

'There's more. The Japanese Prime Minister called twenty minutes later with the same bitch. You know they have no native oil and only limited reserves. Well, he'd had a call from the King of Saudi Arabia himself, who said basically the same thing as Gaddafi. The President's very upset. We all know what happened the last time these bastards capped their wells and refused to ship oil.'

'If the Arabs believe the threat, and won't sell their oil to nations like France and Japan, then the little guy in the street sure isn't going to have a lot of confidence in his paycheck or his savings account,' Phillip mused out loud. 'Anything else?'

'No. That's enough, isn't it?'

'Yes.'

'We'll talk tomorrow. Gotta go now,' Cobb said, and hung up. Phillip turned his light off and wheeled back into the bedroom.

Veronica was lying on her side propped up on one elbow, reading. She looked up at him apprehensively, knowing what he was going to say after the phone call.

'Killed the mood?' she asked. She put her fingers on his lips and stopped him from speaking. 'Don't, Phillip. Don't ask me to go.'

He stared at her, not saying a thing, trying to understand.

'Send the car away. Let me stay with you tonight.' She had never stayed over; she had never asked before.

Slowly he raised his hand and took her wrist, pulling her fingers from his lips. 'Veronica . . .'

She brought his hand to her mouth and kissed the backs of his fingers where he still held her arm. 'Shhhh, just do as I ask. I want to be with you, Phillip. Don't send me away.'

He placed her hand on the bed, on top of the book. He reached for the phone and punched in a set of numbers. 'We won't need the car any longer tonight; why don't you head home.' He didn't wait for the 'Yes, sir' before he hung up.

Phillip did not want to be alone tonight. The problems could wait until tomorrow. They always did.

Tuesday morning 7:00
CAY SAL BANK

Heather screamed at the top of her lungs.

Nick had just returned from the last currency delivery and was helping with the unloading when he heard her. He had made it a habit to check on her about dawn every day that he could, when he went for his morning run and to check the defenses round the island. Her nightmares were occurring regularly now.

Nick ran into the warehouse and bent over her, shaking her shoulders gently. 'Wake up, Heather.'

She threw her arms round him and inhaled air in gulps as if she were still trying to catch her breath, as if she were still drowning. 'I was so scared, Nick,' she gasped. 'The sea . . . it was red, full of severed legs . . .' She shuddered and inhaled deeply, then exhaled. 'I'll be better in a minute.' Nick rose to make coffee, giving her a moment to compose herself.

Books appeared in the doorway, holding a phone. He moved into the light as Nick started the coffee machine.

Nick got up and walked over to the pile of gold bars. He fingered one of them aimlessly, thinking before he spoke.

'We've got more problems,' Nick said, holding one of the gold bars in the air, almost waving it at them. 'I got sort of a weird tip on it last night. I think Don Saverese may come after this.'

'After what?' Books said, almost yelling. 'I thought those assholes had some honor, some kind of ethics?'

'Gold. After the gold. You said it yourself, Books, when the stakes get this high all bets on human behavior are off.'

'You believe him, your source? Why would he tell you anything?'

'He's got his own beef against the family, an oldtime grudge,' Nick said.

'This is serious about the Mafia if you are right, Nick. How sure are you?'

'Very. The source is good and my instincts say those boys are planning to rip us off.'

Both men thought of the ramifications of taking on the Mafia if they had to.

'Shit,' Books said, breaking the silence. 'How could I have let this slip by me? I just assumed they would be happy with their share; I thought they had some ethics. I guess I watched *The Godfather* too many times. Greedy bastards.'

'Let's not talk about greed,' Nick said.

The confidential informant reports in front of the President and Phillip had all been carefully read and culled by Ralph Cobb. He had asked the DEA, the FBI, the Treasury Department and all the local law enforcement groups he knew to press their confidential informants to the limit to determine exactly how the bogus money was being handled and distributed by the mob. Cobb had to do this without telling the agency or the control agent what they were looking for, exactly.

The result was thirty-seven reports; each report was between three and ten pages in length, and had a cover page marked with a code name and number. Cobb had made extensive notes on the cover pages.

'I've grouped the reports into categories,' he explained. 'Drugs, gambling, loan-sharking and legitimate enterprises. There are other categories as well, like pornography and prostitution. But the categories I have chosen are the main ones. In every case there is great activity and the pattern is the same: an influx of cash to provide unlimited working capital for expansion.'

'Ralph, cut through all that and get to the bottom line for me, please,' the President said.

'The bottom line is that the mob is definitely distributing the funny money, and most of it is going into legit businesses they own or control.'

'How are they paying for it?' Phillip asked.

'In gold, as we expected. There's no question about it.' Cobb picked up a file with the code name 'Wolfman' and tossed it on the table. 'Wolfman is one of their gold buyers. He's running all over the country paying a small premium for gold and filling his hat. He makes a guaranteed profit with every ounce he buys, because the mob stands ready to pay him a premium. It adds up fast, the quantities the Wolfman deals in aren't small. He's a CI for the Justice Department.'

'What does the mob get for the gold?' the President asked.

'Four perfect paper dollars for every dollar in gold bullion they cough up. At least that's our best estimate. The wrinkle here is that this paper is so good that none of the CIs or even our own agency people has put it all together yet. But that's the reason gold is up to almost fifteen hundred dollars an ounce and rising: nobody's anxious to sell. And the irony is that the mob is buying the gold with funny money they are getting for the gold.'

'It's an endless cycle,' commented the President.

'Can't we move against the families on counterfeit charges?' Cobb asked.

'Absolutely not,' Phillip answered. 'Firstly, it would be difficult, if not impossible, to get physical evidence to prove which bills are the counterfeits. I've checked this with the Mint and the Justice Department. Secondly, and more importantly, if we made an arrest of this magnitude against the main Mafia families of America on the counterfeit charges, we would have to deal with mega publicity. We couldn't handle the public heat on the dollar. There would be outrage and panic; and possibly a run on our financial institutions.'

Cobb sat and observed the President and Phillip as they mulled and dissected the problem.

A new intriguing thought had entered Cobb's brain as he listened to the President speak – 'Get the mob to do your dirty work.' In order to expedite his plan, he would have to use his CI.

When the meeting ended, Cobb called the man at home and told him to be at the Secret Service building first thing in the morning. Cobb would be waiting to open a side door and usher him in personally.

Tuesday afternoon 2:00
NEW YORK CITY

Carmine smoothed out the poster-sized prints with the palms of his hands as if he were smoothing out a pizza. Don Saverese waited patiently as Carmine covered the surface of the Don's massive mahogany desk with the photos; all other items had been removed. The Don held the tiny Ferrari in his hand, running the car across his palm with his thumb. Its paintwork was chipped as a result of its many tumbles and crashes.

Carmine stood back when all three enlarged photos were finally smoothed out on the surface of the desk. The Don walked up to study them. He indicated the liberty ship. 'This is an old ship, no?'

'It was used as a troop transport in World War Two. The pilot who took these photos was a veteran of that war. The large name painted on the side,' Carmine traced with his fingertips the area along the sides of the huge ship as he spoke, 'Mako Marine Institute, is the cover name for the counterfeiting operation. It poses as a privately endowed mariculture project.'

'Clever, like this sovereign rights business.' The Don's eyes roved over the pictured areas as he spoke. 'A very special kind of mariculture project that needs fifty-foot steel towers on each corner of the island with tarpaulins covering what seem to be machine guns, and wired-off areas around the shoreline that look like minefields. These little pointy nests that are covered, what are they?'

'SAMs, heat-seeking surface to-air missiles, was the pilot's guess.'

'And these?' The Don pointed at posts that stuck up from the sand and criss-crossed the island.

'Surveillance posts. They send electronic beams that connect to each other; it creates a solid eight-foot-high electronic web that nets the island in invisible currents. If any are broken, the system is activated and the giant heli-arc lamps located on these towers go on.' Carmine pointed out the light towers. 'This system was installed by a man who knew what he was doing and who was given a big budget to do it.'

'Nick,' the Don stated. 'He is an expert. It was his business for many years. He did my compound in New Jersey, and supplied all the families with the latest surveillance tools.'

'There's more,' Carmine said. 'These antennae indicate that a very complex radar system has been installed on the liberty ship. I went to an expert that we use in Florida, a man who was in Vietnam, who now flies for us in Colombia. He told me there is an advanced low-level radar system that must operate from the bridge of the ship. It can spot just about anything that comes in, at any altitude.'

'If Nick set this up, it will be well done. But everything that is made by a man can be outsmarted by another man. I will need this pilot who flies for us. I want him and Bruno Pugliese to get together. What else?' the Don asked.

'These subs.' Carmine pointed at three dark-grey steel cigars. 'Diesel-driven World War Two models. They may be using them for the European deliveries.'

'They are of no concern. When we take the island, we will sink them. Where is the gold?'

'It hasn't moved. We triangulate it every two hours and it is here.' Carmine put his finger on the Butler factory building.

'Is that where they produce the money?'

'Probably.' Carmine pointed to the second Butler building. 'See, both buildings are well air-conditioned and they have these very large dehumidifiers to take the moisture out of the air so they can dry the paper quickly.'

'Is this what I think it is?'

'Yes, it is the barge they brought down from Hoboken, with our paper from the dump, still stored in it.'

411

'So, the gold appears to be stored in this building.' The Don dropped the tiny Ferrari directly in on top of the Butler building. He checked his notebook and said, 'The next delivery is in five days.'

Carmine rolled up the large photos into tubes that he taped tight.

'I'll keep those, Carmine,' the Don said, extending his hand. 'For Bruno.'

The Don walked Carmine to his office door. He stopped when they reached the door and slid a brown paper bag under Carmine's arm. 'Carmine, you have been of great service to the family. And now I feel you deserve a rest. Take some time off now. Please take what is in this package and spend it for your pleasure.'

The men looked at each other and said nothing. Don Saverese hugged Carmine and said goodbye. He watched from his one-way glass window as Carmine walked through the car showroom and disappeared onto Columbus Avenue. The Don breathed a sigh of relief. Carmine was broken, of no use anymore. But the Don did not want to harm him, it would almost be like harming himself. They had known each other for so long, had been through so much.

Carmine walked steadily for three blocks; he knew what was in the envelope. He had a particular destination in mind. He shouldered his way against the waves of Yuppies, endless armies of the same person. 'They all look alike!' Carmine thought to himself. 'Why do they want to look the same and why do they strive so hard for what I carry under my arm in a brown paper bag?'

He waited for the light to change and walked past three storefronts that displayed expensive, trendy clothing and shoes. He stopped at the fourth. It was a store he knew; it looked lonely and out of place. It was the recycled clothing shop for the St Vincent De Paul mission.

Carmine walked inside and located the drop box for clothing and other items just inside the door. He slipped the unopened brown package into the collection box, and walked back out onto Columbus Avenue. He pulled his collar up round his neck to protect him against the cold, biting wind that whistled down the wide avenue.

He sighed deeply, wanting clean air in his lungs, and started to walk again. He wondered how his life had become so complicated once more. Things had been so simple in prison.

A smile crossed his face as he tried to imagine the St Vincent De Paul store manager when she opened the brown bag. By the feel of it, there was at least a quarter of a million dollars inside the plain brown paper bag.

Wednesday morning 8:00
CAY SAL BANK, BAHAMAS

'Books, why haven't we put the gold from the last two shipments in the blue hole?' Nick asked.

'Instincts, based on what you told me about the wise guys. If they're planning to hit us, then we've got to be under surveillance again, and I don't want to lead them to the vault. I have a new hiding place in mind, a special vault.' Books stood up and stretched. 'I planted a little tidbit in the *New York Herald* that should stir up some shit in the next twenty-four hours.'

Books headed for the navigational chart on the wall. 'Nick, I got a call from Bruno Pugliese this morning. They want to double up the next load, make it four billion in paper. And they want to make the swap right here.' Books tapped his finger on a spot less than ten miles from where they were standing.

'Right in the middle of the freighter lanes, close to us, twice the amount. That's just great!' Nick said. 'When?'

Books turned his head from the map. 'In four days.'

'Got a plan?' Nick asked.

'I want you to go and see Don Saverese. I have a plan, a special plan for him.'

An hour later, when Books was finished explaining his total plan and what he wanted Nick to do in New York, Heather understood. She understood exactly why Books wanted Nick to go to the mainland; it might help get her off the island.

Wednesday midday 12:00
NEW YORK CITY

The Secret Service helicopter flew Cobb from Washington to the heliport on the East River under the 58th Street Bridge. From there he took a cab to Arturo's restaurant on Houston Street in the Village. It was a popular local restaurant he knew and liked.

It was Cobb's policy always to arrive late for this kind of meeting because he didn't want any criminal ever to keep him waiting.

Cobb had been to this restaurant several times, but no one recognized him; no one ever recognized him. Cobb was not a man people remembered.

He saw the CI sitting in a booth in the furthest corner in the rear of the restaurant. Cobb had met the man only once years ago and they had struck a deal. The CI would ferret his way back into the mob and wait, like a landmine, to be activated. He would be called upon only for the most important kind of information and would be used only once.

In return, he was allowed back out on the street five years earlier than expected, with a chance to live with his family. But his son had died just months before he was released, and he had never had a chance to get to know him.

Carmine Calabrese looked up from his espresso coffee as Cobb slithered into the red leatherette seat across from him. The two men looked at each other for several long seconds.

The waiter came, and they broke their stares.

'Two espressos, please,' Carmine said softly to him.

Cobb pushed the sugar bowl across the red and white plastic tablecloth, out of the way, so there was nothing between the two men. 'It's time now, Carmine, time to pay. I want to know everything about what's going on between Don Saverese and Books St John.'

Cobb sat quietly for forty minutes as Carmine explained. He made Carmine repeat himself several times in the more complex parts. Finally, Carmine explained about the gold, and the fact that the Don was going to steal the precious metal on the next delivery.

'I need to see him,' Cobb said.

'Don Saverese?'

'Yes.'

'When?'

'Today, tonight – soon as possible.'

'Why?'

Cobb said nothing. He just looked at Carmine, wondering how he was going to set up the meet without blowing his cover; but that was Carmine's problem.

'Why? Because I'm going to make him an offer he can't refuse, that's why.'

Ellis Island was the location. Choosing a suitable place for the meeting between Don Saverese and Ralph Cobb had been very difficult. Both men arrived by helicopter. Don Saverese had arrived thirty minutes early, so he could explore the buildings and walk the same path as his Sicilian grandfather had once walked long ago.

The coolness of the Great Hall sent shivers down his back; he thought he heard the tired scuffling footsteps of the hordes of people who had walked on this floor and changed their lives, the course of history, and the lives of the millions who now populated the land as a result of their journey.

The Don closed his eyes and stood in the center of the hall; he tried to imagine passing through these portals, unable to speak the language, with wife and children in tow. A paper name tag tied to the button of your coat was the only legal proof of your identity, your existence. The teeming masses flowed through this very building, the room he was in, many fleeing oppression and prison, or creditors. All with one common thought: freedom, and a chance at a new life where the only requirement was hard work and perseverance. The Don strained to keep his eyelids closed, and frowned, trying to imagine his grandfather holding his grandmother's hand, squeezing it in excitement and fear. His own father clinging to his mother's skirt, looking up at her with dark wondering eyes.

The Don's face relaxed and he smiled; happy that he had given Mr Lee Iaccoca a donation to help restore this place. The country must never forget where its strength and greatness really came from, and how it started, with plain people prepared to work.

'Don Saverese, he is here,' Carmine whispered as Cobb

walked towards them, his steps echoing through the great hall.

Cobb was surprised to see how small Don Saverese was: hardly an inch taller than himself. Both men had agreed to bring only one bodyguard. The fewer people who knew about this meeting the better. Carmine was the middleman.

The two men shook hands and took a polite measure of each other.

'I am honored that the head of the Secret Service should want to meet me, a humble businessman,' Don Saverese said as they started to walk.

Cobb stopped and looked at Carmine and his own bodyguard. He signalled with his head for them to leave. Don Saverese snapped his wrist for his own bodyguard, Bruno Pugliese, to leave also. The two men strode through the Great Hall, unescorted.

Cobb spoke. 'We can cut the bullshit, if you want, and probably save a lot of time.'

'As you wish,' the Don said. Both men walked in step; they looked like two tiny soldiers dressed in longcoats as they walked across the great cold expanse of stone floor.

'There's no need for you to deny anything or to explain. I'm not wired, and I don't care how we got here. I only care that we figure a way outta here that's good for us both. And by us I mean the United States Government and the families you represent.'

Don Saverese stole a furtive glance at Ralph Cobb. So small, deceiving, he must be very good to have risen to his position, the Don thought; be careful.

Cobb continued, 'I know what you guys have been doing. Buying excellent funny money from Books St John and giving him gold in return. I've seen samples; I know how good it is. I also know you have been conspiring with them for some time. Including supplying them Federal Reserve shredded currency from your Waste Products dump in the Meadowlands. We want the operation stopped, and we want you to help.'

'Who do you represent? Who do you speak for?'

'The US Government,' Cobb said.

'Go ahead.'

'I'm assuming you know where they operate from. Do you?'

'Yes, perhaps.'

'All right, here's my deal. Go in and take them down. Destroy the island. Make it look just like a cocaine drug war skirmish. Plant drugs on the island, at least ten kilos and do the regular stuff that the Colombians do – you know.'

'I don't know,' Don Saverese said calmly.

'Play rough, real rough, cut off the hands on some of the bodies, cut the heads off as if it were a warning. Just make it look like the hit was done by Colombians. Ask some of your Colombian pals what they do; you might learn something.'

The Don looked at Cobb, 'They have sovereign rights; they are their own country.'

'Yeah, but it will all go against them if it looks like they were just another drug transshipping point. We want it disguised as a drug war on some tiny worthless island. We'll plant the story with the press the way we want; no one will know or care about the truth. And the Bahamians will be glad to get their island back. I'll keep the DEA, Treasury, and Coast Guard away when you go in, and give you a safe route in and out.'

'What do we get?'

'You get the last shipment of funny money and no heat from us later. You can keep what you have made so far.'

'And you?'

'We get the gold and the Black Box.'

'How do you know we will deliver?'

'Because if you fuck us over we will put so much law enforcement pressure on the families that they won't know whether to shit or go blind, and they're going to come after

418

you because we will let them know you turned down our deal which would have solved the problem.'

They came to a barred window and looked through the strips of steel at the Statue of Liberty and Staten Island off in the distance, bleak and cold.

The Don reached up and squeezed one of the steel bars; it was cold to the touch, so cold that it felt hot, burning. He had never spent one minute behind bars, and he wondered what it would be like, what he would have done in Carmine Calabrese's position: would he have become an informant like Carmine for this little man, Ralph Cobb, in return for freedom?

And he contemplated what he would do to Carmine for deceiving him all these years that he had been out of prison.

'So, are you in?' Cobb asked.

'Yes, I'll talk to the other families, but I see no objection from them.' The Don released the bar and rubbed his hands together. He turned to face Cobb.

'Can I be sure you speak for the Government?'

'Yes.'

'I'll take you at your word,' the Don said, a wry smile on his face. They shook hands.

'Fine.' Cobb looked away. He started to walk; the thin smile on the Don's face made him nervous. 'This fucking place gives me the creeps,' he said. 'Too many goddamn ghosts.'

Cobb hastened his pace until he reached his waiting helicopter. He slipped into the passenger seat and slammed the door, glad to be airborne.

Nick circled the block in front of the Club Siracusa twice before he found a parking spot on Bleeker Street. Alfonso, the doorman, recognized him and checked the clipboard until he found Nick's name. Alfonso waved his hand-held metal detector in an arc round Nick's body and grunted an okay for him to pass. Inside, the maitre d' led him directly to the steps that descended to the shooting range located in the basement below.

Bruno Pugliese was waiting for Nick at the thick lead door. He nodded for the maitre d' to leave as he took Nick through to the second door. He pushed the second door open and Nick stepped into the shooting gallery. Don Saverese's oversized ear protectors lay loose round his weathered neck. The smell of cordite was hovering in the air. The Don was reloading his .357 Magnum with a speedloader. He laid the gun down on the table when he saw Nick and extended his hand.

'Nick, a pleasure to see you.'

'The pleasure is mine.'

'Join me for a little shooting.'

Nick was surprised. It was a great honor to be asked to shoot. Holding a loaded weapon in the presence of Don Saverese was a high privilege afforded few.

'Thank you, I believe I will.' Nick wondered if the Don had made the offer to gain his trust, or to lull him into overconfidence.

'Bruno, help Nick select a pistol. Nick, you can choose any pistol that hangs over the initials D.S.' Bruno took the keys and opened the two glass cases containing the guns.

Nick hadn't held a gun in his hand since that deadly night in Paris. He wondered how his aim was now.

He selected a Colt .45 model 1911. It was standard issue

for the US Army, accepted in the 1920s and still used by the military. The automatic pistol delivered a knockout punch at short range. This particular gun had mother-of-pearl handles and a filed-down hair trigger; about two pounds of pressure was all it took to fire. It was the same model that he had used on Sean O'Reilly.

Bruno handed Nick the empty clip and six cartridges. Nick clicked the cartridges into the clip one at a time. They felt good in his hands, slim, cool and deadly. The bullets, military-style metal jackets, slid easily into place; he inserted the clip into the pearl handle and slapped it in the last quarter-inch smartly with the palm of his free hand.

'Be my guest, Nick.' The Don motioned for Nick to shoot first; a new target was hanging on the line a hundred feet away.

Nick spun, joined hands, and snapped up his gun. The sudden action caused Bruno's hand to fly to his breast and waiting shoulder holster. The Don placed his hand on top of Bruno's to calm him.

Nick fired six rounds in less than four seconds. When he was done there was no center left in the target. The heavy caliber slugs had torn the heart out of the paper target, leaving a gaping hole. Bruno pulled in the line quickly hand over hand and tore off the spent target. He handed Nick six more cartridges as he inserted a new target onto the line.

'No. Thank you. That's enough for now. These things make me nervous.' Nick handed the gun back to Bruno and moved out of the shooter's position. The Don moved in, slipped the sound-mufflers up over his ears, and waited for Bruno to move the target down to the end of the range. When the target stopped, the Don fired; he fired slowly and precisely, centering each bullet in the target. When he was through, the center had disappeared.

'Want to try that one?' the Don asked, pointing to a new Beretta still on the hook inside the glass cabinet.

'No, thanks.' Nick stepped aside as the Don hung up his

ear mufflers on the wall. He handed the .357 Magnum to Bruno who put a red sticker on the handle, indicating that it should be cleaned, and hung it in the glass cabinet.

'Drink, upstairs, with us?' the Don asked.

'Yes, thanks.'

'To your health – *salut*, Nick!' The Don held his glass of Sambuca in the air. Nick touched the rim with his glass of Scotch on the rocks. The Don continued, 'I had an amazing experience this afternoon. I went to Ellis Island, something I've always wanted to do. Been there?'

'No, just floated past on a boat once or twice.'

'Very impressive inside. It has a starkness and power that is real. You know, Nick, it gave me an immediate and greater understanding of my grandparents, and my father. I wish I had gone there before. There was real human drama happening on that island at the turn of the century; you can feel it in the walls, in the floor. A second chance for all who passed through those doors. Those people had great respect for the Government, for the law; perhaps it was gratitude for being given a second chance in this country. Still, enough of this waxing philosophical. Nick, what is it that you have on your mind?'

'It's not me, Don Saverese, it's my friend Books St John. He has asked me to come and personally deliver this message. It concerns the next delivery of four billion in paper.'

'Yes, go on.' The Don squirmed in his seat slightly. It was an unconscious body signal that Nick recognized, but couldn't put his finger on. It was something people did when they were nervous.

'Books has asked me to verify the gold on this shipment.'

'What! What do you mean?'

'I'm to verify that you have put one billion in gold bullion on board the delivery ship and I am to accompany the load to the delivery point.'

'Outrageous! My word should be enough.'

Don Saverese had not gathered one dollar in gold bullion.

It had never entered his mind that he would need the gold. His plan was to take the paper and then exterminate the entire crew. Then he would execute Carmine Calabrese. Finally he would assault the island, destroy it. A nice neat package.

'Your word is certainly good with me, Don Saverese, but I am representing Books St John, and this is a condition for the delivery. If I don't see the gold loaded and personally accompany the vessel, there will be no delivery. I'm sorry.'

There was no question in Nick's mind any longer that Don Saverese was planning to rip them off. Books had been right when he said, 'If Don Saverese protests, then the tip-off was correct.'

'Nick, why are you asking for this now? This is our twelfth delivery. We have never had a problem. Has someone said something that bothers you and your friends?'

'No. My associate is becoming paranoid as the stakes rise for us all. I'm sorry, but there is no negotiating on this point.'

'Well, then he shall have it as he wishes. You may accompany this shipment.' The Don signalled for the waiter to refill the three glasses. The Don raised his glass and Nick and Bruno followed. 'To our biggest delivery and continued success.' The Don smiled as they clinked glasses, but there was no warmth in the smile. He and Bruno left as soon as he finished the drink, leaving Nick sitting alone in the booth.

The Don tapped his toe impatiently as Alfonso the doorman signalled for his chauffeur. The jet-black Maserati Quattraporte limousine sidled up to the curb and waited for him to enter. The Don slipped Alfonso twenty bucks as he opened the door. He kept the window closed as they eased into the Greenwich Village traffic. He had to think; there was much to do in the next forty-eight hours. And he had no idea how he was going to get one billion in gold in such a hurry without bringing in the other families.

Wednesday night 7:00
WASHINGTON, D.C.

The down-link was in operation and the heads of state of all the involved countries sat anxiously waiting for the President.

He was late. When he entered he was as angry as Phillip had ever seen him. Cobb followed, sitting next to him sheepishly, fidgeting with his papers. Phillip knew the signals. When the President was angry he tapped his pencil point on the paper in front of him, sometimes leaving hundreds of black dots imprinted on the white vellum. He also wore his Ben Franklin glasses down on the tip of his nose so he could see over the frames and you got the full effect of those ice-blue eyes that could emit such a chilling fire.

The President pulled his glasses up the bridge of his nose sharply, forced a smile, and began. The faces displayed on the screen stopped their conversations, adjusted their seats to attentive positions, and leaned in as if to hear better.

The President nodded to Phillip, indicating to him to send the fax. He addressed the screen. 'Please read what we are sending to you now. It is an article that was planted in the Sunday edition of our *New York Herald* newspaper.' In seconds, each representative was holding a copy of the article. The President sat fuming inwardly, giving them time to read it, knowing some of them had to make their way a little slower through the language barrier.

COUNTERFEITING IN THE CARIBBEAN

A reliable but unidentified source has revealed to this newspaper that a large-scale counterfeiting ring is operating from the Caribbean. They are allegedly using high-technology techniques to produce near-perfect currency paper. This paper money is being distributed in Europe as well as in the United States, and may involve the currencies of many nations.

Our source indicates that the Secret Service is currently investigating the operation. The Secret Service would not comment on the scope or validity of this report.

The *Herald* believes this story is important enough to assign a team of seven investigative reporters to follow up leads and thoroughly investigate all sources. Supposedly, this operation is producing bogus money in the billion-dollar-per-week rate on a constant basis.

If this report is true concerning the volume of money being printed, it could pose a bigger economic problem to this nation than drugs.

At last, the President spoke. 'It was an anonymous tip that the *Herald* received. They would have paid no attention to it except that there were twenty thousand dollars of counterfeit money stuffed in with the letter, with the note: 'A picture is worth twenty thousand words.' The *Herald* had experts examine the currency and they confirmed that it was real, or so good that they couldn't tell the difference. We can see it got their attention. The *Herald* publisher told us that he is giving the story top priority.'

'Why would they send such a thing?' the French President asked. 'And to include the actual money?'

'It is obviously some form of extortion; they want to put pressure on us, media pressure. This is a potential disaster,' the British Prime Minister said.

'We are positive that the Mafia in this country, and the Union Corse in Europe, are handling the distribution,' the President interrupted. 'At least a billion a week, maybe more by now. We have finalized our assault plan to destroy the island, which we will review in four days. The plan will be faxed to each of you at the conclusion of this meeting. We would like your comments.' The President organized the small pile of papers he had in front of him and continued, 'Our top priority must be to stop the media in their pursuit of this story, and to execute our plan for the destruction of the counterfeiting operation as soon as possible.'

'There will be one more meeting just before the assault. Thank you for your time.' The President smiled and clicked off his transmission, not wanting to answer any more questions. The faces on the screen disappeared.

The President gathered his papers and left. Phillip and Cobb followed.

Thursday night 10:00
PARIS, FRANCE

Nick waited for Colonel Le Clerc at the Colonel's private table; he ordered a cognac, then turned to watch the sex show. The stage had been set in heavy red damask curtains with a king-sized bed center stage. The bed was surrounded by mirrors on the walls, ceiling, and headboard. Two small, beautiful Oriental women and the Prince of Pigalle were making love as if there were no one else present. The Prince of Pigalle was trying to live up to his legend, performing in every possible position and using every orifice. The mirrors were angled, and gave the scene the depraved, surreal look of many more people on the bed. At this moment, the man was lying on his back with one woman squatting on his face, the other impaled on his stiff penis. The women faced one another, embracing, their hands exploring each other's bodies, kissing, using their tongues, and obviously enjoying it. They seemed oblivious of the man who lay below them as they writhed on top of his body, lost in each other.

'Degenerate animals. You think they would tire of this. But no! It only seems to make them want more. The men like it because the Prince of Pigalle always excites the women – some kind of primeval penis fantasy, who knows?' The Colonel smiled as he sat down and offered his left hand for Nick to shake. Then he stuffed his wooden right hand in tighter against his chest, using his good hand. 'Young children are the only participants forbidden here, Nick. Although it goes on in many of my neighbor clubs, it will never take place here. With adults, grown people, who cares what they do to each other.' The Colonel waved away three of the club girls as they were about to join them.

'It's good to see you, Colonel.'

'And you, Nick. You must be a very wealthy man by now; perhaps you are ready to retire soon.' The Colonel smiled and raised his glass of brandy. 'To retirement, while we still are alive to enjoy it.'

'You're thinking of retirement?' Nick asked.

'I am retired. Have been for years; this is my retirement home, this madhouse.'

The crowd in the club roared and cheered, breaking into applause, when the girl sitting on the man's penis acted out her paroxysm of orgasm.

'She pretends well, see how she rolls her tummy; she could be a star of the cinema, no?' The Colonel clapped for the girl and her orgasm. 'Let's get out of here and go upstairs; Michelle is waiting for you. Besides, this bores me, I've seen it too many times.' He smiled and gave a shrug. 'I must be getting old for sure to talk like this!'

When they arrived at the top of the stairs, just before they entered the apartment, the Colonel turned and smiled at Nick. 'Remember what I said, money's no good to you if you are too dead to spend it. And money's hard to come by for most people; they can't print it, like you. Look what those three on the stage in the bed will do for a few francs, huh? You're a young man. Enjoy life.' He winked, and opened the door.

Michelle Descartes sat on the couch waiting for him. She wore a severe deep green Chanel dress and a string of perfect pearls. They glistened ivory-white against her dark skin. She tossed her long, flowing brunette hair over her shoulder and nodded at Nick, extending her hand.

She told him of the seizure of the *Aigle Corse* by the Russians.

'We have problems, big problems,' she said. 'Gold is drying up and the price has climbed to sixteen hundred dollars an ounce; we are starting to get heat from all the governments of Europe. They are working us over hard. We have lost much of our powder trade to seizures, and they are pulling our people in off the streets for small infractions of the law.'

'Do you want to stop?' Nick asked.

'No. But we would like to have only one delivery a month, twice the size.'

Nick stared at her, trying to read her face. It was the same pattern as with the mob. Was it a setup or not? Just because she was a female and more believable to him didn't mean she was telling the truth.

Nick looked at Le Clerc. The Colonel looked away.

'Okay,' Nick said. 'Where and when?'

'Bay of Biscay in seven days, four billion in these currencies.' Michelle handed him a list: 'US dollars — 2 billion; French francs — 500 million; German marks — 500 million; Swiss francs — 500 million; English pounds — 500 million. Value in US dollars twenty-four hours before delivery. The London Gold Market quotes will be used — US dollar equivalents.'

'We'll be there,' Nick said. 'Is there anything else?'

'No. That is all we need discuss,' she answered.

'Fine. I have to be off. I have a plane waiting at Orly.'

'I'll walk you to the door,' Colonel Le Clerc said.

As they went through the club, the threesome on the stage were slipping into their robes. The show was over. Some of the regular patrons, dressed in their formal uniforms for the night, were yelling at the two girls to take their robes off and join them at their tables; they waved franc notes in the air as an inducement.

The Colonel shook his head sadly from side to side as he opened the door to let Nick out into the brisk Paris night. 'Ah, the human condition. Will we ever rise out of the swamps, the human sludge? We should live so long, eh, Nick?'

'Goodbye, Colonel.'

'I hope it is only adieu, *mon ami*.' The Colonel gave Nick a hug and eased him out onto the street. He closed the door without looking back.

Friday morning 9:00
CAY SAL BANK, BAHAMAS

Heather sat on the dock next to Percival Smathers as the newly-printed money was loaded into the three Bertram yachts. The full green garbage bags which contained the shrink-wrapped packets of money were stuffed into the yachts; four billion just about filled the three boats to capacity.

Percival rose and went to the bow of the Bertram at the end of the dock to talk to Books. Books was mounting a tripod that would hold an M-60 machine gun. He had already installed M-60s on the other two yachts. Percival noticed that M-60s were mounted on the flying bridges as well. 'Expecting a war?' Percival asked, offering Books a swig of beer.

'Thanks.' Books took a long gulp and went back to screwing the leg of the tripod into the strong fiberglass deck surface.

'So why all the hardware all of a sudden?'

'It's just getting to be that time; the stakes are getting bigger and the greed barometer is climbing.'

'Yeah, and no more walks on the beach. You activated the Claymores, so the beach is no longer a beach, it's a minefield.'

'Right. Gimme another swig of that beer, will you?' Books reached out for the Budweiser. 'Looks like we're about to run out of money,' Books said, pointing at the empty pallet in front of the small fork-lift truck.

'Well, I guess I'll just have to go get another billion.' Percival smiled and extended his arm toward Books, holding out the Budweiser, then went to join Heather.

Together, Heather and Percival watched as the last pallet of green garbage bags full of money was loaded onto the Bertram.

They stood in silence, bathed pink-yellow in the glow of the lowering sun. They watched Books as he worked quickly, with purpose, like a movie director on a set, moving from boat to boat until the three Bertrams were loaded and ready to go. Books had enlisted the aid of all the submariners in the loading procedure and made sure everyone was checked out on all the weapons. The throats of the mounted M-60s on the bows were cleared and all the individual weapons, the stainless steel Ruger Mini 14s and the Glock handguns, were inspected and fired against floating targets on the flats. Everyone carried butterfly clips and plenty of backup ammunition.

'Gives me the creeps!' Heather said.

'Me too. Scares the shit outta me. It's Miller time,' Percival said, reaching into the ever-present Igloo cooler, pulling out two dripping bottles. He handed one to Heather.

'Thanks. I think Books really likes this part,' she said, silently toasting Books who was standing on one of the flying bridges.

'Who wouldn't?'

'I wouldn't!'

'That's 'cause you ain't a boy, Heather. Hell, Books gets to play with guns, drive boats, trade paper for gold on the high seas in the dead of night, deal with a Mafia chieftain, fuck with the US Government, and most importantly he gets to run the show, be the head honcho, get called "el Jefe" by the other boys. And tonight he gets to feel his own adrenaline boil. Shit, it's a never ending hard-on to a guy like Books; it's better than lust.'

'Thanks for reminding me, Perce. I think it was lust that got me here in the first place.'

Percival looked at Heather and clinked the long neck of his beer bottle against hers. 'Lust for what, Heather?'

She shrugged and waited a few minutes before answering, watching the men work.

'Maybe lust for life, Perce. Maybe I have a little of that pirate stuff inside me, the same stuff that Books has, boys' stuff. Maybe I get a little rush too.'

Friday evening 5:30
NEW YORK CITY

The rush-hour traffic was snarled on East Side Drive, but the driver refused to cut off and drive through Spanish Harlem; Nick couldn't blame him. The cab crept along with the flowing East River, moving only slightly faster than the outgoing tide.

It was sunset; the flotsam and jetsam of human existence floated along with the black murky river: a window frame, a door, and three green garbage bags.

The garbage bags collided with the remnants of a pier that extended into the river. The first two bags careened off the pilings and continued on their journey; the third bag scraped the abrasive gray barnacles and split open, spewing its guts into the dark waters. The contents of the bag was the stuff of daily life – milk cartons, cans, newspapers, cereal boxes, used condoms.

The cab inched past a stalled bus and the driver hit the gas. The car lurched free and picked up speed until they were cruising along at seventy miles an hour, as if they could regain the minutes lost in the traffic jam. The rushing air flowing through the open windows felt good on Nick's face. There was something special about New York: energy! Paris had beauty, romance, art, and a past, but New York was immediate, here and now. The world's great existential city. It was Nick's birthplace, his city, and he loved it.

He took one last deep breath of the tar, salt and sweet rotting garbage scent of the brackish East River air before they turned off at the Bowery exit; it made his nostrils constrict and tingle. Minutes later the cab pulled up in front of the Club Siracusa.

Alfonso the doorman recognized Nick, but it didn't stop the wand-waving search for deadly metal objects. When he was finished, Alfonso held the door open for Nick, who was escorted by the maitre d' directly to the Don's corner table.

Bruno Pugliese looked up at Nick but said nothing. It was the Don that offered the polite greeting.

'Ah, Nick, right on time. Sit here, please!' The Don waved at the chair opposite him with the back of his hand.

Bruno nodded at Nick and pulled the chair out with his foot. They ordered drinks.

'You have been travelling, Nick?' the Don asked.

'Concorde to Paris; makes it a daytrip.'

'I haven't been to Paris in years, although I have a few friends over there,' the Don said as the drinks were set down in front of them. '*Salut!*' he said, hoisting his glass of

Sambuca. He placed the glass on the table and stared at the floating coffee beans. 'Tomorrow is the big day. Does that suit you, Nick?'

'Fine.'

'You will meet with Bruno on the Miami River near the airport at six in the morning.'

Bruno slipped a piece of paper into Nick's coat pocket with the exact address.

The Don continued. 'Two shrimp boats will be used; they are expected to arrive at the meeting co-ordinates at two in the morning. You may accompany the shrimp boats if you wish. They will be ready to depart when you arrive.'

'The gold will already be loaded?' Nick asked.

'Yeah,' Bruno grunted.

'I'm sorry, but I have to inspect it as I requested.'

'Inspect it in da boat,' Bruno said.

'Tight quarters, and I don't feel like climbing around in the stinking bilges of a shrimp boat. You wouldn't like it either, Bruno,' Nick said, looking at him.

The Don shrugged. 'As you wish. Be at the dock at five and you can inspect it before loading.'

'I'll be there.'

'A lot of gold, one billion.'

'Not as much as you might think, Don Saverese.'

'Whaddya mean?' Bruno asked.

'When we started, gold was five hundred dollars an ounce; it's a little under two thousand an ounce now and rising. Four times higher than when we started, so it's one quarter of the original amount.'

'Details! No matter. Gold is gold! Let us get on with it,' the Don snapped, waving his hand in the air as if he were shooing flies.

It was the first time Nick had ever noticed anger in the Don's voice, and the first time the Don had not once looked him in the eye.

Friday night 8:00
FEDERAL RESERVE, NEW YORK CITY

The sheets of paper in Phillip's hand vibrated ever so slightly, trembling, as if a tiny independent wind blew just at them. The pages were a summary of the M1 and M2 for the last twenty years.

The M1 indicator represented all United States bank reserves plus currency held by the public. The M2 reported currency plus demand deposits at all commercial banks.

M1
December 1971 –   86.6 billion
December 1981 – 169.8 billion
December 1990 – 347.6 billion
M2
December 1971 – 230.4 billion
December 1981 – 364.6 billion
December 1990 – 722.9 billion

It was time to move. The money was now flooding in as if someone had opened the dam gates. And it wasn't just happening in the United States; it was worldwide.

It was time to activate the rest of the plan.

Phillip called Ralph Cobb to see how far advanced the air-assault plan was, but Cobb was not in his office.

Saturday evening 5:00
MIAMI RIVER

Nick walked through Miami Airport to the baggage claim. He strolled out of the baggage area and walked over to the Hertz desk to rent a car. He filled out the forms and took the Hertz bus to the car rental compound. A pretty blonde in shorts pointed him to his parked Ford Escort baking in the Miami sun.

Nick checked his rearview mirror to see if he was being followed. He drove to Miami River Road, a small marina on the river. The building was steel and windowless. The walls extended slightly past the edge of the Miami River with canals dug back into the land to allow for private enclosed slips. Bruno Pugliese was waiting in the small outer office. Nick entered the office and shook hands with him. Bruno was alone.

'Nice to see ya, Nick,' Bruno said. 'Good trip?' Bruno took a seat across from him on a broken-down stuffed couch. The office walls were covered in old nautical charts; magnets of different sizes and shapes were used to hold the corners of the charts to the steel walls.

'You packin'?' Bruno asked.

'Just this Glock.' Nick reached into his small shoulder bag and pulled out the pieces of a plastic gun; he placed them on the desk. Only the barrel was metal and that was hidden inside Nick's Walkman.

Bruno examined the gun for a second. 'Glocks are Austrian, ain't they?' he asked, to show Nick that he was up on his weaponry.

They walked into the boathouse. It was expansive and had a hollow feeling, the same feeling as a massive airplane hangar. There were no supporting beams or columns; the roof was hung from outside supports.

A long thin barge was centered in the middle of two finger piers. Two steel, high-powered shrimp boats sat on either side of the barge. These were the best of the shrimp boats, new high-powered models almost a hundred and fifty feet long. The boathouse was packed with other smaller boats but there were no workers to be seen, only armed guards and crew who wore black watch caps, blue jeans and black turtle-neck sweaters like uniforms.

Nick and Bruno walked to the barge. Bruno nodded at the two men who stood in the stern of the barge. They pulled the tarp back about ten feet. The barge was packed with gold bars that shone yellow in the late afternoon sun.

'So, dere ya go! Just like youse asked,' Bruno said, pointing at the load.

Nick said nothing. He jumped onto the stern and knelt, examining the gold bars. He hefted the first one that came to hand. It had the weight of gold, that incredible dense weight that is unique to gold.

'Pull the tarp,' Nick said to the two men in the stern.

They looked at Bruno for their cue. 'You got plenty to look at dere, right in front of you.'

'Bruno, don't give me any shit! I have to call Books with a signal when I complete my inspection of the load and an hour after we are on the high seas.'

'OK, do what he says.'

The two men climbed down the length of the small barge, balancing on the gunnels, carefully folding back the tarp.

'Bring the fish scale over here,' Nick said.

He set the scale on the dock and yelled down to the two men who had climbed back into the boat, 'Dig a hole in the center and hand me every fifth bar you pull, and the bar on the bottom. Bruno, go over to the tool bench and get me a hacksaw.'

'Hey get your own fuckin' hacksaw. I ain't your slave.'

'Bruno, I know you ain't my slave but if you want to get out of here by six maybe you could help out.'

'Yeah, yeah,' Bruno said, signalling one of the men to get the hacksaw.

For the next forty minutes Nick examined the gold bars. They checked out. Finally they got to the bottom of the center hole. Nick carefully took the last bar and, using the hacksaw, he cut it in half. The soft metal, 99.9 per cent pure, like all gold bars, melted easily under the blade. Gold of this high grade was easy to cut. Nick took the two half-bars and examined them in the afternoon sun. They looked perfect. He was looking for alloys or perhaps a lead center. But these were the real thing.

'Good as gold,' Nick said smiling at Bruno.

'Whadja think? Think we would fuck with youse after all this time?'

'I got a paranoid partner.'

'Me too. Only he's my boss, not my partner. So can we load?'

'Yeah.'

'Good,' Bruno said signalling for the men to get busy loading. 'This is hot work; how about a beer in my office?'

'Sounds good, but I'll have mine out here. I like watching people work,' Nick said.

'Suspicious prick, ain't ya,' Bruno mumbled as he headed for the small refrigerator in the office.

Nick sat on a rickety wooden chair out of reach of the shrimp boat outriggers as they were swung over the barge to lift and swing the pallets of gold from the barge into the refrigerated holds that were designed to carry shrimp – pink gold, as the Key West fisherman used to tell Nick.

It was gold all right, Nick thought, not pink shrimp. He and Books had thought the Don would not risk real gold, but they were wrong. What the hell was really going on?

Saturday night 8:00
NEW YORK CITY

Don Saverese hung up his desk phone. Bruno did not sound
well; perhaps he should have sent someone who did not suffer
from seasickness, but there was no one the Don trusted as
he trusted Bruno.

The first part of the plan was completed. Nick had
contacted Books and informed him that the gold was loaded
and that they had left the Miami River. There would be one
more call between Nick and Books confirming that the
shrimp boats had entered the Gulf Stream when they were
thirty minutes from the rendezvous point.

Good, now he could start to see the picture in his mind.
It was rare that the Don ever wanted actually to go on a job,
but he had wanted to go on this one. He wanted to see all
that gold stacked up in one place. He made a note to thank
his friend at Handy and Harmon, the precious metal dealers,
for lending him that much gold. He had to give them cash
collateral. But who cared? He would have his money back
the morning the gold was returned to the bank in Miami.

In fact, the gold would never be risked. It would never
complete its journey to the meeting place.

Clever ideas, where do they come from? the Don wondered
as he padded down the rear metal stairs to the garage. From
putting one's mind up against the ultimate tests, solving the
toughest puzzles and riddles, that's where great ideas came
from. 'That's where the fun of life comes from,' he said out
loud to himself.

At first he'd thought it would be impossible to acquire so
much gold in three days, that he'd have to use a substitute
like painted lead. But that would have been foolish; there
was no substitute for gold. Gold was gold, like a rose was
a rose.

438

The Don opened the thick metal fire door and entered the garage. A lone mechanic was working under a red Ferrari that was suspended in the air on a hoist. The man worked smoothly, not too fast, not too slow, with the precision and sureness of a surgeon.

The Don watched without the man knowing he was there. The shiny new car had to be ready in the morning for a junk bond salesman who worked for the Don's brokerage firm on Wall Street.

The mechanic made twenty dollars an hour and he earned it. The Don noticed the grease under the man's fingernails as a hand reached for a socket wrench, calloused knuckles that had been beaten against hard metal for over twenty years, a thick strong wrist used every day to power stubborn nuts and bolts.

The man earned an honest day's pay for honest work. He had no desire to think of hundreds of millions of dollars, and gold, and dealing death.

The Don admired the mechanic; in some inexplicable way he yearned to be able to do what he did.

The Don slipped back through the fire door and up the metal stairs to his office to await the next call from Bruno.

Sunday morning 2:00
GULF STREAM

Nick sat on the bridge glancing from the coast to the geodetic chart, number 11013, of the Straits of Florida, that was spread out on the chart table in front of him. His finger traced the quadrant numbers on the chart as he checked the Loran printout on the screen in front of him.

They were almost there; six miles from the meeting co-ordinates, thirty minutes away from the final exchange. Bruno swallowed another seasick pill and handed Nick the satcom phone.

Nick dialed and waited.

Books answered. 'This is Marlin One.'

'Marlin One, this is Poseidon; the dolphin are running free tonight.'

'I read you loud and clear. We picked you up on the radar about twenty minutes ago. See you soon,' Books said, signing off.

Nick hung up the phone.

Bruno spoke. 'That was pretty clever of youse guys. The fish code, and a last-minute call to make sure we was really here on the spot and everything. Probably got a code for different things like whether you was in trouble or not, right?'

'Maybe, Bruno. But what the hell is the difference?'

'The difference is you ain't as smart as you think you are, dat's the fuckin difference.' Bruno calmly popped his .357 Magnum from the quick-draw holster under his arm and pressed the cold gray steel barrel against Nick's temple.

It hurt. But Nick remained still.

'Slip on these clippers!' Bruno dropped a pair of handcuffs into Nick's lap. 'You know how dey work, put 'em on.'

Bruno picked up the mike, dialed a closed frequency and spoke. 'OK, you can come on. We have to make the switch easy; they have us in the radar.' He removed the gun from Nick's temple and squeezed the bracelets tighter round his wrists. 'Let's go.'

Bruno walked Nick to the stern. Two sister shrimp boats appeared out of the darkness. They had been trailing, travelling without lights. Within minutes they were rafted up against the sides of the gold-laden boats. The four boats were dead in the water for less than sixty seconds as Bruno, Nick, the crews and gunmen switched vessels without a word.

The two empty vessels continued on their way while the

two gold-laden vessels fell behind, eventually turning round and heading back to Miami with the gold.

Nick returned to the wheelhouse with Bruno. 'Clever, Bruno. The gold was never in jeopardy; just flash it and take it back.'

'Yeah, by nine tomorrow morning it will be in the back door of the bank in Miami. And your cash will be in trucks heading for eager hands in many cities.'

'Nice and neat. The Don is very thorough.'

'Yeah. That's why he's the Don, he's not like you Ivy League fags; now shut the fuck up.'

Minutes later three white dots flashed on the horizon. Bruno dragged Nick out onto the wheelhouse deck and yelled through the bullhorn, 'OK, there they are! Those flashin' lights. No fuck-ups, just follow the fuckin' plan.

'And you, you don't try nothin' or you're dead. Just do what you're told.' Bruno pushed Nick down the wheelhouse steps.

When Books and the three yachts were almost alongside, Bruno bellowed into his bullhorn, 'Turn on the strobes.' Suddenly the black night was lit up like a Hollywood set. The lights were pointed directly at the three stunned yachts. Bruno strongarmed Nick onto a fishbox that raised them above the level the gunnels. The crew on both shrimp boats had taken their positions; their guns were trained on the three boats and their occupants.

'Are you nuts, Bruno? You can't get away with something like this,' Books yelled from the yacht.

'I already did. See your pal here? Do anything stupid and I'll blow his brains all over the fuckin' deck.'

'What do you want?' Books yelled.

'The cash. What the fuck do you think we want? Stop stallin' and pull up alongside us and unload.'

Books picked up his radio microphone and spoke into it. Nick heard only two words but he knew what they meant: surface now!

Suddenly there was a whooshing sound as a submarine rose out of the black water into the glare of the spotlights. It was an apparition out of a Second World War movie. The bow popped up out of the water like a thick pointed knife only to settle as the water streamed down the fuselage to the conning towers which now stood upright out of the water like a battlement. Two men ran from the conning tower to man the five-inch gun. Two other men stood in the con holding Laws rockets on their shoulders like bazookas. The sub settled exactly between the yachts and the shrimp boat. The enormous amount of water displaced by the sub rocked the shrimp boats from side to side.

The surprise wasn't over; a second sub shot into the night air behind the shrimp boats. The bow whooshed out of the silent ocean, splitting the quiet. Then it settled down, and the conning tower with the Mako Marine Institute insignia became visible. The men of the second sub followed the same drill as the first. Two men ran towards the bow to operate the five-inch gun and two men appeared in the conning tower carrying Laws rockets on their shoulders. The water displaced by the second sub met the first set of waves and caused a cross-chop. The shrimp boats rocked violently, their extended outriggers almost touching the water as they dipped deeply into the swell.

Nick heard it, a deep, thundering rumble, in Bruno's big belly as he grabbed for the rail and vomited overboard. He tried to keep Nick in view as he automatically hung his head over the side.

Books saw it happen and took the advantage. He yelled, 'Fire!' The fiery tails of two Laws rockets screamed into the night, one from each sub. The rockets hit the unmanned wheelhouse of the second shrimp boat and exploded, blasting bright crimson and yellow as they destroyed the wheelhouse. The crew dove into the ocean to save themselves.

The explosion caused Bruno to take his gaze off Nick and look up at the burning shrimp boat. Nick moved with great speed. He slid his handcuffed hands under Bruno's belt in the center of his back. He used the belt to lift Bruno up off the rail. Bruno's feet flailed as he fired his pistol wildly in the night. He screamed as he flew off the gunnel into the murky moving waters of the Gulf Stream.

Books and the crew opened fire on the strobe lights and in seconds they were black.

'Everyone hold your fire!' Books yelled into his bullhorn and the night went silent. 'Nick, you all right?'

'Yes.'

'The gold's gone, right?'

'Yeah, they switched boats.'

'All right. Everyone listen to me; all I want is Nick and you're free to go. Even that asshole Bruno.' Books focused his bridge light on Bruno, who was clinging to some debris that had flown off the wheelhouse. 'There's nothing to fight over. You were going to rip us off and now you're not, that's all. There's nothing worth dying for. And I assure you in the next thirty seconds your boats will be nothing but splinters if we open up on them. Just be cool. Hand over Nick, collect that asshole Bruno down there and get on your way.'

Bruno spluttered out one strong 'Fuck you' between gulps of sea water.

One of the Bertrams came in close enough for Nick to jump onto the bow. The boats dispersed as quickly as they had gathered. The subs slipped gently under the surface as the yachts headed for the dark horizon.

Bruno was pulled into the shrimp boat with a rope ladder. 'Well, at least they didn't get the fuckin' gold,' he said aloud as the crew lashed the second disabled shrimp boat to their stern.

Sixteen miles away the other two shrimp boats were running without lights at a steady eight knots, in single file about a hundred feet apart. They were on the alert for the Coast

Guard; it would be tough explaining away all the gold in their holds.

The Captain of the first boat was the best in the Don's fleet. He had been a smuggler for many years and he knew what to look for. But this baffled him.

It was a thin sliver on his radar screen that looked like a tiny toothpick in the middle of the ocean, but there was no doubt that it was metal.

'What the fuck?' he said to no one in particular. He cupped his hand over his eyes and glared out the wheelhouse window into the dark night. He saw nothing. They were on a collision course and there was less than half a mile between them. The Captain veered to the port and the trailing boat did the same.

The thin metal needle moved and centered itself, realigning with them for collision. 'I don't like this!' the Captain said to his First Mate.

'Alert the crew we got trouble. Tell them to lock and load, it could get hot.'

The First Mate left the wheelhouse on the double.

The Captain fired up his spotlight, something he never liked to do; he preferred running in the black with no lights. It was out there all right; an oblong form lying still in the water, not moving. As the shrimp boats moved, the image got larger. He swept the water with the white beam of light and then he hit it, a white insignia of a mako shark on some kind of a low-slung hull.

They were only fifty yards apart when it came into full view in the single beam of light. 'It's a fucking submarine. I can't believe this shit,' the Captain said softly.

The voice of Ernie Sands filled the night air. 'Captain, stop your engines and come out onto the bow of your boat along with all your crew, hands up! Do it now! We are armed with rockets and have a five-inch gun aimed right at you. Be smart, do as you're told. If you do not, we will sink you where you sit.'

A single rocket snaked out of the conning tower, its thin

fiery tail wiggling past the two shrimp boats only a few feet above the outriggers.

Ernie Sands' voice filled the air again. 'Just a warning shot. We have two Zodiacs over the side for you. Get into them. Abandon your boats. You have thirty seconds or you're dead.' The quiet finality of Ernie's voice echoed from the sub across the expanse of ocean; it sent shivers through the men in the shrimp boats. The Zodiacs were pushed towards them.

'All right. Abandon ship, men!'

Five minutes later, Ernie Sands was whistling a tuneless melody behind the wooden helm of the first shrimp boat as he set the automatic pilot on a course for the Cay Sal Bank. When he was done he went forward to the bow and took a deep breath of fresh air before he lit his cigarette. The sub was laying off fifty yards to starboard, as an escort; the second shrimp boat was manned and a hundred yards behind him.

'Not a bad haul tonight, for a bunch of salty old fucks who should be sitting rocking themselves to sleep on a porch somewhere,' Ernie said to the stars and the moonless night.

Sunday morning 8:00
NEW YORK CITY

The call was from Miami.

'How can you still be alive?' the Don asked Bruno. 'One billion in gold gone, and you're still alive?'

There was only silence on the other end of the line. Bruno knew he was sitting on death's shoulder. He had lost both the gold and the money.

'There was nothing we could do, it was a set-up.' Bruno

started to repeat his story and quit mid-sentence. 'Maybe there's somethin' we can still think of.'

'Handy and Harmon will be waiting for delivery of that gold right now. I'll have to pay for it in cash, Bruno. How the hell do I account for one billion in gold? I don't have that kind of cash sitting around, and the tax people . . .' He let his sentence drift off. The Don had to think.

Handy and Harmon would wait for a day or two before they moved, and that would be enough time for him to think of something.

'Bruno?'

'Yes, Don Saverese?'

'I spoke hastily; you have been loyal to me for thirty years. We will deal with this matter as we have dealt with everything else over the years, my friend. We will deal with it by reason.'

'My life, as always, is in your hands. I will do as you wish,' Bruno answered.

The Don hung up and went to the window that looked down on his showroom. It was almost nine and the sales people were starting to file in with their coffee and bagels, newspapers tucked under their arms; life for them was simple.

The Don pulled his tiny Ferrari out of his pocket. Something was very wrong here. There was no question those people had been warned. They were ready for Bruno, armed and waiting. Those subs, the extra armed men, the rockets, the whole scenario was well planned.

They were tipped off, and there was only one man in his organization who was a traitor to him, Carmine Calabrese. He would pay with the one thing that he had left to give: his life.

Now the Don had to call and tell Ralph Cobb that he had failed on his end of the deal; he had lost his leverage. Now he was totally vulnerable to Cobb.

Sunday morning 7:15
MARSEILLES, FRANCE

Michelle Descartes spoke softly to Captain La Farge. He was an elegant man in his sixties with a full shocking-white head of hair flowing from a low, blunt hairline just above his thin eyebrows and broad nose. The full lips and trim body gave her the feeling that he should have been an orator in the Roman Senate, not a career smuggler who was a qualified captain for any vessel, any ocean. He had smuggled hundreds of millions of dollars' worth of contraband over the years for the Corsican Brotherhood. Michelle had decided to take Captain La Farge completely into her confidence.

'The exchange will be made here.' She pointed at the chart just off the Azores on the west coast of Africa.

'And then?'

'Back here to Marseilles and our warehouse.'

'There will be many currencies this trip?'

'Yes, English pounds, French and Swiss francs, German marks, and US dollars.'

'Amount?'

'Four billion in total, the largest amount ever. It may be the last; things are hot on the Continent and getting hotter. The manufacturer is also having his own problems, so we have asked for only one shipment a month.'

'That means one billion in gold.'

'Yes. The gold is in Toulon; it will start arriving tomorrow. You will load it directly onto the freighter. Be ready to sail by Wednesday noon.'

The freighter sat looking old and tired at the wharf; several different shades of blue covered the hull where it had been painted over the years. There was nothing remarkable about the vessel, it looked like any of thousands that plied the waters of the Med and the coasts of Africa. The engine room was the only thing out of the ordinary. Gleaming new Caterpillar diesels waited to be put into service. And if examined carefully enough, the seam scars on the port side of the vessel where welders had burned a hole to put in the new engines and then later sealed the hole closed could be seen. But the hull was sound and the old freighter could do an honest twenty-five knots. The less time at sea with precious cargo, the better.

'Good, I think you can leave the rest to me.' Captain La Farge smiled benevolently. He liked her spirit and had long ago come to grips with 'women's will' as he called it; having a female boss did not bother him as it did some Frenchmen.

'I'm sorry to hear that your uncle is failing.'

'Yes. He couldn't stand any bad news right now.'

'You mean he still keeps informed on day-to-day operations?'

'When they involve a billion dollars in gold, he does.' Michelle smiled.

'That I can understand.'

'You are the best man in the fleet, Captain.'

'Ah, flattery. I love it, Mademoiselle.'

'It is the truth, Captain. And in a way you hold my fate in your hands.'

'As I have held your father's and your uncle's fate several times, in the early days. But we never hesitated to take chances.'

'There are many people who would like to see me fail.'

'Let us not even talk of such matters; your uncle would never permit it. Once decided, it is full speed ahead. I will do my best for you. Do you expect any treachery?'

'Always,' Michelle answered with a smile.

'That I know; treachery sleeps in every man's heart. I meant to say, do you expect any *particular* treachery?'

'No.'

'Then let the dice fall where they may. I will, as always, anticipate the worst and hope for the best.'

448

'Bon voyage, Captain.'

La Farge raised his espresso coffee and they touched cups; there was a slight dry rubbing sound from the lips of the styrofoam cups as they came together.

Sunday morning 10:00
WASHINGTON, D.C.

The big screen flashed green, then bled white and broke into live animated squares as the satellite-transmitted faces came into sharp focus on six large screens, each about the size of forty-inch TV screens. There were two faces on each screen.

The British Prime Minister was the first to speak. He went through a summary of the events that had led this group to where they were: times, places, names, estimated amounts of counterfeit currency produced, and locations. It took him the first ten minutes of the meeting to complete the analysis. The US President had asked him to do it.

When the Prime Minister had finished, the President addressed the group. 'Those are the facts of the situation, but the main reason we are here is that it was inevitable.

'Simply put, paper money is obsolete. It is as obsolete in this age of electronic communication as the horse and buggy was when the Model-T took over the roads.' The President sipped from his water glass and continued, 'It was inevitable that someone would modify computer and laser-copying technology to permit them to print perfect money. So, we really have two problems that we must tackle today, and we must tackle them head on. First, we must find a way to put these people out of business, and then we must find a way to stop the same thing from recurring.'

'Easier said than done,' the French Prime Minister commented. 'If the Black Box can be made once, it can be made again.'

'I agree,' the German Chancellor said. 'Once an idea like this has been spawned, and described by the press, it seeps into the air. Others will try the same method, or an improvement.'

The President nodded. 'Yes, they will. Therefore, after we have dealt with the immediate problem, we must deal with the larger problem of the use of an antiquated system of paper currency as the accepted medium of exchange. We must eliminate the use of paper money, and we must do it together as a unified action – and quickly!'

Phillip sat next to the President, ostensibly taking notes, but primarily he was watching the reactions of the distinguished panel of faces before his eyes. This was the ultimate punch line; Phillip saw the power of those words as it registered on the faces in front of him.

The Japanese Premier was first to respond. No one had to explain the 'underground cash economy' to this group. 'Yes, billions are lost in taxes by people trading in cash. Untraceable transactions are the bane of every government in existence. Stop people from using cash and you stop tax evasion, or at least cut it down.'

The British Prime Minister raised his chin and leaned forward. 'I have a suggestion to offer,' he said, clearing his throat. 'I suggest that we consider moving immediately to the use of the "Lifecard"; all the mechanics are in place for the countries represented here. Wherever a Visa or Mastercharge or American Express or any other card is acceptable, a Lifecard is acceptable.'

Phillip, with a nod from the President, took up the theme. 'We all started working on the Lifecard project five years ago, and all of us are about at the same level of development. The card is ready to go, especially now that the common market is a reality. This is my card.' Phillip held it up to the camera. It was the size of a regular credit card, with 'The United States of America' written across the top in currency green over a bald eagle. Below the eagle was a one-inch picture of Phillip, two sets of numbers and a hologram. 'As you can see, the card designates that it is a United States card, it contains a picture of the owner, and carries a hologram to prevent counterfeiting. There are two sets of code numbers. The first number, or the key number, is the social security number, which is given to each American citizen at birth; the second number is the person's new Federal Banking registration number, which provides a central banking function for the individual. But all payouts and receipts continue to pass electronically through a commercial bank chosen by the cardholder. A person's entire financial life is recorded on this number. The social security number traces everything else: employer, education, police record, automobile registration, addresses, tax payments, passport – it provides an instant life history.'

'Now is the time to introduce the Lifecard,' the British Prime Minister urged, 'as we begin economic unification of Europe through the common market with one currency and one passport for all citizens of Europe. The counterfeiters have given us the perfect excuse to replace paper money quickly with the Lifecard.'

In the ensuing silence, the vast implications of such a move whirled through the brains of everyone present.

Phillip broke the silence. 'The Lifecard will also solve the biggest social problem we all face, drug dealing. With approximately one year's use of the Lifecard there will be only limited cash left floating in the system and every transaction will be traceable. How could drug dealers sell drugs and launder money?' He paused, then went on, 'And if drug traffickers do use the card, we can trace them; private, untaxable transactions will cease. The untaxable, cash, underground economy will be brought out into the sunlight. If the underground economy can be taxed, it will provide extra revenue so that there will be no need to raise taxes for ten years. We will be able to pay off our deficits and still have a windfall of funds.'

'The people of the United States and Canada will never stand for such a restriction of personal freedoms!' the Canadian Prime Minister interjected.

'What's the alternative, Mr Prime Minister?' Phillip asked. 'A bunch of hoodlums printing money in every basement in the country? If one of these machines can be built, then more can be built. The people of our countries must face the facts that paper money is archaic and obsolete.'

'But other counterfeiters couldn't get the paper,' the Swiss Prime Minister said, 'now that we have cut off the source.'

'They could bleach out one-franc notes and use the copier to make one-hundred-franc notes; a hundred-to-one mark-up is well worth the effort. I've seen it done many times in crude ways. With this advanced technology there would be no controlling it. It would be like a cottage industry,' the French President said.

'This image you create of a copier in every basement is ominous indeed,' the Canadian Prime Minister conceded.

'If we seize this opportunity, in one year paper money will be as scarce as silver dollars, replaced by the Lifecard,' the Japanese Prime Minister commented.

'But, even though I reviewed your attack plan, I still don't see what we do. How do we punish them?' the German Chancellor asked.

'First, the operation must be destroyed, their ability to manufacture currency must be eliminated,' the US President responded.

'I agree,' the French Prime Minister said, raising his voice. 'We are in immediate risk of having our oil cut off by the Arabs. They are close to not accepting paper of any kind.'

'I suggest that we put it to the vote and that the majority decision carries the group. And I suggest we vote in secret, right now,' the President said.

452

Everyone nodded their assent and the voting began. In front of each head of state was a fax machine. The responses traveled directly to the US location for tabulation. Phillip noted each and then handed a small piece of paper to the President. 'The vote is unanimous,' he announced. 'They must be destroyed.'

'We can stop them but we shouldn't punish them,' Phillip said. 'If we hang them out to dry in a court of law, the extent of their counterfeiting will become known. Besides, our legal footing isn't any better than it was before. They operated as a sovereign country, not subject to our laws, and they dealt through third parties to distribute their product. The legal implications are very thorny and complex. We must do what we have to do to eliminate their operation and we must do it fast.'

'And the others, the Brotherhood and the Mafia? What do we do with them?' the French Premier asked.

'We do nothing,' the British Prime Minister said. 'If we are sure that the manufacturing has stopped, we do nothing, nothing at all. We let it die, along with the value of the cash they have amassed.'

'Who will eliminate them?' the French President asked.

'We will,' Phillip said. 'It started with us and it will end with us. The plan you all have studied for four days is ready for implementation. We will proceed when the time is right.'

Everyone nodded their assent, and the screen was washed clear.

The President buzzed for Ralph Cobb, who had been monitoring the meeting.

'Well, how do we deliver on our promise?' Cobb asked as soon as he entered the room.

'I will leave that up to you two gentlemen. Finalize your plan and execute it,' the President said, gathering up his papers. 'I'm late for another meeting.' And abruptly he was gone.

Cobb and Phillip knew why he had left, as many Presidents

before him had left crucial meetings at critical moments. It was the first rule of the intelligence hierarchy of politicians. Always leave one escape route open in case things go wrong, because sooner or later something would go wrong. Leave a way to deny involvement. Deniability was the stanchion that long-term survivalists built on, and the President had been a survivor for a long time.

Cobb knew that if they blundered in their plan to take the perpetrators out of the picture, it would be his ass thrown to the wolves, not the President's.

WEEK EIGHT

Thursday night 11:45
MARSEILLES, FRANCE

It had been many hours since Captain La Farge had seen the subs disappear into the dark Atlantic and the Azores drop off his stern. It had been clear sailing, surprisingly smooth seas and light winds for this time of the year. The jagged Rock of Gibraltar, the solid sentry, had slid past on his port side as he entered the Mediterranean Sea. Things had gone very well. The transfer at sea of cash for gold had gone without a hitch, and now as they approached the port of Marseilles, they were on the last leg of their journey. The crew knew better than to use any extra words with Captain La Farge when he was working. And to Captain La Farge, working meant only one thing, smuggling.

The rough skeletons of waterfront cranes, thick, solid oil-holding tanks, and the squat warehouses of Marseilles popped up on the horizon, a silhouette city against the setting sun. Captain La Farge ordered the engines back two thirds. The First Mate, who was standing next to the Captain, looked at him questioningly but remained silent and followed orders.

'We'll wait until dark,' Captain La Farge offered by way of explanation.

'*Oui, Capitaine,*' the First Mate answered. He had served with La Farge for over twenty years and never once had either of them seen the inside of a jail.

'Things are going too well,' the Captain added. 'I'm used to trouble. Tonight makes me worried.'

The First Mate gave the Captain a long look. La Farge had never said such a thing to him in twenty years. He slipped his hand under his shirt and felt for his cross. It was mahogany and had come from Madagascar. It felt cool and smooth in his hand. The cross hung at the end of a well-worn wooden rosary that he wore every time he was on a mission such as this. Saying a prayer was his long-time secret and he believed that the rosary had protected him from many dangers, storms and strife over the years. His lips hardly moved as he said a fast, silent decade of Hail Marys in the darkness of the bridge, his fingers creeping from bead to bead.

When he was done with his silent mouthing, La Farge leaned over and whispered in his ear, 'Say one for me while you're at it, *mon ami.*'

The Captain's whispered words sent a shiver of fear shooting down the First Mate's spine right to the tips of his toes.

At midnight Captain La Farge could feel the liquid softness of the Mediterranean disappearing under the hull, replaced by the scummy harbor water of Marseilles.

The shipyard cranes and warehouses were dark disjointed figures on the near horizon, blending into and out of the blackness as the moon peeked out through the passing clouds. As they passed the wharfs, La Farge could see the dim lights of the waterfront bars.

His forward speed was three knots as he entered the narrow 'Corsican Channel' as he liked to call it. It was a row of twenty warehouses bulkheaded by one long wharf. La Farge headed for warehouse number seven. He had specifically asked for warehouse seven; it was his lucky number and he wanted everything working in his favor tonight, although once into the Corsican Channel and with warehouse row looming ahead, he knew he was safe. Many people were on the Corsican payroll, and these warehouses were special; they were given only the most cursory of inspections by French Customs and newly arrived ships were often not inspected at all.

Six longshoremen stood ready on the wharf to cast the lines to the waiting deckhands as Captain La Farge eased the rusty old ship into her berth. The dilapidated old freighter had four billion in assorted currencies in the hold. The entire stash filled only half of one of the smaller sealed holds.

Once the hawsers were secure, a signal was given and trucks pulled out of the warehouse onto the dock. The money was to be loaded into the trucks and dispersed to five separate holding locations.

La Farge lit a Gauloise. He inhaled deeply, then exhaled, letting the smoke envelop him in an aromatic cloud. The smell of a smoldering Gauloise had many good associations for him. He always smoked at the end of a run and never during; it was the final reward that he reserved for himself. And the fact that he didn't smoke under pressure reassured him that his will was stronger than his fear.

He leaned out over the steel railing to watch the cargo net swing over the gunnel. It contained about a quarter of the green garbage bags in the hold; one billion dollars. The heavy cargo net dropped gently. It scraped the concrete pier and flopped open; a few of the garbage bags rolled onto the concrete. They were quickly picked up and thrown into the open backs of the waiting trucks. The bags made a puffing sound as they squashed up against each other. It was a pleasant sound to the Captain's ears.

He looked up at the blinking moon and watched the dark clouds ease past the yellow disk in an almost surreal design, a design Picasso might have painted. At first he thought his eyes were playing tricks on him. There were specks hovering high up, dark birds. They flashed in and out of the erratic moonglow. From the corner of his eye he saw the cargo crane swing over the freighter a second time, carrying another load of garbage bags. He strained his eyes and looked skyward again, then yelled to the First Mate, 'Bring the night glasses!'

La Farge slowly spun the rubber lens grommets of the infrared military-issue binoculars until the specks came into focus. He counted seven attack helicopters watching them from above.

He swung the night glasses down to the wharf and watched as the doors to the first truck were slammed shut and the second truck was loaded. The first truck began to roll towards the high chainlink fence and the road that led to Nice. He saw dark figures move towards the fence. They were blurs dressed in black and they carried automatic weapons; he spotted at least twenty police commandos with his trained eye. The night exploded as the Sûreté blew the iron fences with small charges of plastique. La Farge watched the fence posts rise in the air and fall to the ground as if they were toothpicks plucked from the ground by an invisible hand.

Flashing lights and the shrill sound of police sirens filled the air. La Farge ran to the port side and saw police boats fill the narrow channel. Every escape route was cut off.

The hollow sound of helicopter blades was suddenly audible as the choppers dropped like dead black birds from the heavens, stopping their descent only feet from the ground. The high-power spotlights on their noses burst into hot white beams and immediately lit up every square inch of the wharf.

A hand-held loudspeaker could be heard above all the other noises. 'This is the Sûreté. You are all under arrest. You will stay absolutely still, hands high in the air, or be shot.' A group of ten police ran up the gangway and onto the ship as the patrol boats that had silently entered the Corsican Channel nudged their noses up tight to the freighter's rusty hull.

The First Mate moved over closer to the Captain, his hand inside his shirt as he said his rosary.

The sergeant of the Sûreté squad hit the bridge with two men. He recognized La Farge.

'Ah, Captain, we catch all the big fish tonight.'

'You were waiting for us.'

'Perhaps.'

'Never before have we had trouble in this restricted area,' La Farge said, referring to the unspoken protection granted to the Corsican Channel and the group of twenty warehouses.

'Orders for this operation came from the very highest authority. A matter of national security, we were told.'

Their discussion was interrupted by the screech of brakes as a French television crew and their truck came to a skidding halt in front of the sprawled-out net. Two portable video cameras focused on the piles of shrink-wrapped currency as they were divided into piles of French and Swiss francs, German marks, English pounds and US dollars by the officers of the Sûreté.

'Who invited the TV cameras?'

The sergeant shrugged. 'Who knows, monsieur? Perhaps they come uninvited.'

La Farge extended his hands towards the handcuffs. 'I doubt it.' The cuffs clicked closed.

The Captain thought about Michelle Descartes and what this would mean to her. She had just paid out one billion in gold and would receive nothing in return; everything would be confiscated. More importantly, she would be challenged now for the leadership. Her judgement would be questioned. She could only hope that her uncle stayed alive long enough for this huge financial loss to be dimmed in the memory of the Brotherhood.

La Farge watched as they handcuffed his First Mate. His manacled hand slipped back under his shirt to the rosary.

'The man's faith is unshakable,' the Captain mumbled to himself.

'What? What was that you said?' the sergeant asked.

'*C'est la vie*,' La Farge smiled. 'The older I get, the less I know, and that's the only thing I know for sure.'

The sergeant shrugged, and moved to the bow to herd the prisoners ashore.

Enzio Luchese, the ruling Don of Chicago, sat in the passenger seat of his black Lincoln with his car phone jammed into his ear. It was a conference call. He had the Detroit and the Los Angeles Dons on the line.

'So you heard, I'm sure,' Enzio said. He spoke in a clipped style, not quite sure about the security of the line.

'Who hasn't, for Chrissake. It's all over the Miami waterfront. It ain't good,' the Los Angeles Don said.

'Why? Why would he do such a thing, cutting us out like that? We had a fuckin' deal; plenty to go round, no need to be selfish. I heard he lost a billion dollars in gold trying to go round us,' the Detroit Don said calmly.

'You checked the others?' the Los Angeles Don asked.

'Yes. Everyone agrees that the Feds are going to come in and really put the boot to us – IRS, FBI, the fucking works. We have to give them a signal that we are out of the game.' Enzio had the deep powerful voice of the baritone opera singer that his mother had wanted him to be. He knew the power of his voice and used it. He was a big man, with a broad, flat face, fleshed out by the bulk of almost three hundred pounds hanging from a five-foot-eight frame.

'The other dons agreed?' the Detroit Don asked.

'Yeah, to a man. None of them like getting fucked. It was greedy and stupid of our car-lovin' pal.'

'Yeah, life is short; a person should enjoy their pleasures. Ain't that right?' the Los Angeles Don grated.

'We drew names out of a hat,' Enzio Luchese said. 'You know it has to be one of us, up close and personal as they say on the television.' He let the silence hang on the line, then continued, 'I changed the rules at the last minute; the others already agreed. If you agree, then this is the way it's going to go down: not one of us does it, the three of us do it. We can all get to him and there won't be no fuss. We was partners and it only seems fitting that we're all present to pay our respects when our partnership ends. Whaddya say?'

Another short silence.

'I could use some target practice,' the Los Angeles Don finally said.

'Yeah, me also. My eye ain't been so good lately. 'Course I ain't had nothin' real good to shoot at in years; couldn't hurt to have a little practice.'

'All right, it'll be done. We'll meet in New York. *Capisce?*' Enzio said.

'We'll be there,' the Los Angeles Don said.

'*Ciao, signores.*' Enzio boomed his goodbye in his deepest, most resonant voice.

Enzio slipped a tape into the car's player and waited for the first notes of the aria from Pagliacci to fill the car before he burst into song at the top of his voice.

The driver continued to stare straight ahead and said nothing; he was used to it. He had heard the phone conversation and he knew what it meant. Don Saverese was going to die.

Friday dawn 6:35
CAY SAL BANK, BAHAMAS

Six American Apache attack helicopters from the USS *Kennedy* flew low across the Gulf Stream into the rising crimson sun. They flew at top speed in a tight V formation. Their rotors gave off a deep base line that made vibration ripples on the calm surface of the flats as they broke away from the Stream and approached the Cay Sal Bank.

They whizzed over the heads of eight Zodiac rubber assault boats that carried a dozen men each. The men, Navy Seals, hardly looked up. Their faces were blackened and they were concentrating on the role they would play when they hit the island. Their orders were clear: if there was any armed resistance, they were to 'do what was necessary' to neutralize the enemy.

As the island came into view, the helicopters slipped from a V formation into a straight line with a hundred yards separating them. Each helicopter had designated targets. Their orders were to leave the two Butler buildings intact and destroy everything else so the waterborne attack force would not be compromised.

The leading helicopter zeroed in on the first guard tower and fired; the rocket's fiery tail ended in an abrupt explosion that turned the wooden structure into a burning ball of fire-splinters that fizzled in the salt water as they landed. The helicopter fired a second rocket directly into the next guard post and it also burst into flames. As the helicopter made its pass, the Gatling guns mounted on the bow raked the fine white coral sand, setting off the Claymore mines in rapid succession like erupting volcanoes. The helicopter veered off and was lost in the new sun.

The following helicopter came in higher, firing four rockets so fast that they looked as if they had one tail. They slammed into the stern of the liberty ship first and ran up the rusty hull, four direct hits. The boat seemed to explode in slow motion, first the stern, then amidships, and finally the bow. The ship rose out of the water like a dying monster, metal debris flying, sending a deadly shower of shrapnel over the island.

The second helicopter had come in for the subs, but they were gone, so he took the secondary target. The first rocket made a direct hit on an anchored Bertram. The fiberglass boat splintered and melted under the blast leaving only a small section of the bow intact, tethered to the mooring. The two other yachts disappeared in the same way, leaving the small harbor littered with plastic and the minimal contents of the Bertrams.

The fourth pilot was a weekend sailor and he winced as he pulled the trigger that obliterated *Desperado*, the beautiful maxi racer. The rocket hit the sailboat directly amidships, dislodging the mast. Like a giant needle, it was launched end over end, sailing in an arc over the water until it landed on one end, sticking abruptly up from the sandy flats like an empty flagpole.

The fifth helicopter came in over the fiery harbor and let loose with four rockets. The chopper veered up and away as the missiles slammed into the steel sides of the barge holding the paper. The explosions raised the barge out of the water so high that the ocean poured in on the opposite side. When the barge settled, the side the rockets had hit had disappeared. The rockets had been loaded with a special charge that was not incendiary. The attackers wanted the paper to be water-soaked and ruined. They did not want it to burn, giving off toxic fumes that might harm the waterborne assault force that was just then hitting the beach, with the sixth helicopter escorting.

The main targets of the assault group were the Butler buildings. The rubber boats had a shallow enough draft to run on the flats. They hit the island at four points, two boats grinding to a halt on the coral sand at each location. The men leapt out of the boats at a full run, crouching and breaking up into deadly clusters of firepower. Two assault teams hit the factory first, quickly laying 'DET' cord at the base of the front and rear doors. As the cord was exploded, the men filed through the front and rear doors. At the same time the second two teams were blowing the doors to the warehouse. As the metal doors imploded into the warehouse, the strike force followed.

There was no one inside the warehouse or the factory.

The attack groups quickly scoured both buildings for possible hidden areas or escape hatches. There were none.

The squad leaders in the factory called in their findings. 'The island is abandoned, not one living soul.'

Ralph Cobb received the news aboard the USS *Kennedy*. Phillip sat next to him. 'What equipment did you see?'

'We got a copier and a computer with a small black box in between,' the squad leader said.

Cobb looked over at Phillip with a smile on his face. 'I guess we surprised the hell out of them.'

'Don't be too sure; I've been through this before, Ralph,' Phillip said. 'Is the technician in your group?'

'Yeah,' the squad leader replied.

'Have him open the Black Box as he was instructed.'

The second assault group stood inside the warehouse. It stank. The vats of slurry were still warm. After they secured the building and the perimeter they wandered round the pallets of printed money almost in a daze, carrying their guns in the port position. There was pallet after pallet of printed cash. Each pallet had the flag of the currency nation implanted on top. In the corner were stockpiled sheets of blank currency paper.

The leader called in his report to the *Kennedy*. 'Hard to describe what I got here, just mountains of goddamn money. Pallet after pallet of cash money, billions.'

'Okay, break up your team. Position twenty men outside the warehouse building, forming a perimeter, and four men inside. Captain, you remain inside. You read me?'

'Yes, sir, I'll set it up. Hard to believe it's like the damn Mint here.'

'We know,' Cobb told him. 'My men and I will be there in a few minutes to take over. From then on it will be the Secret Service's responsibility. But till then it's your job.'

'Yes, sir.'

Cobb turned to Phillip. 'Where the hell did they go to?

There was action on that island last night. Now they're gone and so are the subs; very strange. It's almost like they were tipped off.'

'How? No one outside of our group knew what was going down tonight. We didn't even inform our allies,' Phillip said. 'Maybe it's coincidence. Maybe they just decided to leave on their own and it coincided with our attack.'

'Yeah, and maybe pigs can fly. I'm not a big believer in coincidence. Are you?'

'Not really,' Phillip said. They were interrupted by the first team leader. 'Sir, we've just about got this black box open.'

'I'm not hopeful,' Phillip said quietly to Cobb.

'The first panel is just sliding out now and the technician is looking inside with a flashlight.'

'And?' Cobb prompted.

'It's empty, sir,' the team leader said.

'Shit,' was all Cobb could think of to say. History was repeating itself.

Friday evening 7:45
PUERTO RICO

Nick, Books, Heather and Perce stood in the San Juan airport shaking hands with the over-the-hill gang as they boarded a Pan Am flight to New York. Each man had a slight protrusion under his shirt that spanned his stomach. They seemed like well-fed tourists. The tummy bulges were caused by two rows of tightly packed one-hundred-dollar bills that added up to a hundred thousand dollars for each man. There was no Customs and Immigration when entering the US from Puerto Rico.

Ernie was the last to board; he lingered to talk to Nick. 'I could stay, you know. I got nowhere to go in a hurry. I could help you raise those submerged subs.'

'No, Ernie, we'll manage; take your fate the way it's handed out. You're supposed to go and have a good time now with your ill-gotten gains. Besides, who knows how this will all turn out; it could get rough.'

'But Perce's staying.'

'Perce is a different story,' Books said as he walked over, Heather behind him.

'Goodbye, Ernie,' Heather gave him a hug. 'We'll miss you.'

'Likewise.' Ernie turned and boarded the plane.

It was dusk in San Juan. Books, Nick, Heather and Perce watched the silver Pan Am 747 disappear into the setting southern sun.

'Let's go to the casino,' Books suggested, 'and spend some of this cash – verify the reality, you know?'

'Hell, yes,' Perce said.

The casino was located inside the San Juan Hilton, a sprawling gaming room that looked like the inside of any Hilton in the world.

They all started off with ten thousand dollars. Books headed for the craps table, Perce to the blackjack, Heather to the roulette wheel to play the colors, and Nick went to the bar, where he settled onto his Naugahyde bar stool and ordered a Scotch on the rocks. He wasn't in the mood to gamble.

The raid on the island was still the lead story. He studied the bar television as it showed the wreckage of the island and the currency piled up on pallets, and the submerged barge with the water-soaked currency paper. Nick had to look away when he saw the drowned *Desperado*; blasted and demasted, it looked violated.

They had been lucky. It had been Books' idea just to abandon the island, taking only the Black Box innards aboard *Ubiquitous*; and the subs, loaded with cash and gold, manned by the over-the-hill gang. The three subs, slightly submerged, had eased along the Great Bahama Bank, through the Windward Passage and down along the southern side of Puerto Rico. Nick, Heather, Books and Percival rode shotgun on *Ubiquitous*.

The three subs surfaced just before dawn to slip over the reef line and into the natural caves of the property. The caves were invisible unless you were positioned directly in front of them at sea level. The subs were unloaded, then were taken out to the natural reef and sunk with full ballast tanks in sixty feet of water.

The two-man crews exited the subs through the escape lock-outs, leaving everything ready to re-enter and raise the subs at a later time.

A follow-up story flashed onto the TV screen over Nick's head; it showed a raid in France where billions in currency had been confiscated from the Union Corse. It was suspected by the media that this raid was connected to the destroyed island in the Bahamas and a massive counterfeit ring but there was no proof.

'A cool million for your thoughts,' Heather said.

'I was just thinking how convenient those caves were. Books purchased the land two years ago. I like seeing a plan unfold where I play a major part and all I get is surprises, my lines fed to me after the scene is set.'

'We'd have had an even bigger surprise if we'd stayed on that island last night.'

'Yeah, a fatal surprise.'

'I wonder why there were no pictures on TV of the suspected culprits,' Heather mused.

'Probably because the world powers don't want to disclose everything and I imagine they're still unsure of the legal ramifications of the "sovereign rights" issue. A lengthy trial would do no one any good.'

'So they'll just kill us and solve their problem?' Heather asked.

'It doesn't seem to be bothering Books,' Nick said, pointing at Books, who was pitching the dice with total concentration, as if the money on the table was his last.

'What do we do now, Nick?' Heather asked. 'I'm ready to join the over-the-hill gang and get the hell out of here.'

'Somehow I don't think that's the right move, Heather,' Nick said as he watched Books gather up his winnings and head for the cashier's cage.

'I'm going back to the table. It takes my mind off things,' Heather said.

'Sure; I'll see you later,' Nick responded. 'Good luck.'

Nick ordered a new Scotch and stared down into the amber liquid, watching an oily slick form as the ice slowly melted into the alcohol. He remembered the rum punches he had with Phillip on Martinique only a couple of months before, and the cable he'd received from Books that had asked him to join him in the Bahamas. His mind raced ahead to the New York docks . . . kicking Phillip's wheelchair when he had blackmailed him over the shooting in Paris . . . and later, his confession to Books that he had been sent by Phillip to act as a spy. Then the blue hole popped into Nick's brain and all that gold, and the circling shark, and the kiss he and Heather had stolen on top of the mountain of gold. What the hell was Books going to do with so much gold and all the wealth it represented? What a strange man Books was. Did he ever care for Heather? It did not seem to bother him at all that Heather was out of his romantic life. What a smart, cagey bastard he was leaving the island just before the attack.

Then it struck him like a bolt of lightning. He wolfed his Scotch and ordered another. 'I can't believe this! I just can't believe it,' he said to himself.

'You all right, Nick?' Books said as he sat down next to Nick.

'I'm better now!'

'Why's that?'

'I know, you know,' Nick said.

'What? What do you know?'

'What you are really up to.'

'Yeah? Well, keep it under your hat. I'm not sure I know myself,' Books said, getting up quickly. 'I'm not sure I ever really knew,' he said, walking away.

Saturday afternoon 2:30
NEW YORK CITY

Don Saverese had the entire Club Siracusa range to himself. He slipped the ear protectors on and looked to see if the red light was lit above the sound-proof door. The light glowed red like a tiny beacon. Bruno stood sentry outside, his back to the sound-proof door, facing the outer lead door.

The Don turned to face the empty range. He walked to alley three and sent a fresh target down the electrically operated wire clothesline. His ear mufflers stopped all sound and filled his brain with a void that by its very silence had a unique sound, noisy emptiness. 'The brain compensating,' the Don said to himself, testing the ear mufflers to see if he could hear. He heard only a slight murmur. 'Yes, that's all I hear, white noise.'

Don Saverese turned to make sure, one last time, that the door was locked and the red light was still glowing.

He spun to the target and fired six fast rounds from the chrome-plated Smith and Wesson .357 Magnum. He ejected the spent cartridges from the cylinder onto the side table and pressed the button to retrieve the target. He felt the hum from the motor as the half-inch-thick wire brought the target back to him, but he couldn't hear it.

Three holes, dead center, three in the second ring. Good.

The Don smiled as he reloaded with the speed-loader. He knew that everyone was using the new automatics, the Beretta 21 and the plastic Glock, guns that held seventeen rounds in the clip. But he would stick with old reliable. A couple of rounds should do the job and no chance of jamming. He smiled to himself; if you had to fire a full clip of seventeen rounds, then you were in the wrong place at the wrong time.

The smile disappeared as he sent a new target down the line and planted his two small feet in position. The target came to an abrupt halt and waved slightly like a palm frond for a second, then it steadied itself, hanging quietly, waiting for the Don.

This was going to be the perfect score, six out of six, bull's eyes. Slowly, five seconds apart, the gun exploded in the cellar range. The Don only heard six soft puffs as the bullets exploded, about as loud as a small child clapping.

He pushed the button and squinted as the target came grinding back to him. He could see that there was a white hole where the center used to be. He reached for the target as it approached.

Bruno stood outside, the red light glowing over his dark curly hair. There was a soft warning knock as the lead door in front of him opened. Bruno's hand went to his holstered gun but stopped when he saw who it was. He recognized the Dons from Los Angeles, Miami and Chicago. They smiled at Bruno and pointed at the red light, asking for permission to enter. Bruno nodded and turned to open the sound-proof door; as his hand reached the door handle the first bullet entered his brain. Blood and brains splattered against the padded door. Enzio Luchese grabbed Bruno by the collar and pulled his body away from the door so they could open it.

Don Saverese stood with his ear protectors on and both hands extended in the classic police position for shooting a pistol. All he heard was the soundless white noise; suddenly his wrist was encircled by a large meaty paw. His gun hand was twisted behind his back, the gun snatched from his fingers. Even through his ear protectors he recognized the deep basso-profundo of Enzio Luchese. He could feel it as he was turned round to face away from the target wall.

Plastic restraining cuffs were quickly slapped round his left wrist, his arm was lifted up and clamped to the target retrieval wire. His right wrist was pulled up and the same thing was done with it. He was trussed and bound to the wire, both his hands over his head, and he stood on tiptoe.

Enzio ripped the grasshopper-eye mufflers off Don Saverese's head.

The three men surrounded the Don. Enzio's enormous bulk dominated. He spoke. 'Why? Why do you treat your partners so bad? We had a deal with that funny money, and you had to go around us.' Enzio tugged the Don's wrists to make sure they were secure. The plastic restraining cuffs dug into his wrists, but the Don showed no sign of pain.

'You wondering what happened to Bruno?' the Los Angeles Don said softly, almost in a whisper. 'He's gone. All the families are against you. You brought us unbearable heat from the Feds. Maybe when they see you dead they will lay off a little.'

'I can talk to people in high places, use my influence,' Don Saverese said. Before he finished his sentence, the Detroit Don reached into a pocket and pulled out a roll of steel-gray duct tape. He ripped a four-inch strip off and slapped it across Don Saverese's mouth. The Don's eyes widened, not in fear but in surprise that he would be treated in such a manner.

Enzio pointed at the open sound-proof door. The Los Angeles Don slammed it shut. The red light automatically went back on.

'That's better,' Enzio said. 'Now we don't need this fuckin' tape.' There was a loud zip as Enzio Luchese yanked the tape off the Don's mouth. 'Let's have a little dignity here. Right, Don Saverese? After all, that's why we came personal to do you, out of respect. We could have sent anybody, but the five families agreed that we would do it ourselves. Now if you can take this like a man, we'll treat you like a man, but we got to make an example; no man is above the code.'

Enzio nodded at the other two men, then grabbed Don Saverese by the small of his back, using the Don's fine leather belt as a handle. He raised him off the floor and held him dangling two feet in the air.

Enzio nodded at the Los Angeles Don, who started the electric motor that drove the target cable. 'Think it will hold?' he asked.

'He don't weigh much,' Enzio said as he tossed Don Saverese's feet over the railing and released his hold. The Don's torso was pulled down to the end of the shooting alley.

Don Saverese said nothing as he was pulled along, dangling by the wrists. He had sent many men to their deaths; he knew that once it was decided there were no appeals, no reprieves. So he would die with dignity. Abruptly the wire stopped at the first station, twenty-five feet away from the three Dons.

'Naw,' Enzio said, 'take him down to the fifty-foot mark.'

The Los Angeles Don started the cable once more and Don Saverese was dragged another twenty-five feet. The tips of his black Gucci loafers scraped the rough concrete and rolled over spent lead slugs that had bounced off the padded fire wall and rolled back down the alley. The Don dropped his eyes and studied the tips of his shoes; they were being scraped white by the concrete. For some reason it made him think of his mother. Such expensive shoes, these beautiful black loafers, being ruined for no good reason. The hum of the wire was reassuring to him; it meant he was still alive. He thought of his father and how hard he had worked all his life, and it flashed through his mind that everyone winds up at the same spot, standing alone in the circle of death. The wire stopped.

He now knew what the target saw when it looked up the shooting alley. Three heads were down there, with large bulbous ears protruding, ugly insects.

The crack of Enzio's Beretta filled the shooting range. The

slug hit Don Saverese square in the breast pocket, moving his body sideways a couple of inches. It felt like a hard, brass-knuckle punch to the ribs. The skin was unbroken; the bullet had hit the tiny Ferrari in his pocket and ricocheted off into the wall. For a second the Don thought the gods were with him. And for some strange reason, at that moment, he wondered what would happen to his numbered Swiss account. There was still twenty million in cash, on account. No one would ever claim it; the fucking Swiss would get it.

The second shot was the ear-splitting sound of a long barreled .44 Magnum. Don Saverese saw the red flash from the barrel. It was the last thing he ever saw as the hollow-tipped lead slug entered his head just above his ear and exploded his brain.

Saturday afternoon 5:00
NICE, FRANCE

The little breath that crept into René Descartes' lungs was pure bottled oxygen. A harness of two small tubes was strapped to the base of his nostrils, and the stream of oxygen was ever-flowing. His eyes, closed most of the time, were open now, trying to focus on his beloved niece.

His blue eyes were rheumy, wandering, the creeping film of death blotting his vision. But when he heard her voice and saw her outline, his mind filled in the rest.

His voice was raspy, and it was a great effort to talk. But he had carefully explained to her before he was hospitalized that it was the most important thing left in his life, to see her become queen of the Corsican Brotherhood. He was to

475

be kept fully briefed on all that transpired until his last breath, no matter what the doctors said.

Michelle spoke in a quiet somber voice, almost a monotone. She went slowly, even though she believed he was listening intently and she could speak faster. The slow smooth sound of her words was calming to her and took some of the sting out of what had happened.

It was difficult to talk of her failure: the loss of the gold and the four billion in cash, the incarceration of Captain La Farge and his crew; the headlines; the heat. And her impending crisis within the Brotherhood for the leadership. She faced a hopeless situation.

'Cursed, cursed . . .' Descartes whispered above the bubbling oxygen.

Michelle leaned over and put her ear closer to her uncle's lips and listened. He seemed to gain strength for a second.

'The money was cursed from the beginning. The Russians taking it, and now the Sûreté. I should have known when I met that young man. There is never anything free. I should have known. What good is your life if you never know, never learn?'

Michelle thought she saw his shoulders shrug a little. 'I should have known,' he gurgled, patting her hand. He had exhausted himself with the effort of speaking.

'No, Uncle, everyone was fooled. The great Mafia chieftains were also fooled. I have had news that Don Saverese is dead, killed by his own people.'

This news greatly agitated her uncle. His hand went for the transparent plastic tube in his nose as if to pull it out, to rise from the bed and protect her, but it dropped feebly by his side, fingers limp and listless.

'Easy, Uncle, please. I know what I have ahead of me.

With supreme effort he spoke again. 'Remember what I said a long time ago,' he whispered. 'I was right. They must come to you with a deal, they must come. They will never want the full story revealed. They must come, Michelle.'

She patted his hand. 'Easy, Uncle. This can wait.'

'No. This cannot wait. When they come, you have to be ready. You must have it thought out.'

Michelle could see the color draining from his face; his fingers were like a trembling, dying bird in her hand. His will was all-powerful. It was ruling his dying body.

He continued in a voice that was hardly audible. She could feel the gasps of air tickle her ear as he spoke. 'They will need to save face, they will need a story they can give to the public, to avoid panic. You must do whatever is necessary. People, loyal people in the Brotherhood, may have to be sacrificed. Do it. Do what they ask; do what is necessary.'

She knew instinctively that any more words would kill him. She spoke in his ear. 'I will. I will do whatever is necessary to preserve the Brotherhood!'

'To preserve yourself!' he whispered. 'To preserve yourself.' His eyes shut.

'Shhh. That is enough now,' Michelle said, and she started to hum the mockingbird lullaby that he had sung to her as a child. A slight smile crossed his lips; the sound soothed him.

She laid her head on his chest and hummed the tune in a quiet, strong voice, as he used to sing to her. Slowly she felt his chest rise and fall as he caught his breath. The humming turned into words and she sang until the breathing was regular again and he was asleep.

She stopped singing and let her head ride up and down with his breathing. She sighed and closed her eyes for a few minutes. She knew that he was right; he was always right.

Tears formed round her closed eyes. They were not tears for her dying uncle or for the danger that faced her. The tears were because she knew she would never again be loved the way this man loved her.

Saturday evening 8:00
PUERTO RICO

At sunset they heard the heavy bass notes of a single military helicopter emerging out of the lowering sun, and they ran out to the verandah. The Huey, framed by a red glow, hovered over the estate. It looked like a prehistoric bird emerging from an egg of fire. Two giant head and tail rotors spun in sequence, suspending the brown bird hesitatingly in the air, waiting for visual permission to land. It bore the single white star insignia of the Army.

Books went down and stood in a clearing in front of the beach walk and waved the chopper down onto the beach. The rest of them followed him.

The four of them had to avert their eyes against the swirling, biting sand as the helicopter touched down and the mighty rotors slowly came to a thumping halt. The silence was broken by the cargo bay door as it creaked open and a hydraulic ramp emerged, sliding out of the bay onto the white coral sand like a long dark green tongue. Four Green Berets came trotting down the ramp, two of them carrying a long, rolled-up, narrow exercise mat. They unrolled and laid it from the end of the ramp to the edge of the boardwalk leading to the beach house. They moved back to stand sentry.

Then the sun was gone and darkness encompassed the tiny encampment. The only illumination came from the interior of the helicopter; it lit up the ramp and the empty cargo bay. Heather moved instinctively closer to Nick and held his arm. Nick's hand slid down to the .45 in his belt.

An iron wheelchair appeared at the head of the ramp, silhouetted in the light, stuttering in its movement for only a second before slowly gliding down the ramp and onto the mat.

Heather looked at Nick, confused, as Books walked up to

478

Phillip. The two men shook hands and smiled at each other.

Phillip nodded at the four Green Berets and they moved back up the ramp double-time. The ramp slid up behind them and the cargo bay doors closed.

'No need for them here now,' Phillip said to Books.

Heather squeezed Nick's arm; he just stood there. Phillip slowly pushed his wheelchair until he was only inches from Nick.

'Hello, Nick,' Phillip smiled.

'I wondered when you would show up,' Nick said, and looked over at Books. 'I figured it wouldn't be long.'

'How long have you known?' Phillip asked.

'Known for sure? Only a day or so. It was clever, very clever, of you, Phillip. You too, Books,' Nick said, nodding at Books.

'What kind of games are you guys playing?' Heather asked.

'Not games,' Books said. 'This has never been a game.'

'Let's go inside and talk,' Phillip pointed at the house.

The group moved and formed a circle round Phillip and his wheelchair as they walked up the boardwalk. Perce ran to light the gas lamps, turning them to their highest brilliance.

Once they reached the verandah, Phillip stopped his chair.

'My name is Phillip Sturges, Miss Harrison.'

'The mastermind of this incredible scheme. You are, aren't you, Phillip?' Nick interjected.

'I suppose so, Nick. Books helped. Could you please help me up these steps?' Nick grabbed the handles of the chair, turned it, tipped it and pulled it up the steps backwards. They all entered the sitting room. No one spoke; the hissing of the gas lamps was the only sound. Nick paced in front of Phillip's chair. He was the first to speak.

'The whole idea was so you could pick up more gold to back the dollar. The United States now has the world's largest gold reserves, right?' Nick asked.

'We always had the world's largest gold reserves, Nick. Now, we just have more. I've always been a fundamentalist:

479

just like a rose is a rose, gold is gold – the age-old barbarous metal that men will kill for. Even though we are entering the age of high technology some things stay constant.'

'Like greed and deceit,' Nick blurted.

Phillip raised a hand and continued. 'Books called me today, and said that he felt it was time for you to be fully informed about what has been going on.'

'Fully informed?' Heather asked. 'Who could ever believe you?'

'You must listen to me. There are bigger issues at stake here. And one of them is whether or not you people eventually wind up in jail,' Phillip stared at her. 'This entire operation was planned two years ago, after I first learned of the power of the Black Box from the Zed Corporation. Nick is right to say the object of all of this has been gold, not paper. It was the objective of the United States Government to own most of the gold in the world, and the Black Box was the means by which to achieve that end. We, or I should say you, have picked up most of the street gold, to the point where any further accumulation would have an adverse effect on the price; it's high enough at twenty-two hundred dollars an ounce to stop.'

'So, I'm right, all this gold we have been piling up has really not been for you, Phillip?' Nick asked. 'Or Books.'

'No, it was never for us. It was destined for the US Treasury, to back the dollar, to bolster it, strengthen it, primarily against other world currencies. On the average we did very well on the exchanges you made – close to dollar for dollar.'

'You!' Heather snapped. 'You and Books, you did well; we all just got used, lied to, tricked and deceived. You bastards. From the beginning this was all your idea. We were just pawns in a bigger game.'

'Your game, Heather Harrison, was revenge, and for your revenge, you committed crimes. You thought you would get back at the Zed Corporation by stealing the Black Box, then

480

counterfeit a few million dollars in the bargain. But it grew; it got out of your control,' Books said.

'It was never in my control!' Heather yelled.

Phillip interrupted. 'Calm down and look at this for what it is. No one here is innocent. So what if everyone present is here to serve his or her own best interests, first and foremost. But no more; as of this evening it changes. We want you all to go to work for the United States Government; this doesn't mean you can't serve your own ends as well.'

'That's a nice story, Phillip, but how about the whole story; this time no more tricks. There is more going on here than gold, a lot more, isn't there, Phillip? What is it? The collection of more gold is not enough motive for the United States to risk getting caught and discredited.' Nick asked. 'What the hell is going on here; and what is it that you want us to do?'

Phillip talked for thirty minutes without interruption. When he was finished, everyone finally understood what was going on, and that the gold was not the main issue. The main issue was the death of paper money and with it, the death of the 'underground economy'; the elimination of paper, for ever, as legal tender and the substitution of plastic; plastic that was used to withdraw cash to pay for groceries, gasoline, dinners, and the rest of the necessities of life.

They had been an integral part of the worldwide birth and acceptance of 'The Lifecard'.

Sunday morning 8:00
PUERTO RICO

Heather sat on the flying bridge of Nick's boat *Ubiquitous*. Nick was below in the galley, cooking.

She was trying to understand what she felt. She was still numb from Phillip Sturges' sudden appearance last night. The pieces were coming together; she was assembling the jigsaw puzzle in slow motion.

She smiled. The whole thing suddenly appeared like a giant practical joke, a huge sting — but on whom? She chuckled to herself as she fingered the dials on the console in front of her. Books had been on the hustle with her from the moment he had met her in the art gallery in London.

Even the sex. The smile vanished. Books was smooth like a practiced whore, a gigolo leading her along, step by planned step, until finally she wanted what he wanted all along — that they steal the copier. Her face relaxed as she thought about how clever these men were. Beyond sophistication, they bordered on the diabolical, they were magicians, nothing was as it appeared. And Nick, below her at this very moment, cooking. Did he only figure out what was going on a few days ago or was he the most subtle part of their devious plan?

She heard the salon door below slide closed behind Nick and she smelled the food, breakfast of dehydrated eggs, canned bacon, and slightly burned toast in the still tropic morning air.

Nick handed her a plate and said, 'So, feeling defiled, abused, used, raped, deceived, and tricked?'

'And worse.' She was starving; she ate quietly, finishing her eggs before she spoke. 'Why didn't you tell me you had it figured out?'

'I wasn't sure. I was looking for a way to confirm it before I told you. Besides, I didn't have it *all* figured out. The Lifecard was a surprise. And there was a reason we weren't told, you know.'

'Yeah. We wouldn't have done it.' Heather blurted.

'Well, next time let me know if you're speculating, will you? It's my life, too,' Heather added, biting into her burned toast. She sat thinking for a minute. Then she laughed.

'It is funny, Nick.'

'Except that it's so serious.'

'Ironic,' Heather added. 'They took my desire for revenge and used it for themselves.' She examined her burned toast.

'Sorry, the toaster has a mind of its own; maybe you could design a better one for us,' Nick said.

'For us?' Heather said, crunching again into her toast.

'Yeah, for us.' Nick turned her chair so that it faced him directly. 'I want there to be an us, after this.' He held his hand out.

She dropped her toast onto her plate and looked up, grinning and blushing. She took his hand. 'I don't think we'll owe anybody anything, anymore,' she said.

Nick interlocked his fingers with hers. 'Let's go below.'

Without another word they slid down the ladder from the bridge into the salon. Nick took her hand and led her gently into the master cabin.

They fell into each other's arms and made love, for all their frustrations, fears, and hopes.

WEEK NINE

Monday morning 9:15
CAY SAL BANK, BAHAMAS

Nick was inside the blue hole, watching the team of Navy Seals work. The US Navy had sent a helicopter for him in Puerto Rico, and shuttled him to the *Lexington*, an assault carrier idling against the flowing Gulf Stream, waiting only miles from where they were. He had led the dive team through the opening into the dome. The first thing he did when he entered the great bell-like structure was feed the shark, this time a nice steak, compliments of the Navy. Whenever he entered the dome, the shark would come and circle the rock until Nick dropped food there. Then the shark would eat it and disappear down into the black abyss that formed the far side of the bell. In the many times that Nick had been inside the blue hole he had forgotten the food only once; that time, the shark never stopped circling the rock.

Inside the natural vault it was a riot of refracted light. Sporadic beams of distilled sunlight bounced off the rectangular squares of gold haloing the cache in a glistening, soft, blue-yellow fuzz where it was stacked high against the wall of the blue hole.

The team of US Navy Seal divers had a meticulous plan to extricate the gold, and they followed it to the letter. Nick floated above them, looking down as they sent the gold bars rolling along the stainless steel conveyor belt and out onto the waiting metal grids that lay on the white coral sand. Rubber mats covered the steel mesh grids, so the soft metal would not be damaged. The bars were caught as they flopped off the conveyor, and stacked carefully on the grid. When each grid was full, it was replaced by another. The full grids were lifted by strong steel cables to a waiting landing craft on the surface where the gold was lifted aboard by a crane and inventoried. When the craft were loaded, they plowed off to the waiting mother ship, the *Lexington*.

'This is probably the only thing I'll miss,' Nick thought to himself, 'this wonderful domed cathedral of nature.' The divers were very skillful and they had been warned to move carefully so as not to set up a sandstorm of silt. They had been briefed on the potential danger of the bottomless side of the bell, and all of them had seen the massive hammerhead when Nick had fed him. They gave the rock a wide berth.

'Keen beans, these guys, full of their youth,' Nick thought.

He turned his vision upwards toward the center of the dome to watch the slow rate of ascent of his bubbles. He drifted up with a string of bubbles that he blew out. *Life* was captured in those bubbles; without those bubbles there was no human existence. Each one changed its shape with the pressure, like a malleable, clear crystal.

When his bubbles hit the hard surface of the dome ceiling, they split up into smaller bubbles and were finally transformed into hundreds of tiny spheres of gas.

From Nick's floating perch, way up in the center of the dome, the men below looked like ants working on an ever-decreasing anthill of gold.

God, it was all so strange what men did for gold.

This gold came from below the earth, had been stored below the ocean, and now it was being moved to a concrete cave in the bowels of Fort Knox.

'This dome has that effect on me,' Nick mused to himself. 'It makes me think lofty, useless thoughts. Thoughts that don't really matter. What matters is human nature. And human nature is down there below me in the form of twenty highly-trained young men who are doing the bidding of their elders, trying to get that gold organized so it can be re-hoarded, no longer by Books but by the US Government, and used as leverage against other hoarders who believe the yellow metal is more precious than life itself.

'But what the hell difference do wealth and power make anyway? We're all dead in less than a hundred years,' Nick concluded, as he propelled himself downwards toward the tiny opening.

Wednesday afternoon 2:15
FORT KNOX, KENTUCKY

Books St John, Heather, and Nick sat silently in the back of a stretch limo that had been waiting for them in the Louisville airport. They had traveled south along the black Ohio River on Highway 31 until they exited at Bullion Boulevard and took a left under the underpass.

Nick strained his eyes through the one-way dark glass, looking for the Depository as the limousine turned onto Gold Vault Road. The Depository was at the end of the road, a much smaller building than he had imagined; it was a two-story, squat rectangle of granite, concrete and steel.

The limo turned and stopped at the electrified steel fence that surrounded the building. Sentry boxes could be seen at each corner. The electric car window hummed as it dropped into the door. A voice echoed out of the metal box. 'Halt. State your business into the speaker.'

'We have priority clearance. The password is twenty-four carat,' the driver said.

'What's better than twenty-four carats of gold?' the voice asked.

'A twenty-four carat diamond,' the driver replied as he had been instructed.

The gates swung open and a single rotating TV camera on the roof stopped and focused on the incoming limo. Two men standing sentry at the Depository door snapped to attention. They were both armed with M-16s. One of them quickly descended the five steps and opened the door. Books slid out first and was followed by Nick. They walked through the green marble entrance and under the simple chiseled words: 'United States Depository'.

Phillip was parked in his wheelchair in front of the vault door.

It took three people to unlock the vault door. No one person was entrusted with the combination. Two men, employees of the Depository, stood beside Phillip, working on the combination.

Phillip extended his hand, 'Hi, Nick.'

'Hello, Phillip.' Nick took Phillip's outstretched hand. Books smiled and in turn shook Phillip's hand.

A trim, petite brunette approached. She smiled at them. 'Hi, I'm Elizabeth Bartlett, head of security.' She moved to the massive vault door and spun the lever quickly right and left to her combination. She leaned against the door and it swung open slowly, a huge mouth.

'The Depository,' she proclaimed.

Phillip was first behind her through the door. Nick followed and as he entered he looked up at the massively strong ceiling above him; it was woven with steel plates, steel I-beams, and steel cylinders laced together by hoop bands and encased in concrete.

They passed a series of compartments, small solid steel cells. Elizabeth was silent as she walked, not looking back, obviously in charge of her territory. Her tight skirt moved silkily against her trim bottom.

She stopped two compartments from the end of the hall. 'This is it.' She opened up the compartment. The two guards took a step forward, but she gestured with a hand for them to remain in the background. 'These compartments are seven feet wide, nine feet high and sixteen feet long. They can hold thirty-six thousand bars. This compartment has a little over twenty-five thousand bars.'

A bar was smaller than the outstretched span of Nick's fingers. It was now clear to Nick why Books had specified this exact size to Don Saverese and Michelle Descartes, to keep the bars the same as the rest of the gold in the Federal system. Each bar was now worth more than $850,000 dollars at current world prices.

The gold bars did not quite fill the room. It held over sixteen billion dollars in gold, enough to actually buy certain small countries, Nick thought.

Nick heard clicking footsteps on the marble and turned to see who was approaching their little group. The glare of the overhead fluorescent lights made it difficult to see the face of the man who was walking towards them. He was a big man, with broad shoulders, a wide chest, and a full head of well-combed hair. He walked alone down the corridor with the purposeful strides of a man who always knows where he is going. He carried a small package in his arms.

'You must be Nick Sullivan,' he said, extending his hand as his face came into the direct light of the compartment. He moved on to Heather. 'And you are of course Heather Harrison. You do nice work, Heather.' The President smiled.

In his arms he carried the Black Box. He handed the box to Phillip to examine.

'And you are Books St John,' the President said, moving nearer the compartment. 'The banker.'

The President stopped when he saw Elizabeth Bartlett standing inside the compartment. 'And you?' he smiled.

Elizabeth stammered, her eyes wide. 'We were told we would be getting a senior VIP today, but we weren't told who it would be. It's very nice to meet you, Mr President. I'm Elizabeth Bartlett, head of security here at the vault,' she said, regaining her composure. She extended her hand for the President to shake.

'It's nice meeting you. Maybe you and your two associates could leave us for a minute.'

'Well, yes, fine,' she said, thinking about the regulations. 'Seeing that it's you, sir, and Mr Sturges, we will wait down the hall.'

The President waited until they cleared the area, then spoke to them all. 'I wanted to thank you and I wanted to say it in person.'

Phillip reached up, handing the Black Box back to the President who examined it for a second before speaking. 'A very small item to be so powerful.' He smiled his wonderful smile, a smile that had much to do with winning him the Presidency. 'And I also wanted to see just what all that gold looked like.'

He came closer and, in a low voice, said, 'You people did the impossible. The price of gold is over two thousand dollars an ounce, so all the gold in this building has risen five times in value over the last nine weeks. Gold will always be important in international transactions. The value of this single room is many billions; it comes as a direct result of your efforts.' The President paused to look at each of them. 'In this age of high-technology,' he went on, 'money is obsolete. It's now obvious to every nation that we must eliminate paper currency.

'When we do eliminate cash and introduce the Lifecard, all the hoarded currency will have to surface to be redeemed, or lose its value. Think of what that will mean for the economy of our country. We will declare a one-time amnesty to allow people to surface with their hidden hoarded cash and pay only a small back-tax penalty. This compares with losing it all if they don't. We are talking about billions of dollars in uncollected taxes from the underground economy. This is what we set out to accomplish; what we *needed* to accomplish. We never wanted to fill the jails.'

The President took their measure, looking them straight in the eye. 'Now you know the importance of this operation. We can now implement the Lifecard program. No important nation will object. The Lifecard will start a new economic way of life. Electronic money is as important an economic innovation as when paper money was introduced in the 1860s.'

Nick turned away. He felt nothing, like he was inside an empty void, a vacuum, a tiny pawn in a huge economic chess game. A game he had entered because of his love and loyalty for these men.

The President continued, 'I have a small reward for each of you.' He reached into his pocket and handed an envelope to Books. 'This is but a token of our thanks.' He walked to Nick, withdrew two small books from his pocket, and handed one of them to Nick. 'One of these is for you Nick, and one is for you, Miss Harrison.'

Nick flipped the small black booklet over in his hand and saw 'Bank of Zurich' written on the outside. He opened the book and saw a two million-dollar balance in a numbered account. He snapped it shut.

'Good. Well, that should do it. And don't forget to declare this money during the amnesty period, folks.' The President smiled. 'Once again, thank you for your help,' he said wryly, waving for Elizabeth Bartlett and the two men to return.

Elizabeth stood aside as Phillip wheeled out from the compartment threshold. 'One last thing, sir,' she said as she slammed the door shut. 'We would like you, Mr President, and Mr Sturges, to sign this.' She handed the President a white sheet of paper. 'This sheet will be immediately laminated and placed on the door. We will seal it right now.' She signalled the two guards forward. They wired the door shut and formally sealed the closure with sealing wax.

The President examined the document claiming 25,340 bars. He looked at Phillip. 'Did you actually count them, Phillip?'

'No, sir, these two men conducted the count,' Phillip nodded at the two Depository guards, 'as well as two men of my choosing from the Federal Reserve. I'm happy with the count.'

The President laid the document on top of the Black Box in Phillip's lap, scribbled his initials on the amount and signed in the signature column. 'Well, I must be on my way.' He smiled and shook each person's hand before he left.

The group watched the sturdy figure walk down the hall to join two waiting Secret Service men.

Books turned. 'I'll also say goodbye. I have an appointment in New York.' He walked over to Nick and shook hands. 'I hope we can be the friends we once were, Nick.' Books let his words hang in the air. 'I have only the best feelings toward you.' Books next went to Heather. 'Goodbye, Heather, don't think too badly of me, please. I did . . .'

'Books, just leave it alone. I understand now.'

He kissed Heather lightly on the cheek and went to Phillip. 'Phillip, I'll see you when I see you, right?'

'Right, Books,' Phillip said, gently squeezing Books' hand with both of his.

Nick, Phillip and Heather watched as Books started down the marble-floored hall.

He waved back without turning.

Elizabeth Bartlett started to walk down the hall with a man on each side of her. Her bottom swayed in rhythm to her steps.

Phillip looked up at Nick and winked. 'Women are lucky; they start with some natural advantages.'

'Some women are luckier than others,' Nick smiled, looking at Heather.

'How about a push out of here?' Phillip asked.

Nick hesitated for a second, then smiled at Phillip as he stepped behind the chair and grabbed the two handles and started to push. Nick walked very slowly; for reasons that were a mystery to him he did not want this to end.

Just before they reached the Depository steps and the ramp, Nick released Phillip's chair from his grasp. He and Heather moved in front of Phillip. Nick extended his hand. 'Goodbye, Phillip. We won't see each other for a while. I need a rest.'

'I'm sure you do, Nick.'

Phillip looked at Heather. 'I think I'll have this Black Box gold-plated or something. In a few years we can look at it and maybe we will laugh.'

'Smile, maybe,' Heather said.

Phillip squeezed Nick's hand and pulled him forward. 'See ya, brother.'

'Yeah,' Nick said. He and Heather started to walk away.

'Nick, there is one more thing.'

Nick turned. 'Books told me that there were some bars of gold missing from the blue hole, about ten. Know anything about that?'

'No,' Nick said.

'I didn't think you did. I told Books to forget about them, round the total off; there would have been slippage, you know . . .'

'Yeah, Phillip, I know.' Nick lifted a corner of his mouth in a slight smile and turned with a wave. Nick took Heather's hand. It was time to head to Puerto Rico, to *Ubiquitous*; they had to stock up on boat supplies.

He did not look back. He could feel Phillip's eyes on his back. Then he heard Phillip shoo the security men away from his chair to let him negotiate the ramp on his own.

They drove slowly out to *Ubiquitous* in the Whaler, just above trolling speed. 'God, I missed this, Nick; I'm hooked, you know?' she said, slipping off her seat so she could sit next to him in the stern. 'I'm hooked on the wild, beautiful ocean and you.'

Nick squeezed her hand; silently they made their way to *Ubiquitous* sitting quietly at anchor. He started the powerful diesel engines of the Rybovich sportfisherman, then went forward to the bow and flipped the electrical switch on the power winch that pulled the anchor chain. He sat on his haunches as the links fell into the chain locker like a steel snake coiling itself for a long rest. The anchor slid into the stainless steel sleeve on the bow pulpit and Nick made his way to the flying bridge. Heather had changed into shorts and a halter top.

'Destination?' she asked.

'I have one planned stop which we will hit in a few hours; after that we have no schedule, no plan. We just follow the nautical charts to wherever they take us. Okay?'

'Aye, aye, Captain. You lead. I follow.' She rose from the pilot's seat on the bridge and kissed him hard on the lips and whispered, 'I hope you lead me below to the cabin soon; I missed you.'

Nick said, smiling, 'Me, too! Now that I finally have you with me I just want to get a good distance between us and civilization as fast as I can.'

For the next three hours they rolled south with the gentle swell of the ocean and hugged the Great Bahama Bank until they finally dropped below the twenty-fourth parallel. Nick headed west toward the Cay Sal Bank.

'Nick, are we . . .'

'I just have a brief stop to make and then we're on our way.'

'Just trust me, honey, and keep quiet. Is that what you're trying to say, Nick?'

'Something like that.' He smiled.

Two hours later Nick dropped the anchor. The Cay Sal Bank was barely in sight.

'Are we where I think we are?' Heather asked. 'Over the blue hole?'

'Maybe,' Nick laughed, 'and maybe not.'

'I think it's maybe. I think we are over the blue hole. You going down to visit our toothy friend down there?'

'Yes.'

'I'll wait, and work on my tan. I've had enough drama in my life for a while.'

'As you like.'

Nick strapped on his tank, slipped on the strap to his nylon goody bag, checked his speargun, mask, and regulator, then gently somersaulted off the gunnel into the familiar clear blue water.

He dropped swiftly through the tepid water and crabbed along the white sand, following familiar landmarks until he reached the opening. It was still there; the Navy Seals had not blown it when they removed the stash. Nick swam lazily over to the tall coral head fifty feet away and clicked the safety off the speargun. A lane snapper about two feet long was circling the base of the coral head. Nick waited until the fish passed a second time and shot him. The spear penetrated the snapper just behind the dorsal fin and gills.

He left the fish on the spear as he retraced his movements back to the opening. The stainless steel rollers were still there. Nick smiled to himself, wondering what archaeologists two thousand years in the future, would make of the rollers. He traveled through the slim tunnel on his belly, feeling the rollers turn beneath his stomach. He landed with a familiar thud on the white sand inside. The fish on his spear was dead now, and he ran the thin shaft through the body until it was free as he swam over to the rock and placed the fish on top as his offering to the shark. He would wait for the shark to appear for his dinner. Nick floated inside the bell. He wore only a T-shirt and a bathing suit and his gear. The pressure of the water felt good to him, soothing, healing as he slowly rose to the top of the bell. The blue laser shafts of light were criss crossing and hit his body like massaging friendly fingers trying to remove the grit of life. Nick rolled over and looked down at the rock fifteen feet below him now. The shark was making ever-decreasing circles over the rock, following its pre-programmed, primordial pattern until finally snatched the snapper and disappeared into the bottomless gloom on the far side of the bell.

Nick turned one last time and took benediction from the pin-pricks of blue light. Then he sank slowly back to the rock.

With his hand, he rubbed the sand under the rock in a small gentle circle, watching the white granules drift off, until he saw the first gold bar appear. He unclipped the bag from his belt and slipped the rectangular bars into the bag, one at a time, as they emerged from the sand. When he had the ten bars, he pulled the cord tight and closed the bag. They weighed over two hundred pounds, but underwater it was only a small fraction of that weight.

Nick made his way across the bottom of the blue hole just above the sandy bottom. He took one last look at the rock.

The shark was back.

It hovered over the rock. Then it slowly flicked its tail and glided forward, moving twice as fast as Nick. He was only feet away from the opening when they came eye to eye. The shark stopped for a second, then it flipped its tail and shot up the domed wall to the apex of the bell and came shooting down the far side, gaining speed as it skimmed along the wall until it disappeared in a blur into the bottomless, dark abyss.

Nick sighed in relief, a block of bubbles burst out of his mouthpiece and drifted away from him as he made his way into the small entrance. Nick wondered if the shark knew he was leaving for the last time and was saying goodbye, while it was left for ever trapped in this tiny world.

Nick dragged the bag behind him over the rollers and swam to the anchor line. He pulled himself up the chain and clipped the bag to the line just below the surface and swam the rest of the way to the back of the boat unencumbered.

He broke the surface and pulled himself onto the teak dive platform.

He sat in silence for a few seconds, looking at the dim outline of the islands that formed the Cay Sal Bank. There were no buildings visible; everything had been leveled. It was as if they had never been there.

'How was it?' Heather asked.

'Uneventful. It's time to leave,' Nick said, rising from the diving platform and springing over the transom.

'Okay with me. I've had enough of this place.'

'Come to the bow with me while I crank up the anchor,' he said.

Nick detoured slightly and started both powerful diesel engines.

Together they stood on the bow pulpit as the anchor chain was retrieved by the electrical motor. Nick saw the bag and stopped the chain. He slipped over the gunnel into the water. 'Give me a hand, please.'

The gold sparkled though the mesh bag in the afternoon sun. One by one he took the ten gold ingots out of the bag and passed them up to Heather. She laid them out on the deck.

'What's all this?' she grunted, pulling the last bar over, then helping Nick use the anchor chain to heave himself back aboard.

'Insurance; I don't trust paper money,' he grinned.

'And I hate the idea of Lifecards that tell your whole story.' She knelt down and put her arm round his shoulders. 'Anything else you're not telling me?'

'Anything else can wait. I just wanna run away with you,

hang out, and watch you invent stuff.' Nick smiled. 'That's what this gold is for, so we won't have to ask for any loans if you invent some incredible machine for the benefit of mankind.'

'Mankind is too complex for me; my urges are more basic. I have no immediate urge to invent anything, except maybe a baby.' She hugged his shoulder with her arm.

Nick touched her hand and rose, placing the ten gold bars in the bag. Together they carried it to the bow hatch and dropped it onto the cabin carpet. Nick went aft, engaged both engines from the lower station, and sat in the captain's chair. He set the course on automatic pilot and headed into the Gulf Stream. Heather came to stand next to him.

'Where are we headed, Captain?' Heather said, putting her arms round him.

'Great Inagua and the Windward Passage, but it may take a week. I know a few lost and lonely keys along the way; the first one is only an hour away.'

'The sooner the better.' She squeezed him, standing on her toes so she could kiss him square on the mouth.

EVERYBODY WANTS IT...

MONEY FOR NOTHING

JOHN HARMAN

'Hitting an old lady over the head with a brick and stealing her handbag is a crime. Anything else is just business.'

Five men, all Establishment figures and at the top of their professions, set out to make themselves a fortune – illegally. Within a year, they are multi-millionaires. They also cause a revolution in one of Her Majesty's protectorates, the brutal slaying of a platoon of British soldiers, the bankruptcy of a major company and the imprisonment of an innocent man. They are also accessories to murder . . .

No one ever connects them to these events and no one misses the money. It is the perfect crime. Until, more than twenty years later, a beautiful girl tells Jerry Pilgrim the whole incredible story as they lie together one morning in a big bed in a small cottage in Northamptonshire. For Jerry, the knowledge of a secret that could destroy some of the country's most powerful men is just too tempting, so he sets out to commit his own audacious crime.

But someone else knows the secret too. For, wherever Jerry goes, death goes before. You see, everybody wants . . . money for nothing.

'Harman's absorbing novel slices deep into the fraud and outrageous crime that motivates even the most seemingly stable pillars of society.' *Yorkshire Post*

FICTION/THRILLER   0 7472 3123 0

A selection of bestsellers from Headline

FICTION

GASLIGHT IN PAGE STREET	Harry Bowling	£4.99 ☐
LOVE SONG	Katherine Stone	£4.99 ☐
WULF	Steve Harris	£4.99 ☐
COLD FIRE	Dean Koontz	£4.99 ☐
ROSE'S GIRLS	Merle Jones	£4.99 ☐
LIVES OF VALUE	Sharleen Cooper Cohen	£4.99 ☐
THE STEEL ALBATROSS	Scott Carpenter	£4.99 ☐
THE OLD FOX DECEIV'D	Martha Grimes	£4.50 ☐

NON-FICTION

THE SUNDAY TIMES SLIM PLAN	Prue Leith	£5.99 ☐
MICHAEL JACKSON The Magic and the Madness	J Randy Taraborrelli	£5.99 ☐

SCIENCE FICTION AND FANTASY

SORCERY IN SHAD	Brian Lumley	£4.50 ☐
THE EDGE OF VENGEANCE	Jenny Jones	£5.99 ☐
ENCHANTMENTS END Wells of Ythan 4	Marc Alexander	£4.99 ☐

All Headline books are available at your local bookshop or newsagent, or can be ordered direct from the publisher. Just tick the titles you want and fill in the form below. Prices and availability subject to change without notice.

Headline Book Publishing PLC, Cash Sales Department, PO Box 11, Falmouth, Cornwall, TR10 9EN, England.

Please enclose a cheque or postal order to the value of the cover price and allow the following for postage and packing:
UK & BFPO: £1.00 for the first book, 50p for the second book and 30p for each additional book ordered up to a maximum charge of £3.00.
OVERSEAS & EIRE: £2.00 for the first book, £1.00 for the second book and 50p for each additional book.

Name ....

Address ....

....

....